P9-DHF-792

She was a virgin.

He had seduced and taken a complete stranger—a lady—without a single consideration for the consequences. He'd thought . . . .

Oh bloody hell he hadn't been thinking at all.

He reached for the bed curtains and yanked them open. Moonlight hurt his eyes as it poured over the bed, over fair flesh and golden hair and blue eyes wide and unblinking as she stared up at him.

"Melissa . . . no . . ." Her name was a shocked whisper on the air, of dismay, of wonder.

Melissa Seymour.

Oh God. Not her. Anyone but her.

## Praise for Eve Byron

"An utterly beautiful and moving love story with a deep and powerful message of hope that will set readers' spirits soaring."
*Romantic Times*

"A truly satisfying love story."
Arnette Lamb

## Other AVON ROMANCES

DESTINY'S WARRIOR *by Kit Dee*
EVER HIS BRIDE *by Linda Needham*
GRAY HAWK'S LADY *by Karen Kay*
THE MACKENZIES: CLEVE *by Ana Leigh*
SCARLET LADY *by Marlene Suson*
TOUGH TALK AND TENDER KISSES *by Deborah Camp*
WILD IRISH SKIES *by Nancy Richards-Akers*

*Coming Soon*

STOLEN KISSES *by Suzanne Enoch*
TOPAZ *by Beverly Jenkins*

*And Don't Miss These*
## ROMANTIC TREASURES
*from Avon Books*

FALLING IN LOVE AGAIN *by Cathy Maxwell*
FLY WITH THE EAGLE *by Kathleen Harrington*
LYON'S GIFT *by Tanya Anne Crosby*

# DECEIVE ME NOT

# EVE BYRON

AVON BOOKS  NEW YORK

This is a work of fiction. Names, characters, places, and incidents either are the product of the author's imagination or are used fictitiously. Any resemblance to actual events, locales, organizations, or persons, living or dead, is entirely coincidental and beyond the intent of either the author or the publisher.

AVON BOOKS
A division of
The Hearst Corporation
1350 Avenue of the Americas
New York, New York 10019

Copyright © 1997 by Connie Rinehold
Inside cover author photo by Shea Balika
Published by arrangement with the author
Visit our website at http://AvonBooks.com
Library of Congress Catalog Card Number: 96-95487
ISBN: 0-380-79310-5

First Avon Books Printing: August 1997

AVON TRADEMARK REG. U.S. PAT. OFF. AND IN OTHER COUNTRIES, MARCA REGISTRADA, HECHO EN U.S.A.

Printed in the U.S.A.

WCD  10  9  8  7  6  5  4  3  2  1

To Ann McKay Thoroman and Carrie Feron
for many reasons.

Damaris Rowland because . . .
and
Arnette Lamb for making my brain itch.
You asked for it; you got it!


With special thanks to:
Virginia Rifkin, Audra Harders
and
the members of the AOL authors' loop,
past and present,
for always being there no matter what.

God bless you all.

# Prologue

**S**ilence.

It was as heavy as the air in the closed room, as smothering as the fear swelling in Melissa's chest as she watched her father lying so still in his bed, one side of his strong jaw hanging slack. He'd taken ill five days before and had yet to awaken.

*Ill* seemed a puny word for the seizure he'd suffered, his face red and contorted and his eyes rolling back in his head. She hadn't seen his eyes since. And every day since, Mother had held on to her hand so tightly it became cold and numb as they held vigil over him.

*Please, Father, please open your eyes and smile.*

Sometimes she wondered if this body she watched was really her father. It didn't seem possible that the man whose eyes sparkled as he listened to her relate the wonders she'd found in the latest book he'd brought her, who played Blindman's Bluff with her, who dared to unravel her hair ribbons when Mother wasn't looking, could lie so still and lifeless.

She shivered and focused on his chest beneath the covers, watching for movement, assuring herself that

1

he was alive, and believing he would be himself to-morrow.

She had to believe it. There were so many things he had yet to teach her, so many things she wanted to share with him in spite of Mother's exasperated sighs whenever they stole away to collect leaves or watch the birds or catch rain on their tongues. They always asked Mother to join them but she always shook her head and cautioned that soon Melissa would have to learn less about the world and more about being a lady.

Father said that she was only ten and there was plenty of time for her to become a lady.

Melissa wondered what else there was to being a lady. Every morning she listened to her mother's lessons and then put them into practice until she received a coveted nod of approval. She knew her manners and curtsies. She knew to be silent in adult company and speak softly when addressed. She knew all the latest fashions and what to wear at which time of day. She even knew most of the details of how to be a good wife.

She didn't care about being a lady or a wife. She'd much rather read with Father and go for long walks with him where they would both take off their shoes and feel the textures of grass and leaves and even mud squishing between their toes. Of course, they were careful to stop at the stream to wash off before they returned home with their shoes properly in place.

As Father had said, she had plenty of time to be grown-up. And when that happened, she was determined to fall in love as Mother had with Father and live in the country, where her children could run barefoot and even laugh out loud if they wished. Even if they were girls.

She'd heard Mother laugh, but only when her parents were alone together. It wasn't proper for a true lady to allow her emotions to spill out for all to witness. A true lady was demure and reserved and kept her feelings to herself. Melissa supposed that was why Mother never hugged her or kissed her when others were about. When they were alone, Mother hugged her very tightly and smoothed her hair and whispered how much she loved her as if it would be scandalous to have the words overheard.

Melissa didn't much like it when they had guests. She never knew what to say and felt horribly confined by the crowds that often came for Mother's parties and balls. At least she was still too young to take meals with company and only had to make brief appearances.

When she became a lady that would change.

*Now, Arabella, there is plenty of time for Melissa to become a lady,* Father often said.

Melissa stole a glance at her mother and wondered if her time had run out.

Mother had been silent since Father had collapsed. She stared straight ahead, her eyes wide and her face so very, very pale. And she held on to Melissa's hand as if she would collapse too if Melissa moved away from her.

Melissa's hand ached and she was sleepy and she badly needed to visit the privy.

"Melissa, darling, please do be still," her mother whispered.

"Melissa?" It was a hoarse whisper in the silence.

Melissa looked up. Father's eyes were open and his jaw seemed straight again.

Mother gasped and lurched forward toward the bed, her hand still clenched around Melissa's.

Her gaze caught by her father's gray eyes, Melissa followed willingly.

"Love you, 'Bella," he said, and swallowed.

"Oh, Edward, I love you so very much," Mother choked out. "You must get well. You must. I need you—"

His hand rose slightly from the bed toward Melissa. She placed her free hand in his and almost jerked away. He felt cold. Horribly cold.

"You have Melissa," he said, his words slurred. "A good girl. . . ." He closed his eyes and swallowed. "My joy, Melissa. My strong and very wise girl. Take care of your mother . . . for me . . . she'll need you . . ."

His eyes never opened again.

Silence. Worse than before, heavier and more stifling.

Melissa could barely breathe as she stood beside her mother, her hand held tightly until it went cold and numb, as all the people who had come began to walk away.

The bishop had finished his sermon with wet eyes and a sad "Farewell, old friend."

Others wept as well.

Edward, Earl Seymour, had been laid to rest.

Forever.

The word screamed in Melissa's mind as she stared at the stone walls that held her father. He was dead. Mother had said so in a quiet voice that sounded dead, too. And then she'd only said what she had to when someone approached to say they were sorry or that they would miss Edward.

Melissa wanted to let the scream out. Why were they sorry? He wasn't *their* father. *They* weren't left alone. *They* didn't love him as she and her mother did. And she wanted to know why they walked away, already talking of a party or ball or horse auction, if they were missing him. She would miss her father most of all and she couldn't even think of what to do in the next minute.

Except scream. *Why did you have to die? Why did you leave me? I'm only ten. I need you! Mother needs you! I don't know what to do.*

But she pressed her lips together and walked beside her mother from the chapel into the house, then stood silently while guests again said stupid things and asked if they needed anything.

*I need my father! I need my mother to hold me! Why isn't Mother crying? Why doesn't she scream at everyone to go away?*

She said nothing while the words screamed and screamed in her head.

And then silence again as the last guest left and the butler shut the door without a sound.

Her mother sank onto a settee and pulled Melissa down beside her.

"I'm afraid." The words slipped out of Melissa's mouth before she could stop them, and she thought that if she would be reprimanded for those, she would say it all. "Will you die, too, Mother?" Tears slipped down her cheeks and she hiccuped.

Her mother blinked and looked down at her, her mouth working until Melissa thought she was going to have a seizure as Father had.

"Please don't leave me, Mother. I'm afraid."

Arms wrapped around her and crushed her as her mother began to rock back and forth, her words coming in between sudden gulping sobs. "I'm afraid too, Melissa darling . . . I will never leave you . . . you are all I have now . . . I will never let you go."

Melissa's breath seemed to get caught in her chest, swelling until her heart beat faster and faster and her skin turned cold with fear as her mother repeated it over and over again.

"I will never leave you . . . you are all I have now . . . I will never let you go."

*My strong and very wise girl. Take care of your mother . . . for me . . . she'll need you . . .*

Melissa stroked her mother's back and murmured "Shh" over and over again, trying to comfort her. She didn't understand why she was suddenly more afraid than ever. All she knew was that she wished she hadn't said anything.

She wished she were alone in her room, where she could curl up by the window and stare at the woods where she and her father had wandered barefoot, and then finish reading the book they had begun the night before he became ill.

And as she listened to her mother sob harder and harder into her hair until it sounded like the scream in her head, Melissa wished for silence.

# Chapter 1

*April 1821*

"**H**ave I told you how beautiful you look tonight?" Bruce said smoothly, finding it easier than usual to lie to his paramour. Sometimes, her taste in gowns leaned toward the dowdy, and tonight it was downright frumpish. Still, Joan Sinclair was an attractive woman with her liquid brown eyes and long straight hair that rippled around them when she rode him behind the bed curtains. The anticipation of another such frolic was justification enough for the clanker he'd just told.

"Flattery will get you everywhere," she murmured.

Bruce was counting on it. He never would have agreed to attend her parents' house party if he hadn't been certain there was something in it for him, namely a night in her bed without worrying that her husband might wander in as he had done last week.

Even now, Bruce shuddered at the memory of Henry Sinclair arriving home early from wherever the hell he'd been off to and barging into Joan's chamber to speak to her about their eldest son's progress at school. The man had no consideration.

In that moment, Bruce had understood why Joan always insisted that the bed hangings be closed before they made love. Not that Henry wasn't aware that his wife had a lover, but Bruce was sure he wouldn't appreciate actually finding said lover in the act. But that wouldn't be a problem tonight. Joan's husband was at home with a chest congestion.

He touched her arm, a discreet little caress designed to draw her attention and no one else's. After all, she was a married woman and it wouldn't do to be too familiar in public. "What time shall I come to your room?" he asked.

"Midnight or after, I should think," Joan replied.

Bruce bit back a grin as he scanned the guests milling about Baron Longford's drawing room. He loved house parties and all the sneaking about. It added an element of excitement—

The thought dissolved as his gaze snagged on Melissa Seymour.

Now, there was a beautiful woman.

As a rule, he found classic English beauties mundane, but where he saw others as being merely pink and blue and yellow, Melissa's fair skin had undertones of rose, her round eyes were a soft, clear blue shining with innocence rather than calculation, and her hair gleamed like pure gold.

What drivel, he thought as he slanted his mouth in mockery of his purple musings. Melissa was the same as the others, all pink and blue and yellow, only more so. It was her silence and lack of animation that fascinated him. It offended his confidence that she would not find him as charming and amusing and irresistible as other women did. It challenged his ingenuity to wring a reaction from her.

Deliberately, he fixed his gaze on her full bosom, then followed the lines of the silk gown that draped over her like a jealous lover, showing her off while holding lascivious glances at bay.

But not his. Bruce had a knack for tracing every fold of fabric and translating it into the feminine taper of a small waist, the provocative curve of softly rounded hips, the intriguing length of smooth, shapely legs. And if he could get past the appalling innocence in Melissa's eyes, he would find great delight in uncovering every tantalizing inch of her.

It really was too bad that she disliked him. At least, he assumed she did, since he'd come close to ruining her three years ago. He grinned at the memory. Put like that, it sounded as if he'd compromised her, when in truth he'd only threatened to initiate some gossip about her and a thoroughly unsavory member of the ton. It would have been a shame to ruin such a lovely creature as Melissa, but he'd have done it without compunction and for what he considered the noblest of reasons.

Of course, if one were to ask Melissa's mother, she'd paint him the blackest of self-serving rogues. But then, Arabella, Countess Seymour, saw things only from her own perspective.

And who among the ton—except his family—would believe that Bruce Palmerston, Viscount Channing, had even a nodding acquaintance with loyalty, much less good intentions?

It was exactly what he wanted them to think.

His gaze narrowed on Melissa as it occurred to him for the first time that she was quite alone. Where the devil was Arabella? She never allowed her "darling Melissa" out of her sight, particularly when he was around. If Melissa disliked him—being too gentle a lady to entertain anything so harsh as hate—then Arabella despised and damned him.

Something glittered and gleamed on the edge of his vision, drawing his attention.

He blinked and cocked his head.

Good God, how could he have missed Arabella? She stood not a foot away from Melissa, wearing a king's ransom in diamonds at her neck and wrists and even threaded through her hair. Her hand fluttered to her heart as she laughed at a remark made by Baron Longford.

Obviously, she hadn't realized Bruce was present. She was too relaxed. But that wouldn't last, he knew. As soon as she discovered he was in attendance, her spine would stiffen and her nose would rise in the air and she would hustle Melissa as far from him as possible. Arabella didn't dare "cut" him, given his lofty connections, but she could avoid him.

He found her ingenuity in accomplishing just that to be supremely entertaining.

And if their gazes accidentally met, she would give him a look that would freeze brandy, which in turn would encourage his wicked streak to surface. He'd go over to her then, just to see how uncomfortable he could make her with social chitchat and an occasional innuendo designed to outrage her into mouth-flapping silence.

But tonight wasn't the time to indulge in such antics. He had other things on his mind.

He slid his gaze away from Arabella and took one last look at Melissa, enjoying the heat that flared through his body. He loved looking at her far more than he enjoyed tweaking her mother.

Sighing, he returned his attention to his lover.

"Are you quite finished with your perusal of Melissa Seymour?" Joan hissed.

Bruce kept his expression neutral. He hated getting caught. "I'm sorry, darling. What did you say?"

"You heard me perfectly well."

Sometimes a lover was more trouble than she was worth. It was beyond him why Joan should be jealous of his merely looking at another woman when she had a husband. Nevertheless, he was in no mood to have that particular discussion. "Have I told you how much l love you, tonight?" he purred, using the quickest means he knew to placate Joan. Women did so need to hear those three little words. And he aimed to please.

Joan turned her face away from him.

Bruce rolled his eyes in impatience. Apparently, it was going to take more than pretty words to mollify her tonight. "Why don't we discuss this later, in bed?"

"I've been thinking that perhaps it isn't a good idea for you to come to my room, after all. I'm not sure I'm comfortable receiving you in my mother's house."

"As you wish," Bruce said easily without bothering to remind her that Lady Longford had given this house party as an excuse to see *her* lover. Few things annoyed him more than coy games. He simply refused to play.

Joan opened her mouth, then shut it again, apparently thinking better of expressing the hurt that flickered in her eyes.

He favored her with a lazy and knowing smile, bowed over her hand, and strolled away, knowing that once the guests had settled down for the night

Joan would be more than willing for him to slip into her bed.

In the meantime, he'd have no trouble entertaining himself. People were dancing in the ballroom and debating politics in the library. And there was always the card room. He was confident a place would be made for him at one of the tables.

He paused in the middle of the drawing room to change direction and caught a glimpse of Joan from the corner of his eye. She stood where he'd left her, her hand extended as if she wanted to call him back and recant her earlier refusal to entertain him in her boudoir.

She would definitely welcome him in her bed tonight.

He turned and focused on finding the clearest path to the card room. His gaze collided with Arabella Seymour's.

She shot him a venomous look, then gestured for her daughter to precede her into the ballroom.

Without a word, Melissa complied.

Bruce's mouth flattened. For some reason it had always annoyed him that Arabella treated Melissa like a trained lapdog, never allowing her to stray far from her master's side. Melissa's ready obedience to her mother always made him want to shake her and shout at her until she shouted back. Anything that showed there *was* life in her. Anything to prove her vocabulary extended beyond "Yes, Mother."

He'd love to hear her say "Yes, Bruce."

But it wouldn't happen. Arabella kept too tight a lead on Melissa. He wouldn't be surprised if one night he walked into a ballroom and found Arabella holding on to the ribbons of Melissa's dress as she danced.

Bruce grinned. Suddenly, he had a strong urge to dance.

Abruptly, he turned on his heel and strode after them. As usual, the Ladies Seymour had awakened the devil in him.

He had long ago tired of Arabella's bitterness. So he'd threatened to ruin Melissa. He'd only done it to prevent her mother from destroying two people who were dear to him. She had wisely taken him seriously and refrained from spreading her poison. It was ancient history, and three years was much too long to carry a grudge. He had no hard feelings. In fact, he felt a certain amount of admiration for Arabella.

Three years ago, she'd been on the verge of bankruptcy. Today, she was a wealthy woman. She'd recouped her fortune by selling off her family heirlooms and art collection and buying shares in a trading ship, a practice she continued even today.

It was extraordinarily bold of her. Only a few men in the aristocracy, himself included, defied convention and engaged in business. It was scandalous for a woman to do so. Arabella, of course, believed her activities were a closely guarded secret. And they were. As far as Bruce knew, society had swallowed her tale of an unexpected inheritance and only he was aware of how she'd acquired her fortune. But then, he made it his business to know everyone else's business.

The orchestra struck up a waltz as he stepped into the ballroom and quickly located Melissa and Arabella. Without breaking his stride, he veered toward them and halted directly in front of them. "Arabella, Lady Melissa, how good to see you," he said.

"Lord Channing," Arabella replied with a stiff and frigid smile.

Melissa dipped a perfect little curtsy and said nothing as she lowered her gaze to the floor.

"I believe this is our dance, Lady Melissa," he said, knowing she would neither meet his gaze nor dispute his claim. To his knowledge, she never disputed anyone. He arched his brows at Arabella. "With your permission?"

Her mouth tightened, but she nodded stiffly, having no choice but to acquiesce. There were too many people within earshot for her to say no.

He offered Melissa his arm.

Without lifting her gaze, she placed a trembling hand very properly on top of his wrist and meekly walked beside him to the dance floor.

His conscience pricked him unexpectedly. He really shouldn't force her to do this when it so obviously overset her. But as he spun her into the waltz he reminded himself that he'd danced with her many times before he'd threatened her with ruination and she'd behaved in exactly the same manner. She'd always kept her gaze focused on his shoulder and held her body as far away from his as possible.

He wanted to pull her a little closer, but he knew that would be pushing his luck. At least he was close enough to enjoy the sweet scent of her, the rise and fall of her breasts beneath her sky blue gown, the gleam of candlelight on her hair. But tonight it wasn't enough. He was in the mood to hear her voice, to know that it was as soft and gentle and sweet as her disposition. "The orchestra is very good tonight, don't you think?" he asked.

She nodded slightly.

Perhaps a little flattery was called for. "Has anyone ever told you how beautiful you are?"

She flushed a beautiful pink, and her hand trembled in his. Yet, still, she said nothing. And still she didn't look at him.

Perhaps wit would accomplish what charm did not. He could tell her the joke about the ballerina and the juggler—no he couldn't. It was too naughty for a debutante's ears, he thought as he admired her silky skin and the way the light fell over her cheekbones, defining the hollows beneath. Her face had matured in the past three years.

His brow pleated as realization dawned. Melissa was no longer a debutante. She had to be twenty-one years of age by now, and on the shelf by the standards of society. "Why haven't you married?" he asked bluntly.

Her head jerked up, and for the first time in their long acquaintance, she stared directly into his eyes. His heart seemed to thud and then stop altogether as everything around them suddenly seemed to fade and recede, as if nothing could survive in the shadow of her beauty. She took his breath away.

Her lips parted as if she were going to answer him. He waited, suddenly wanting more than ever to hear her voice, needing to hear her speak only to him.

The music stopped. Once again, she lowered her gaze.

Bruce watched her for a moment, both inexplicably frustrated by the interruption and completely mystified by his response to Melissa's gaze. Never had he felt seduced by any woman, let alone by a simple look. He was the seducer rather than the seduced . . . always.

And beyond finding amusement in tweaking Ar-

abella, his interest in Melissa was nothing more than
that of a man for a beautiful woman. He didn't give
a bloody damn if she spoke or not. In any case, if
she did speak, it would likely shatter the image of
perfection she projected.

Yet as he guided her back to Arabella, he couldn't
help but feel that he'd been close to learning something important about Melissa. Something that
would have given him insight into her calm and
gentle demeanor. Something that would prove she
was more than a heart-stopping face and breath-
stealing body.

Something that would prove she wasn't as empty-
headed as she seemed.

# Chapter 2

He must think her a complete idiot. Melissa tried to catch her breath and gather her composure as Bruce strode away. She shouldn't be worrying about how she'd behaved. Bruce Palmerston was the last man in the world whose opinion she should care about. She shouldn't react to him as if he were the last man in the world and she was starved for his attentions. Unfortunately, she always worried about his opinion of her. She did care. And her physical reactions spoke for themselves whether she willed it or not.

She had a bad feeling that those reactions were telling her something she didn't want to hear. That against all reason and her own common sense she was attracted to Bruce. She might not be starved for his attentions but she certainly craved them.

She stood by her mother and listened with only half an ear to the conversation she was having with Lady Fitchley. They would be at it for a good half an hour, and while her mother would be aware every moment of Melissa's whereabouts, she wouldn't expect her daughter to contribute to the discussion. What did she care about her mother's search for a French chef when both her body and her mind betrayed her every time Bruce Palmerston so much as winked at her?

If only Mother hadn't educated her in explicit detail as to the intimacies shared between men and women. She'd prefer ignorance to understanding of the images her mind conjured when Bruce was nearby. At least then she could ignore the sensations he aroused. She could fool herself into believing she felt fear and panic rather than awareness. Anger would be better. Dislike for him would be welcome. He was not at all the type of man for whom she wanted to feel an attraction.

Aside from being too handsome, he was too bold, too large, too overwhelming. His too-wry wit and too-astute observations had always reduced her to muteness. By remaining silent, she was in no danger of sounding foolish. Ironically, between her bashful nature and unsettling reactions to Bruce, she behaved like a mindless twit regardless.

*Why aren't you married?* His tactless and inappropriate question had both startled and appalled her. She could not believe that even Bruce would be so bold. Nor could she believe that the answer to his question had run through her mind and threatened to pop unbidden out of her mouth. She'd come so close to telling him that she was waiting to meet a man as painfully bashful as she who would not overwhelm her as Bruce did. For one fleeting moment, she'd felt as if it were the most natural thing in the world to confide in him that she wanted to marry only for love. Thankfully, the moment had been fleeting and the familiar panic had strangled the words in her throat as she'd met his all too penetrating gaze.

It had been this way since a night three years before when he'd used the only weapon at his disposal to stop her mother from creating a scandal involving his friends. Melissa had been that weapon.

Sighing, she stared at the French doors leading out to a balcony and gardens beyond. Doors very similar to those she'd stepped through three years ago, trailing, as usual, in her mother's wake. She'd been appalled then, too, as the evening took on all the aspects of a theatrical farce.

Melissa had just returned to her mother's side after dancing with one of the legions of young aristocrats who roamed the line of debutantes in search of a likely candidate to enhance their wealth as well as increase the size of their families.

Mother had dismissed the poor man without a single concession to courtesy.

Stunned by such offhanded rudeness to the young man, Melissa dared a small frown as she glanced at her mother.

Arabella stood unblinking, her gaze focused on a couple standing in the center of the ballroom.

The Duke of Bassett and Lady Jillian Forbes.

"I see the duke has recovered from his broken foot," Arabella murmured. "And Jillian appears quite agitated with him. Really, she is too common, displaying her emotions with every expression."

Melissa envied Jillian that ability. It took such strength to face society as she was rather than as she was expected to be.

"Come, Melissa, darling," Arabella commanded. "It is time we paid our respects."

"No, please," Melissa said, but she might as well plead with the chandelier.

Her mother stepped forward.

Melissa had no choice but to follow, though she knew the encounter would leave her mother in a black mood for the rest of the evening. On more than one occasion, Jillian Forbes had turned Countess Seymour's caustic remarks back on her, thus earning her wrath. They were the only times Melissa could remember her mother being reduced to speechless outrage. Unwittingly, Melissa had added to her mother's dislike by expressing not only her admiration of Jillian but a desire to seek friendship with her.

Since then, her mother took every opportunity to patronize Jillian with barely veiled insults and maliciously delivered advice on how to deal with her "shortcomings."

Jillian had no shortcomings that Melissa could discern. She was warm and open and quite the most dazzling person Melissa had ever seen, with her shining mass of black hair and vivid gown that matched her emerald eyes perfectly. In comparison, Melissa felt like a pale imitation of vitality with her blonde hair and blue eyes and timid manner. Even the colors of her gowns seemed suddenly shy and insipid.

The Duke of Bassett and Jillian glanced their way and then took to the dance floor.

Arabella came to an abrupt halt.

Relief weakened Melissa's knees. "Please, Mother, may we go home?"

Arabella sent her a quelling look, then returned her gaze to the Duke of Bassett and Jillian, her mouth set in a disapproving line. "I wonder at her brother's wisdom in leaving Jillian with Bassett."

Melissa knew it would do no good to point out that the Duke of Bassett and Jillian's brother, the

Duke of Westbrook, were the best of friends, or that the two families had protected one another for centuries. Her mother had always seemed to resent the bond they shared and had become outright contemptuous when they had expanded their circle to include Viscount Channing.

In helpless silence, Melissa stood shrouded by a sense of doom. The orchestra seemed to grow louder in her ears and time seemed to gather speed as couples whirled by in a blur. All too soon the dance was over and Max led Jillian toward the sidelines.

Again, Melissa's mother gripped her arm and moved forward.

From the corner of her eye Melissa saw Lord Nunnley approach them also.

The Duke of Bassett glanced toward them with a cold and threatening expression.

Lord Nunnley suddenly veered away in the opposite direction.

Her mother again halted abruptly. "So that is the way of it," she said thoughtfully.

The way of what? Melissa wondered as she realized the duke's hostility was not directed at them but at Lord Nunnley. He was always lurking about Jillian, and the way he looked at her made Melissa's skin crawl.

Her eyes widened as Jillian swept past her and disappeared through the French doors leading to the terrace.

"What can the girl be up to, slinking off alone?" Arabella mused.

A moment later, Lord Nunnley followed.

"I'm sure Jillian simply needs some air," Melissa said, the sense of doom that surrounded her reaching out to encompass Jillian as well. Alone, Jillian was vulnerable. With Nunnley stalking her, her reputation was in peril of being permanently damaged. Frantically, she searched the ballroom and found the Duke of Bassett speaking with Viscount Channing.

Suddenly, the duke strode toward the French doors.

Viscount Channing caught Melissa's eye and gave her a brazen wink.

Melissa jerked her gaze away as heat flared inside her. Why did he do that to her? Of course, she knew the answer. Bruce Palmerston was prone to mischief and seemed to find a great deal of pleasure in turning her inside out.

"Come, let us walk on the terrace," her mother said. "It's stifling in here."

"We can't," Melissa said. "The duke is out there."

"Exactly," Arabella said, then took a step in the same direction Jillian and Bassett had gone. "Come, Melissa. If her brother is too lax to look after her, then we must."

Horrified that her mother would presume to interfere in such a way, she opened her mouth to argue.

"Not another word," Arabella warned as she propelled Melissa toward the open doors.

Apprehension nipped at Melissa's heels as she obeyed, wishing she could be anywhere else yet morbidly curious to see what would happen when her mother and Jillian clashed once again. It took little wit to know that her mother sought revenge for Jillian's slights, though she could not imagine what form it would take.

The low murmur of masculine voices carried through the night air, followed by soft, feminine laughter.

"This way," Arabella whispered. "Take care to move quietly."

Melissa held her breath as she trailed behind. Surely things were not as they seemed. If they were, it would give her mother just the opportunity she'd needed to humiliate Jillian.

Arabella exhaled slowly and grasped Melissa's arm, staying her.

Melissa glanced up and frowned as she recognized Lord Nunnley crouched behind a large marble urn. Beyond him, the Duke of Bassett stood towering over Jillian where she sat on a stone bench.

Abruptly, Jillian bolted to her feet and spun, then tumbled forward, crying out in pain as her shins hit the bench.

The Duke of Bassett reached out and caught her by the back of her gown. The fabric ripped and Jillian slammed down to her knees, leaving Basset holding a swatch of green silk.

Arabella gasped.

Lord Nunnley stiffened and flicked a look over his shoulder, then relaxed as Melissa's mother put a finger to her lips.

Arabella turned to Melissa and gestured toward a potted plant standing in the corner. "Go there and wait for me," she commanded in a whisper, then joined Lord Nunnley behind the urn.

Melissa backed away, feeling as if she truly were caught in a Shakespearean farce without knowing her fellow cast members. Of course, she knew of them since gossip in the ton could not be avoided, but her acquaintance with the players was largely limited to recognizing them by sight and reputation.

She did know that Jillian had been nothing but warm and kind to her and that the Duke of Bassett had neither smirked at her nor made the cutting remarks that others thought she was too dense to comprehend. And she knew that her mother and Lord Nunnley would delight in painting a sordid picture of their encounter for the delectation of the ton.

She wanted very badly to call out to Jillian and the duke, to warn them that unfriendly eyes watched them.

"I would not have believed it had I not seen it with my own eyes. He actually has his hands up her dress," Lord Nunnley whispered with a derisive snicker, "or what is left of it."

A hot blush swept over Melissa at such crudity. If the duke had his hands up Jillian's dress she was certain he was merely checking her for injury.

"Do not speak of it. My daughter has been shocked enough tonight."

Shocked? Melissa thought. The only thing that shocked her was the way her mother and Lord Nunnley were twisting the mishap into something ugly. She didn't want to see that side of her mother. She didn't want to know that her mother could be so vindictive.

"Everyone will be speaking of it soon," Lord Nunnley said, his tone filled with menace. "He actually had the gall to threaten me earlier when I happened to walk out for a breath of fresh air."

*Liar!* Melissa thought. He'd been following Jillian. If the duke had not followed as well—the thought broke off as she realized that Channing had warned Bassett of what Nunnley was about.

Oddly, she felt a flicker of admiration for Channing. He wasn't all outrageous behavior and smug arrogance. His loyalty to his friends gave him more depth than the sly dilettante she'd thought him to be.

"Her brother must be informed immediately," Arabella said. "They mustn't be allowed to escape."

"Most certainly," Nunnley agreed. "His Grace, the Duke of Westbrook, should know that his sister and his bosom bow are making a fool of him."

Melissa's arms fell to her sides. She had to do something. She couldn't simply stand by and allow this to happen. She could not live with herself if her timidity was the cause of Jillian's ruin.

She clenched her hands into fists. "Please don't, Mother. I'm certain there is a logical explanation. Jillian fell. It did not look as if His Grace meant to tear her gown."

Arabella straightened and sidled away from the urn. "I will not discuss this with you further. Come along."

Melissa clenched her hands tighter. She breathed deeply and groped for the courage she needed to reason with her mother.

The words died in her throat as Viscount Channing stepped from behind a stone column. "You would be wise to listen to your daughter, Arabella," he said.

Although his voice was silky and pleasant, there was no mistaking the steely threat. Nor was there any mistaking the heat that washed through her at the sight of him. Never had he looked so massive and intimidating . . . nor had he ever been so welcome.

"And Nunnley," he continued, "if I were you I would consider it very carefully before I crossed the Dukes of Bassett and Westbrook."

Melissa again felt a flicker of admiration and a spark of hope. He was here to help.

"You saw as well?" Arabella asked.

"Yes," Viscount Channing said.

"Then you know Jillian Forbes should not be allowed to associate with decent people." Arabella stepped toward the doors opening into the ballroom. "Come along, Melissa."

Anxious to escape the scene and the equally distressing Viscount Channing, Melissa was only too happy to comply. As she passed Viscount Channing, she lifted her gaze and for the first time in her life stared directly into a man's eyes.

*Do something*, her mind cried out to him.

He smiled at her as if he'd heard what she dared not say aloud. A beautiful and slightly sad smile that tripped her heart and turned her legs to liquid. A smile that was both appreciative and reassuring. He would take care of his friends, no matter the cost—

He reached out and ripped the sleeve from her gown.

Melissa blinked and stared down at her bared arm and shoulder. She opened her mouth, yet could form no words.

"Melissa!" Her mother spun around at the sound of fabric ripping, her gaze taking in her daughter's dilemma immediately. Her mouth dropped open and she inhaled sharply.

"Nunnley did it," Lord Channing said blandly.

Melissa blinked at the blatant lie, too fascinated by his quick thinking and calm demeanor to protest.

"That is not true!" Nunnley strode forward. "I was nowhere near her."

She blinked again as Viscount Channing's hand shot out and yanked on the end of Lord Nunnley's cravat, then plowed through Lord Nunnley's hair.

This was madness, Melissa thought wildly. Whatever was he doing? She and Lord Nunnley looked as disarranged as Jillian and the Duke of Bassett.

"This is scandalous!" Her mother ripped off her shawl and wrapped it around Melissa.

"Why don't you give her your topcoat, Nunnley?" the viscount suggested.

"What the hell are you about?" Lord Nunnley rasped as he fumbled with his cravat.

Suddenly, Melissa knew exactly what Channing was about. He was sacrificing her to save his friends. Her admiration for him died. He was cold . . . cruel . . . ruthless. He was everything that terrified her.

"I'm trying to save your life, you fool," Lord Channing barked. "You breathe one word of the exchange between Lady Jillian and the Duke of Bassett, and he and the Duke of Westbrook will have your guts for garters."

What about her life? Melissa wondered miserably. She was ruined just as surely as Jillian was ruined. Tears stung behind her eyes. Thanks to Viscount Channing's quick thinking, there was a good possibility she would be forced to marry the odious Nunnley for the sake of her reputation.

She hugged the shawl closer, acutely aware of her torn gown. "I can't be seen this way," she said numbly.

Lord Channing's gaze softened briefly as it rested on her and then hardened once more as it skipped to her mother and Lord Nunnley. "Forget what you saw. If you or Arabella speak of it, I'll see that you find yourself wed to Melissa in a trice."

Melissa stilled. There was still a chance. He was merely using her and Nunnley as bargaining chips. Yet as she stared at his rigid profile, she knew with absolute certainty that, if necessary, he would carry out his threat without a second thought. He would manipulate and intimidate anyone who stood in his way. He had no conscience.

And still in the back of her mind, she admired his loyalty to his friends and envied his brashness and nerve.

"Arabella, take Melissa back inside the ballroom and leave at once. No one will notice her disrepair as long as she keeps the shawl hugged close."

Melissa couldn't wait to escape. It was over. He was letting them go. In his arrogance he assumed her mother and Nunnley would do as they were told.

Of course, he was correct in his assumption. She wanted to laugh at the realization. As much as her mother wanted to hurt Jillian and the Duke of Bassett, she would never do anything to harm Melissa. And Nunnley was obviously unstrung at the prospect of marrying her. He would keep silent as well.

"You bastard," her mother hissed as her hand closed around Melissa's arm, her nails biting into the flesh.

Viscount Channing shrugged. "So true. Now, begone, and remember not a word or you know what will happen."

"Dry your face, Melissa," Arabella ordered. "Smile. We are just returning from a stroll on the terrace."

Melissa swiped at the tears on her cheeks. Tears she had not realized she'd shed. Without looking back, she fled with her mother along the dark terrace.

It had been three years ago, yet it seemed as if it had happened only yesterday. Nothing had changed since then except that her mother had become wealthy. Nothing was different except that Melissa's feelings for Bruce Palmerston had taken on new dimension and texture.

She blinked and felt her face heat up as she realized she'd been entertaining memories while staring blindly at a point across the room.

*He* stood there, leaning against a pillar, watching her with a small smile curving his wide mouth. She tried to tear her gaze away but she couldn't. His look was too knowing, too intense, the twinkle in his eyes too entrancing, holding her paralyzed as if time itself stood still, unable to move for the reactions that built on themselves with a simple glance or touch from him.

Slowly, lazily, he lowered one eyelid, favoring her with a wink. The heat radiated through her body and curled in the pit of her stomach, a small ember of desire waiting to be fanned.

"Melissa!" Arabella snapped crossly. "Please attend. I wish to see the library everyone has been raving about."

"Yes, Mother," Melissa murmured, and turned away. She wished she hadn't. Her mother's narrow-eyed glare at Bruce was full of outrage, her tight lips evidence that she kept her anger at bay only until they found more private surroundings. She'd seen Bruce's lingering regard of Melissa. She'd witnessed the wink.

Once again, Melissa knew she would pay for Bruce's actions.

As she followed her mother from the ballroom, Melissa accepted what she'd only suspected three years before.

Bruce Palmerston was a dangerous man.

# Chapter 3

B ruce had forgotten how boring house parties could be. If it weren't for Melissa, he'd likely fall asleep where he stood. Oddly enough, he was perfectly content to prop up the wall while Melissa was in sight. Come to think of it, Melissa had been the only source of interest for him at social functions lately, and he'd begun to balk at considering her as entertainment.

Lately, it seemed a great deal more like fascination.

Bruce straightened as Melissa followed her mother toward the doors of the ballroom. Where could they be off to? he wondered. Aside from it being far too early for them to retire, he knew that Arabella preferred to be in the thick of things. He glanced around at the men and women lining the walls of the ballroom. What did he care where Melissa went? He'd come to Baron Longford's to rendezvous with Joan and to catch up on gossip he might find useful in furthering his own interests in both business and pleasure. Every man here knew that more intrigue was hatched and more business concluded at social functions than in their solicitors' offices—or in the House of Lords, for that matter.

As if drawn by invisible strings, his gaze found the flash of Melissa's skirts as she passed through the wide doors. Even from the back, she was a work of art, with her long neck revealed by the upsweep of her hair and the rose petal perfection of her skin above the neckline of her gown. Too bad he couldn't see more of her body. He'd like to uncover it himself, inch by inch, exploring each dip and swell with his hands and his mouth. She'd taste as sweet as her smile—

"You are making a spectacle of yourself over Melissa Seymour," Joan whispered furiously as she materialized at his side.

Startled at having such provocative musings interrupted, he frowned down at Joan. Where the devil had she come from? More to the point, when had she become so damned possessive? He wasn't being any more attentive toward Melissa than usual ... was he? Nevertheless, Joan's censure annoyed him in the extreme as it would when coming from any woman with whom he shared a liaison. He was careful about that, choosing his lovers for their sophistication and lack of desire for permanent ties. Lovers who wanted exactly what he did without any illusions that their liaison might become more personal than the pleasure they found in bed. He might tell them he loved them, but they knew he meant he loved their wit and their company, their beauty and their bodies. They enjoyed hearing words that their husbands neglected to say. Some might call his attitude callous but he thought it more honest than most.

He'd often wondered if his mother would have

been happier and more at peace if her lover had bothered to say the words. If Bruce and his sister, Kathy, hadn't been told as well as shown how much their mother loved them, God only knew what a nightmare their lives might have been. As it was, any cruelties inflicted on them by their mother's husband were bearable because they'd had the comfort of tender embraces and caring words.

"Bruce," Joan said sharply, cutting off his thoughts. "Did you hear me?"

"I heard you," he snapped, further annoyed at his lapse into a past that was engraved in the stones adorning more than one family crypt. That thought threatened to nudge his irritation over an edge he made it a point never to approach. "I'm making a spectacle of myself, rather like you're making a spectacle of yourself with your strident jealousy. If you speak a bit more loudly, you will entertain everyone here."

She paled as the barb found its mark.

Wincing at his uncharacteristic harshness, Bruce tightened the reins on his wandering mind and focused on Joan. She was, after all, the reason he was here. . . .

Wasn't she?

"Forgive me," Joan said weakly. "I don't know why I'm behaving this way. I suppose it's been too long since I've had you all to myself."

He gravely considered her distressed expression and forced his voice to soften. "Yes, well, I understand how trying this past week has been for you, what with your husband being underfoot." Convinced by her returning color that she once again had things in proper perspective, he glanced toward the open doors. "Excuse me," he said, feeling an overwhelming need to escape.

"Yes, of course," Joan said with a strained smile. "I'll see you later."

Apparently she'd changed her mind about receiving him in her bed, not that he'd ever doubted she would. He returned her smile and bowed over her hand. "Later," he said, avoiding reference to when and where he would see her. In her present mood, she'd likely watch the clock and spoil their tryst with recriminations if he was so much as a minute late. In his present mood, he'd likely walk out on her if she did.

He strode out of the ballroom and took the stairs to the second floor of the house, his gaze searching the hallway for a glimpse of Melissa's blue gown and golden tresses. Realizing what he was doing, he muttered a curse and veered toward the library. He'd tortured Melissa quite enough for one night and he wasn't up to any more of Arabella's scathing glares.

His mood lightened as he spied Roger Wentworth stepping through the set of double doors leading into the library. Wentworth was always amusing. At twenty-seven he had a brood of five children and a wife who could outspend the Prince of Wales. It took all his considerable income to keep her as well as his two mistresses. In spite of that he was always on the prowl for the incidental lover.

Bruce followed Wentworth into the long, cavernous room lined with floor-to-ceiling bookcases and furnished with cozy groupings of furniture. A welcoming blaze crackled in the huge fireplace fronted by two large chairs whose backs curved high into canopies that offered privacy.

"Shall I pour you a brandy, old man?" Wentworth asked from beside a cart near the doors that offered an inviting array of spirits and a sparkling collection of crystal snifters and glasses.

Bruce nodded as his gaze appreciatively explored the room that would be a welcome retreat from boredom over the weekend.

He stopped short as his gaze reached the far end of the room. Melissa and Arabella stood at the large bay window with their backs to him.

He backed up a step, intent on leaving before they spotted him. But Wentworth pressed a snifter in his hand, staying his retreat. "Impressive, isn't it?" he boomed. "Who'd of thought the baron would have a fondness for books?"

Arabella stiffened and glanced over her shoulder, her expression stormy as her hand shot out to grasp Melissa's arm.

Bruce blinked and narrowed his gaze on Melissa's back. He could have sworn she flinched away from her mother. It had to have been a trick of the light. He couldn't imagine Melissa doing anything that hinted at defiance.

Wentworth stepped in front of Bruce, effectively blocking his view of Melissa. "It ain't gentlemanly to be entertaining such thoughts about Lady Melissa," he drawled.

"What thoughts?" Bruce inquired dryly.

Wentworth shifted to the side and flicked a quick glance at Melissa. "Thoughts of tossing up her skirts. She's so bloody beautiful it hurts to look at her."

Bruce stiffened at Wentworth's blunt admission. "Then perhaps you shouldn't look at her," he suggested, finding it difficult to maintain a mild tone of voice.

"Can't help myself any more than you can, old man."

"Pardon me?" Bruce said.

Wentworth chuckled. "Don't pretend you don't understand. I've been watching you lust after her for years."

It jolted Bruce to hear the same observation voiced twice within the same hour. It disturbed him to realize that his attentions had been so grossly misinterpreted. "I've merely been appreciating the scenery."

Wentworth shrugged. "So I gathered when you never offered for her. But then, that's certainly understandable. She may be beautiful, but she is also quite stupid. Who wants a wife who can't run a house and bears half-witted children?"

Bruce stifled a sudden urge to vigorously defend Melissa, never mind that he had similar doubts about her intelligence. "Who indeed?" he said simply.

"Just so," Wentworth said with a nod. "But, then, I don't require any of those things from her. I live for the day she finally takes a husband."

Bruce's chest tightened as he caught Wentworth's meaning. He lived for the day Melissa was free to take a lover. That didn't sit well. More disturbing was his confusion over being disturbed at all, whether by the idea of Wentworth's having her or by the idea of her marrying. In fact, it more than disturbed him, and Bruce wondered how he'd allowed himself to be drawn into a discussion of this nature. It was always degrading to the woman. That it was in regard to Melissa made it all the worse. "She doesn't seem the type to indulge in extramarital affairs," Bruce said, biting back the caustic reply he wanted to make.

"Of course she is." Wentworth grinned wolfishly. "And if she isn't so inclined, then I'll just have to persuade her."

*Arrogant sod*, Bruce thought. "You're quite sure of yourself," he said.

"No more so than you are of yourself. Don't tell me you don't plan to add her to the ranks of your lovers at first opportunity."

"Actually, I hadn't thought about it," Bruce said, his annoyance growing by the moment.

"I don't believe that for an instant." Wentworth cocked his brow thoughtfully. "Care to make a wager on which one of us has her as a lover first? Say, a thousand pounds?"

Something swelled inside Bruce and threatened to explode. He raised the snifter to his lips, stalling his reply and concealing his agitation under the guise of sniffing appreciatively, sipping, rolling the liquid over his tongue and savoring the flavor. Yet he tasted nothing in his confusion and shock over the strength of emotion that buffeted him from the inside out. Emotion that felt like anger. Yet anger was the last emotion he allowed himself to indulge, not when he could accomplish so much more by keeping his head clear enough to manipulate conditions to suit himself. Still, Melissa's honor was being besmirched, and he felt a ridiculous need to defend her.

Ridiculous. The only women he'd ever needed to defend were his sister and sister-in-law, and his mother when she'd been alive. Women for whom his love was deep and unquestionable, an integral part of his life and himself that he could no more discount than he could stop breathing. He felt nothing for Melissa but curiosity and lust and perhaps sympathy.

Thankfully, Wentworth turned back to the sideboard to examine the various decanters while muttering something about bitters, giving Bruce time to arrange his thoughts in a rational pattern.

He raised his snifter again and took a larger sip than was decent with fine brandy as he studied Melissa from across the room. She wasn't like any other woman. He'd known it the moment he'd met her. There was a quality about her that drew him and inspired his protective instincts. He'd sensed in her a genuine quality that was all too often missing in members of his society or at the very least buried beneath avarice and malice and fear. And he admired the courage it must take for one as timid as she to face society, not to mention her harridan of a mother, with such serenity. Courage such as Kathy and Jillian and his mother possessed. Courage notwithstanding, Melissa would not fare well in a game of musical beds. Somehow he knew that she would be the loser in such a game.

Why in hell should he care? She was a grown woman well past marriageable age. In another year she would be firmly on the shelf and free to take lovers whether she was married or not. She would be all but invisible. . . .

His eyes narrowed as he saw her shoulders slump slightly at something her mother said. Arabella gave her a sharp look and Melissa's shoulders straightened with a jerk. That disturbed him almost as much as his sudden urge to reduce Arabella to gasping humiliation with a few well-chosen words. But he'd only gone that far once and then only to protect Max and Jillian.

Wentworth straightened and grinned triumphantly as he held up the bitters he'd found in the depths of the sideboard.

Bruce cocked a brow and waited, hoping that Wentworth had forgotten about his proposed wager.

"A thousand pounds too rich for you, old man?" Wentworth asked. "Look at her. She's certainly worth it."

*Damn.* Bruce clenched his hand around the bowl of his snifter, wishing it was Wentworth's neck instead. The idea of making a wager over Melissa turned his stomach, yet he knew he was going to do it. He had to prove to himself that she was no more to him than any other lady of his acquaintance—a source of pleasure to the eye and entertainment for the mind. And if that failed, he needed the wager to justify keeping Wentworth from having her.

Tossing back the rest of his brandy, Bruce again stared at Melissa. "Merely a thousand pounds, for a morsel like her?" he said with a trace of mockery.

Wentworth's brows shot up in surprise. "How much did you have in mind?"

"Five thousand pounds," Bruce said, knowing how tightfisted Wentworth was and trying to set the stakes so high that he was sure to abandon the notion altogether. It would get him off the hook and perhaps remove some of the appeal for Wentworth.

"You're joking," Wentworth sputtered.

"Not at all," Bruce said. "Unless, of course, you want to withdraw the wager."

"Not likely," Wentworth said with a grin. "I'm going to enjoy collecting my five thousand pounds." The clock on the mantel chimed the hour. "Eleven o'clock already. I'd better fly. Haven't even said hello to our host."

*Bloody hell*, Bruce thought as Wentworth strode away. He'd never expected his bluff to be called. Now what? Suddenly, he became aware of Arabella's stony glare. Realizing that he was still staring at Melissa, he quickly glanced away and cursed under his breath as he remembered Joan's and Wentworth's observations.

Apparently, he was going to have to start employing more discretion. He could discount Joan's comments, but to have them repeated by Wentworth meant there was something to them.

The rustle and graceful ripple of blue silk drew his gaze back to Melissa.

She'd turned partway, her head lowered and tilted in his direction, her hand at her side absently fingering the skirt of her gown, like a caress.

Heat blossomed in his groin.

She watched him from beneath lowered lashes, her lips parted slightly, her cheeks glowing with a soft blush.

His breath caught in his throat as he saw something in her eyes that he'd never seen before. Something speculative and seductive that sent a lightning bolt of excitement through his body.

It couldn't be. Yet the expression in her eyes was one of a woman who desired a man. Suddenly, he had the feeling that he had completely misjudged Melissa Seymour, that every opinion he'd formed about her over the years was wrong. And then he told himself that he imagined it as he continued to watch her watch him from the corner of his eye. He had to prove he was right before he made a complete ass of himself.

Abruptly, he turned his head and stared fully at her as he curved his mouth in a slow, lazy and completely knowing smile.

She flushed and jerked her head away to stare at the bay window, her hand clenched around a handful of her skirt, mangling it.

He hadn't been wrong about her after all. She was a timid mouse, unable to cope with the most innocuous of a man's attentions. For all her twenty-odd years, she was a child who didn't know the first thing about seduction. She was as harmless as his teasing of her.

Feeling that all was right in the world again, he turned on his heel to leave.

Joan stood in the threshold of the library doors, venomously glaring at him, then at Melissa and back at him again. Without a word, she whirled and quickly walked away, her skirts swishing back and forth like a broom making a clean sweep.

Sighing, Bruce strode out after her, knowing what she'd seen. But she'd reached the end of the long corridor and disappeared around a corner. He considered following her and changed his mind. He really didn't think it was a good idea to try to make up with her now. He'd wait and do it later in the privacy of her chamber.

He frowned. Where the devil was Joan's chamber?

With another sigh, Bruce headed toward the grand staircase. He'd have his man, Smithy, locate Joan's room and procure a key from one of the maids.

"Bruce Palmerston should be horsewhipped," Arabella grated between clenched teeth. "How dare he trail us from room to room? How dare he stare at you as if you were not wearing a stitch of clothing?"

The same way she dared to stare at him, Melissa thought as she tried to suppress the guilt that clenched in her stomach. But she couldn't, no more than she could rid herself of the swell of embarrassment that threatened to crowd out her breath.

"He hasn't the decency to conceal his baser instincts," Arabella fumed.

Apparently, Melissa didn't either. For just as surely as Bruce had undressed her with his gaze a moment ago, she'd done the same as she'd watched him from beneath lowered lashes.

And he'd caught her.

His mistress had caught them both.

Now she understood that old saying about looks being able to kill, only she wasn't sure who Joan Sinclair wanted to kill most, Melissa or Bruce.

It was an odd feeling knowing that someone was actually jealous of her. Actually, it was rather a nice feeling, like satisfaction, and perhaps a small bit of smugness. Nicer still was knowing that Bruce had, for those few moments, been as fascinated with her as she had been with him, that he had indeed been undressing her with his gaze. From the way he'd smiled at her—slow and lazy and quite provocatively—she had little doubt that he'd found her as pleasing as she'd found him—

"Never has a viler man been born." Arabella continued to glare at the place where Viscount Channing had been standing a moment before.

Melissa stifled a sigh and nodded absently. The best thing she could do was keep silent, pretend attentiveness and allow her mother to vent her spleen. Thank goodness the library was empty.

Melissa frowned at the pulse throbbing at her

mother's temple. Perhaps she'd vented enough. If she frothed too much more, she would end up with a headache and have to spend the next day in bed. And while Melissa might enjoy the freedom that would give her, she didn't want it at her mother's expense. "Let me pour you a glass of sherry to settle your nerves, Mother," she said as she moved to the sideboard.

"The only thing that will settle my nerves would be to give Channing the dressing-down he deserves. I have had enough of his antics."

Panic fluttered in Melissa's stomach. She'd never heard her mother speak in terms of confronting him. Knowing Viscount Channing's penchant for mischief, that would only make matters worse. "Just leave him be, Mother."

"Just leave him be? You would not say that if you had seen the way he looked at you."

Melissa's face flamed as she quickly turned to the sideboard and picked up a crystal decanter. Of course her mother would assume she had been looking anywhere but at Viscount Channing.

"He is nothing more than a scapegrace."

"Mother, please," Melissa said as she poured sherry into a glass. "Someone might overhear you."

"Someone has overheard you," a deep voice drawled.

Melissa swallowed a gasp as she turned to see a small man rise from one of the canopied chairs fronting the fireplace. Her panic doubled as she recognized him as Robert Palmerston, the Earl of Blackwood.

Bruce's father.

Shooting a quick glance at her mother, Melissa was unsurprised that she appeared completely unruffled. She was very good at recovering herself when the need arose. For Melissa it was not so easy and in this instance it was impossible.

She wanted to sink into the floor and disappear. Of all the people in the world to overhear, why the earl? He didn't need to hear her mother's attack on his son. He'd had enough tragedy in his life.

At least in Melissa's opinion it was tragic.

The Earl of Blackwood had only recently returned to England after an absence of more than a decade. According to her mother, he'd fled the country under a cloud of shame because his wife had been in love with another man and was openly conducting an affair with him.

The late Countess of Blackwood must have been completely heartless and completely selfish to have done such a terrible thing to her husband—and to their children. Because of her, Viscount Channing and his sister had grown up without their father.

A lump welled in Melissa's throat as the earl crossed the short distance between them.

"Blackwood," Arabella said smoothly.

"Countess Seymour," he replied with a nod. "I collect that you don't care much for my son."

Arabella straightened her shoulders and lifted her chin. "I shan't take back a word of it. In fact, there are a few other invectives I could heap upon him."

Melissa felt the blood drain from her face. She hadn't expected her mother to go on the attack.

"And what would those be?" the earl inquired in a flat voice, his face expressionless. "Scoundrel? Rake? Hell-born babe?"

Melissa inhaled sharply and prayed that her mother would change tactics.

Arabella lifted her chin. "Those will do nicely, thank you."

What was her mother doing? Melissa wondered as her hand flew to her heart.

"It's quite all right, Lady Melissa," the earl said, turning his gaze on her. "I'm well aware of what Bruce is. Why do you think I remained in the shadows while he was here? I've found we get on much better if I ignore him whenever possible."

The blunt admission shocked Melissa. How could the earl say such a thing about his own son? While it was true that Viscount Channing always overstepped where she and her mother were concerned, he was held in very high esteem by the rest of society.

Melissa slid her gaze to her mother. If she had had any reaction to the earl's statement, she gave no indication.

"Unfortunately for me, that is not an option," Arabella said. "He seems to take great delight in being completely outrageous whenever he is near my daughter and myself."

The earl gave a sympathetic smile and folded his hands behind his back. "Perhaps I could have a word with him. In the meantime, allow me to offer my apologies for any offense Bruce has given." That said, he bowed, turned, and strode out of the library.

"So the earl and Channing are at odds with one another," Arabella said thoughtfully. "How wonderful. He may be just the ally we need."

"Perhaps," Melissa said, uneasy at the calculation in her mother's voice. She wasn't at all sure she trusted a man who so willingly and easily spoke ill of his own flesh and blood. It was the height of disloyalty.

Something was not right here. She could not imagine Viscount Channing being equally disloyal to his father, especially in view of the earl's recent heroic actions. He'd saved his daughter and her husband from certain death when a thwarted suitor had tried to kidnap Lady Kathleen and, failing that, had wounded her husband, the Duke of Westbrook. The earl had arrived just in time to kill the deranged man before Lady Kathleen could be harmed.

Society had been fawning over the earl ever since and sighing over the melodrama of it all.

Melissa, too, had sighed—in admiration of a man who so openly loved his children, and in grief for her own late father, who had loved her in such a way. Such sentiment was distressingly rare in the ton, where marriages were impersonal and children obligatory.

"Well, are you going to pour me a sherry or not?" Arabella said.

Melissa focused on the decanter in her hand, poured a measure into a small stemmed glass and handed it to her mother.

"Really, Melissa," Arabella said after taking a healthy sip of the wine. "You've been inordinately distracted this evening. I feel as if I'm talking to air half the time." She pressed the back of her hand to Melissa's temple. "Are you ill?" she asked, her brows drawn together in a fretful frown as she studied Melissa's features.

"I'm quite in the pink, Mother." She stifled the urge to press her fingertips to the bridge of her nose. If she didn't find solitude soon, she would be the one with the headache. "I'm simply tired. It's been a long day." *And a longer night*, she added silently.

Arabella's features smoothed in relief as she set

her glass down. "Of course, darling. I'm also a bit weary. Why don't we retire? If we're fortunate, Joan will have sent Channing packing and we can enjoy the rest of the weekend without his presence."

Melissa followed her mother from the library, too dismayed by the prospect to reply. She hated the thought that Bruce and Joan Sinclair would be together for the next two days.

She hated the thought of his leaving even more.

# Chapter 4

**"I**t is beyond me why Lady Longford gave us rooms at opposite ends of the hallway," Arabella grumbled as they reached the door to the room assigned to Melissa. "I can understand that it may not have been possible to manage adjoining chambers, but at the very least she could have situated us across the hall from one another. I'd feel much more comfortable knowing you were nearer to me."

Secretly pleased with the accommodations, Melissa didn't reply to her mother's endless stream of complaints as she pushed the door open and stepped inside. She hadn't expected the same luxury of distance from her mother at a house party as she enjoyed at home, where their rooms were at the opposite ends of the house.

She turned to say good night, the words arrested on her tongue as she saw the deep frown of distress creasing her mother's brow. "I'll be fine," Melissa assured, forcing a gentle tone and trying not to be annoyed. She loved her mother but felt suffocated by her overprotectiveness.

Arabella sighed deeply, not looking at all convinced. She, too, stepped inside and closed the door behind her, then examined the ornate dressing table set against one wall, the large canopied bed heavily draped with gold velvet, and the woven carpet with its carved pattern in forest green, rose and gold. "Be sure to turn the key in the lock. There are no inside bolts on these doors. Gentlemen will be prowling the hallways at all hours in search of their lovers. It is not unheard of for someone to blunder into the wrong room."

Melissa's annoyance gave way to sudden guilt. She supposed her mother's concern was justified, and she knew it was rooted in love. "I will," she promised with a tender smile and a pat on her mother's arm.

Still, her mother seemed reluctant to leave her as she stood by the door, her gaze fixed on nothing more than air, her beautiful face still distressed by a frown. "Mother," Melissa said softly, "will you help me out of my dress? I really don't feel like summoning a maid."

Arabella immediately smiled and stepped closer. "Of course, darling," she said brightly. "Now, turn around and be still. The buttons are quite small."

Melissa obeyed and kept silent, knowing that her mother would begin to chatter now.

"Did you notice that Channing was nowhere to be seen as we said our good nights and returned upstairs?" Arabella asked as she unfastened the buttons.

Melissa squeezed her eyes shut. She didn't want to discuss Viscount Channing. She didn't want to remember the smoldering look he'd given her in the library. "Perhaps he was tired and went to bed early."

"I'm certain he went to bed early." Arabella snorted. "So did Joan Sinclair; I noticed she was absent as well."

Something lurched in Melissa's chest, a sensation so intense her knees weakened. Viscount Channing and Lady Sinclair were together. The sensation grew in her chest, crowding out air.

"All finished," Arabella said. "Now, let me get all those pins out of your hair."

Suddenly, Melissa wanted nothing more than to be alone. She crossed her arms over her chest and turned. "No, I can manage. Thank you." She kissed her mother's cheek. "Good night."

"Nonsense," Arabella said.

Once again, annoyance pricked Melissa. She battled it back and appealed to the one concern she knew would send her mother running for her room. "I see the beginnings of dark circles beneath your eyes." Her mother prided herself on her youthful appearance and went to great lengths to preserve her beauty.

"Dark circles," Arabella said as her eyes widened in alarm and she pressed her hands to her face.

Melissa nodded, shamed at the lie. But it was the only way to send her mother off without hurting her feelings, and the need to be alone was growing by the second. "I'm sure they'll be gone by morning. All you need is a good night's rest."

"Yes, of course. Good night, darling," Arabella said, then glanced back over her shoulder. "Are you certain I can't help you with your hair? A few more minutes won't hurt—"

"I'm certain, Mother." Melissa saw her mother out and dutifully turned the key in the lock, her anger over Viscount Channing's and Lady Sinclair's being together ticking inside her like a timepiece that had been wound too tightly. She walked slowly toward the bed, shedding her clothing as she went while telling herself that she was being irrational.

Whatever was the matter with her? she wondered as she stepped out of her gown and tossed it on a chair. It was none of her concern what Viscount Channing and Lady Sinclair did. She would give it no more thought.

She shed her chemise and tossed it on top of her gown, unmindful of the fragile lawn edged with cobweb-fine lace. Nude, she reached for the night-gown lying across the foot of the bed, and absently stroked the shimmering white silk and embroidered lace before slipping it on over her head.

She shivered and wished that tonight she had a heavier one, something with long sleeves and a high neck. But her mother believed a woman should always wear beautiful things from the skin out, and Melissa loved pretty lingerie—the way it felt against her skin, the way it rustled in the silence and flowed around her body like a cool breeze . . .

She smoothed the gown over her body and shivered again at the memory of Bruce's gaze sliding over her in just such a way, like silk warmed by the touch of flesh.

Lady Sinclair probably received Viscount Channing wearing a similar confection.

"Stop it," she said aloud as she stalked to the dressing table and snatched the pins from her hair, then briskly pulled her brush through the strands, determined to put Viscount Channing from her mind. But she kept seeing him, kept seeing his smoldering blue eyes roam over her body.

She shook her head to clear it. What did she care

if he'd looked at her as if he wanted to make love to her? He'd been looking at her that way for years.

Well, not precisely that way, she corrected. Tonight it had been different. In the past, she'd always known he'd been teasing her. Tonight, she'd seen no humor lurking in the depths of his eyes. Tonight, she'd seen only unconcealed desire in her expression and seduction in his smile.

And for that brief space of time, she had wanted to be seduced . . . by him.

Her hand stilled in midair as yearning swept through her, leaving her body aching in the most intimate places. She stared at herself in the looking glass, seeing the glazed expression in her own eyes. It was desire . . . for him.

It frightened the wits out of her. Is this what he'd seen as he'd stared at her, his gaze caressing her from across the room, beguiling her into seeing no one but him, feeling nothing but the pleasure his smile suggested? She'd felt it then as she did now, lingering over her in an almost cherishing way.

*Wishful thinking*, a voice murmured in her thoughts.

She tore her gaze from her reflection and shook her head with a jerk. What kind of woman was she? How could she have such lustful thoughts about a man her mother hated with every fiber of her being? A man she should hate for the way he'd humiliated and used her.

Perhaps she could have hated him as her mother did if she hadn't seen the compassion and regret in his eyes on that long-ago night. But she had seen it, and she'd known that she would have done the same thing if her friends were being threatened.

If she had any friends. Even as it formed she

brushed the thought away. Friends or her lack thereof were not her immediate problem.

And yet, she remembered wishing on that night that Bruce was her friend. In his actions, she'd seen a capacity for love that knew no bounds and a loyalty that recognized no rules.

She'd wanted to experience the kind of love one wasn't born with. She'd wanted to know what it was like to have someone besides her mother care enough about her to want to protect her, no matter the cost.

She'd always been attracted to Bruce, but after that night she'd become increasingly fascinated by him. He was a scoundrel and a rake, yet she'd seen him treat his women with tenderness and respect. In fact, she thought he spoiled them outrageously. He was ruthless in his dealings, yet she'd heard the emotion in his voice when he'd spoken of his sister and friends.

She wanted to hear that same emotion in his voice when he spoke her name. And tonight she wanted him to whisper sweet nothings into her ear rather than Joan's. Worse, she wanted it to be her room he entered for the night.

Tonight, she didn't want him to be her friend. She wanted him to be her lover.

And now she wanted to feel shame for her thoughts, but the memory of him was too fresh in her mind, her attraction to him too overwhelming.

And completely impossible.

She tossed her brush down and rose to make a slow circuit about the room, wishing she could snuff out thoughts of Bruce as easily as she snuffed the candles.

As she climbed into bed she was certain of only

one thing: She would keep her gaze well away from Viscount Channing in the future, and she would try very hard to remember that while he was witty and charming, he was also ruthless and altogether too sure of himself. He might very well love his family and friends, but his habit of keeping company with married women made it quite clear to her that he had no interest in marriage.

She wanted marriage, a man's love. She wanted to love as her parents had loved.

It made no sense that she wanted all that and Bruce too.

What he'd done to her with one blatantly sexual look from across a large room contradicted everything she'd believed about herself—that she would marry only for love and that until then no man would interest her. Yet Bruce more than interested her, and she feared what might happen if he bestowed another of those burning looks on her during one of their forced dances.

She didn't want to think about it. She *wouldn't* think about it one moment longer, she decided as she settled back against the pillow and closed her eyes.

Instantly, they popped open again as the light of the full moon fell directly on her face. Sighing, she pushed up on her elbows and studied the bed hangings. She would have to get out of bed to close them.

A click echoed through the air, stalling her as she realized it was a key turning in the lock. She turned her head toward the door as it slowly opened.

*It is not unheard of for someone to blunder into the wrong room.* Fear paralyzed Melissa as her mother's warning echoed in her ears. Oh, God, it was happening. But how? She'd locked her door. She wanted to cry out, but sound froze in her throat.

With a candelabra held high, Joan Sinclair stepped into the room, her eyes narrowed as she searched the room. "I was looking for someone, I thought he might be here."

The fear drained out of Melissa so abruptly she felt as weak as a baby, as Joan's words caught up with her. *He?*

Lady Sinclair could mean only one man. Viscount Channing.

Melissa felt her eyes grow wide and her brows shoot straight up. Joan had thought that Bruce was here?

"Obviously you're alone," Lady Sinclair said. "I apologize for the intrusion."

Melissa could only nod, speech still beyond her grasp, as she watched Lady Sinclair back out the door.

She didn't know whether to laugh or cry. What sort of woman did Lady Sinclair think Melissa was?

Exactly the sort of woman she'd been fantasizing about being a few short moments ago.

The door opened again. "Be sure to lock your door from the inside, I seem to have lost the key," Lady Sinclair called out and was gone.

So that was how she'd gained entrance, Melissa thought numbly. This was Lady Sinclair's parents' house. She would have access to all the keys.

She must be desperate to find Viscount Channing to stoop to such a thing.

A smile spread across Melissa's face.

They weren't together.

She frowned. Why was she so pleased? She shouldn't be. She *wouldn't* be, she told herself as she climbed out of bed and once again locked her door. It was nothing to her.

Remembering to pull the bed curtains, she gave them an angry yank, then slid through the opening, overlapped the ends of the curtains to give herself complete darkness, and punched her pillow into place.

With a weary sigh, she again settled into bed, determined to think of nothing but a night of dreamless sleep. As she drew the counterpane up to her chin, the corners of her mouth once again curved in a smile.

Bruce and Joan were not together.


One-thirty in the morning. The full moon hung low in the sky, casting a silver wash over the terrace and grounds. Bruce had sat on the balustrade for over an hour, too restless to be confined in his bedchamber and too agitated to concentrate on the games going on in the card room.

He closed his pocket watch and slipped it back into his pocket. Surely, Smithy had discovered the whereabouts of Joan's room and procured a key by now. And hopefully enough time had passed for Joan to have calmed down. He had to admit that she had every right to be unhappy with him. He was unhappy with himself for breaking his own rule to never treat a lover with anything but respect and courtesy. If he'd learned anything from the earl—his legal father and his mother's paid "husband"—it was that there was rarely any reason to be cruel. If he'd learned anything from the late Duke of Bassett—his true father and his mother's lover—it was that selfish disregard for the feelings of others was perhaps the worst cruelty of all.

He winced at the memory of the hurt he'd seen in Joan's eyes, not once but twice that evening, never mind that he'd been completely unaware of doing anything untoward. Aware or unaware, he'd satisfied some lascivious streak in his nature at Joan's expense.

It still rattled him to know that Joan and Wentworth thought the worst. Who would have thought Melissa could wreak such havoc in his life without saying a word? But then, Melissa had always had an odd effect on him, stirring his lust as well as holding his attention to the exclusion of all else. Three years ago, he'd damned near recanted his threats to Nunnley and Arabella when he'd seen Melissa's panic. And he'd damned near begged her forgiveness when he'd seen comprehension of his actions dawn in her eyes followed by understanding and a brief flash of admiration.

Since when had he cared whether anyone admired him or not?

Yet, that night, he had cared enough to almost forget about protecting Jillian and Max.

For some unknown reason, shy, timid, and quite possibly dull-witted Melissa brought out all the softer emotions he reserved for his family and friends. For reasons too unsettling to ponder, beautiful, sweet, innocent Melissa held his attention, his interest, and engaged emotions too strong and complex to be considered soft. He wanted no part of any of it.

For reasons that were becoming increasingly clear to him, he had to leave her alone.

She was dangerous. With Melissa, he seemed to lose his power to reason.

With one last look at the moon, he swung his legs

over the edge of the wide balustrade of the terrace and made his way to his room.

The moment he stepped in the door, Smithy lurched to his feet. "Well, it's about time."

Bruce's lip twitched. Only Smithy would have the nerve to complain. But then he was no ordinary servant. Having been with Bruce for nearly twenty years, there was no part of his life to which Smithy was not privy. They'd gone through hell together. And then Smithy had gone through hell with Bruce's sister and her husband while Bruce was abroad. The man had more than earned his right to familiarity.

"Sorry to keep you waiting," he said mildly, then frowned as he realized the tightness of Smithy's expression was due to strain rather than weariness. "What is it?"

"Did you know the Earl of Blackwood is here?"

Bruce went cold inside at the mention of the man who had made his and his sister Kathy's childhood a living hell, the man whose name they bore and whose title Bruce would one day inherit. The man the world believed was their father.

A grand lie.

A lie that Bruce and the earl had no choice but to perpetuate for the sake of everyone involved. Too bad the earl hadn't stayed in America. Things had been much easier when there had been a continent between them. But there wasn't, and Bruce preferred to concern himself with what he could change or control rather than what he could not. "Father is here?" he said mockingly as he sauntered farther into the room.

Smithy's jaw tightened. "It ain't funny. Watch your back. He's like a snake lying in the grass waiting for you to step on him."

"True, but you and I both know he's not poison-ous anymore. He wouldn't dare do anything to harm me." Bruce smiled as he recalled the threat his brother-in-law had made to the earl while Bruce had been away. Damien had promised the earl that he would destroy his name, his wealth and his power if any harm should ever come to any member of his family. A promise that had resulted in grand irony when the earl had shot a man to save the lives of Bruce's sister, Kathy, and her husband, Damien, when he would have preferred to see them disposed of once and for all.

His heroic actions had been proof positive that the earl had taken Damien seriously.

"If you're so bleeding sure of the earl, why didn't you know he was here?" Smithy asked, his eyes gleaming with suspicion. "Why is he hiding from you?"

"Actually, avoiding is more accurate," Bruce said. "I imagine he doesn't want to be put in a position where he has to be cordial to me. God knows, I don't want to be anywhere near the man."

"I can have us packed and out of here within the hour. We can be home by noon."

One might think Smithy was afraid of the earl, but Bruce knew better. He knew the urgency stemmed from what Smithy felt was a lack of caution on Bruce's part.

But Bruce refused to live his life constantly look-ing over his shoulder, and he refused to pack up and leave every time he found himself at the same social function as the earl.

"I don't think it is necessary to go that far." He raised a brow and changed the subject. "Did you have any trouble locating Lady Sinclair's room?"

Smithy shook his head. "None at all. Your lady showed here looking for you not ten minutes after you left."

"Joan was here?" Bruce said, pleased. Maybe he wouldn't have to grovel as much as he'd thought, or perhaps she'd come to give him a stinging set down in private. Either way, he'd at least have the opportunity to make it up to her without having to apologize to her through a door shut firmly in his face. "Did she leave a key and directions to her room?"

"'Course not. She's a lady. She pretended she'd knocked on the wrong door," Smithy said. "I followed her. Her room is in the east wing, last one at the end of the corridor."

"Very good," Bruce said. "Were you able to procure a key?"

Smithy fished in his pocket. "She left it sticking in the outside lock when she went in."

"Excellent." Bruce grinned and pursed his lips in a tuneless whistle as he shrugged out of his coat, poured water into a basin to wash up and clean his teeth, and fixed his mind on the night of pleasure ahead.

But as he dried his face and ran twin brushes through his hair, his thoughts slipped into the blue depths of Melissa's eyes.

# Chapter 5

**A** figure darted furtively into a corridor.

Apparently, he wasn't the only tardy lover tonight, Bruce observed as he ducked into a small alcove and waited for the count of ten, then cautiously tilted his head, looking left and then right to make certain no one else was lurking about.

The halls appeared empty. But that wasn't surprising; the hour was so late that the couples who'd planned a tryst were already trysting. He waited another thirty seconds, then proceeded down the passage to the room Smithy had seen Joan enter.

As he reached Joan's door, he quickly glanced over his shoulder one more time. Satisfied that he was quite alone, he quickly let himself in, locked the door behind him, and pocketed the key Smithy had purloined.

His smile broadened as he glanced toward the bed. She had released the hangings—a sure sign that she expected to use her bed for more than sleeping. Joan always felt more secure behind the privacy of thick bed curtains. And she liked the idea of separating herself from the world; she'd said it heightened the pleasure to be completely blind with only the senses of touch and taste and smell and the stimulation of naughty words drifting through the night air.

He had to admit that it did add to the excitement on occasion, but so did seeing the soft flesh and provocative contours of a woman's body poised for sex. Tonight, he welcomed the anonymity of darkness and hoped it would blot out his thoughts as well.

The light of the moon literally glowed on the gold bed curtains like candle flame reflecting off mellow walls, beckoning and seducing with shimmer and shadow on the silk velvet. An appropriate setting, Bruce thought, a golden temple designed to enhance passion and heighten desire.

He slipped out of his jacket and dropped it on the floor.

From behind the bed curtains came the sort of sigh produced by sweet dreams or sweet anticipation. Which was it? he wondered. Was Joan lying in the darkness, aware that he was here, or was she asleep and thus affording him the pleasure of slowly bringing her to awareness?

His manhood stirred as he hoped for the latter. Waking Joan with his caress might be rather sensuous. She had a tendency to rush through lovemaking and overlook the eroticism that came with savoring each touch, prolonging the pleasure.

He tugged at his neck cloth as he slipped off his shoes, then swiftly and silently stripped off the rest of his clothes. Stark naked, he moved toward the velvet-shrouded bed, his footfalls making no sound on the thick carpet.

With care, he slipped inside and eased down beside her, quickly releasing his hold on the curtain to shut out the shaft of moonlight that followed him inside.

He lay still for a moment. He always felt slightly disoriented when first entering Joan's black cocoon. The darkness was so complete he couldn't make out her silhouette, though her deep, even breathing told him she was indeed asleep.

Rolling to his side, he propped himself on one elbow and, like a blind man, reached out for her, his hand trailing over the curve of her hip, then traveling upward to gently cover her breast and thumb one nipple through her silky nightgown. As it tightened beneath his fingers a soft sigh carried through the darkness.

"That feels nice, doesn't it, darling?" he whispered.

She started and inhaled sharply as her hand jerked up to tightly grasp his, stilling the play of his fingers on her flesh.

"I'm sorry, I hurt you tonight, Joan," he said with all sincerity. "My behavior was inexcusable."

She remained silent, her grip on his hand like a vise.

Obviously, she was still angry with him. He should have kept his mouth shut rather than remind her of his transgression. Still, he noted with a grin, she hadn't pushed his hand away from her breast but simply held it there, keeping it from roaming to more intimate places. Never one to waste an opportunity, he intended to put this one to good use, knowing that with the proper encouragement, Joan never took long to melt in his arms.

With her hand still clamped over his, he slowly kneaded the tantalizing mound. Just as slowly, her hold relaxed, as if she'd decided to accept what he was doing now rather than punish him for what he'd done hours ago.

"I've waited all evening for this moment, darling," he said as he nuzzled her earlobe. "Waited to do this . . ." Silk slid beneath his hand as he gently lowered a strap over her shoulder, down her arm, over her hand. She lay still as he bared her breast, found it with his hand and lingered there with the barest whisper of a touch. "And this." He lowered his hand and eased the hem of the gown up, over her legs and hips. Lust clenched in his belly at the thought of how she must look, her legs and belly bared and one breast free, the rest draped in luminous silk.

He lowered his head and nudged the fabric away from her other breast, then skimmed his tongue over the center.

She arched her back to press herself closer, her nipples hard nubs against his palm and mouth, her hand tightening over his, yet not pushing him away, not resisting his caresses. . . .

Encouraging his touch.

"Oh, Joan, I love you."

He raised his head to nibble at her ear, down the length of her neck and back up again to drop a light, teasing kiss to her mouth. "Forgive me," he murmured, heat curling in his belly at the softness of her flesh and the fullness of her breast that overflowed his hand. . . .

It was a perfect breast.

It wasn't Joan's breast.

He stilled, his hand on her breast and his groin barely pressed against her hip. A lush hip. An unfamiliar hip.

"I beg your pardon," he whispered, not knowing what else to say.

She didn't move, didn't release his hand or shrink away from him. All he heard was breath being carefully regulated . . . by her . . . by himself. And then he didn't hear her breathe at all, as if she were frozen, waiting for him to say something, do something.

He didn't know what to do. He had neither the urge to laugh at having made such a mistake nor the inclination to leave her now, before he compounded the error. He should leave as silently as he'd come, saving them both from the embarrassment of recognition, but he could not. Something compelled him to remain, to see what happened next. Something dark and seductive and almost desperate—

She hesitantly guided his hand to her other breast.

Desire streaked through his body, scorching him, reducing his thoughts to ash. That he didn't know who she was inflamed him more. And by her very silence he could only assume she didn't want him to know her identity. It was an erotic fantasy come to life. A fantasy that he had no intention of passing up when she lay so pliant beneath his hand, her breath catching with every movement of his fingers on her breast.

In less than a heartbeat, his erection grew to painful proportions.

He leaned over her and ran his tongue between the crevices of her fingers, still splayed over his, then grasped her wrist and turned it, pressing a kiss to her open palm before he placed it on his chest. "I can think of other things for you to do with your hand. . . ."

Her body trembled then, and he sensed a poignant

vulnerability in the suddenness of it, as if the woman beside him were struggling with herself—and perhaps with her conscience. That she knew his identity seemed likely, as he'd seen no strangers at the house party. That she wanted him to continue was obvious in the way she lay without moving, without protesting. Was she, too, indulging in a fantasy as she would never have the courage to do openly? That, too, spoke of vulnerability.

She was a puzzle, yet one he had no immediate need to solve. Not when desire rose in him stronger and more insistent than he could ever remember. Not when he had the sudden need to make this unknown woman comfortable with what he was doing . . . with what she was obviously asking him to do. He wanted to give her all the pleasure he could. He told himself that it was no less than he ever did for his lovers, but he knew this was somehow different, somehow special. How many times in one's life did one have the opportunity to *be* a fantasy as well as live in one, even for a night?

Her fingers fanned out on his flesh, a timid venture that encouraged him to rotate his palm over one nipple, then the other. Had he ever felt such softness? Had he ever known such a response as she arched and shuddered with pleasure and her nipples swelled and puckered?

He lowered his head and took her mouth in small teasing nips at one corner, over what turned out to be a full lower lip, to the other corner, then skimmed his tongue over the delicate peaks of her upper lip.

Her hand drifted up his chest to his shoulder, slowly, hesitantly. Her head moved, her mouth following his, clinging to his kiss and parting slightly as she panted softly in the darkness.

Unable to resist, he slipped his tongue between her lips, tasting her, inhaling her warm, sweet breath as his hand skimmed down her midriff, over her belly....

A light dew misted her skin as she quivered and heated beneath his touch.

His hand glided lower ... over soft curls and softer flesh ... on the inside of her thighs ... between them.

Her legs parted and her hair brushed his face as she tossed her head from side to side.

She was hot and wet and ready for him.

The air inside the bed curtains was heavy and sultry with the scent of desire as fever burned inside him and demand for release throbbed in his groin. The darkness felt like magic, a spell enveloping him, holding him, caressing him as she caressed him, over his shoulders, his neck, his back. Such simple caresses to inflame him so.

He covered her body with his as he took her mouth again, deeply, exploring every corner and hollow. His hand stroked above her thighs, parting her moist folds, seeking, finding and stroking deeper.

The silence became more complete as she seemed to hold her breath and her body became like fluid, flowing around him as her knees bent slightly and her legs gripped him on either side of his hips.

Any lingering doubt vanished. This lady knew exactly what she did and what she wanted.

And never had he wanted anything so fiercely as he wanted the woman beneath him ... now ... quickly. He pressed against her, into her.

No. Not now. Not yet.

He bit back a groan as he forced himself to pause,

to slide down and rest his head on her breast. He wanted it to last. He wanted to savor every nuance of the woman who was a part of the night, more than a shadow yet less than real to him. He wanted memories of the fantasy, of taste and smell and texture and sound after the moment had passed.

Yet she made no sound other than a sigh, a caught breath, a whisper of flesh brushing over fine linen.

*The least she could do is moan a bit*, he thought as frustration bit at him. He needed to hear the sound of her voice blending with the darkness. . . .

To hear her say "Yes."

"I love you like this," he whispered as he stroked her more intimately, more urgently.

She whimpered and twisted beneath him, seeking him, opening her legs wider in demand.

"Your body is eloquent," he whispered as he slowly moved toward her, yet denying them both fulfillment. "Will you not speak? Tell me what you want." He traced her lips with his thumb. He dipped his head and again took her breast in his mouth, drawing on the nipple as his hand probed a little more deeply inside her, knowing she wanted him, needing to hear her say it was so.

He pulled away completely, withdrawing his touch. "Tell me you want this," he said softly, clearly—a demand and a challenge.

She whimpered and writhed and tossed her head from side to side, yet still she said nothing. Her hips arched, reaching for his shaft as her hands gripped his waist, pulling him to her.

He could not wait. Rising above her, he slid his hands beneath her hips, lifted her to meet him, entered her in one hard thrust.

She stiffened. She trembled and gave a stifled cry.

She buried her head against his shoulder and sank her teeth into his flesh.

He froze above her in horror.

Damn it to bloody hell. She wasn't a woman; she was a virgin.

He throbbed and ached and shuddered as his body demanded he surrender. He held it in check, commanding his body to obey his restraint, unable to move at all for fear of losing complete control.

She was a virgin, perhaps someone's sister. . . . He shuddered again and clenched his teeth as he lifted away from her, out of her in painful increments, willing himself not to let go, not to plunge deeply into her and find release.

But before he could completely leave her body, she cried out and grasped his hips again, slid her hands around him and flattened them against his buttocks, pulling him down.

"I cannot do this," he said hoarsely as he pressed his forehead to hers.

She raised her head slightly, her mouth meeting his and moving in what could have been the one word he didn't want to hear, to feel.

*Yes.*

Her hands pressed harder, urging him to sink into her. To drown in her. She trembled, and a sob escaped her, sounding like a word . . . a plea. Again, her mouth reached for his and opened for him. She wrapped her legs around his waist and arched, taking him—all of him—inside her.

He wanted to thrust again and again, to meet her each time she arched against him, creating friction, driving him mad until he didn't care who or what she was.

*A virgin.* He recited it like a litany, refusing to let

go, to take the pleasure she offered, to give her more
until they were both spent and sighing. Every muscle in his neck tightened with the force of his effort
not to move, not to thrust, and not to spill himself.
He shook his head to clear it and groaned as she
quivered and tightened around him, holding him inside her with the force of her own release. It rocked
him and shattered him and threatened to overwhelm
him as her spasms caressed him in the deepest intimacy of all.

By her faltering caresses, he'd judged her untu-
tored, yet not innocent. Never innocent. How could
she, a virgin, find such pleasure so quickly and easily? So completely? How could he have become so
lost in fantasy that he'd lost his mind as well?

How could he continue to want the fantasy even
as reality pounded on the door to his mind?

He reeled with the discovery that he had seduced
and taken an unknown woman—a lady—without a
single consideration for the consequences of such an
act. Of course, he knew the answer. He'd thought—
he'd chosen to think—her a woman like so many
others of his acquaintance, frustrated and neglected
and needing an exciting interlude to relieve her
boredom. He'd thought to enjoy the provocative
mystery of her. He'd thought . . .

Oh, bloody hell, he hadn't been thinking at all.

He still wasn't thinking as she held him inside her
and continued to tremble against him, around him.

A virgin no more. His fault. His insanity.

He jerked away from her and grimaced as her
body tightened in one last spasm, refusing to surrender him easily. As he gained his freedom, he
reached for the bed curtains and yanked them open.
Moonlight hurt his eyes as it poured over the bed,

over fair flesh and golden hair and blue eyes wide and unblinking as she stared up at him—

"Melissa . . . no . . ." Her name was a shocked whisper in the air, of dismay, of wonder.

Release came swiftly on the heels of comprehension as his body completed what he would have denied it, spilling his passion onto the sheets as his mind grappled with confusion and shock.

Melissa Seymour.

Oh, God. Not her. Anyone but her.

Yet Melissa stared up at him, her beauty ethereal in the moonlight, her flesh moist and glowing like pearls, her eyes an almost translucent blue glazed by passion, her hair spread around her head on the pillow like a halo—an angel corrupted.

His gaze swept her body, her legs still parted, her breasts swollen and heaving as she caught her breath in the aftermath, her arms lying limp on either side of her, a fantasy come to life.

He banished the thought and replaced it with the truth. He had taken Melissa Seymour tonight as he had taken her a thousand times in his dreams.

A virgin. Never had he taken a virgin.

And she had allowed it, welcomed it, knowing who he was. Worse, her lack of shock and outrage during his seduction hinted that she knew more about the act than any virgin ought to know. The way she'd opened for him left him in little doubt of that.

Neither, he thought grimly, could he doubt that as a result of his stupidity and her willing enthusiasm, life as he knew it—life as he'd made it—would come to an end.

# Chapter 6

**"I** should have known it was too good to be true," Bruce muttered just loud enough for Melissa to hear.

Too good to be true? It had been better than true. Being held in his arms had been wonderful. Being stroked and caressed by him had been breath stealing. Being beneath him as his body became a part of hers had been sheer ecstasy.

Ecstasy . . . a word she'd always thought rather silly and melodramatic until now.

She floated on it still, that cloud of rapture that drifted just beyond the world, separating her from loneliness and stifling restrictions. Separating her from everything and everyone save Bruce, whose hands created magic and whose beautiful body seemed to fit so well into hers.

And his body was indeed beautiful with power etched by silver moonlight and midnight shadows over his broad chest and wide shoulders. As beautiful as his face with its strong lines softened by the creases in his lean cheeks that deepened when he smiled and the slight cleft dipping into his firm chin.

As beautiful as his blue eyes that shimmered like light penetrating her thoughts.

"Why?" he asked hoarsely.

Melissa didn't know what to say. She never knew what to say when Bruce was near. But now, as she lay on the bed staring up at him, her body was too full of sensation, her mind too full of answers for her to utter a single sound.

Now she knew why she'd been both drawn and repelled by Bruce. Now she knew why no other man held her attention. And now she understood what her mother had meant when she'd said that coupling produced pleasure. She'd had a hint of the pleasure her mother spoke of when Bruce first touched her, when he bowed over her hand and boldly brushed his lips to the backs of her fingers, when he held her in the dance. Then, she'd both feared and enjoyed his touch. Feared because of the way her hand tingled and her body flushed and her heart seemed to lurch and stumble in her chest. She'd enjoyed it because of those very same sensations. Sensations of excitement and anticipation.

She'd always been attracted to him. Now she could have no doubt that she'd always wanted him.

Tentatively, she slid her hand across the space between them, reaching for him, her fingers opening over his thigh, caressing.

He jerked away from her.

She parted her lips, wanting him to again lie down beside her and take her back to that other place where she had no concerns beyond what she felt and what she wanted. That world had been a revelation to her as she'd emerged from the fog of sleep, at first too stunned by Bruce's presence to know what to do. Her body, however, had no such timidity and had come alive at his first caress, the sensations he evoked a thousand times stronger than ones prompted by her imagination. By the time she'd fully awakened, she hadn't wanted to stop him. She hadn't even considered it. She hadn't even cared that his "I love you" hadn't been meant for her.

But he sat stiffly on the edge of the bed, his face pale and his eyes bleak as he stared at her.

"Why?" he repeated, an edge of demand in his voice.

Still, she couldn't speak. How could she tell him that her loneliness had been particularly acute tonight, or that her thoughts had been particularly rebellious as a result?

He turned away from her.

She thought he was angry, yet he showed no sign other than the tension in his naked back and his fist gripping the edge of the velvet bed hangings. Never had she seen Bruce angry, not that night on the balcony when her mother had threatened Jillian and the Duke of Bassett, and not at any other time. Society adored him for his easy manner and scandalous wit even as no one ever doubted that he would make a formidable enemy if challenged.

His shoulders heaved as he inhaled deeply. "You knew who I was all along," he stated flatly.

She swallowed and nodded as he glanced at her over his shoulder.

"You were willing."

Again she nodded. Of course, she had been willing. She'd thought of nothing but Bruce all evening long, had fallen asleep with the image of him in her dreams. She'd enjoyed being selfish, indulging only herself. She'd reveled in the rebellion of acting on instinct rather than obeying rules.

"You were a virgin," he said harshly, an accusation.

"I'm sorry," she blurted. And she was sorry. Sorry that she hadn't had the experience to please him as he'd pleased her. Sorry that her knowledge did not extend to how to behave in moments like this one.

He rose abruptly and began gathering his clothes. "I, too, am sorry."

She watched as he paused in the center of the room and frowned, apparently searching for his trousers. He stood so tall and straight and proud, his flesh silvered by moonlight, his gaze approaching and halting on her. And as she stared his erection grew, a stiff and bold silhouette rising from his body.

Startled at the sight of it, she sat up and stared down at her bared breasts and the nightdress twisted up around her waist. Bruce had been inside her! It didn't seem possible, yet the memory of the sharp thrust of pain even as she accepted him inside her, stretching and conforming to him, was too vivid to deny.

"Now you are shocked," he said with a twisted smile. "And now you understand the consequences of what occurred."

"But you didn't ... I mean, you waited ..." she stammered, and slid a glance at the sheet as she fumbled to push her nightgown down over her hips and pull it up over her breasts.

His mouth twisted. "You mean I bungled the job?"

Bungled? If he had bungled what would it be like when he did not? Could there possibly be more? The thought intrigued—

"Nevertheless, you are a genteel young woman

and I have compromised you." He stalked back to the bed, loomed over her. "Take a good look, Melissa. Consider what it means to be in a room alone with a naked man, much less in bed with him." He leaned over her then, holding her gaze as he supported his weight with his arms stiff and his hands planted on the mattress. "Do you understand? You are compromised. You can no longer give a husband your innocence."

She shook her head. She did not want to marry just any man. She wanted to marry a man who loved her enough to accept her as she was, virgin or not.

"Since I am the one who received that particular gift, I will become your husband." Bruce straightened away from her. "Do you wish to speak with"—he grimaced—"Arabella before I approach her?"

The mention of her mother hit her like a wave of cold water threatening to drown her. "Why?" she asked, hearing the high note of panic in her voice.

"I should think that is obvious," he said as he shoved one leg, then the other, into his trousers and pulled them up over his hips, then sketched a mocking bow. "It is customary to petition the parents of the woman one wishes to marry."

She shook her head. "But I don't wish to marry you."

He raised his brows. "At last, you speak a complete sentence. It is, however, the wrong one."

"Why?"

He sighed and picked up his shirt. "Again, the answer should be obvious."

"No," she said vehemently. "There is no danger . . . no one need know . . ." Her tongue seemed to wrap around itself then, losing the words she wanted to say. She swallowed and tried again. "It isn't necessary."

His gaze sharpened on her. "You're certain of that?"

She nodded. "Mother told me all about . . . I mean, I know there will be . . . no . . . consequences."

"Your mother," he mused, "acts as if you're the bloody crown jewels and every man wants to steal you, yet she has told you 'all about it.' " He faced her with his hands on his hips, his shirt hanging open over his chest. "And you can't move right nor left without being told, yet you accept me in your bed and urge me on when I would have stopped."

She winced at his opinion of her. Yet he was right. Her mother did guard her as if she were the crown jewels. And she always did what she was told whether she wanted to or not.

Until tonight.

Until Bruce had happened into her room and given her the perfect opportunity to be as bold and brave as she'd always dreamed of being. . . .

Just once.

"Why did you do it, Melissa?" he asked softly as he walked toward the bed and sat down beside her, his hands reaching for her arms, then retreating as if he didn't trust himself to touch her.

"I wanted to," she replied honestly.

"You wanted to." He raked his hand through his thick auburn hair. "Yet you don't want to marry me."

Watching him warily, she shook her head.

"May I ask why?"

She lowered her gaze to her hands, suddenly a coward again, afraid to tell him she would marry only for love for fear he would laugh at her. He'd laugh at her for certain if she told him she couldn't marry him because her mother would never allow it.

She would be devastated if Bruce laughed at her.

He waited for her answer with narrowed eyes. "Why, Melissa? Marriage is usually the reason why a woman like you beds with a man."

"I don't want to marry," she repeated lamely. *Except for love*, she added silently. *And you do not love me.*

"You want me to keep quiet and pretend what happened is a figment of my imagination?"

She nodded hopefully.

"I cannot do that, Melissa," he said as he abruptly rose and strode across the room, picking up the rest of his clothes and donning them as he went along. Reaching the door, he turned back to her with the mocking smile she knew so well. "I can, however, give you time to reconsider."

She closed her eyes at the sound of the latch turning.

"I'll keep silent for now, Melissa," he said softly. "But this matter will by no means be forgotten."

A lump formed in her throat and her chest ached as the door shut quietly behind him. Mechanically, she reached over and pulled the bed curtains closed, then stared into the darkness as Bruce's parting words taunted her. Compromised. She'd given to him what only a husband had a right to claim. Bruce would keep silent . . . for now.

She began to shiver then, hard, racking shivers that had nothing to do with the cold. Grabbing a pillow, she clutched it to her chest and curled around it, more frightened than she'd ever been in her life.

She had given herself to a man. To Bruce, the one man she should have avoided.

She hadn't taken a single breath of a moment to consider that Bruce might want to put a face to the body he'd caressed and kissed and . . . She swallowed against the aching lump that grew larger in her throat at the sudden and vivid reminder of exactly what he'd done to her body. She struggled with the rush of warmth in her veins, in her belly and below. It hadn't occurred to her that she might relive the sensations at every thought of what she'd done, that she might yearn so strongly for more. Nor had she considered that Bruce of all people would never just walk away and forget what had happened.

For the first time, she wondered if she might be as simpleminded as so many others thought her to be.

*Others.* Panic thrust the lump higher in her throat. Bruce had said he would keep silent for now. But what about later? She knew firsthand that he would have no compunction about seeing to her public ruin if it would serve his purpose.

Ruin.

If word got around about tonight, she would be inundated with masculine attention, none of which would involve proposals of marriage.

Her mother would be shattered.

She groped for the covers and pulled them up over her shoulders. She had given in to impulse. And then she had hoped he would fade into the night and she could think it all a wonderful dream.

She sobbed once into the pillow at the realization that dreams, once fulfilled, could be regretted. That dreams were only perfect until they became real.

Bruce had made it real by opening the bed curtains and insisting on marriage. By taking her and what they'd done seriously. No one took her seriously except her mother. To the rest of the ton she was nothing more than a shadow of the Countess Seymour, as anonymous as she'd been while Bruce had been making love to her. No man had even bothered to pay his addresses to her since her first Season.

More than once she'd overheard them quip that they would prefer impressment than brave the Countess Seymour's glacial stare.

Except Bruce, who took obvious delight in baiting her mother. She'd always thought it was because very little mattered to him other than his family and close circle of friends. And because he approached everything in his life with a reckless irreverence as if he'd faced the worst and challenged fate to best it. To best him.

So why had he behaved as if *her* future mattered to him? Why had he tempted her with a compromise on her dreams? Instinctively, she knew he would be a kind and solicitous husband and a loving father. And for a brief and deranged moment she had considered agreeing to marry him while her heart thudded in excitement and her blood raced at the possibilities. Bruce would make it so easy for her to believe he did love her. She'd almost believed it when he'd whispered the words and his hands had woven a magic spell over her flesh.

But it wasn't enough to *almost* believe. Not when everyone knew that Bruce loved every woman he touched. The best that could be said for him was that he loved them one at a time.

In any case, her mother would never allow it.

Shortly after her come out, Melissa had realized her mother did not intend to allow her to marry anyone. Ever.

A tear slipped down her cheek. How long had she dreamed of becoming brave enough to defy her mother and do as she pleased? Just as soon as she found the right man, she'd told herself. Just as soon as she could bear to hurt her mother. She'd even dreamed of eloping as Bruce's sister had done with Damien Forbes, Duke of Westbrook.

If Bruce had mentioned such a thing she might have been further tempted to agree. To belong to a family, and to have one child or a dozen. To share with Bruce the pleasures of marriage.

She squeezed her eyes shut and curled more tightly around the pillow hugged to her chest. She wouldn't have done it. She hadn't the daring to consign herself to a lifetime with a man as vital and flamboyant as Bruce. And her mother would be devastated by such an act. Melissa was all she had, all she loved. She would forgive Melissa for ruining herself more easily than she could face living alone.

Melissa couldn't abandon her, not for a man who offered love to a woman as he would a trifle.

She shivered again as tears began to flow down her cheek, knowing she wept neither for panic of impending scandal, nor in fear of her mother's certain anger, nor out of regret for her own actions. She wept with hard, wrenching sobs only because when Bruce had said "I love you" tonight he hadn't been saying it to her.

Of all the virgins in all the world, why did he have to stumble upon this one in the dark? Bruce wondered as he hastened to his room. Why the one woman whose innocence went beyond the physical? The one woman who never failed to capture his attention and stimulate both his best and worst instincts? He really had no choice but to insist they marry, even if it meant condemning himself to hell.

Arabella would be his mother-in-law. The mind boggled at the prospect.

If he were to take it seriously, Melissa's refusal would spare him that.

She'd spared him little else. Like guilt. It beat at him from the inside out and shouted profanities in his mind. He had taken an innocent. He had taken Melissa. At a house party, no less, where anyone was likely to be lurking in the halls ready to seize on any tidbit of gossip they could unearth and enhance with strokes of imagination.

He couldn't abandon her to that.

As if his thoughts had delivered a cue to his own doom, a door opened and closed and a shadow appeared in the candlelit corridor. Bruce ducked around a corner and flattened his back against the wall, waiting for whoever it was to pass.

But "whoever" appeared to be the Earl of Blackwood, his so-called father, speaking to a servant.

Bruce clenched his fists, chafing at the urge to run the other way. Never had he run from the earl, not when he'd been a boy and the man had beaten him to a pulp, and not when he'd been sickened by the earl's deliberate attempts to nettle him with paternal solicitude in the company of others. Yet now he hid in the shadows, afraid to face him and risk discovery of where he'd been. Afraid for Melissa as he'd been afraid only once before in his life—the night he'd threatened her mother and prayed she would heed him. To this day he couldn't say what he would have done if Arabella had called his bluff. For certain he would have carried out his threat in order to protect Jillian and Max. But he would have trapped himself as well by honoring the silent vow he'd made to see that Melissa didn't suffer for his actions. How he would have accomplished it, he hadn't a clue.

He shifted restlessly and strained to hear more of the conversation taking place around the corner. How much could the earl have to say to his servant? Particularly the servant Bruce identified as Tommy, a lumbering oaf who belonged on the docks rather than stuffed into Blackwood livery and prowling the halls of a baron's estate.

Damn it! Were they to discourse all night?

A devil of mischief whispered in his thoughts, prompting him to brashness. He stifled a chuckle and reminded himself that if ever he were to exercise caution, now was the time. Now was not the time to brazen it out with the earl.

But then again, why the hell not?

He straightened from the wall and smoothed down his jacket, checking to make sure his clothes were in proper order, then sauntered around the corner whistling tunelessly.

The earl glanced up and immediately curled his lip in distaste. Tommy faded into the background as much as his size and red-and-black livery would allow.

Bruce halted and raised his brows, affecting a look of surprise. "Blackwood. Fancy meeting you here. Don't tell me you're off to an assignation." He gestured toward Tommy. "I'd advise you to leave him in the kennels, though," he said conspiratorially, "unless you feel you need protection from the lady."

The earl brushed off the sleeve of his coat as if Bruce had touched it and left a spot of muck on the fabric. "Tommy," he said, ignoring Bruce, "you may retire for the night." With a regal nod, he turned on his heel and entered the room five doors down from Melissa's, dismissing Bruce as well.

Bruce gave Tommy a brief salute, resumed his whistling and continued to saunter down the hall toward his own rooms.

A close call that. At least the earl's refusal to acknowledge him confirmed that he had no idea that Bruce had passed the last hour in Melissa's room. Bruce shuddered to think what the earl would do with such information.

Bruce wasn't sure what to do with it himself.

He pushed his hands into his pockets and strolled the distance to his room as if he were simply walking off a bout of sleeplessness. He'd been observed doing stranger things, like nettling Arabella at every opportunity and dancing with Melissa when other men quailed at the prospect of not only having to brave Arabella but spend the length of a dance with a woman who met attempts at conversation with a blank stare.

Until tonight. Melissa's unexpected assertiveness had rendered Bruce speechless for the first time in his life. He wasn't sure what shocked him most; that the first complete sentence she had spoken to him in three years was "I don't want to marry you," or that she didn't *want* to marry him at all. Miffed and inexplicably rattled that Melissa was so definite in her refusal, he'd been unable to form a single convincing argument. He'd offered marriage; she'd refused.

She'd cut his pride to the bone by wanting to relegate the experience they'd shared to a figment of imagination. He knew Arabella despised him, but that was no reason to turn down a perfectly sincere offer of marriage from a man considered to be a prime catch.

As he entered his room and leaned back against the closed door, he realized that more than his pride was involved. Melissa had always been special in his eyes. He felt like a cad for taking her without first discerning her identity, never mind that she could have spoken up and stopped him at any time.

Never mind that he'd been so consumed by her artless passion, he wasn't at all certain he could have stopped.

For the second time that night, he stripped off his clothes, not caring where they fell, while telling himself that she had given him the perfect gift. He'd wanted her for years yet would never have knowingly taken her. Tonight he had indulged in a fantasy and she'd insisted it remain that way.

She'd made it very clear that she'd known exactly what she was doing, that she'd wanted to do it. He smiled wryly as he sprawled, stark naked, on the bed.

She'd cleared his conscience for him.

If he had any sense he would accept her gift with good grace and then put as much distance as possible between them. A gentleman would honor a lady's wishes.

But then Bruce was a gentleman only when it suited him.

He had but to decide whether, in this case, it suited him or not.

# Chapter 7

**M**elissa couldn't decide whether she was relieved or disappointed to find that Bruce was absent from Lady Morton's rout. For eight days she'd approached every social occasion dreading an encounter with Bruce. For that same eight days, she'd returned home from every social occasion feeling hollow.

She'd neither heard from nor seen Bruce.

She really ought to be vastly relieved.

In her highest moments, she hoped he was avoiding her. In her lowest, she feared that he was avoiding her. Regardless, it appeared that he hadn't meant what he said. Or perhaps he had meant it and simply changed his mind. Perhaps he had decided to honor her request.

If only she could honor it and forget the night had ever happened. But as time passed, she thought of it more and more, remembering the sensations he'd evoked of heat and feather touches, of closeness and powerful strokes. She'd always avoided closeness, finding it stifling and confining, yet Bruce had lain on top of her and she'd felt only freedom from fear and loneliness and the limitations of her own meek nature.

She wanted to feel it again.

She wanted to see him again—

Instead, she saw his father approach.

"Countess Seymour, Lady Melissa," he said, greeting them with a courteous bow. "You are by far the most interesting ladies in attendance tonight."

Melissa replied with the proper words and regarded him warily. His compliment was odd, to say the least. Any other man would have remarked on their appearances. But to say they were interesting? The compliment was pleasing in itself, but she hadn't forgotten how easily he'd spoken ill of his son to complete strangers that night at the Longfords' house party. Every time she saw the earl, the sympathy she felt for Bruce as a result of his father's venom drowned out all other considerations. Bruce was a scoundrel, to be sure, but she'd never known him to harm another, and she'd certainly never heard of him deliberately heaping insults on the head of another, as so many members of the ton were wont to do. Of course, he'd threatened her once, but his reasons were justified and she'd forgiven him almost instantly—

"Lady Melissa, may I have this dance?" the earl asked.

Startled, she glanced at her mother. Why on earth would the earl want to dance with her?

Arabella, too, appeared startled, but recovered quickly with a gracious smile. "Go on, darling. You haven't danced all evening."

Melissa recognized her mother's friendly acquiescence for what it was. The earl was safe. And he was interesting himself. Her mother had spoken of him more than once.

Placing her hand atop his, Melissa walked beside him to the dance floor. Perhaps he would reveal something about Bruce, give her some hint as to where he'd been for the past eight days.

"You seem preoccupied," the earl said as he swung her into the dance.

"I'm weary," she murmured.

"And troubled, if I'm any judge." He smiled. "A matter of the heart, I'll warrant."

The organ in question lurched, then settled back into place. He couldn't possibly know anything about her and Bruce. "No, of course not."

He stepped back, performed the required bow, pulled her close again and circled her. "A shame that a lady of your beauty and sweetness should be so alone."

Her gaze shot to his, surprised that he would recognize what others had not. Despite her mother's constant presence at her side, Melissa *was* alone. Yet, for that brief moment, she felt less so as the earl's gentle concern reminded her of her father. She sighed, giving in to the sense of comfort and understanding he projected. It had been so long since anyone had noticed she had feelings of her own.

"I hope you have not fallen in with a bounder," he said.

"No." A mischievous rascal. A flamboyant spirit. A secretive soul. Bruce was all those things, but definitely not a bounder. For his mischief was performed with care, and his spirit was also generous, his soul kind. She was certain of it.

"Then I suggest the man must be quite blind to

ignore you. Tell me his name and I shall open his eyes."

The mechanics of the dance saved her from having to answer. In any case, she would not reveal to anyone the name of the man she loved.

She stumbled and would have fallen but for the earl wrapping his arm around her waist to steady her. She barely heard his concern as he smoothly recovered both her and himself and led her from the dance floor. The music seemed to drift far away until it was only an echo of the word that had rolled so easily from her mind, as if it had nested there for a long time and was ready to hatch.

*Love. For Bruce. Impossible.*

Yet she knew it was true.

Dazed, she didn't know if she'd responded properly to the earl's thanks for the dance as he delivered her to her mother's side. She must have, for he lingered to engage her mother in conversation.

She edged away from them, needing time and space in which to gather her composure and marshal her thoughts into some kind of order. Her back connected with the wall and she gratefully leaned against the support as she reeled under the weight of her realization.

She was in love with Bruce. When it had happened, she didn't know. Nor did she know how it had happened. If she had known, she might have been able to stop it.

If she'd known she might have been able to save herself from her own foolishness.

Uncaring if her posture was correct, she sagged against the wall as realization tumbled over realization. No wonder she'd been so tempted to marry him. No wonder she'd welcomed his mistake in stumbling into her bed. No wonder he both terrified and fascinated her. What could be more fascinating than chasing a will-o'-the-wisp? And what could be more terrifying than the thought of trying to hold it once caught?

She had unwittingly caught him. Thank heavens she'd had the sense to let him go before she became entangled in her own trap—

Heat suddenly prickled up her spine. Something like a touch crackled over her, traveling from head to foot. She glanced up and stared, held in the gaze of a man staring at her from across the room.

A man whose blue eyes and deep copper hair were enhanced by his evening clothes of dark, elegant blue.

Bruce stood nonchalantly near the large fireplace, his shoulder propped against the mantel and one hand raising a drink to his lips. And still he watched her over the rim of his glass, soberly at first and then the familiar twinkle crept into his eyes as he directed a slow, lazy wink at her.

She could only stand mute and frozen for the battle raging between her heart and her mind. All else seemed to recede—the dancers, the small knots of people, the room itself. Only Bruce seemed close though the entire width of a room separated them. Too close as he stood watching her with arched brows, waiting for . . . what?

She knew then that he had not forgotten, would not forget, what they had shared in the darkest hours of night. He would wait and watch, and one day he would demand the answer she had refused to give him.

\* \* \*

"Melissa darling, what ever is wrong with you? Are you ill?" Arabella leaned across the coach and pressed the back of her hand to Melissa's forehead. "You've been so listless lately."

"I'm quite well, Mother," Melissa replied as she held perfectly still, willing herself not to flinch away from her mother's concern, willing herself not to show her fear that her mother had observed Bruce staring at her so blatantly. Or that she had seen Melissa sink in misery as Bruce had set his glass down, pushed away from the mantel, and disappeared. "I am simply finding the Season tedious," she added truthfully.

Arabella sat back and stared at her daughter. "How can you say so? The Season is all that stands between us and tedium."

"I'm sorry," she murmured, and hated herself for it. What had she to be sorry for? She'd only spoken her mind.

"Of course you are, darling. I expect you are suffering from a headache brought on by those ghastly musicians Lady Morton engaged for tonight's rout."

*And the incessant gossip, and the heavy food, and the pitying looks I received from all the matrons of the ton,* Melissa added silently as she recalled what she'd overheard tonight and every other night they were in company. Tonight of all nights she hadn't needed to hear what others thought of her, what Bruce must think of her. Yet she had stood against the wall, listening with morbid curiosity because it was less disturbing than wondering where Bruce had gone and with whom he might be passing the night.

"Poor Melissa," a dowager had whispered loudly from behind her fan.

"Such a pretty girl," a young widow offered. "It's

really too sad that she can't say boo to a goose."

"Still, she'd make a biddable enough wife," their hostess chimed in. "I'm certain any number of men would welcome her silence and her obedience."

The dowager snorted. "Arabella has that gel so firmly tied to her corset strings you couldn't pry her loose with a crowbar. No backbone is her problem. She'd rather cling to her mother than lie beneath a man."

Melissa had recovered from the shock of hearing so blunt a statement just in time to realize she was smiling smugly. If they only knew what she had done.

Her next thought turned smugness into anguish. She had given herself to the man she loved. A man who might love her, but only in the moments he would be with her, and then only as an indulgence, like a sweet to be sampled before moving on to another confection, another whim.

Her headache had begun then, a throbbing pain that increased as another group of people speculated on the affairs of one Viscount Channing.

"Did you notice that Joan is keeping company with Lord Lynley?"

"Yes, just as I noticed that Channing has been notably subdued. Who dispatched whom, do you suppose?"

"Why Channing, of course. What woman in her right mind would willingly give *him* up?"

What woman indeed? Melissa wondered bleakly as she rested her head against the squabs and closed her eyes. Traffic was unusually thick this evening and the ride home would likely take twice as long.

Those ladies had been right in their brutal chatter. She had no backbone at all. If she had, she might

have had the courage to brave marriage to Bruce
rather than languish in her mother's cosseting
household. Perhaps the momentary illusion of love
and the fulfillment of passion would have been
enough. She might even have enjoyed it, for Bruce
Palmerston was nothing if not entertaining . . . and
fun.

It had been a long time since she'd had fun.

Bruce hadn't enjoyed himself so much in years.
When was the last time he'd climbed a tree? he wondered as Smithy stood beside him, shaking his head.

"I'd take the trellis," Smithy advised as Bruce
grasped a low branch and tried to swing his legs up
to a fork in the trunk.

"Damien had great success climbing a tree in the
name of chivalry," Bruce argued. "I've a fancy to do
the same in the name of romance." He swung free
for a moment, his long legs dangling almost to the
ground.

"His Grace had no choice. You have a good,
sturdy trellis."

Bruce dropped back to the ground, disappointed
that Smithy was right. The last time he'd undertaken
the task of climbing a tree he'd been a good bit
younger and without the weight and bulk of a man's
body to haul around. The trellis it was. "Go find
some amusement, Smithy," he said tersely, "before
you ruin all my fun."

"And how will you be getting home?" the man-
servant asked.

"Just leave my horse tied to that large oak in the
park across the way."

"I'll be waiting under that same oak. Just don't be
taking all night for your lark," Smithy replied. "And

don't be taking that poor girl neither," he mumbled just loudly enough for Bruce to hear.

Bruce shook his head, knowing he should reprimand Smithy for his cheek, and also knowing he would do no such thing. Smithy was the most unconventional of servants, a condition that had served him and his sister well over the years. And where else would he find a man-of-many-talents who enjoyed mischief as much as he did?

Satisfied that Smithy was well concealed with their horses across the street, Bruce turned to examine his objective—a balcony jutting out from a narrow set of doors constructed of mullioned glass and thankfully open to the night air. A room that was conveniently dark in a house that was equally dark but for a lantern over the front door and dim lights glowing from the entry hall and spilling out from the kitchens.

The trellis led directly to the balcony, and it was sturdy and in good repair.

It was all too bloody convenient for words. One would almost think Melissa was expecting him. But if she were, he'd surely not be driven to such lengths to speak to her.

Several times since the debacle at the Longfords' house party, he'd entered a ballroom or drawing room and abruptly turned on his heel upon seeing her in the crush. She always looked so panicked when among so many people, as if she were suffocating. And she always seemed to be standing in a corner or against a wall, as if she needed something solid to support her. He'd not had the heart to approach her the few times he'd seen her. Not with all of the ton watching and Arabella standing guard with her viper's tongue at the ready. He'd have been too tempted to match her venom with some of his own, and that would never do.

Not when he had made up his mind to become her son-in-law.

He couldn't trust himself to behave a proper gentleman. And if he did, everyone would surely surmise that something was afoot.

He'd repeated the same ritual tonight, arriving late at the Mortons' rout and immediately homing in on Melissa. She'd been dancing with Blackwood of all people. And she'd actually been replying to whatever the earl said to her. He'd watched her, grimly intrigued that Melissa had appeared so at ease and responsive with the one man in the world she should avoid at all costs.

Bruce's stomach had turned at the possibilities presented by the sight. Was the earl courting Melissa? Was she so dim that she could not see the cruelty lurking behind the earl's congeniality?

It mattered not. Seeing her so at ease with the earl had made him suddenly comfortable with his decision to pursue marriage with her. Blackwood never bestowed his attention on anyone unless he thought to use them in some way. And Bruce would do anything to protect Melissa from Blackwood. Anything at all.

That the earl had lingered with Arabella, lavishing her with obviously amorous attention had relieved Bruce to the point of making his knees disgustingly weak. The earl's behavior had left Bruce no doubt that he was after Arabella rather than her daughter.

Now, there was a combination—the devil and the pit viper. A match made in hell.

Careful to keep out of Melissa's sight, he'd observed her for a while longer after the dance had ended. Melissa had never appeared so isolated and fragile to him, so easily broken, as she stood apart, staring out over the crowd while Arabella and Blackwood chatted. He'd wanted to go to her, to tease her into one of her winsome blushes, to take her mind off whatever held her apart from the world. Yet, while he might play the engaging rogue with other ladies of his acquaintance, Melissa made him feel as if the role fit him like a poorly tailored coat.

God only knew what he might say or do in his brashness, and Melissa couldn't be trusted not to give away what he would keep secret. She obviously knew nothing of duplicity and bluff, and the last thing he wanted to do was alert anyone to potential gossip. Particularly with the Earl of Blackwood standing only a few feet away from her, charming Arabella to the soles of her feet and watching Melissa like a hawk.

He'd known it was time to leave when Melissa had glanced up and caught him watching her. Her face had flushed and her lips had parted, reminding him of how they'd tasted, of how she'd looked in the wake of passion. Of how badly he'd wanted her a thousand times since.

And then the earl had looked right at him. Arabella's gaze had followed, and a block of ice seemed to form between them and him.

The earl was up to something, he was sure. He would deal with it in due time, though he had a feeling that by removing Melissa as a playing piece, he would also check whatever the earl was planning. Regardless, dealing with Melissa presented the greater challenge.

And the most pleasant.

He sighed and grasped the trellis, beginning his

climb and gauging the best way to proceed without becoming tangled in the foliage climbing up the latticework. It wouldn't sit well if he were found dangling from the trellis, done in by a climbing rose.

Deciding that he should be able to reach Melissa's bedchamber and wait for her with no trouble, his mouth twisted in self-mockery as a thorny vine laden with blooms slapped him in the face. No trouble indeed. Here he was climbing a structure made of little more than sticks and sneaking into her rooms after eight days of unsettling indecision and worry.

Worry for Melissa. There might be no possibility that she was breeding but he greatly feared that might change. She'd displayed an incredibly passionate and sensual nature behind closed bed curtains. A nature that, once awakened, was not so easily subdued. He'd seen it in Kathleen when he'd come upon her and her husband in the gallery or the garden or anywhere at all. It had shocked him to see his usually aloof and rigidly controlled sister exhibit such passion for her husband without regard to who might come upon them. Since he'd returned from the Indies to find her married to one of his two closest friends, it had become necessary to whistle or call out when strolling anywhere in one of their homes just to warn them that they were not alone.

Yet, with Kathleen, such open displays of love would have come after she'd given her feelings grave consideration and conducted many arguments with herself.

Melissa had taken him into her body on an impulse, because she'd "wanted to." Heaven knew what trouble she'd get into if she felt so inclined again. And she would. She'd enjoyed it too much to take a vow of chastity now.

Thoughts of Melissa making love with another man had deviled him for eight long days.

That worried him most of all. Why should he care about who she chose to sleep with? She'd made it clear enough that she was capable of making her own choices. Except that she wasn't. Not really. And though he made sure no one else knew about it, Bruce had a damnable propensity for concerning himself with strays, misfits and lost souls.

He'd never seen anyone who looked as lost as Melissa. In an odd way she was as much a misfit as he. She just didn't possess the guile to hide it.

Was she even aware, he wondered, that the choice she had made was telling in itself? She'd known exactly who he was that night. The knowledge had driven him in circles these past days. She'd known *him* and wanted *him*. He assumed that meant she harbored a certain attraction to him.

Infatuation, he'd told himself. A silly thing she hadn't the sense to control. Yet Melissa was long out of the nursery and, thanks to Arabella, knew enough about coupling to understand exactly what she was getting into.

She was naive only about how it might affect herself as well as him. Had she actually expected that he would go on his way while she pretended she'd merely had a pleasant dream? Did she believe that he was so lacking in honor that he would leave her in so cavalier a fashion and forget the incident had ever happened?

Yet his indignation had diminished as he discovered that he was equally naive. He had no bloody idea of how it affected him, much less how it had affected Melissa. Could she have been exercising her own sense of honor by refusing to allow him to exercise his?

The thought intrigued even as it appalled him. Blast it, he was the man. It was up to him to accept the consequences regardless of who seduced whom in the end.

Another thorn scraped his cheek and he impatiently slapped it away. Of course, Arabella would surround her home with thorns. He glared upward, certain the house had acquired another level in the last few minutes and the damn trellis had grown taller as well.

If his luck held, Melissa and Arabella would not return from the Mortons' rout for at least another two hours, giving him time to reach Melissa's room and then leave again if he should be so fortunate as to talk himself out of this madness. He didn't *have* to marry her. They could go on as if nothing had happened. And if she should marry later, there were ways to fool a bridegroom into believing his wife pure. He knew all that. No doubt Melissa did too. So why was he risking life and limb to see her and convince her to marry him?

But he'd used the same arguments a thousand times to no avail, thanks to his damnable conscience. A conscience he was adept at concealing from everyone but himself.

Beyond that he was loathe to ponder.

Reaching the top of the trellis, he peered through the sculpted marble columns of the balcony rail and frowned at the potted flowers and plants scattered over the small space. He would have expected that all things Melissa would be neat and uniform in their arrangement. He'd also expected that Melissa's rooms would adjoin her mother's rather than being situated in the opposite wing of the house. Yet lately he'd found in Melissa other small signs of rebellion that negated his conceptions of her.

All the more reason to marry her. The girl—woman, he corrected himself—was too gentle and straightforward to properly rebel against anything, let alone the rules of society and the stranglehold of her mother. To do it properly she required an experienced accomplice.

Namely himself.

Bruce stretched and grasped the top of the rail, cursing its width that didn't allow a proper hold. Thoughtfully, he turned to study the thick branch near his shoulder. He knew he should have climbed the tree. Sighing, he eased to his left, swung his leg over the branch, and heaved the rest of his body over to half straddle, half hang from the swaying limb.

He made the mistake of looking down and felt his stomach lean in the opposite direction. With a deep breath, he righted himself inch by precarious inch, then straightened slowly, careful to keep his balance while gaining his feet. Refusing to contemplate what fate awaited him should he miss, he leaped from limb to balcony.

He danced in midair twenty feet above the ground and fought to angle his body toward the house. His foot caught on a twig. Desperately, he extended his arms and hooked them over the rail. He grunted and his breath whooshed out of his lungs as his lower body crashed into the foundation of the balcony.

With a heave, he swung one leg, then the other, over the rail and dropped to the floor of the balcony . . . right on top of a pot of pansies. At least his body had muffled the sound of breaking pottery. At least he still had a body that was reasonably whole.

What had possessed him to play bloody Romeo when he wasn't even certain bloody Juliet would welcome him? Surely no woman on earth was worth this.

He shifted and glowered at the soil and blooms scattered among fragments of the pot.

His mouth stretched into a wide grin as he reminded himself that everything happened for a reason, even accidents. Brushing the debris aside, he carefully lifted the flowers, dusting dirt from each in turn. He rose and grimaced at the stab of pain in his groin, then stuck the stems into the top of his waistcoat. No doubt he was growing more than one impressive bruise from his collision with the balcony.

Dismissing the discomfort, he slipped through the open doors. His vision already well adjusted to the darkness, he surveyed Melissa's bedchamber by the light of the moon, not daring to employ a candle. Again, she surprised him. He'd thought her chambers would be pink and white and literally frothing with lace and ruffles.

Instead he discerned an assortment of vibrant colors—though he couldn't readily identify them in the silver glow of the moon—and rich furnishings with simple lines. To be sure, there was white in abundance, and lace adorned the windows and overlaid what appeared to be silk in the hangings and canopy of the bed, but it was an elegant lace rather than a prissy one. Rather like fine cobwebs ending in deep, pointed scallops. He wandered around the room, examining the papers littering the top of a small writing desk arranged perpendicular to the French doors, the books stacked haphazardly on the floor beside the fainting couch that angled from the other side of the same doors, the ribbons jumbled in the midst of bottles of scent and painted porcelain-backed hairbrush and comb on a dressing table.

It appeared that Melissa, so perfect in her toilette, had less regard for order in her private sanctum. Judging from the size of her room, the scarcity of furnishings, and the small areas of clutter, she appreciated both plenty of space and the freedom to indulge in her whims. She obviously also enjoyed sunlight and fresh air if the open doors and placement of her desk and the slight depression in the seat of the fainting couch were any indication. He grinned, imagining her bottom fitting perfectly into that spot, and thought it would fit just as well in his lap.

He squinted and focused on the objects lying on the chaise, the large overstuffed chair, the bed and on the floor in front of the fireplace. He'd never seen so many cushions. One, directly in front of the hearth, also held depressions—two, to be exact—as if she'd stretched out on her stomach and propped her elbows on the pillow. Apparently, Melissa was fond of sprawling wherever it took her fancy to light.

There were enough cushions to accommodate two.

His curiosity about Melissa growing by leaps and bounds, he angled his head and made out some of the titles of her books: philosophy, romance, Shake-speare, an instruction on how to conduct a proper household . . .

Dreams and romance and poetry. Idealism, tragic heroines, and practical housewifery. No doubt she was skilled with a needle as well. He lifted a coverlet that was crumpled on the chaise and, sure enough, found a half-embroidered cloth of some sort hanging out of a sewing basket.

His grin slipped as he stroked the threadbare fabric of the coverlet. It was obviously old and well-favored by Melissa. Everything he saw pointed to expectations, and perhaps hopes, of marriage.

So why in blazes had she rejected him?

He dropped the coverlet and walked over to her dressing table to finger the various hair decorations. Picking up a length of wide yellow ribbon, he pulled the pansies from their precarious position in his vest. The perfect touch, he decided, and tied the ribbon around the stems in a perfect bow. How fortunate he'd had a sister to teach him such things. His ladies had always appreciated his skill and patience in tying bows. Of course, he'd learned the intricacies of corset laces and petticoat tapes on his own.

How fortunate that Melissa had a fondness for romance. He prided himself in his ability to pander to that side of a woman.

He glanced around the room, his gaze pausing on the worn coverlet, then scowled at the bow and tore it free. He retied the ribbon and fussed with it until it suited him. Perfect bows were not for Melissa. Everything in her room spoke eloquently of a distaste for perfection and uselessness: the depressions in the cushions and fainting couch, the dog-eared books, the helter-skelter way the flowerpots were arranged on her balcony—

A coach rumbled in the courtyard below, then voices drifted upward from the entry hall.

The Ladies Seymour had returned early from their social engagement.

Bruce searched the room for a place to hide until he could be certain Melissa was alone. Given Arabella's hold on her daughter, it wouldn't surprise him if she insisted on tucking Melissa into bed every night.

*Bed.* He turned toward the far wall. Why not? He might as well begin his confrontation with Melissa as close as possible to where it could very well end.

For the only conclusions he'd managed to come to in the past eight days were that he wanted her with a need that was beyond his ken and that, if he couldn't convince her to marry him with logic, he'd damn well convince her with passion.

# Chapter 8

**N**ot one of his more inspired ideas, Bruce decided as he blew a dust ball away from the carpet near his nose. The pansies tickled his chin, and his arm was becoming numb. But it was too late to find another hiding place.

The door opened and he heard the soft pad of footsteps on the carpet. A moment later the light of a candle cast a golden glow in the room. Two pairs of elegantly shod feet topped by frothy hems came into view. Identifying the soft yellow as Melissa's gown, he smiled. Recognizing the gold to be Arabella's gown, he rolled his eyes and grimaced.

"If you aren't in the pink by tomorrow, I will summon our physician," Arabella said.

"I'm feeling much better now that I've had some air," Melissa replied wearily.

A shoe sailed past Bruce's narrow line of vision. Another skidded beneath the bed. He wondered if Melissa disliked shoes or was merely venting frustration by kicking them off. She had pretty feet, he mused as he watched as her toes spread and seemed to stretch on the carpet as if they had waited all day for freedom—

"I'm glad to hear it, darling," Arabella said in a tone hard as granite. "And since you are feeling better, there is no reason why I shouldn't ask why you encouraged Channing to openly flirt with you this evening . . . Turn around so I can unfasten your gown."

Melissa's toes curled into the carpet as if they were clenching. He tilted his head a bit, fascinated by that small display of anger.

Melissa sighed. "Viscount Channing behaved no differently than usual, Mother."

Intrigued by the turn of conversation, Bruce inched forward just enough to see a bit more of the room through his screen of lace and layered his hands beneath his chin. Silk rustled and visions of Melissa's gown opening, revealing her smooth back an inch at a time, were becoming more vivid by the second.

"You were staring at him," Arabella accused, "encouraging him. No wonder he finds such delight in harassing us."

Bruce remembered all too well how Melissa had stared at him, as if she were reaching for him with her gaze, clinging to him even as he walked away.

"You know how much I loathe Channing," Arabella continued without giving Melissa a chance to reply. "And yet you persist in accepting his attentions."

Bruce could not help but smile at that. If Arabella knew her "darling Melissa" had accepted more than his attentions she would no doubt go into apoplexy.

Perhaps he should reveal himself and tell her.

"I'm afraid I was woolgathering and didn't notice him until he was walking away," Melissa said.

*Good girl.* Bruce silently praised Melissa's quick

thinking, grateful that she wasn't the simpleminded twit he'd first thought her to be. He couldn't abide a vacuous female.

Yet he had been drawn to her even when he'd thought her dim. Discarding the reminder, he concentrated on the conversation and the more pleasant sound of the whisper of silk.

Arabella clicked her tongue. "I suppose you'll tell me next that you didn't see him wink at you."

"Of course I saw him wink," Melissa admitted. "He always winks at me, and every other woman in proximity." Her voice softened. "Mother, I fear you will tear my gown."

He saw Arabella's shod feet move back a step and could almost picture an expression of horror on her beautiful face.

"Channing should be shot," Arabella muttered as if she blamed him rather than her own anger for nearly ruining Melissa's gown. "Forgive me, darling. It's just that men like him delight in duping girls like you."

Bruce's grin slipped as he kept his tongue behind his teeth. He'd never duped a woman in his life. If anything, Melissa had duped him.

"He's far too obvious to dupe even someone like me, Mother," Melissa said in a resigned tone.

Silence followed as if Arabella were digesting her daughter's observation.

"Thank you, Mother. I can do the rest."

Arabella sighed. "Please understand, Melissa. I can't bear the thought of him hurting you. You know I'll *never* allow anyone to hurt you." Both vehemence and fear trembled in her voice.

Sudden insight chilled Bruce as it all became clear to him: why Arabella never allowed Melissa out of her sight; why Melissa had no friends; and why every potential suitor had been turned away. Arabella pampered and guarded her, not to protect her from the cruelty of society but to protect herself from being abandoned. Arabella was afraid of being left alone and would therefore enforce her daughter's loneliness.

Arabella used Melissa's meekness to encourage the popular belief that Melissa had windmills in her head.

Arabella hadn't meant "hurt" but "have."

If she had her way, Arabella would never let Melissa go.

If he had his way, Arabella would have no choice.

Melissa's head pounded from the inside out, and she knew that if she didn't find her bed in the next few minutes, she would collapse wherever she happened to be standing. At least her mother had become subdued in the last few moments, giving her the opportunity to form more replies to any further accusations.

"Really, Melissa, I don't know why I bothered to find a proper French maid for you. More and more you leave her to her own devices."

"I'm sorry, Mother." Melissa winced. She'd done it again—apologized when she could find no logical reason for doing so. Still, she was so grateful her mother had dropped the subject of Bruce Palmerston that she would offer a dozen apologies if it would divert her mother's wrath. "But really," she added for good measure, "Nicole fusses so to have everything just right, and I am too weary for her attentions tonight."

Arabella's beam of approval at the confirmation of

Nicole's skills faded into a frown of concern. "Of course, darling. I'll just have a posset prepared for your headache."

"All I need is sleep." Hearing the edge to her voice and instantly regretting it, Melissa summoned a weak smile and leaned forward to press a kiss on Arabella's cheek. "I'm certain I'll drop off without a posset, but thank you for your thoughtfulness." Without giving Arabella time to insist, Melissa escorted her to the door. "Good night, Mother. Sleep well."

"Do get some rest, darling," Arabella said as she stepped into the hall. "Robert—I mean, the Earl of Blackwood—will be calling on us tomorrow."

That didn't surprise Melissa. The earl had lingered with them the rest of the evening, providing more fodder for the gossip mill. Melissa had been grateful, for it left her to suffer Bruce's absence in her own company. It was the first time in memory since her father died that her mother's attention had wandered more than one thought away from her.

"Good night, darling." Arabella turned and walked toward the curving staircase that separated the two wings of the house.

Melissa shut the door and leaned against it, grateful, as she was every night, that her mother's rooms were in the opposite wing. It had been a hard-won victory to move her rooms so far away, and had only been accomplished because her mother had promised her her heart's desire when her investments had paid off so handsomely. Since she could hardly tell her mother that her heart's desire was a man who loved her as much as she loved him, some measure of isolation and privacy seemed the next best thing.

Her musings fled as privacy beckoned in the silent

room. A cool breeze greeted her from the open French doors, clearing her head. The scattered shadows of familiar objects provided immediate comfort.

She pulled her gloves off and unclasped her necklace, then dropped them both on the mantel next to the candle her mother had lit. Holding the taper in one hand, she untied the sash beneath her breasts with the other and let it fall to the floor. Sighing, she reached back to finish unfastening her gown as she turned toward the bed . . . and froze.

A man lay on his stomach beneath her bed, his head and shoulders revealed beneath the lace bed skirt, his chin propped in one hand as he solemnly regarded her.

A man with thick auburn hair, deviltry in his blue eyes, and a nosegay of pansies in his free hand.

Bruce Palmerston.

He pressed his forefinger to his lips, cautioning her to silence.

She couldn't utter a sound. Her heart raced and heat pooled in her belly. Anticipation rose like another shadow in the room as she continued to stare at him, unable to do anything but stand dumbly in the center of the carpet, shocked by his appearance, stunned by the implications of his presence.

He had neither forgotten nor dismissed her. He certainly hadn't honored her wishes.

He looked obscenely at ease lying beneath her bed with lace draped over his shoulders.

She was obscenely pleased to see him.

He looked prepared to stay.

Suddenly, she was ready for him to stay. Her breasts tingled. Her breath was a lump of desire in her throat. Her body felt hot and liquid. She raised the candle higher like a shield . . . or a weapon.

He blinked and glanced around the room. "Good God. Don't tell me Arabella actually allowed you to do this to your chamber."

*Her chamber?* As if she'd never seen it before, she followed his gaze to lustrous, forest green silk beneath white lace, over vibrant yellow, coral, violet, and green cushions scattered over the white damask fainting couch, chair and dressing table bench, to silk wall covering painted in a delicate and graceful design in those same hues accented by simple white moldings. It had never occurred to her how others might react to her preferences in color and furnishings. At the time, she'd known her choices were unconventional. She'd also known that in her mother's house, no one but the inhabitants would ever see it. It was hers, and the decor pleased her.

She wondered if it pleased Bruce.

He glanced around again and shook his head in bemusement. "As lovely as it is, I can't fathom Arabella permitting you to do this," he commented as if he'd come only to examine her furnishings and perhaps have a spot of tea. But then he pinned her with a shrewd stare. "Or did you present her with a *fait accompli*?"

She flushed with guilt and lowered her gaze, too caught up in his offhand compliment to reply. Lovely . . . he'd said it was lovely. Her mother had said it resembled a seraglio. It had been one of the many times she'd wished her mother would not speak so frankly with her.

Bruce slid out from under her bed and sprang to his feet as if he was well conditioned to the practice. "Clever girl," he murmured, without mockery or sarcasm.

Her gaze flew up to his, saw the gravity in his

eyes, the gentleness in his smile . . . the approval. He meant it. Her room was lovely, and now she was *clever*. Heat burst and pleasure billowed inside her. Her mother told her she was beautiful and sweet, yet always added a footnote of criticism. Others called her beautiful and sweet, yet whispered that she was boring and most likely "dim." No one had ever called her clever for any reason.

She watched as he approached her at an idle stroll, his steps silent on the fitted carpet, his hand outstretched, offering her the nosegay tied with a gay yellow bow. A bow that was large and flamboyant, like Bruce.

"You tied it yourself," she said inanely.

"Of course."

She blinked and studied the posies more closely. "With my ribbon."

"It was handy," he said with a shrug.

She glanced at the balcony, noted the shards of pottery shoved into a corner. "They're my pansies."

"I could hardly carry flowers while climbing a tree. In any case, these are sure to please you since you chose them yourself."

Again she blinked. Nonsense. It was all nonsense, yet he made it sound perfectly ordinary and acceptable.

*No!* She shook her head and reaffirmed her first thought. *He* was all nonsense and she was encouraging it. She'd encouraged him once before and look where it had led.

*To ecstasy*, a voice whispered in her head.

*To ruin and regret*, she argued silently. Ruined the moment she'd realized that she loved him. Regret that she loved Bruce rather than some quiet, bookish man as shy as she was.

Her body argued with her as Bruce took her hand, turning it palm up a moment before he lowered his head and brushed his lips and his tongue over the sensitive flesh, caressing the backs of her fingers with his thumb as he wrapped them around the stems of the pansies and released her.

More heat. More tingling. More pleasure and longing. She didn't feel in the least shy, and knew that ruin and regret would surely multiply if she didn't do something, say something to drive him away. If he touched her again she would be lost.

"Why are you here?" she blurted.

"To ask your preferences for our wedding," he replied blithely.

Excitement beat like thunder in her chest. The idea appealed, no matter what she'd decided to the contrary. With Bruce standing so close, compromise on her principles seemed less and less abhorrent. But to marry Bruce she would have to hurt her mother, someone who *did* love her, and sneak about while she was at it, as if she acted out of shame.

She inhaled deeply. "None," she said firmly. If she could not celebrate her marriage, and the reasons for it, she would have no marriage at all.

He crooked his forefinger beneath her chin. "Melissa, we must marry." A corner of his mouth angled up in a wry smile. "I fear I cannot live with my conscience otherwise."

*And yet more nonsense*, she told herself firmly as she turned away from his hold and walked to the French doors. "I'm certain you'll find a way," she said crisply.

"What of your conscience, Melissa?" His voice was close . . . too close. The heat of his body was directly behind her; his breath feathered across the nape of her neck. She had nowhere to go to escape him unless she jumped from the balcony.

Given the urgency building in the pit of her belly, that might be a good idea.

She felt the whisper of a touch on her head and then the weight of her hair falling from its arrangement of curls on her crown. Felt his fingers comb through the mass and skim her back, her waist . . .

"What of your conscience, Melissa?" he repeated between nibbles on her ear. "Would it not be even more pleasant to indulge ourselves freely at any time we wished?"

Pure pleasure shivered down her spine.

"And what of your memories? Are you not tantalized every time you remember that night? How you enjoyed my touch . . . here . . ." He slid one hand around her waist, up to her breasts, while the other nudged her gown from one shoulder, then the other. Somehow, he'd freed the rest of the fastenings on her gown while playing with her hair. All that held up her bodice was his hand circling her breast, cupping it.

He'd make an excellent pickpocket—

"And here . . ." he continued as his hand traced the dip at her waist and glided lower, over her hip, around to her belly, kneading it and inching lower still. "Does the memory not haunt you as it does me? Don't you want more?"

Yes, it haunted her, a ghost that lived in her memory, seducing her at every reminder of Bruce. And more? She wanted more than she could possibly have in a single lifetime. "Please stop," she said, thankful that at least her voice remained steady. He must stop, now, before she stopped caring about anything else but Bruce, his touch, the stroke of his body inside her. . . .

"I think not," he said as her gown fell to her waist, leaving only her thin chemise and corset to cover her. "Not yet." He found her nipples and toyed with them, his hands large and startlingly masculine against the wispy lawn fabric of her shift. "Not unless you convince me that is what you want."

Suddenly she was conscious of how her corset pushed up her breasts, how her swelling nipples strained against the fabric and then nothing at all as he loosened the ribbon of her chemise enough to draw the neck down to the tops of her stays. Shame chided her for her lack of protest; modesty prodded her to cover herself, to move away from him. She paid them no heed, for they were nothing compared to sensation and need. She trembled and bit her lip, waiting for him to go on, praying he would never stop.

Her gown slid over her hips and pooled on the floor around her feet.

"Convince me, Melissa," he urged as his hand feathered over her waist. Her breath whooshed out as her corset loosened to his touch, then fell away.

She stifled a whimper and clenched her hands and waited for Bruce to touch her beneath her chemise.

But Bruce was no longer touching her anywhere.

"Turn around, Melissa. Face me and again tell me to stop," he said, his breath no longer caressing her flesh.

The breeze washed over her legs above her stockings to the hot place between her thighs. The perfume of flowers wafted into the room, mingling with the scent of Bruce and the musk of desire.

Her legs would barely support her, much less allow her to turn. And she couldn't face him, not with the truth sliding from her lips. "I can't," she said, and it was like release. Her body became moist and burned hotly with the flame he'd ignited. But she couldn't move, couldn't take the step she wanted to take, couldn't do anything but stand with her knees locked and her love for him swelling in her chest. "I can't," she repeated, and it was a shudder that rocked her to her soul.

She heard him exhale, felt him behind her, closer and closer until again his hands wove magic on her skin. "Why can't you, Melissa?" he asked, the question barely more than a breath against her neck. "Tell me."

*Why?* Because she couldn't send him away. Because she couldn't stop wanting him. And because she knew her only shame was in not having the courage to ask for what she wanted. "I don't want to," she admitted around a shaky breath.

"Tell me you want what I want." She shook her head as he traced the line of her spine, drawing her chemise down until it would go no farther. He encircled her with his arms and his palms stroked her breasts as he completely loosened the ribbon securing the neckline, then slid the garment down, letting it slip from his fingers to the floor. Only her pantalettes and stockings and garters remained. "Tell me you don't want it to end."

His voice trailed off as his tongue replaced his hands on her spine, down . . . down to her buttocks, sliding her pantalettes down until they, too, fell around her feet. His fingers wandered between her bared thighs, circling the sensitive flesh with the lightest, most provocative of caresses. And then the sound of his breathing in a heavy and seductive rhythm replaced his demand for answers as his fingers found her, stroked her.

She gasped and her legs threatened to give way. The moon emerged from behind a wispy cloud and bathed the balcony before her in silver light. Magic light. Cushions appeared—from the chaise, she supposed—and Bruce lowered her to lie upon them, then straightened and began to remove his clothes ... slowly ... deliberately ...

Her gaze followed every movement as he shrugged out of his coat, his waistcoat, his shirt. She held her breath as he unfastened his trousers and slid them down over strong legs. He seemed even larger now, stronger with his muscles tensed and his body looming over hers.

Desire roared in her ears as she stared at him, seduced by the sight of his erection rising so boldly, insistently ...

Moonlight bathed her with cool light from the open window, and Bruce warmed her as he descended over her.

She opened to him, wanting him inside her, but he held himself above her on his elbows and his mouth began a leisurely stroll over her neck, her shoulders, her breasts, and below to the flesh of her inner thighs above her stockings. He raised his head and met her gaze. "We can have a lifetime of this, Melissa—"

She cried out and grasped his shoulders, trying to pull him down. She bent her knees on either side of him and arched her hips, wanting him inside her.

His mouth quirked in bemusement as he remained poised above her. "A lifetime, Melissa. A lifetime to be like this wherever and whenever we wish. I wonder if it will be enough."

She parted her lips, inviting his kiss, needing to silence him before he convinced her he spoke the truth.

He took her mouth, yet still denied her his body. His tongue plunged deep, making promises that tempted her to believe him, to believe he would want her for a lifetime.

And then he tore his mouth away from hers and his breath puffed over her in short, hard pants. "I cannot wait forever for your answer."

She wrapped her legs around his waist, meeting him. He groaned and plunged into her.

The only pain she felt was from pleasure as he drove into her again and again. The only fear she knew was that it would end. And then she knew nothing at all but ecstasy as he stiffened above her and thrust again, once, twice, three times, giving her all she could ever expect from him.

She sobbed as she accepted, her body tightening around him, taking from him, absorbing him, and wanting more. . . .

A lifetime.

A promise that would last only as long as the moonlight that was even now bleeding into darkness.

A promise made with his mouth and his body and his hands but not his heart.

They became nothing but shadows beyond the dim glow of a single candle. Bruce continued to make promises to her, with his hands gently caressing her and stroking her hair, with his mouth dusting soft kisses over her lips, with his eyes that gleamed like silver-blue steel in the night.

A night in which she had both begun and ended a lifetime.

\*   \*   \*

Bruce lay beside her on the cushions, spent and regaining his breath as he idly fingered the various fabrics of her clothing puddled on the floor, and struggled with unfamiliar feelings of confusion, uneasiness, ineptitude. Melissa had succeeded in seducing his body before he could seduce her mind. He'd meant to stop, to leave her before it was too late to protect her. He'd wanted a yes from her before passion robbed them both of speech. Until this moment he hadn't realized how much he'd wanted that yes.

But Melissa was stubborn. Far more stubborn than he could ever have imagined. Too stubborn to accept his proposal of marriage even as she accepted his body inside her as if that was all she wanted.

Surely not.

Why not? His stomach knotted as he realized that his passion was all any woman had wanted from him. But then he'd chosen only those women who wanted nothing more, women to whom he offered nothing else. Marriage had never been a consideration until now. Marriage had never been a need that stalked him as it had for over a week, luring him with promises of a life that revolved around the rituals and natural order that he'd never known.

Rituals and natural order that his sister Kathy now enjoyed. That his half brother, Max, enjoyed. And children. He'd always wanted children. Kathy often said that it was because he was a child himself with his mischief and manipulations. She'd also said that he needed the stability of family to balance his drive to remain one step ahead of the rest of the world. He hadn't bothered to correct her, to tell her that it was boredom and dissatisfaction that drove him.

That he explored all possibilities and created others because he needed to find his own place, his own peace.

In the space of a breath, he denied such maudlin thoughts. What he needed was Melissa in his bed every night, waiting to take him to levels of pleasure he hadn't known existed. It was that—and only that—he craved. A woman who took what he offered without guile and gave in the same way, expecting nothing from him but the honesty of the moment.

It rankled that she didn't expect more.

Still, he wasn't sure what to say to her, what he could say to convince her that she should expect more, that he would gladly give it to her.

Feeling awkward, he picked up a garment and studied it, frowned at it. A garment he had heard about yet never seen. "Pantalettes," he mused. "How odd to find you wearing something so risqué."

She sighed, and it sounded like relief. "Mother says they make sense," she said in a rush as if she were pouncing on the forbidden subject of intimate clothing to divert him from the proper one of marriage. "She finds them particularly sensible in the cool evenings, and the only reason they are considered shocking is because men find them—" Breathless, she stopped abruptly.

He could imagine her biting her lip in consternation. "Inconvenient?" he supplied. "There is that, I suppose, if one is too lazy to appreciate the added anticipation of removing them."

From the corner of his eye, he saw her flush crimson from head to foot. "Arabella's opinions aside, how do *you* feel about wearing them?" he asked, puzzled by how important her answer was to him.

She flushed a deeper crimson and looked away. "I'd already had my maid purchase some for me," she admitted in a barely audible voice. "I—I get cold, you see."

Something inside him unclenched, relaxed, at her confession. He felt ridiculously smug that she should confide in him at all, and idiotically pleased to have further evidence that she listened to her own mind on occasion. It gave him badly needed assurance that her actions at the house party had been a result of an intelligent decision rather than the whim of a flighty mind.

He rolled his eyes at the absurdity of placing so much importance on her choice of undergarments when more weighty matters had yet to be addressed. One would think he was basing his own decisions for the future upon whimsy rather than his usual careful deliberations.

That he'd been acting more on instinct than calculation was a suspicion he'd successfully ignored since the house party.

Abruptly he turned to his side, facing her. "I've a fancy to take a leaf from my sister's book and elope," he blurted, anxious to settle the matter and at a loss for a more charming way to present the proposal.

*Elope.* The word tasted sour in his mouth. Kathy had told him how wretched hers and Damien's flight to Gretna Green had been. He didn't really want that for Melissa, yet saw no other choice. Not after his revelation about Arabella. He suspected that she would rather see her daughter ruined in the eyes of society than allow her to have a life of her own.

No wonder Melissa was content with moments stolen in the dark of night.

She lay silent beside him, her gaze fixed on something he couldn't see.

He groped for the throw draped on the chaise behind him and tucked it around Melissa. If he was going to have a rational discussion with her, he didn't need the sight of her body driving him to distraction. "We can be in Scotland and married within a week," he said softly. "We might even enjoy a honeymoon at Westbrook Castle. It's large enough that we could be there for months without running into anyone."

She shuddered and blinked. "No."

"Not Westbrook Castle," he said, deliberately misinterpreting her meaning. "Perhaps a cottage by the sea. Rustication does have a certain romantic appeal."

"No."

"Melissa," he said carefully, "I understand that you might want a proper ceremony, but it's not possible."

"I know." She hadn't moved except to curl up beneath the throw. Her hair gleamed an ethereal gold in the light of the guttering candle. Her face appeared translucent, fragile.

Bruce wanted to gather her close, to hold her and stroke her hair and her cheek, to reassure himself that she was real. Instead, he clenched his fists and hardened his heart against what he knew he had to say. "Melissa, Arabella means to keep you with her. She will never allow you to marry."

She turned her head and met his gaze. "I know."

*She knew?* Frustration bit at him as he stifled the many questions he wanted to ask. It appeared that from the beginning of their strange relationship she had known more than he. "I see," he said flatly.

"You knew it was me in your bed at the Longfords' house party. You know that your mother will keep you a prisoner all of your life. Pray tell me what else you know—in complete sentences of more than two words."

She caught her lip between her teeth, then turned her head back to again stare at the ceiling. "I know that my mother loved my father very deeply. And I know that she loves me."

Bruce had to strain to hear her, she spoke so softly. But at least she had spoken. "I love you also, Melissa," he said, offering her what she had a right to hear, what everyone had a right to hear and so often didn't. Yet, this time as he spoke, the words sounded new to him and somehow unique, as if he'd conjured them for Melissa alone.

She sighed. "I know that, too. And I know that you will continue to love me until you leave me tonight, or until you cross paths with another beautiful woman whom you will love until you leave her."

For the second time in his life, he was speechless, finding no glib rebuttal or logical argument to confuse her. Besides, how could he address her perceptions of him when they were so bloody accurate? "At least you know you are beautiful," he muttered, feeling the coward.

"I have a mirror," she said matter-of-factly.

Bemused at her lack of coy protest, he stared at the night beyond the doors, his mind a maze of thoughts he hadn't the time to sort out. The horizon was no longer a blurred line separating sky from earth but a smudge creeping toward the city. In a few hours time, dawn would be heralded only by a dirty thumbprint of light behind a dense gray curtain of fog.

Enough was enough. The time for persuasion was past. "We could converse in circles all night and into next week. But the only way this matter can be resolved is in marriage. A quick, secret marriage."

"I will not marry you."

He plowed his hand through his hair. "You continue to refuse me but you have yet to tell me why."

Again she met his gaze, steadily, unflinchingly. "I will not marry without love."

His mind reeled at the conversation that seemed to chase its own tail. "Melissa, has it not occurred to you that if we are married, we will be together and I will, of course, love you all the time?" He gave her a slow, lazy smile. "So you see, your doubts are for naught."

Two tiny lines appeared between her brows as if she considered his logic. And then she reached over to him and stroked his cheek. "It's very kind of you to offer marriage—"

"Kind? Kindness has nothing to do with it. It's time that I married. I would like children before I'm a doddering old man." He paused, knowing that he was as near to being rattled as he'd ever been. The reasons why he should feel so eluded him at the moment. "Melissa, I want to marry you," he said slowly, calmly. "And it is imperative that you marry me. I fear I've done something unforgivable tonight. You may be breeding as a result. I would see to it the child has a name and a future."

Her hand fell to her side. "And I fear I've done something stupid," she said tonelessly. "Please go now. There is nothing left to be said."

*Stupid?* What stupid thing had she done? he wondered. He should ask, but she had completely turned away from him and curled into herself beneath the throw. She looked so damn vulnerable he didn't know what to say for fear that she might break if he uttered a sound.

It was a mistake to try to speak with her now. He should have known better. Women wanted smooth caresses and pretty words after making love, not demands—and certainly not logic.

He rolled to his feet and picked up his clothes, donning them in silence as his mind ran away with him. Caresses and poetry were overruled by urgency. He'd had to risk his neck to get to Melissa tonight. God know how and when he'd manage to see her again, especially with Arabella's nose to the ground, sniffing for him like a hound out for his blood.

Dressed, he approached Melissa once more and watched her, waiting for her to move, to acknowledge him, to do anything at all. "I suppose I can carry you off," he quipped, unsure whether he was serious or not. "I assure you that by the time we arrive in Scotland, I will have convinced you that I am right."

She moved then, sitting up and staring at him. "And I will hate you for it for the rest of my life."

Disturbed beyond comprehension by her calm statement, he instinctively slipped into the role he had set for himself so many years ago. His mouth angled upward at one corner in a mocking smile as he gave her a formal bow. "In that case, I'll take my leave of you. Sleep well, Melissa."

The throw slipped, baring her breasts to his gaze as she stared up at him.

His manhood stirred and threatened to rise against him. In defiance, he leaned over her and grasped her under her arms, lifting her until she had no choice but to stand. Wrapping his arms around her, he hauled her to him, chest to chest and thigh to thigh, and took her in a deep and thorough kiss, ravishing her mouth with his, plundering until she hadn't even a breath left for protest.

He tore his mouth away before he was similarly robbed of breath and reason, and cupped her chin with his hand. "A lifetime, Melissa. We will have it in marriage. It is up to you how we accomplish it."

"Please don't come here again," she said.

"As you wish . . . for now." He set her aside and raised his hand to cup the back of her neck. "This is not finished, Melissa. It will never be finished."

Before he could display his frustration with her, he stepped away and left the way he had come, noticing neither the swaying branch of the tree nor the prick of thorns on the trellis.

He was only aware of the single sob drifting down from the balcony and then a silence that reflected his own loneliness.

Suddenly her room seemed like a dark and empty cave as Melissa listened to the rustle of leaves and the snap of twigs. Soft footfalls brushed over the grass and faded into nothing. Bruce was gone like the fantasy he seemed when he wasn't winking at her and teasing her . . . kissing her and stroking her with powerful thrusts of his body.

Absently, she leaned over to retrieve the throw and wrapped the worn fabric around herself like a cape.

Already the passion they had shared seemed unreal, like a dream that awakened her in the night. Except she was already awake. He'd been real and the passion had been real. Bruce was truly a part of her now. Perhaps he was a part of her for all time.

A lifetime, if his seed had taken root inside her. A seed she'd allowed inside herself. A seed that, even now, she thought she would welcome.

Bruce's child, inside her, like the mustard seed of hope.

*Stupid.* The word reverberated in her mind as she stared at the sky outside, felt the light brush of lace over her legs as the hangings at the French doors billowed out in a sudden breeze. Bruce had not given her hope. Not for anything lasting. Not for anything strong upon which a future and a family could be built. His words of love were empty and meaningless, uttered in exactly the same way as the night he'd mistaken her for Joan Sinclair, and doled out as if they were a sweet given after a feast.

And even if she could hope that he might love her in time, what would she do with a man such as Bruce Palmerston? Wait for him to visit her in their home? To fall apart every time he touched her, then pick up the pieces at her leisure after he left? Honorable he might be, but he was also vibrant and restless. She'd seen it in the way his gaze seemed to be everywhere at once, absorbing everything even as he stood indolently propped against a pillar or a wall, the very picture of amused boredom. She'd witnessed it in the way his mind constantly worked to turn words and actions inside out and against the one who spoke them. A man of good heart he might be, but he displayed little regard for anything but his own pleasure and manipulations.

As he'd manipulated her tonight.

And she'd allowed it. Welcomed it. Enjoyed it.

She blinked at the silence surrounding her, at the fog that was rising from the streets and curling over the marble boundaries of her balcony, reaching her, enshrouding her like the panic that suddenly took hold of her, crushing her.

*A child.* What would she do with a child? She knew nothing of children or their needs. She couldn't even reach into her memories and draw from them. She'd never been a child, not really. Once her father had commented that she'd been born old. A good thing, he'd said, for someone must look after her mother when he was gone. A year later, he'd slipped away from them.

He'd been wrong. Her mother had never needed anyone to care for her. Her only need was to do the looking after, to control and hold fast to all that was hers.

Including her daughter.

*A child.* How could she raise one? In her mother's house and under her mother's thumb, allowing her child to be told what to do and how to do it, what to think and when? Another child like her who would be too timid and afraid to do anything but comply. Yet Melissa knew she complied for another reason as well. She both loved and pitied her mother, one feeding off the other until she no longer knew which was the stronger. It had never mattered before.

A child would make it matter.

Bruce's child. It should be a happy thing to contemplate having a child by the man one loved. Yet all she could do just then was hope with all her heart that another woman would love Bruce as much as she did. That another woman would be the one to give him children.

For beneath all the reasons why she shouldn't want a child lay the most compelling one of all—her fear that out of loneliness and need she would cling to her child as her mother clung to her.

She shivered and realized that she stood virtually naked and surrounded by fog that separated her from the rest of the city, shrouding her like her mother's love. It struck her as symbolic, an omen perhaps, or a warning that her small portion of the world would forever be separated from the wide landscapes of Bruce's world.

She had indeed been stupid to think, even for a moment, that she could be a part of his life simply because he said so. He was too proficient with words, too crafty. And she'd been so pitifully eager to believe him.

Sick at heart and shamed to her depths by her own gullibility, she sank to her knees on the bed of cushions and wrapped her arms around her middle. Suddenly, she felt old and far wiser than she cared to be as her thoughts circled the possibilities that might spring from her actions.

*A child.* Whether it came to be or not, her self-indulgence had created a secret that would haunt and torment her for all her days and nights. Especially the nights. And whatever happened as a result of her own foolishness, she knew that she would have to face it alone and live with it alone.

# Chapter 9

"**S**mithy, damnit, where are you?" Bruce called in a loud whisper laced with barely contained impatience. The park was a silent bower of shadows looming overhead and crouching on the ground. A light fog crept over it all and swirled around his feet. Clouds hovered low in the sky with a promise of drenching rain.

The horses snorted and pawed the ground, impatient to be untethered from the tree and turned toward home.

Smithy was nowhere to be found.

Fear beat a path through Bruce's body, speeding up his pulse and racing in his veins. Dread held him still, watching, listening. If anyone had harmed Smithy—The thought twisted his stomach. Smithy had been with him all of his life, first as a companion ten years older than he who watched over him when he'd been too young to watch over himself, then as a friend who taught him the ways of the world outside the cloister of the aristocracy, and then somewhere along the way he'd become that rarest of things, a *trusted* friend. Smithy had taught him how to fight and survive with brawn as well as wit. In the eyes of the world, Smithy might be only a servant, but to Bruce he was family.

Suddenly, a bush rustled. Twigs crackled.

Bruce swung around and assumed a fighting stance, ready to defend himself against cutpurses or anyone else who dared to interrupt his search for Smithy.

A groan reached him riding low on the fog.

He reached toward the horses, searching for a weapon. Smithy's cudgel was missing. Groping along the ground, he found a rock and hefted it, then followed the sound, using as much stealth as his riding boots and the dense foliage allowed.

"Over here," a voice called from beyond a stand of bushes.

Reedy as the voice was, Bruce recognized it as Smithy's. Relief nearly dropped him to his knees. He breathed deeply, shoring himself up, telling himself that Smithy was alive. Alert for danger, he crouched low and circled the area before closing in.

"Took you long enough," Smithy said around a moan as Bruce reached him. He lay flat in the middle of a flower bed, leaves, broken stems and detached petals scattered in his hair and over his clothes. Signs of a struggle were everywhere in trampled grass, divots, and twigs broken from the bushes. Smithy's small cudgel lay at his side.

Smithy struggled to raise up on his elbows.

"Don't move," Bruce ordered. "Where are you hurt?"

"In my pride mostly," Smithy muttered, then winced. "And maybe a place or two on my head." He probed the back of his skull and then gingerly felt around his left eye. "Blighter took me by surprise."

"What blighter? What happened?" Bruce asked as he helped Smithy to his feet.

Smithy shook his head and winced again as he bent to retrieve his cudgel. "Not here," he said ominously. "Been strange folk lurking about. Let's get home first."

As if it were an omen, thunder rumbled in the distance.

Bruce helped a weaving Smithy back to the horse and hefted him up into his saddle. Mounting his own horse, he grabbed Smithy's reins, knowing the servant was too disoriented to manage on his own.

"Mind the shadows," Smithy slurred. "It's a perfect time for nightcrawlers to be about."

Bruce grunted and aimed his mount toward home, keeping his gaze alert and ever moving while appearing to stare straight ahead. On a night like this the "nightcrawlers" would dare to venture into better areas like this one using the cover of fog and rain to accost "swells" returning home from social engagements.

Fortunately, he and Smithy would not have to ride far to reach his town house. Even more fortunate was their earlier decision to ride, rather than walk, the short distance to Melissa's house. Bruce had thought it prudent to have the advantage of a swift horse beneath him should a good plan go awry.

Shadows shrouded in mist detached from the side of a vacant residence and skulked closer, obviously thinking a gentleman on horseback with only a swaying servant to protect him easy pickings. From the corner of his eye, Bruce counted four men.

Why not? The entire evening had been a disaster from beginning to end. Being set upon by vermin was merely the climax, and one he had no patience for.

If the odds weren't so against him, he wouldn't have minded cracking a head or two about now.

On the other hand, it might not be necessary.

He pursed his lips and began to whistle softly as he slowly shortened the reins on Smithy's horse, drawing him closer, where he could reach the cudgel.

"Give me the reins!" Smithy whispered as he came abreast of Bruce. "They're on foot. We can make a run for it."

Bruce knew better. Smithy was in no condition to hold his seat at a fast trot, let alone a canter. If he didn't keep his wits about him, he'd either be too dead or too broken to worry about marriage or anything else. He had little hope that his years of learning fisticuffs with Smithy and later at school would save them.

Sweat broke out on his brow as he eyed the men closing in on them.

It was his wits or nothing.

"Blast it, man," he growled loudly, "I forbid you to go mad on me before we reach home and I can shoot you." He lowered his voice, though not enough to keep the men stalking them from hearing. "I told you the squirrel that bit you was rabid. I could have put you down then. But no, you had to run. Good thing I found you before you sank your teeth into that tavern keeper."

Smithy flashed his teeth in a quick grin. "I ain't rabid, I tell you," he whined, then slipped into incomprehensible mutterings and growls.

"Not rabid? I suppose it's the ale making you froth at the mouth."

"You ain't shooting me. I took down three men tonight and I'll take you down too."

As if by divine providence rain began to fall in a steady downpour, soaking them within seconds.

Smithy's body jerked in a series of spasms as he let out a string of demented shrieks and mewls. "The rain . . . stop the rain . . . thirsty . . . so thirsty . . . I'll twist your head off with my bare hands if you don't stop the water from touching me. . . ." His mouth worked and bubbles appeared on his lips.

The men paused and collected into one large huddled shadow.

"Cease at once! Or I'll be forced to draw my pistol, put you out of your misery in the gutter, and leave you for the rats."

The shadow broke apart; the band of thieves scattered and disappeared.

Smithy straightened in his saddle and wiped the spittle from his mouth with his sleeve. "Quick thinking, milord."

His horse balked as Bruce sagged in his saddle and gave thanks that Melissa hadn't completely addled his brain.

Straightening, he tossed Smithy his reins. "It appears you are recovering. I suggest we make haste before I lose those wits altogether."

They reached home in silence, leaving small rivulets of water in a trail from entrance hall to stairs to Bruce's chambers. Bruce tossed Smithy a linen towel and used another to dry his hair. Exhaustion clamped down hard on him as Smithy headed for his own quarters to change. With slow, heavy movements, Bruce exchanged soggy clothing for a dry pair of breeches and a dressing gown, poured a glass of brandy, and sprawled in a chair by the fire to wait for Smithy to tell him what had happened in the park.

As if he really wanted to hear about yet another problem.

Melissa, shy and gentle as she was, had perplexed him more in a few days than all the problems he'd faced in a lifetime.

He'd always been quite adroit at handling problems.

Until Melissa.

Tonight, he'd not only been at sixes and sevens over how to handle her, it had damn near flummoxed him when he and Smithy had been confronted with danger. Quick thinking indeed. He'd actually known a few moments of complete panic and confusion before inspiration struck.

No doubt because his brains had had to climb from his crotch to his head in order to function properly.

Why in hell had she refused him? How could she refuse him after giving in so easily to his passion? Heaven knew he was ready to give his soul for more of *her* passion as well as her companionship.

He had a nasty suspicion that he'd already given his heart. Why else would he place such a high value on her company and conversation?

Staring broodingly into his glass, he remembered telling Melissa he loved her—words he'd said too many times to too many women over the years. Words his mother had longed to hear from her lover and never had. Bruce hadn't wanted to be guilty of withholding the words, and he'd made it a point to never accept a woman's gifts unless he felt some fondness for her. Melissa had been right. He did love his women while he was with them, and always made certain they knew it. But he'd never used the words to get a woman into bed, only offering them to shore up a lover's sagging spirit or to appease a reluctant lover's guilt over what she was doing. He'd never viewed it as deceit, knowing that he said the words only to women who took such sentiment as lightly and pragmatically as he offered it, aware it would last only as long as the moment itself.

Yet tonight with Melissa there had been a distinct difference. The words just slipped out with no forethought, as if saying them was the most natural thing in the world. Tonight, the words had tasted different on his lips, sounded different to his own ears, felt different as they sank into him, curling up inside him as poignantly as Melissa curled up on the cushions. He'd felt a tenderness for her, a need to give her all that was in him to give.

He'd certainly done that. Never had he been so reckless in his lovemaking. At least his carelessness might aid him in convincing her to marry him—an issue he seemed to be embracing with a great deal of enthusiasm.

He took a hasty swallow of the brandy, willing it to numb his emotions so he could think more clearly. But the memory of Melissa's taste and scent overpowered the fine liquor, intoxicating him far more than spirits ever could.

More than any woman had ever intoxicated him with a beautiful face, an alluring body, and lively wit.

He'd savored every word and sentence Melissa had uttered, enjoying the sound of her voice, the expressiveness of her features. For all her shyness and lack of conversation, Melissa had never bored him, and since their interlude at the house party, he'd spent an inordinate amount of time wondering what was hidden beneath her lowered gaze and timid manner. Definitely not a slow wit, for when she'd finally met his gaze he'd seen comprehension and intelligence, as if she understood far more than he did of the situation.

Oddly, he wasn't surprised, as if on some level he'd always known that Melissa had as much depth and mystery as the proverbial still waters.

He knew nothing of such tranquillity. His childhood had been filled with too much strife, his adulthood with too much purpose. Threaded through it all were memories he chased away with constant challenges to himself to exceed his own limits, to create possibilities, to court the absurd and make it work for him. He could not recall the last time he had entertained less than a dozen thoughts at a time.

He frowned as he realized that for over a week he had been preoccupied with only one thought, one goal. Melissa . . . only Melissa.

Always Melissa.

She could be with child. His child. And if she wasn't, she would be soon enough. Bruce knew himself well enough to know he would not stray from his course. He wanted Melissa and had a feeling that he would always want her. Obviously Melissa wanted him. Knowing that, he would not—perhaps could not—maintain the discipline to stay away from her. Nor would he be able to exercise the control necessary to avoid pregnancy, even if he wanted to.

Yet, in the past, he'd never had a problem controlling himself no matter how strong his desire, how seductive his lover.

Always his vow to never sire a bastard child had ruled him.

Until Melissa. In her embrace, he had forgotten everything, risked everything, including pregnancy.

His child would be born a bastard over his dead body.

His hand clenched around the snifter, snapping the stem.

Strong, blunt fingers appeared to catch it before it spilled into his lap. "A fine state you're in," Smithy said from his side.

Bruce rubbed the bridge of his nose. "It has been an eventful night in one way or another."

"Aye, that it has." Smithy took the chair across from Bruce's with the ease of familiarity.

Noting the frown underlying his friend's bland expression, Bruce knew there was more to come. "What blighter?" he asked, picking up the conversation aborted earlier in the park. "Who attacked you?"

One side of Smithy's mouth slashed upward in a wry grin. "I attacked him first."

"Why?"

Smithy met his gaze, sober, intense. "He was watching from the park, then trying to climb a tree to get a better look when you and the lady disappeared. He was slobbering and rubbing himself, having a grand time. " He shrugged. "I dragged him from the tree and clubbed him."

Bruce snorted. "A Peeping Tom."

"Maybe. But that was his pastime. Watching you and the lady was his work." Smithy leaned back and winced as the knot on the back of his head connected with the back of the chair. "I found a fancy purse full of coins on him. He admitted he was hired to spy on the two of you before I knocked him out."

"Who?"

"Didn't say. Or wouldn't. His lights winked out before I could persuade him to talk." He shook his head in disgust. "I thought he'd be out for the night and turned my back on him. Next thing I knew he'd come up behind me and whacked me a good one with my own cudgel."

Thoughtfully, Bruce rubbed the underside of his chin with his knuckles as he assessed the various shades of purple surrounding Smithy's swollen eye. "So he is being paid well enough to take a beating rather than reveal his employer."

"Aye. And judging from the size of the purse and the quality of the leather, his employer is dead serious about keeping it that way."

Bruce's mind took off at a gallop, running through possibilities, and passing others by. His first thought was of the earl, but he immediately discarded it as being improbable. The earl had far more to lose by deviling Bruce than he could possibly hope to gain.

"Not Arabella," he said thoughtfully. "If she had known about myself and her daughter, she would have confronted me then and there with claws unsheathed and teeth bared." Yet Arabella seemed the most logical choice. Bruce knew he had enemies; no one with his wealth and power was free of them. "I doubt it would be a jealous husband. Most of them are only too happy to have their wives diverted so they can frolic with their mistresses."

"A jealous husband would call you out or have you killed," Smithy pointed out.

"Yes, angry men have no imagination," Bruce mused. "It would appear that someone is out to collect information, Smithy."

"Blackmail," Smithy intoned.

"That would be my guess." Every muscle in Bruce's body tightened at the thought. Little could be done to harm him, but Melissa was another matter entirely. He didn't give a bloody damn if someone bled Arabella dry, but he wouldn't have Melissa hurt. And she would be. Blackmail of this sort was a violation of mind and spirit that murdered innocence and destroyed trust.

Both were qualities that set Melissa apart from other women he knew, what made her special.

"You're falling right into it by dallying with an innocent," Smithy said, adding weight to Bruce's concern.

"She dallied first," Bruce reminded him, trying to ease his tension with lightness, trying to order his thoughts with perspective. "I am merely seeking to make it right."

Smithy rolled his eyes. "By seducing her tonight?"

"If that will accomplish my purpose."

"Did it?"

Bruce sank farther back in his seat, stretched out his legs and crossed them at the ankles. "No. She again refused me." And now more than ever, he felt an urgency to change her mind. To protect her with his name.

A name that had been bought and paid for with loneliness and misery.

It was about time the name of Channing did some good.

"Too bad it couldn't be the earl," Smithy said, as if he'd been trailing Bruce's thoughts. "He'd like naught better than to do you harm."

"Yes, but as you said, it couldn't be him. You and Damien saw to that while I was abroad." Bruce almost smiled at the reminder of how his brother-in-law, the Duke of Westbrook, had tormented and threatened the earl if harm should come to him or any member of his family, particularly his wife, Kathy, and her brother, Bruce himself. It also included Bruce's and Kathy's half brother, Max, the Duke of Bassett, and his wife, Jillian, who happened to be Damien's sister.

He did smile then, at how convoluted his family had become in the last few years, since Max had learned of their relationship. Bruce and Kathy had been alone for so many years, growing up in fear and isolation, until they had discovered they were the bastard children of Max's father and the earl was merely a name and legitimacy to them, purchased by their mother's lover. And then the earl had been banished to America by the combined power of the Dukes of Bassett and Westbrook, and Bruce had been sent away to attend the same school as their sons. He and Max and Damien had become fast friends, and that had been enough for him. He'd never expected more. But then Damien's sister had drawn him into an intrigue to trick Max into marrying her and he'd been caught.

Damien had beat him to a bloody pulp. When Max had learned of Bruce's manipulations, he'd taken up where Damien's fists had left off. To stop him, Kathy had spilled the soup, revealing their bond of blood. Following the long-held traditions and loyalties of their two families, Max and Damien had closed around himself and Kathy, guarding their backs as surely as they guarded one another's.

Without question or prejudice, Bruce and Kathy had become links in the family circle forged by Max's marriage to Damien's sister.

And when the Earl of Blackwood had dared to hurt Kathy, Damien had stepped in—with Smithy's aid—ruthlessly using his power and wealth as well as Max's to persuade the earl that his well-being depended on that of all the members of his family, legitimate or otherwise. The effectiveness of Damien's actions had been proven when the earl had shot a madman who threatened to kill Damien and Kathy in the name of love.

It had been priceless, knowing the bitter gall the earl had to swallow to protect the two people he hated most in the world. To this day, Bruce found great pleasure in seeing the earl struggle not to howl in rage every time someone congratulated him for his "heroism" in saving his daughter and son-in-law from certain death.

"It's not the earl." Bruce sighed. "I'm certain of it."

"He has too much to lose," Smithy agreed glumly.

Rising from the chair, Bruce paced to the mantel. "Damn."

"What are we going to do?" Smithy asked.

"You are going to keep a very sharp eye out," Bruce said. "And I am going to get Lady Melissa Seymour to marry me by hook or by crook."

Chuckling, Smithy rose and poured two small measures of brandy from the decanter on the table by Bruce's chair. "It's about time." He handed a snifter to Bruce. "Things have been a mite dull since Lady Kathy got herself kidnapped and married. I was afraid you'd gone all respectable and proper like." He held up his glass in a mock toast, downed the contents and sauntered out of the room. "Mayhap you should follow your brother-in-law's example and kidnap the lady," he tossed over his shoulder as he stepped into the hall and shut the door.

*And I will hate you for it for the rest of my life.*

Melissa's statement ran through Bruce's mind as he swirled the brandy in his glass, more interested in watching the play of firelight on the liquid than in drinking it. If it had come from any other woman, he'd have known she didn't mean it, that the threat was—depending on the woman—either a challenge or an invitation.

Coming from Melissa, it had been a promise.

The prospect of her hating him defeated him before he could form a single outrageous idea. Yet between Arabella's stranglehold on Melissa and some unknown enemy hiring spies, nothing but outrageousness stood a chance of working. That and a sharp mind, he reminded himself. Melissa displayed an uncanny ability to see right through his usual machinations.

He should have seen it sooner—the intelligence in her eyes as she observed the world and the people around her, and the gentle kindness with which she treated everyone who crossed her path. Those qualities alone required strength, as did the quiet defiance she'd displayed in furnishing her room to suit herself rather than her mother. Nor could he doubt that she had conviction. He'd heard it in her voice every time she'd said no to him. He'd seen it in her steady gaze and calm expression when she'd told him she'd welcomed him into her bed because she'd "wanted to," and again when she'd asserted that she would marry only for a love that was shared.

Melissa spoke few words, yet those she did utter wielded a power that could not be ignored.

Power over him.

Bleakly, he stared into the fire and admitted that he was very likely in love with Melissa. Nothing else could explain why he was so determined to marry her when she was so adamantly against it. Nothing else could explain why he couldn't come up with a single plan, outrageous or otherwise, to achieve his ends. Nothing else could explain his sudden lack of confidence in his own charm and resourcefulness.

He pushed away from the mantel and idly wandered around the room—a habit he had developed to ward off agitation and to promote clear thinking. It had been crucial if not vital that he learn early in life to think, to use his mind to overcome obstacles and solve problems. And it kept him too preoccupied with the present to ponder the past. He'd become accustomed to juggling a dozen thoughts at a time, to taking control of every situation in which he was even remotely involved, to managing his life and his emotions rather than merely drifting in the wake of circumstance.

As he was drifting now.

He hadn't seen it coming. He had complacently believed his own conceited assumptions that nothing would happen to him unless he willed it. That at a time and in a way he deemed proper he would find a woman with whom to share his life, his heart, and his future. He would love her because he wanted to love her. Never would he tie himself to a woman without love, and he would not raise children in anything less than a loving household. A loving family.

He had never once considered loving Melissa. Melissa, who was too timid and conventional to make a good match with him. Melissa who surely was too beautiful and sheltered to have any character, conviction or strength. Long ago he'd pegged her as being one who *did* drift with the tides of society.

He'd been wrong.

She wore pantalettes.

He smiled wryly. Who would have thought that Melissa would defy convention by wearing a garment usually sported only by courtesans, regardless of whether her mother approved or not? Melissa had defied Arabella in other ways, with her choice of furnishings for her room, with her agreements to dance with him though she could have employed a dozen reasons to refuse. . . .

Yet, she had never refused him and had taken him into her bed and her body with an honesty that completely disarmed him.

His body came alive at the memory of just how honest she'd been.

Could he be any less honest? He swiped his hand over the back of his neck as he continued to stroll around his room, instinctively sidestepping obstacles of chairs and chest and the odd table or two.

*Love.* Unlike his half brother and brother-in-law, he felt no need to avoid such a state. He'd always expected it would happen one day. But he'd expected it to happen slowly, methodically, predictably. He would meet a woman who appealed to him and with whom he had everything in common. Love would come with time and familiarity like the comfort of oft-worn boots. They would plan their lives and manipulate circumstances to suit themselves, each pursuing interests separately, then coming together whenever the mood struck.

Usually so observant, he had failed to understand the nature of the emotion that flourished between the other members of his family. He'd been too cocky to consider that he might be caught off guard by anyone, least of all Melissa. He'd been too complacent to realize how far Melissa had knocked him off balance.

*Love.* He'd been too certain of his own ability to manipulate his life to accept that he could be rendered vulnerable by an emotion.

Now, after the fact, he was beginning to understand.

*Love.*

With every thought, the suspicion grew stronger that he did love Melissa. He needed time to get used to that. A creature of impulse, he'd always been careful to never act on those impulses without careful deliberation . . . until now.

Now he would have to catch up to himself, take control once again and convince Melissa that she could not live without him.

That resolved, he grinned and turned toward his bed. He did some of his best thinking while asleep, habitually waking several times a night as one idea or another popped into his dreams.

Tomorrow he would awaken with a clear head and a good plan.

# Chapter 10

~~~~~~⟡⟡⟡~~~~~~

**N**othing came to mind.

Bruce stared blankly at the sunlight pouring in through the open window hangings and then at Smithy, standing beside the window with his arms crossed over his chest. The voices of his household staff consulting with his butler, punctuated by the bang of pots, drifted up from the kitchen. Outside, hoofbeats pounded and coach wheels clattered on the cobblestones as maids and gardeners and stable hands of the neighborhood called to one another across fences and stable yards. He'd gleaned some very interesting bits of information by listening to their gossip over the years.

This morning it sounded like so much babble.

"It's near noon," Smithy said with a raised brow.

Noon? Bruce cocked his head and frowned. It couldn't be. He never slept past dawn, never slept through the sounds of activity in his house or intrusion into his bedchamber, becoming instantly alert at the slightest break in silence. Yet he had slept through what had been left of the night and half the day as well.

He'd slept soundly.

He never slept soundly. He was always too busy thinking.

"If this is what she's going to do to you, I think you should forget her," Smithy said with a glower.

*Her . . . Melissa.* Bruce's face began to ache with the intensity of his frown. He *had* dreamed. Of Melissa.

"I get nervous when you get serious."

Forcing his jaw to relax, Bruce jackknifed into a sitting position and all but jumped from his bed. Pain shot through his groin, nearly doubling him over. "I am often serious." He panted as he walked carefully toward the tub of water Smithy had prepared and vowed never—ever—to emulate Romeo again.

Smithy snorted. "You're always serious," he corrected, "but not where anyone else can see."

"Anyone but you, Smithy, and since we're alone I can be serious if I wish." He sank into the water and gasped at the heat. "I want to bathe, not be parboiled," he said through gritted teeth.

"After last night I figured you might be needing to warm up some sore muscles." Smithy tossed him a cake of soap. "Been a long time since you climbed up a trellis and then swung from a tree to see a woman."

"I've never done such a thing," Bruce murmured as the heat soaked into him. "And you are right. I've got the devil of an ache in my middle from slamming into that damned balcony."

"You've got the devil of a bruise."

Bruce glanced down and winced at the array of purples and blues adorning his groin.

"A little lower and you would have broken it . . . bent it at least."

Groaning, Bruce sank lower into the water and closed his eyes.

"More invitations came today," Smithy said.

"Put them with the others and find out which ones the Ladies Seymour will be accepting." Opening one eye, he followed Smithy's progress as he poured a cup of coffee and picked up a plate of pastries. Bruce always ate breakfast while bathing. It saved time. "You are still meeting Arabella's coachman at the local tavern for a nightly game of chess, aren't you?"

"Twice a week," Smithy corrected as he set the coffee and pastries on a table by the tub and fidgeted with the arrangement like an old woman straightening priceless figurines.

Bruce recognized agitation when he saw it. "What is it?"

"Don't need to find out nothing."

Suddenly alert to just how agitated Smithy was, Bruce sat up, not noticing the wave that splashed his chest and spilled over the sides of the tub. "You already know something?" he guessed.

"Aye, I know, all right. And I don't like it one bit." Scowling, he disappeared into the dressing room and emerged with clean clothing. "Countess Seymour rattled the rafters of her house after she got an invitation this morning. Had her coachman take her to the dressmaker's and leave her for the day. He came by here to pass the time."

Wishing Smithy would make a long story short, Bruce reached for his cup and drank deeply, scalding his tongue. "Blast it, Smithy, why don't you just stick an apple in my mouth and turn me on a spit?"

"It might be kinder," Smithy said with an ominous lowering of brows. "Trouble's brewing, sure as the sky is blue."

Bruce blew on his coffee and took a cautious sip. "And from where might this trouble be coming?"

Smithy shrugged. "The earl has bought a house outside London."

Which told Bruce precisely nothing he didn't already know. "I have concerns more pressing than the earl," he said wearily. He'd had a bellyful of the earl before he'd reached ten. Now he preferred to pretend the man didn't exist. "And I already knew that he'd purchased the Wyndham estate. God knows what he'll do with a house that size. It's damn near as big as Versailles and just as pretentious." He set his cup on the table and reached for a pastry. "Come to think of it, the place might just be large enough to hold *his* pretensions."

"He's having a house party there at the end of the Season in four weeks' time."

Bruce brushed crumbs from his chest. Something about Smithy's tone promised doom. On the other hand, if what he suspected was coming bore any resemblance to what Smithy was working his way around a bush to tell him, life might become very interesting indeed. "Pray continue, Smithy," he drawled as anticipation jumped in his chest.

"The countess and Lady Melissa will be going."

"With bells on, no doubt." Pleased to have his deductions confirmed, Bruce finished off his pastry in two bites and began to lather his body. "Arabella seems inordinately taken with the earl."

"You needn't sound so happy about it," Smithy grumbled.

"Anything that distracts Arabella from her daughter makes me happy. Otherwise I might have a bit of trouble seeing Melissa."

"A bit of trouble," Smithy muttered with a pointed glance at the bruise on Bruce's groin followed by a roll of his eyes. He planted his hands on his fists, the very image of disapproval. "It would be best if you didn't see her."

"What happened to 'things have been getting a mite dull' and your fear that I was becoming normal and proper?"

"I changed my mind."

Bruce met Smithy's glower with a raised brow and searching stare. He had to take his old friend seriously. Second to himself, no one enjoyed a good challenge more than Smithy. And second only to himself, no one refused to admit defeat more vehemently than Smithy. It was Smithy who'd taught him the infinite number of ways to skin a cat. Nothing was impossible; retreat was unthinkable. Yet Smithy was advising just the opposite. *That* was impossible. "Too late," he said blithely, forcing himself to ignore the unease inching up his spine. "I can't possibly become a bore now. And neither can you." He gasped as Smithy dumped a pail of water over his head to rinse off the soap. Water cascaded off him as he rose and blindly groped for a towel. "Blast it! First you cook me and then you try to drown me."

Smithy shoved a length of linen into his hands. "Ain't doing nothing to you except trying to get you to think straight."

Bruce wrapped the towel around his hips and snagged another pastry. "Just what do you consider straight thinking?"

"Take the nick to your pride and leave Lady Melissa alone. Walk away from this one."

Suddenly Bruce felt completely limp. Sagging into a chair, he tossed the remains of his breakfast into the fire, his usual appetite gone. "Lady Melissa has already done a thorough job of hacking my pride to bits."

"Then why bother with her?" Smithy poured fresh coffee into Bruce's cup and handed it to him.

Bruce took a sip and stared into the cup. "It would seem I have no choice. My pride is not the only thing involved."

Smithy sank into the chair facing his. "I hope you're talking about your John Thomas," he mumbled.

Bruce smiled halfheartedly. "Unfortunately, I possess at least one other organ which seems to be quite attached to the lady."

"Damnit!" Smithy hit the arm of his chair with his fist. "You went and done it. You fell in love."

"I suspect so," Bruce drawled. "It bears further investigation if I am to have any peace of mind."

A look of utter defeat on his weathered features, Smithy sprawled backward in the chair, his chin resting on his chest. "So it'll be more climbing in windows," he said flatly. "Don't know if I have enough cudgels to handle the others interested in watching Lady Melissa."

"By all means keep your weapons within reach," Bruce said soberly, then finished his coffee and leaned forward. "Though I have something less hazardous than sneaking into Melissa's chambers in mind. If someone is being paid to watch her, I can't risk exposing her to scandal."

Smithy rolled his eyes. "Better worry about what you might be risking. The earl—"

"Is *not* plotting against me," Bruce interrupted

tersely. Apparently Smithy had changed his mind about the earl as well as Melissa. Next, he would be accusing the king himself. "More likely Arabella has hired someone to keep an eye on her daughter. Or perhaps one of Arabella's enemies. Half the ladies in the ton would like nothing more than to put the cat in a cage, preferably in another country, which is where she would have to go to escape the gossip if Melissa were to be publicly shamed. The other half would delight in blackmail to bolster their husbands' strained purses." Rising, Bruce strolled to the clothes Smithy had laid out on the bed and began to dress himself. He'd never had the patience for the fussing and fretting of a valet. "It is my intention to get Melissa to the church before that happens."

Smithy's chin sank lower onto his chest. "I don't like it. Ever since I heard about the earl's house party I've felt like spiders are crawling over my head. He's up to something."

"He's no doubt up to getting a new wife to add to his respectability and his consequence. Arabella Seymour is a beautiful woman as well as a wealthy one."

"Countess Seymour is still young enough to have children," Smithy ventured.

"Yes she is." Bruce adjusted the knot of his stock and picked up his waistcoat. "And if the earl should get her to the altar and if she has a child, I will happily bow out as heir to the Blackwood fortune. I've always planned to give it away; you know that."

"The earl will care more about a child of his inheriting the title."

"And I would gladly relinquish that, too, if I could. Unfortunately, it would create more curiosity than I can satisfy without dragging Kathy and Max into it. The title will have to remain mine."

"Mayhap the earl would think the title good enough reason to plot against you," Smithy said darkly.

"I have more wealth than he. My connections are certainly more powerful than his. And he values his position and reputation too much to gamble them even against the title I will inherit. What can he do?"

A sigh heaved Smithy's chest. "Don't know. It's just a feeling I have. Whatever you do, have a care." He rose from the chair and trained a suspicious eye on Bruce. "What *are* you going to do?"

Bruce smiled and met Smithy's gaze with an innocent expression. "I am going to play the dutiful heir and attend the earl's house party, of course. The Wyndham estate offers a veritable plethora of discreet locations for a lovers' tryst." He rose and tossed the towel aside. "And in the meantime I think I will lurk in the park across from the Seymour house and make the acquaintance of any suspicious characters hanging about."

*Suspicious* was too mild a word for the man who was dressed just a bit too impeccably and strolled too nonchalantly through the private park that served the area. If he had a right to be there, Bruce would have recognized him. If he was a newcomer to the vicinity, Bruce would have known everything about the man down to how often he used his toothbrush before he'd even moved in.

Bruce made it a point to know who and what surrounded him and why.

This man did not belong in a residential area inhabited by wealthy aristocrats. At best, he was perhaps a lesser son of a noble who didn't care how he acquired the wherewithal to pay his rent. At worst, he was an educated man of shady character and vocation who affected a respectable nature.

Bruce leaned toward the worst as he observed how the man's gaze constantly shifted while appearing to focus directly in front of him, easily skirting obstacles when anyone else staring ahead would have tripped several times over. And that riding coat and doeskins were entirely too new, with no signs of wear on the sides of the knees, and too tightly tailored to allow him to ride without splitting a seam or two. Odds were the man didn't even own a horse.

Whoever had hired him learned quickly. After last night's fracas, the mastermind behind the men watching the Ladies Seymour had apparently decided to disguise his wolves in sheep's clothing.

Bruce allowed himself a smug smile at his foresight in "stumbling upon" the local constable during that worthy man's daily constitution and engaging him in conversation, all the while keeping a close eye on the park. At least Melissa hadn't completely addled him.

"I say," Bruce exclaimed in mild curiosity, "did you know that one of our neighbors was robbed a few nights ago?"

Gordon paled and slowed in his tracks. "I didn't ... I mean, it wasn't reported ... surely I would have—"

"No reason for you to know," Bruce interrupted the constable's sputtering. "The party in question didn't want it bandied about, but I felt it wise to alert you to the problem. My man Smithy noticed an odd fellow trying to get a peek into the Seymours' upper windows, and I myself was accosted on my way home."

"I assure you, my Lord, that I and my men made our usual frequent rounds last night," Gordon said as his face flushed deep red.

"Of course you did," Bruce soothed, afraid the man would go into apoplexy any minute. "I often wonder when you sleep."

"Hmph . . . yes, well." Gordon's color returned and his chest puffed out. "'Tis a position of trust I hold here, sir. I would not shirk such responsibility." He scowled as his gaze darted about, no doubt searching for cutthroats behind every bush. "But damn, why wasn't the theft reported?"

Bruce bit back his smile. He'd begun to wonder when the constable would get around to asking more pointed questions. He leaned closer to Gordon and adopted a confidential tone as he embellished his story about last night's fictional robbery. "It seems that the gentleman's wife was robbed of all her family jewels, which unbeknownst to her had been duplicated in paste earlier this year. Her husband had gambling debts, you see." Bruce counted to five, giving Gordon time to digest the Banbury tale he'd concocted.

"Bad business that," Gordon muttered, shaking his head. "Only a matter of time till the paste dulled and she found him out. Last year Lady Barton took after Sir Barton with gardening shears after she found out he'd gambled away her dower house. Chased him down the street, she did. I had the devil of a time getting him out of harm's way."

"Exactly why the theft wasn't reported," Bruce said. "The gentleman was understandably relieved to have them removed so propitiously before his lady could discover his deception. Afraid you—being such a conscientious fellow—would recover the pieces, he is having them replicated yet again in paste, then he convinced his wife that if it were made public and the jewels not recovered, everyone would know they weren't real."

"Hmm, yes, I see," Gordon said. "Better to keep it quiet and let everyone believe she still has the real thing." Again the constable scowled. "Still, I should know who was robbed so I can keep an eye out."

"It's unlikely he'll be robbed again, having been quite thoroughly cleaned out already," Bruce said. "You have far wealthier residents here who would be easy pickings for a skilled thief."

Gordon hooked his thumbs into the pockets of his waistcoat. "Quite right, of course. Someone was watching Countess Seymour's house last night, you say?"

"Yes, and don't forget the attack on my person. One would think an entire band of thieves was at work here." Satisfied that the constable was indeed following the trail he'd laid, Bruce gave him another count of five. "Has someone finally purchased the Hawthorne town house?" he asked.

"Now, if they had, you would have been the first to know, my Lord," Constable Gordon said dryly.

"Hmm, true, but I've been a bit distracted lately. It could be that I missed something."

The constable chuckled. "I'll worry when that happens."

"All the same, I haven't seen that fellow be-fore . . ." He allowed his sentence to trail off as he nodded toward the man making yet another slow circuit of the section of the park facing the Seymour house. "Since the park is for the use of those residing in the area, and he is clearly enjoying its benefits, I must assume he belongs here."

The constable's gaze shot toward the park. "What

the devil? He doesn't live around here. Cheeky bloke, trespassin' where he don't belong," he huffed, and veered off toward the park gate. "And with one of our ladies about to take the air, too. Can't have that." He hitched his pants over his belly and hurried toward the man with his fists clenched.

Bruce's amusement at the constable's habit of referring to the residents of the area in the possessive faded as he idly glanced over to the lady in question. His breath kicked in his chest at the sight of Melissa entering the park with her maid. He should have guessed she would take Arabella's excursion to the modiste as an opportunity to have some time to herself and that she would prefer it in the open air.

It was frightening how well he was beginning to know her.

Pursing his lips in a soundless whistle, he continued his stroll while keeping an eye on the park, not wanting anyone to associate him with Constable Gordon's actions. Nor did he want anyone to think he'd noticed Melissa, much less cared what she was about. Few people noticed Melissa beyond admiring her as if she were a life-size fashion doll.

He was having the devil of a time noticing anything but Melissa. She had defied propriety by not donning a bonnet, and sunlight shimmered in waves over her golden hair, caught at the nape of her neck with a ribbon. A simple pink muslin gown molded to her legs with the gust of a breeze as she walked, staring straight ahead, remote, seemingly detached from the world around her.

Could Helen of Troy have been as beautiful?

He winced at the cliché. If he was going to wax poetic, one would think he could at least be more creative about it.

He forced his attention to Gordon and stifled a grin. The good constable had grasped the intruder's arm and was ushering him out of the park. Within minutes, Bruce knew, the spy would be well away from the vicinity. Gordon knew well how fortunate he was to have a post in such a neighborhood, and he watched out for "his charges" with all the zeal of a sheepdog guarding his flock. There were far worse duties than dealing with the occasional trespasser or directing traffic after a carriage accident in one of the city's most prosperous residential areas.

If he didn't miss his guess, no one venturing in or out of the area would now escape the good constable's scrutiny. Those who belonged here would be carefully watched and those who didn't would find it next to impossible to linger.

Now only Melissa and her maid remained in the park with no one to observe them but the lovesick son of the confectioner standing outside the fence and holding the bars like a prisoner in Old Bailey.

And himself.

God, he hoped he didn't look as cow-eyed and desperate as the young swain waiting for a word from his lady.

# Chapter 11

**H**e stood outside the spired fence, staring at them, the expression on his boyish face urgent.

Melissa had seen him before—on a street corner when she and her maid were browsing the shops, and many times standing as he was now outside the park, watching until Melissa took pity on him and found an excuse to leave her maid alone for a few moments.

Beside her, Nicole fidgeted and repeatedly took deep breaths as if she wanted to speak yet didn't dare. Her French maid was a sweet and homely child, hand picked by Countess Seymour for her skills and her reticence.

Melissa smiled faintly. Nicole was older than she by a year, yet she thought of her maid as a child. But then, she thought of most of her contemporaries as children, frolicking about and squeezing every drop of pleasure from their youth. She'd long since stopped wondering what it would be like to frolic.

Now that she thought about it, she supposed that the uncensored knowledge her mother had given her, coupled with the enforced opportunities to constantly observe society, had jaded her.

She couldn't help but smile at that. Sweet, innocent Melissa Seymour was jaded. Fancy that.

She didn't fancy it at all. If she were as sweet and innocent as others thought her to be, she might be quite happy to marry Bruce and allow herself to be fooled into believing it made him happy as well.

Disgusted that she should still nurture such regretful thoughts, Melissa studied the young man from the corner of her eye and wondered what position he filled in which household. She'd wanted to ask Nicole, but hadn't wanted to become involved for Nicole's sake. Her mother would go into conniptions if she were to discover that the maid she had imported from France carried on a romance behind her back. It wouldn't do to lose so valuable a servant to marriage, for then, even if she remained in the household, Nicole would not be available at all hours of the day and night. Arabella wanted her servants under her roof and under her thumb.

Usually Melissa simply turned her back and hoped Nicole took the opportunity to exchange a few words and perhaps a kiss with her beau. Melissa never peeked, or asked questions. If she neither saw nor heard anything, she couldn't give them away.

Not so long ago, she'd thought it would be wildly romantic to indulge in a furtive rendezvous with one's lover. It hadn't occurred to her that it might be frustrating and without satisfaction. It hadn't occurred to her that it couldn't possibly be enough.

It hadn't occurred to her how lonely it could be to have to hide what should be a matter of celebration and joy.

The young man pointed to Melissa and mouthed

some words she couldn't make out, no doubt urging
Nicole to find a way to come to him. Melissa sensed
that her maid was furiously shaking her head and
casting frantic glances her way.

Were they lovers? Melissa wondered. Not likely.
Not unless the young man climbed the tree to Nicole's upper-story room.

Heat climbed up her body at the thought. Excitement billowed at the memory that followed. Few
men were as daring as Bruce. Even fewer were so
charmed that they could flaunt the rules and not be
called to account for the transgression. Neither scandal nor outrage seemed to stick to Bruce as it did to
anyone else who defied propriety. He simply smiled
engagingly and twisted logic to suit his ends, leaving those around him blinking and bewildered and
too caught up in their own concerns to sort it out.

Nicole shifted for the hundredth time and took
another deep breath that failed to produce a request
for a few moments to speak with her young man.

How sad. Melissa had always thought her own
meekness pathetic. Seeing it in someone else, she
thought it tragic. Especially since Nicole's love was
obviously returned. Melissa wanted to believe that
if she were so fortunate, she would find the courage
to reach out for what she wanted no matter who
waited to slap her hands.

"Who is he?" she asked, surprising herself.

"Mademoiselle?" Nicole said with a note of panic.

Melissa turned toward her and smiled. "He is
very handsome."

Her face turning scarlet, Nicole nonetheless held
her gaze, her eyes steady and bright and defiant.
"Yes, mademoiselle, he is."

A pang of envy twisted in Melissa's stomach at

Nicole's fortitude. "I've been wondering who he is."

"He is son of the confectioner, mademoiselle," Nicole said quickly, as if she wanted to tell Melissa everything she could before her courage failed. "He delivers cakes to your house and others here. I meet him when I first arrive. He—"

"Loves you very much," Melissa said as she stood and made a show of smoothing her skirts. "I believe I will take a walk through the trees. You needn't accompany me. The park is quite empty. I'll be back in a half hour or so."

Nicole tilted her head and her hands twisted in her crisp white apron. Her lip trembled. Even the mobcap on her head quivered. "Mademoiselle?"

"I'm certain you can entertain yourself, Nicole." Melissa nodded toward the young man. "I suggest you invite him inside the fence and find a spot behind a tree in case anyone passes by." Though Melissa didn't mention her mother, Nicole's expression indicated she understood her meaning.

Glancing over to the fence, then back at Melissa, the maid sprang to her feet, grasped Melissa's hand and pressed it to her cheek. "I did not lie when I tell my Ben you are kind," she whispered. "I tell him I like you and wish you were like me—a maid—so we can be friends."

Startled, Melissa lowered her gaze, at a loss as to how to answer. Never had anyone expressed a wish for friendship with her. She frowned as she realized what Nicole had said. "You did not wish you could be like *me*, so we could be"—she swallowed and groped for the word she'd never had the occasion to speak before—"friends?"

Nicole released her hand and stepped back, shaking her head. "My life is not so hard as yours, ma-

demoiselle. I do not wish for your beautiful cage."
Again she flushed. "Please enjoy your walk. I will
watch for your *maman* and find you if she returns
early." She stood with her hands folded beneath her
apron.

Knowing Nicole would not leave her as long as
she stood there, Melissa blindly stepped onto a dirt
path winding through a thick stand of trees, needing
to escape Nicole's astute observations as much as
she wanted to escape her own timidity.

She halted abruptly and turned toward her maid.
"Nicole ... if ... your Ben did not love you, what
would you do?"

Nicole bit her lip and frowned. "I do not know
why he *does* love me, mademoiselle. I sometimes
think he could not, I am so ... so ... *not* pretty, and
I do not sparkle. *N'est-ce pas?* I sometimes am afraid
to believe ..." Her voice trailed off as she shrugged.
"If I think of it I will send him away, and so I make
myself believe him."

Melissa's throat felt as if it were closing. Tears
burned behind her eyes as she took the path, putting
distance between herself and Nicole's confession. A
confession that could have been hers if she had the
courage to accept it.

To accept Bruce and his declarations.

But he had always been too blatant in his caprices,
too fickle in his liaisons, for her to blindly accept that
he had suddenly changed. That *she* had been the
cause of that change. She was the type men chose
for a wife and then ignored, a pretty bauble that kept
well on a shelf in the country.

Bruce would think she was the perfect candidate
for his wife and the mother of his heir. That much
of what he'd said she did not question. But she

would gather dust and become less than nothing in her own eyes if she settled for such a fate.

She would spoil on that shelf in his country manor, her emotions frozen in time while he gave his "love" only in moments measured by convenience.

She was already her mother's doll to be dressed and admired and directed. She would not become Bruce's bauble.

How many times, she wondered, would she have to tell herself that before she finally accepted the truth and stopped hoping she was wrong? She stepped off the path and absently bent one leg behind her, reached back to remove her shoe, then did the same with the other. Sighing in pleasure at the cool prickle of grass through her stockings, she wandered through the trees and willed her mind to ponder nothing more than the breeze that gusted now and then and the scud of wispy clouds overhead.

She stopped short, her hand to her throat, her blood heating as her pulse raced.

Surely the man leaning negligently against a tree while sniffing a flower was an illusion conjured by her thoughts. He couldn't be here, looking for all the world as if he lingered in the park every day. Though it was one of the larger private parks in the city, and his residence in the area entitled him to use it, Bruce was too busy for such idle pursuits as smelling flowers.

He tucked the blossom into the lapel of his riding jacket and straightened. "I have seen shock on your face," he said softly—almost in wonder—as he walked toward her. "I have finally had the pleasure of conversing with you . . . after a fashion," he added with a mocking lift of his brows. "And I have had

the extreme pleasure of experiencing your passion."
He brushed her cheek with his forefinger. "Now, I
witness your tears." He examined the drop of moisture on the tip of his finger, then gave her a smile
tinged with bemusement. "We make progress, I
think."

She clenched her hands to keep from raising them
to her face and swiping away the tears she hadn't
known she was shedding. Tears of self-pity.

Ashamed of her foolish indulgence, and mortified
that Bruce should have seen it, she fought the impulse to hitch up her skirts and run, and met his
gaze instead. "Why are you here?" she croaked, her
mouth so dry her lips felt as if they were sticking to
her teeth.

"I occasionally enjoy a few moments of solitude
in pastoral surroundings."

"To what purpose?" If she knew anything at all
about Bruce it was that he never did anything without purpose.

"To see you," he replied. "I knew Arabella was
gone for the day and I could not bring myself to
waste such an opportunity."

"You're being honest, at least," she said, and
clamped her mouth shut. Never had her tongue been
so unruly as to run ahead of her wits.

Bruce lifted her chin with his forefinger. "I am always honest, Melissa. *Always*. Never doubt it."

*Except when you speak of love,* she argued silently.

"I have my eye on a lovely place in the country,
not too far from Westbrook Castle," he said idly. "A
deserted abbey built of stone with archways and
stained glass and several gardens, each much larger
than this park. The sea is nearby. I can imagine raising children there."

She blinked at the non sequitur as an image formed in her mind of ancient stone overgrown with ivy, graceful doorways open to faintly scented air from the sea, of pathways worn by history and serenity laying over it all like a soft old blanket. And in the distance a castle rising from the ground, a benevolent guardian watching over them.

"You smile," Bruce said softly. "Something else I've never seen." He traced the curve of her lips with his thumb. "The idea pleases you?"

It pleased her, beckoned her, tempted her. Just as his caress tempted her to kiss the pad of his thumb, to open her lips and taste it. She averted her head. "It sounds very nice. But what of Blackwood? Will you not live there one day?"

"No," he said flatly.

She turned her gaze back to him, saw the tight line of his mouth, the distance that had suddenly come into his eyes—a warning, she thought. But warning her against what? Speaking of his home? His father? It occurred to her then that for all Bruce's amiability and participation in society, she knew very little about him. That anyone other than the Dukes of Westbrook and Bassett knew anything about him except what was obvious on the surface. Curiosity grew from there, prompting her to venture further. "I know . . . you don't get on very well with your father—" She halted the flow of words as his face hardened and his body seemed to turn to stone. "I'm sorry. It's none of my business."

"No, it is not," he said tersely, then sighed heavily. In the space of that weighty breath his expression changed from formidable to engaging. "I have not waited three years to converse with you just so we could discuss the earl," he said lightly as he enfolded her hand in his and tugged her along the path. "I would, however, be most fascinated to discover why you have an abhorrence to shoes. Last night you kicked them off so vehemently they literally flew past my nose."

She glanced down at the shoes in her hand, waiting for her face to flame in embarrassment at being caught in so indecorous a state. But she felt nothing but a wry acknowledgment that Bruce had seen far more of her than her feet. How odd that she would have such a thought as if it concerned nothing more untoward than a crookedly tied sash.

"I imagine Arabella would consider your lack of a bonnet a minor offense which you've committed before, but I cannot imagine she knows you stroll about the park getting grass stains on your stockings," he said as he sat beneath a tree and tugged her down beside him.

"Please do not give me away," she said gravely, knowing that she referred to more than her shoes. That in her request was couched a plea she could not form. "Mother is very fragile," she finished helplessly.

"You think I would blackmail you with such information? Or that I would wish to hurt Arabella— or you, for that matter—merely for sport?"

*Yes!* she started to say, but there was an odd note in his voice that stopped her, as if her reply mattered to him. As if it could hurt him. The memory of that brief flicker of apology and regret in his eyes after he'd delivered his cruel threat three years ago cautioned her to answer honestly. "No"—she sighed— "not for sport. I think that you will always do what you believe is right for what you believe are the right reasons."

He grinned. "A compliment. We do indeed make progress."

"I'm quite certain I did not intend it as such." The truth came naturally, as if she had always felt confident in speaking openly with him. "What you believe is often at odds with what others believe."

His smile grew wider. "Inconsequential, since few in our circle comprehend their own thoughts, much less mine."

"It takes a great deal of effort to comprehend your logic," she murmured.

He sobered as he propped his arms on his bent knees and angled his head toward her, regarding her with eyes that seemed to draw her in, hold her in thrall even as they soothed her.

"You appear to comprehend me with little effort." He bent his head and poked his fingers through the grass as if searching for something. "I find it quite unsettling."

She waited for him to signal that he was teasing her with a wink or one of his lopsided smiles. Surely he was teasing. But he did not look at her, and his concentration on the blades of grass seemed singularly intent. She cleared her throat and looked up at the boughs of a tree across from them, willing away the ridiculous urge to cry. "No one has ever accused me of comprehending anything."

"Only because they exercise their mouths rather than their minds. They are afraid to be silent and observe as you do." He lifted his hand slowly to examine a small insect crawling along his palm. "Understanding is an intimate thing."

*Too intimate.* As intimate as sitting so close beside him under a tree doing nothing more than conversing in abstract terms. An intimacy that had little to

do with passion and everything to do with the ease
of familiarity. Why that should be, she didn't know.
In the past, Bruce had given her more moments of
discomfort and anxiety than she cared to count.
Now, she wished they could remain like this forever.

"Many are afraid of such intimacy," he remarked
casually.

As she was afraid. Afraid that if he understood
her too well, his clever mind would find a way to
seduce her into accepting him and what he offered.
"Are you?" she asked softly.

He grimaced as he shifted to sit cross-legged in
front of her, like a child about to share a secret. "I
have no idea." Grasping her hand, he traced the out-
line of her fingers, each in turn, across the tip, down
alongside her knuckles and lingering over the sensitive flesh in between. "Shall we find out?"

He implied so much with that "we." It was no
small thing to court understanding of oneself, particularly when the one in question took such pains
to appear conspicuously shallow. Suddenly light-
headed with the revelation, she inhaled deeply and
held her breath for a moment to calm her quickening
heartbeat. "Why?" she asked.

His brow furrowed as he studied her hands, seemingly absorbed in their shape and texture.

She could almost believe he felt awkward. Earlier
in the day she wouldn't have thought it possible, but
now she had to wonder—

"Because I am determined to marry you," he said,
still not looking at her. "And I cannot think of anything worse than living with a stranger."

Again, he took her breath away with his implications. "Few husbands and wives actually live to-

gether," she ventured. "Most are strangers and prefer it that way."

He met her gaze then, his expression tight, fierce. "I have taken a great deal of time in deciding to marry for that very reason. I will live with my wife and we will not be strangers." Though he spoke in a monotone, he spaced the words apart, enunciating each, it seemed, with deliberate care.

"You will live with her?"

"Of course. Just as Damien lives with Kathy and Max lives with Jillian. Otherwise, what is the point of getting buckled?"

"To produce an heir. To perpetuate your bloodline. To satisfy honor."

"To create a family." He closed his eyes then, as if he envisioned a particularly pleasant dream.

A house in the country. A husband actually living with her. Children.

*Family.* As it had once been when her father lived.

Her throat ached with the memory of all that was gone. Her heart thumped with the idea that she could have it again.

But not with Bruce. He was too restless to be content in such an arrangement. She'd never seen him still—not really. Even when he stood leaning against a pillar or a mantel, his gaze darted and skipped from one place to another, and she'd long ago sensed that behind his lazy winks, Bruce's mind never rested.

He would need a lively household to stimulate him. He would have to love a woman with his whole heart and soul to be content in the same surroundings every day and seeing the same people day after day. His wife would have to sparkle with wit and intelligence and diverse conversation to hold his interest and his heart. His wife would have to be everything that Melissa was not. And while she knew she was intelligent and Bruce was obviously taken with her beauty, she enjoyed peace and routine, and preferred her own thoughts to the chatter and intrigues of others. She was neither stimulating nor challenging.

*Challenging.* Of course! She was a challenge to him. Why hadn't she realized it before? Rarely did anyone say no to Bruce. Rarely did he fail to achieve a goal.

Her rejection had challenged him to pursue her. Marriage to her had become his goal.

And once he succeeded, he would seek something else to provoke his interest.

"You have not answered my question."

Startled from her thoughts, she blinked, then stared at him. "I'm sorry. I don't recall . . ." Her voice trailed off with the lie; never had she been able to actually complete a fib. He'd asked if they should find out whether he feared understanding—a question she dared not contemplate, much less answer.

"No, you were woolgathering. Pleasant thoughts, I hope."

"No, not pleasant at all," she blurted. "I really must go."

His grip on her hands tightened, keeping her from rising, from escaping him. "You are eloquent in your silence, Melissa." His thumb brushed over her eyelids. "Here, where I see your thoughts stray." He smoothed the place between her brows. "And here, where lines speak of your worry when your thoughts stumble back onto your straight and narrow path." He grinned and chucked her under her chin. "And especially here, when you have made a decision and resolve to be good. Like now, when you have most likely reaffirmed your conviction that I am not to be taken seriously."

"I dare not," she blurted. "It would mean disaster for us both."

He rose to his feet and helped her do the same. "Only because you refuse to take me seriously," he said blithely. "Are you so afraid of what you might discover if you did?"

*Yes!* she wanted to shout. She was terrified to learn more about Bruce. Terrified that she would love him more. That she would weaken and marry him. She shook her head. "I simply do not wish to see more."

"Liar," he whispered as he stepped close to her, pressing her back against the trunk of the tree, overwhelming her with his size, his heat, the force of his gaze.

She welcomed it, needing him to hold her, needing the strength of his passion and the urgency of hers to blot out all else but what *she* wanted. She darted a glance left and right, then behind her. It was one thing to exchange pleasantries while passing one another on the path and quite another to embrace against a tree. If she were to be seen conversing with Bruce, gossip would soon have them swinging stark naked from the trees. But, her mother would not be home for another hour or so, and rarely did anyone take air at this time of the afternoon. The path was heavily sheltered by foliage, the park was deserted, and only occasionally did the clatter of traffic pass over the cobbled street outside the gates. No one could see them. She bit her lip against the urge to laugh at the irony of making certain it was safe to be daring.

"Again your silence contradicts you," he murmured in her ear, his breath warm on the flesh of her neck. "All you need do is say no to my caress, Melissa, and I would back away. But you part your lips and wet them with your tongue. Your breasts rise against my chest and your heartbeat echoes mine, racing and tripping over itself."

She sucked in a breath and raised her chin, meeting his gaze and forcing her voice to be strong and sure. "All right," she said, managing a reasonable tone. "All right. My body wants yours. And for now, you feel the same desire."

He cocked a brow and pursed his mouth as if he were fighting a smile.

If he smiled she would raise her knee and—

"Go on," he said gravely. "Our bodies want one another. . . ."

"Yes." It sounded strangled, incoherent.

"And I want you to marry me so we might indulge ourselves to our hearts' content."

"No!" Panic constricted her chest. He was using logic again. *His* logic. She had to take control of the conversation . . . somehow. "You don't want to marry me. Not really," she babbled. "It's your queer sense of honor that demands marriage. If I were like Joan Sinclair or any of the others you would be satisfied to have me as your . . . your—"

"Lover?" He flattened his palms against the tree on either side of her, trapping her.

"Yes." As she said it, an idea emerged. A wild, brazen idea that seemed not only logical but imperative. An idea that would give them both what they wanted if only for a while. Frantic to voice her thoughts and escape, she clutched his arms. "I *am* like them, don't you see? I accepted you twice without protest and I've found pleasure in it. We both know I would do it again." The words rushed out faster and faster now, taking her where she would never dare venture if she had time to employ common sense. If she could find a shred of common sense to employ. Breathless, she paused and gulped in air. "Beyond that we have nothing at all in common. You do not want a woman like me for a wife. I would not make you happy for any length of time. Surely you know that."

His brow climbed higher. "Do I?"

"Of course you do. You *must* know it."

"And, pray tell, what else do I know?" He leaned closer.

This was it—her opportunity to be brave and bold and completely selfish. She had to do it now before panic completely strangled her and drove her gasping to the safety of her mother's house. "You know . . . *you know* . . . that we can be lovers." Now that it was out, a strange calm descended over her. The flush of heat she'd felt rising in her body receded and she no longer had the urge to turn and hide her face from him. She met his gaze without flinching. "We *should* be lovers. We should play out this . . . this . . ."

"Attraction?" he prompted.

She nodded. "Exactly. We should enjoy it while it lasts so that we can go on once it has faded. This way we can walk away from one another without always wondering what *might* have happened. We will know."

With infinite slowness, Bruce lowered his head toward hers, brushed his mouth across hers, settled his lips over hers in a kiss so sweet and gentle she could only stand in numb confusion. And then he raised his head and backed away from her, one step . . . two . . . until he was out of reach. "It is imperative, I think, that we achieve understanding of one another without delay."

"There is no need. Not if we—"

"There is every need, Lady Melissa. And it occurs to me that you are more fearful of the experience than I am."

She didn't blink or speak or move. She couldn't.

"To begin with, understand that you are most definitely not like the others. I am beginning to suspect that in many ways you and I are alike. Understand that while I may prove too besotted to reject you as my lover, I am also determined that you will become my wife. We *will* see each other again, and again, and one day you will say yes to me. I will direct all my resources and efforts toward making it so, and I rarely fail."

If it were any other man making such bold promises—and she didn't doubt that they were promises—she might believe he was in love with her.

But he was Bruce Palmerston, and he was only besotted with her.

"It's all a game to you," she accused. "And you're going to cheat."

He slanted a smile at her. A cocky smile, brimming with mischief. "A game? Hardly that. In any case, you surely must recall that you cheated first."

Contrary to her certainty that she didn't like the sound of that, anticipation crackled inside her. "What exactly are you going to do?" she asked warily.

"At the moment, I am going to play the gentleman and leave you before I forget that we are in a public park and your mother is due home at any moment." With a flourish he retrieved her shoes from where she had dropped them, bent on one knee and slipped one shoe, then the other, onto her feet. Excitement sizzled through her veins as she placed her hand on his back to brace herself. Pleasure reduced her to mush at the deliberate stroke of his fingers over her arch. Her limbs turned to water as he skimmed his hand over her calf, the back of her knee.

He straightened and set her aside, holding her only until she found her balance. "Look at me," he ordered softly.

She lifted her gaze to his. Again he stood out of reach, his features shadowed by a brooding expression—of apology, regret. The last time she had seen such a look on his face had been three years ago when he'd promised to ruin her.

Instead she had ruined herself.

"I am going to court you, Melissa. Think of it as a game if you wish, though it will be one with no rules. I am going to use whatever means I can to convince you to marry me." He sketched a small bow and turned on his heel to stride toward the gate at the far end of the park.

A game. Of course, it was a game to him. How could it be otherwise? And she knew nothing of mischief or outrageousness. She had no idea how to be brash and daring, no idea how to fight both him and herself. She had no idea whether she wanted him to win or to lose.

"It isn't at all fair," she whispered, feeling helpless and apprehensive.

He paused and glanced at her over his shoulder. "I'll be happy to debate the fairness of it with you after we've been married for a few years."

In the time it took her to blink, he had rounded a curve in the path and disappeared.

A will-o'-the-wisp, difficult to catch, impossible to hold.

And she had actually suggested an affair with him.

A sudden burn swept through her at the reminder of her temerity, but not of horror. Not of humiliation. She'd wanted the wild passion and reckless adventure of it. The ecstasy.

Surely not. Surely it had been desperation driving her. Desperation and the certainty that, regardless of what was right or wrong, she would welcome Bruce into her arms simply because she wanted to.

Because she could.

She understood then why Bruce sauntered through life satisfying his whims, collecting his moments, pursuing his objectives with single-minded purpose. It was either that or stand against the wall as she did, watching as the world passed by just out of reach. The sense of triumph and power was heady indeed when one had the pluck to rush out and meet one's opportunities rather than become a part of the scenery, left behind to wish and to regret.

Awareness of the world around her intruded in bursts of sound. Upon first sight of Bruce standing beneath a canopy of leaves, the outside world had seemed very far away, with the rumble of coaches and more distant sounds of city bustle muffled by the hammering of her heart and the soft hum of pleasure in her mind as they'd talked. It had become *her* world to do with as she pleased, with no one to tell her how to stand or where, what to say and when.

Admittedly, she'd gone a little mad with the power of it, but she had also, for once, acted in her own name, taking what she wanted. Now she found it impossible to regret seizing her own handful of moments.

She glanced up at the sky and reckoned that at least an hour had passed. An hour. Never had she conversed at such length with anyone, including her mother. But then, completely absorbed in her own opinions, her mother spoke *to* people rather than *with* them.

It stunned Melissa to realize that Bruce had listened to her, giving every appearance of enjoying discourse with her as much as he'd obviously enjoyed making love with her. He hadn't agreed with her, but he had listened and responded to what she'd said. And then he'd challenged her, as if he thought her a worthy, if not equal, opponent. As if he thought her adventurous enough to at least consider picking up the gauntlet.

She had considered it. She was still considering it.

A game. She waited, expecting to feel distress or apprehension or insult or even anger at the idea. Oddly enough, all she felt was anticipation and excitement. And she felt the peculiar sense of being flattered by Bruce's determination to have his way even if he had to cheat to do it.

It was foolhardy for her to give it a moment's thought. She was not equal to playing such a game with Bruce Palmerston. She would lose, and losers always paid.

Yet knowing this, it was a matter of deciding whether the enjoyment was worth the price. And she could not deny that she'd more than enjoyed being reckless and going a little mad. She reveled in feeling alive.

She strongly suspected that she might have actually had fun.

# Chapter 12

**F**un was intoxicating, addictive. And when it was over, the memory of it popped up without warning to haunt and ridicule and remind Melissa that she was a fool.

She paid the price for her indulgence during the next four weeks, suffering steep descents into misery every time she didn't see Bruce at one social function or another, every time she heard a sound and it turned out not to be Bruce climbing the trellis into her room or approaching her in the park or at a ball or musicale.

She'd never realized how exhausting anticipation could be.

She'd never realized how mercilessly her own actions could turn on her, stabbing her with mortification and shame. Shame because she still felt none for what she'd done and said and thought. She ought to be ashamed, but instead felt a certain pride, a certain sense of power over herself and her life. She—Melissa the timid, Melissa the coward—had done exactly as she'd wanted with Bruce, and then she'd spoken her mind to Bruce.

She'd grown a backbone. A secret one, to be sure, but a backbone nonetheless.

For all the good it had done her. Pride and power were empty accomplishments when one had only oneself upon which to practice them. Still, if she were to be maudlin about it she supposed there was comfort in knowing that she would one day go to her grave with fewer regrets than if she had been a good little girl and sent Bruce away, doing nothing, saying nothing.

She shuddered and glanced around at the extensive gardens and massive manor house. A small company of aristocrats roamed and examined and commented in low whispers about the Earl of Blackwood's new acquisition of property. All were her mother's cronies, very proper and sedate and stuffy. Among the two dozen guests could be found the most rigid corsets and stiffest shirt points in Christendom. Not a single mischievous smile or impulsive thought would be found in this lot. If one were lucky, a droll observation might be heard from time to time, but only in regard to politics or gardening or the difficulty of keeping good servants.

There would be no prowlers in the halls at this house party, no husbands and wives separating under the guise of headaches and weariness in order to meet their lovers. As the only unmarried woman under five-and-twenty in attendance, Melissa really had no idea what she was doing here. The youngest widow was thirty if she was a day, and a bluestocking to boot.

The surety of boredom aside, it was a relief to be at the Earl of Blackwood's house party, where she knew Bruce would *not* be in attendance. Perhaps here, for the space of a few days, she would be able to find a bit of peace by slipping into the old habits of trailing in her mother's wake and having to do nothing more than what she was told. Perhaps she could find respite from her own expectations and be content to observe others having fun—relatively speaking, of course. Baron Moseby would certainly enjoy the nightly card games, Lady Lynnford would spend hours collecting slips from the rose garden, and the aforementioned widow would swoon with delight at having free run of the earl's library. For that matter, Melissa admitted to herself, she, too, would enjoy the gardens and take great pleasure in being surrounded by floor-to-ceiling books.

Sighing, she wondered if that last thought meant she was well on her way to being a stuffy old maid. And then she wondered if spinsters daydreamed about old stone abbeys by the sea and the sounds of children frolicking through the halls. Children with auburn hair and mischievous blue eyes and bright restless minds.

"You appear to be looking for someone," a smooth voice commented at her side.

Startled, she whirled about and nearly collided with the Earl of Blackwood, catching herself just in time to keep from tumbling them both into the hedge. "No," she replied breathlessly, dismayed to hear the resignation in her tone. Bruce would not be here. It was useless to search the guests for his tall form and deceptively lazy posture.

"I imagine a house party is rather dull for you," the earl said. "I really should have included a few of the younger set on the guest list."

"It's quite lovely here," Melissa murmured, avoiding the subject. The last thing she wanted was to be caught between the pitying glances of her mother's friends and either the complete indifference or the spiteful envy of those her own age, depending upon their gender. "I'm looking forward to a few days to myself. The Season can be quite tedious."

"Tedious?" The earl angled his head as if considering a foreign concept. "Most young women would say the Season was exhausting or exciting. Do you consider it a chore?"

"Yes," she said simply, surprised that she should confide even that much to the earl.

"Now that I think about it, I suppose it would be if nothing about the Season interests you." He gave her a sidelong glance. "Yet I sense that you are preoccupied as well as searching for a particular face among my guests."

Her heart jumped into her throat. Was she so obvious? Worse, had she been searching for Bruce's face even here? Could she be such a mooncalf that she now hoped for the impossible?

Her host stepped from her side to meet her gaze head-on. "If you had told me of your interest, I would have been quite happy to send an invitation to the . . . ah . . . person in question."

She could not imagine that the earl would be so ready to accommodate her if he knew who that person was. He'd left little doubt how he felt about his son. And the way Bruce's expression had changed from its usual animation to stony implacability at her mention of the earl had been equally explicit. "There is no one," she said, careful to lower her gaze lest her eyes betray the lie.

*You are eloquent in your silence*, Bruce had said, implying that she could not lie even by omission.

One would think, she thought wryly, that she'd have become adept at deceit in the last few weeks.

"A pity," he mused. "Well, I'm certain you will find the peace you seek. The grounds here are extensive and offer many crannies in which to hide from the general melee of a house party." His brow puckered as if he was coming to a decision. "In fact, I've a maze that is quite unique. It was in appalling condition and I've closed it off while the gardeners do their pruning, but they've been dismissed for the next few days. I'll make an exception and invite you to wander through it at will. The staff will be instructed to turn a blind eye to your trespass and you shall have all the privacy you wish."

"Thank you," she replied, touched that he would show such consideration to her.

"Please let me know what you think of it." With that he nodded and strode away to join another group.

Frowning, she studied his expression from across the informal garden, where footmen had set up tables for a picnic. Had she seen an odd, almost calculating gleam in his eyes as he'd spoken of hiding places? And had his voice been just a bit too casual?

She shook her head, dismissing her suspicions. She really had spent too much time in Bruce's company of late.

Apparently, that would no longer be a problem.

Apparently Bruce had lost interest in the game.

It would be for the best. Heaven knew what he would talk her into, or what she would allow herself to do, if they had another encounter. Like the affair she'd been so brazen as to suggest. Or, heaven forbid, like marriage. Her will became quite foolish when goaded by Bruce's laughing eyes and nonsensical logic.

"Melissa, darling, why on earth are you standing

behind a bush?'' Arabella swept up to her and came
to a halt on the opposite side of said bush. ''The earl
has laid out a feast not to be equaled and awaits our
pleasure. It wouldn't do to embarrass him in the
presence of such an impressive gathering.''

Melissa bit back a smile and a comment as she
recalled her earlier thoughts on the subject.

''Come along, Melissa,'' Arabella commanded.
''Robert has been patient long enough.'' Not bothering to confirm that Melissa complied, she turned
and employed her best gliding walk toward the tables groaning with food.

Sighing, Melissa banished her irreverent thoughts
and skirted the hedge to obediently trail in her
mother's wake. Bruce really had perverted the sense
of propriety her mother had worked so hard to in-
still in her.

Surely providence had saved her from further cor-
ruption.

Providence betrayed her in favor of a dashing
scoundrel smartly dressed in tan doeskins, dark blue
riding coat and high black boots lightly coated with
the dust of the road.

Melissa's fingers turned to liquid as he met her
gaze with a knowing wink and slow smile. Her fork
slipped from her grasp and clattered onto her plate
as he sauntered toward the table she shared with her
mother and the earl. The berry she'd just spooned
into her mouth stuck in her throat as he halted directly across from her and fixed a deceptively somber gaze on her mother.

Arabella set down her glass and glared at Bruce.

''Countess Seymour, how interesting to find you
here.'' Bruce reached for her hand and bent down to

brush his lips over the air above her fingers.

Arabella nodded regally in spite of her obvious wish to snatch her hand away. "No more interesting than to find you in attendance. I wasn't aware you were invited."

Melissa's lips parted in a silent gasp at her mother's rudeness.

"I wasn't," Bruce replied cheerfully as he patted the back of her hand, then released it. "An oversight, I'm sure."

"I see you could not resist the opportunity to foul an otherwise pleasant day," the earl said in lieu of greeting. "Dare I hope you have lost your way?"

Bruce arched a brow. "Dare I hope you will make a scene? Otherwise I fear your guests will think they are attending a funeral."

Calmly, the earl lifted his fork and took a bite of food, chewed and swallowed. "I see that you are determined to wreak your usual havoc. It will be my pleasure to thwart whatever roguery you have devised by welcoming you to my new home and bidding you join my guests." He selected a morsel of lamb and took his time to consume it. "I collect you require a room for the night?"

His mouth slanted in a mocking smile, Bruce slapped his riding crop against the side of his leg. "It will be my pleasure to join such august, if not scintillating, company. And yes, a room would be nice, as long as it isn't in the stables."

The earl nodded toward his house steward and waited for the man to reach them. "Graves, please see that Viscount Channing is shown to a room. The east wing should be to his liking."

"As you wish, my Lord." Graves bowed and

turned toward Bruce. "My Lord, if you will follow me?" He pivoted smartly on his heel.

"Please do follow Graves," the earl said with an edge of distaste. "And do not hesitate to request a bath. If your valet did not accompany you, ask Graves for the services of a footman to clean your boots and brush your clothing."

"That reminds me," Bruce said. "I require a large dressing room with a cot for Smithy. And you might remind your man, Tommy, that where Smithy goes, so does his collection of cudgels."

The earl gave a tight-lipped smile and returned his attention to his meal.

Twisting her hands in the napkin on her lap, Melissa glanced from one man to the other.

Bruce lingered as if Graves hadn't paused a few feet away to await his pleasure, and for the first time he turned his gaze on Melissa. "Lady Melissa, we meet again." He bowed and paused before straightening to peruse the dish of berries and cream in front of her, and by proximity, her bosom. "Now that looks delectable. May I?" Without waiting for her to answer, he deposited his gloves and crop on the edge of the table, plucked up the dish and spooned a berry into his mouth. "We share similar tastes, I see. This is my favorite, and I am quite famished." Selecting another berry, he examined it thoroughly, then lifted his gaze to hers and slowly took the fruit into his mouth, rolling it as he would a taste of fine wine.

Her lips parted as she watched him chew slowly . . . suck in his cheeks slightly as if he were drawing out the juice . . . swallow. Her toes curled as he continued to stare at her with smoldering eyes, holding her mesmerized. Heat and moisture collected between her thighs as he licked cream off the spoon and sighed in pleasure. Flushing, she broke the contact, lowering her head to blindly stare at her hands in her lap.

"Graves is a busy man," the earl said testily. "His duties do extend beyond waiting for you."

"I'll take this with me, then," Bruce replied, and holding the footed bowl in one hand, reached for his gloves and crop with the other.

A glove slid from the table onto the grass.

Bruce leaned over to retrieve it.

Frantically, Melissa groped with her foot for the shoes she'd kicked off under the table and froze as his hand brushed over her instep and around to the sensitive flesh of her arch in a deliberate caress.

She flushed hotter and stiffened to hide the shiver of pleasure radiating out from the pit of her belly. She moved her foot away and rubbed it over the grass, vainly trying to ease the tingle left by his touch.

Angling his head, he watched her with a small, bemused smile as he slowly straightened. Then, in view of her mother and the earl once more, his expression smoothed into one of bland indifference.

The change chilled her and left her bereft of sensation.

Bruce faced the earl's equally bland expression. "Your hospitality is appreciated," he said in a monotone. "I will be sure to enjoy it fully." He flicked a sweeping glance at Melissa, as if he spoke to her rather than the earl.

She felt as if he'd bared her with that fleeting look and stroked every part of her. Quickly, she reached for her glass and gulped too much wine. Her eyes watered with her effort to contain her cough. By the time she was able to focus again, all she saw was Bruce's back as he strolled among the tables, dipping occasionally into the bowl of berries he'd taken from her as he greeted one guest after another with charming smiles and witty remarks that elicited more than one sedate chuckle.

She wanted to slide down in her chair and crumple beneath the table. She trembled so much she wanted to cry. Why had he come? It was obvious he wasn't welcome, and he would have certainly known that. She'd counted on it. She should have counted on Bruce's contrary nature instead.

She'd been a fool to think he would give up so easily.

"It's too easy," Smithy grumbled for the dozenth time as he prowled about the chamber assigned to them, picking up Bruce's discarded riding clothes. "I don't like it when the earl is accommodating."

"The earl is a slave to appearances," Bruce reminded him yet again as he donned fresh clothing. "He would neither create a scene nor overtly evict me from the premises with the cream of society looking on. It would raise too many questions." He muttered under his breath and ripped out the knot in his stock and began to tie it again. "Since I am independently wealthy as well as being"—his mouth slanted in his usual mocking smile—"the darling rascal of the ton, he has nothing to excuse his aversion to 'his only son and heir' but a general disapproval of my behavior. That might justify a certain hostility between us, but it wouldn't explain more drastic actions on his part. After all," he continued without modesty, "most men would welcome a son like me who does not squander the contents of the family coffers nor sully the family name."

Smithy snorted. "Aye, and the cadavers out there wish they had half your nerve." His scowl deepened. "It all sounds right nice, but I don't believe a whit of it. The earl's a sneaky bastard. If there's a way to ruin you he'll find it."

"He knows well enough that the right misstep on his part would encourage me to publicly disgrace him," Bruce reminded Smithy, and wondered if perhaps he wasn't reminding himself as well.

"He knows that if you reveal that he was bought off to give you and Lady Kathy a name, you'll also disgrace yourself, your sister, and your mother's name."

"Ah yes, but he also knows we will not suffer as he would. Regardless of who our father was, Kathy and I are legally legitimate. With Kathy's marriage to the Duke of Westbrook, the earl would be hard-pressed to make any mud stick to her. As for Mother . . ." His voice softened, became husky. "She accepted disgrace long before her death. Now it can't touch her. The earl, on the other hand, would set himself up as an object of scorn by the very people he strives to impress."

"It's too easy," Smithy repeated under his breath.

"You become skittish in your dotage," Bruce replied absently as he stepped back from the looking glass to examine his appearance, even going so far as to turn from one side to the other to check the drape of his coat. "Perhaps I should retire you to a nice cottage in the hills."

Smithy shot him a hard glare. "And since you ain't got the sense to look after yourself, maybe I should find a nice private asylum for you," he spat. "Leastways you'd be safe there."

Bruce ignored his old friend's comment and tugged on his simple blue brocade waistcoat. "I trust I appear sedate enough to fit in with the earl's guests."

"That's another thing," Smithy said, obviously working up a good case of the sullens. "Since when do you preen in front of a looking glass like some prissy coxcomb?"

"Since you began entertaining me with your old-maidish fretting," Bruce countered as he abruptly turned from the mirror, more disturbed by the question than he could admit. He'd never lingered over dressing and rarely gave his reflection more than a cursory glance.

If he didn't have a care, Melissa would loosen more than a few of his screws.

"Is everything ready?" he asked tersely.

"The earl already closed off the maze to his guests, and gave the gardeners the day off. I saw to everything else. Fixed you up a regular love nest, for all the good it'll do you."

It had better do him some good, Bruce thought sourly. If Melissa didn't come around soon, he wouldn't be able to vouch for the sanity of his actions. More and more he acted on impulse, without thought or reason. Like that day in the park. He'd had no intention of being within spyglass distance of Melissa until he'd seen her walking through the gates. Though he'd already taken care of any spies lurking about, he wasn't at all certain he would have cared who observed their *tête-à-tête* beneath the trees. Then there was his shameless and merciless display in the gardens this afternoon. What had possessed him to eat from her dish in full view of everyone, not to mention his foray under the table just to see if she was barefoot?

And now he schemed to seduce Melissa beneath the noses of her mother and the man whose one obsession was to hate him and, if he could, destroy him.

If his own recklessness didn't destroy him first.

# Chapter 13

〜〜〜◯◯〜〜〜

**B**ruce's thoughts of destruction found a new victim as he descended the terrace steps and joined the party.

Arabella stood nearby, beautifully gowned and perfectly coifed as usual, and in her beauty looking as out of place among the staid and stalwart as Melissa did. Particularly, he noted, with a strand of wide lace hanging below the hem of her frock. If he didn't miss his guess, the lace was attached to a pair of pantalettes. And thanks to Melissa, he knew that pantalettes were nothing more than two separate casings for the legs that were secured at the waist of the wearer.

Blessing Melissa for her confidences, he ambled toward his target, a wicked plan fully formed in his mind.

It really was too bloody convenient.

The earl glanced up at him with a peeved expression. Arabella stopped in mid-sentence and favored him with a haughty stare. Melissa colored and stared at the ground.

"Do I pass muster?" Bruce asked with feigned innocence. "I took great care to dress for the occasion."

"Your consideration is heartwarming," the earl spat out.

"God forbid that I should disgrace you. Such actions have a way of returning to haunt one," Bruce said deliberately, knowing the earl would take his meaning. It never hurt to remind one's enemy of a past threat, particularly when one was suffering a belated case of suspicion, thanks to one's servant.

Without giving the earl an opportunity to reply, he carefully stepped nearer to Arabella, placing his feet just so. "Arabella, how lovely you look. Tell me, do you and Melissa always blend by design, or by accident?" He nodded toward Melissa, dressed in a pale embroidered lilac that complimented the deeper shade of her mother's gown.

Melissa frowned as she stared at the ground . . . at her mother's hem.

Bruce didn't hear Arabella's reply as he watched Melissa from the corner of his eye, waiting for her to speak up.

Melissa obliged by leaning forward to whisper in Arabella's ear.

Arabella paled, then recovered, all within the space of a second. She placed her hand on the earl's arm. "Robert, I really must freshen up. Please excuse me for a few moments." Wasting no time, she turned and headed toward the house as quickly as dignity would allow.

"Mother—"

Arabella either didn't hear or was in too much of a hurry to stop.

Lace ripped. Arabella stumbled as the leg of her indecently sheer pantalettes dragged down over her foot. Lurching forward, she caught her balance with astounding grace and abruptly halted.

Melissa's eyes widened.

Like magnets drawn to scandal, heads turned in their direction one by one.

Bruce stifled his grin as he casually stepped away, removing his foot from the lace. "What a macabre sight," he commented as he sauntered toward Arabella. "Here, let me help you, Countess." He leaned over, picked up the bit of froth and held it out to her hooked on his forefinger. "They really should sew the legs together, don't you think?" he said in a stage whisper. "You might suggest it to your modiste. Who knows, you might set a new fashion."

Arabella's chest heaved with indignation. Her nose sought rarefied air, which by attachment lifted her chin a few degrees. To her credit, rather than shrieking in outrage as he'd expected, Countess Seymour took the half undergarment, folded it over her arm and proceeded on up the steps to the house.

The effect was spoiled by the other half of her pantalettes, which dropped farther with every step until it bunched around her ankle. She paused, shook her leg, performed an odd hitch of the hips to free the thing, then continued walking without a backward look.

Bruce grinned in earnest at the bit of fluff lying stretched out over three of the stone stairs.

A woman gasped. Another averted her gaze. Several men chuckled, and one emitted a loud guffaw.

Melissa covered her mouth with her hands.

The earl glared at Bruce. "If you are determined to humiliate me, the least you could do is direct your disrespect *at me*."

"I wouldn't dream of humiliating my host," Bruce said. "On the other hand, I am—as a gentleman—

obliged to behave exactly as Arabella expects. It would be churlish to disappoint her."

"Excuse me," Melissa said in a strangled whisper.

"Pray do not leave us," Bruce said.

"I must," she replied, her voice barely audible with her face turned away from him. "I . . . I have a wretched headache," she continued in a high, squeaky rush. "I'm . . . I'm going to take a short walk and . . . and then go to my room to lie down. Please tell Mother that I will see her later . . ." Her voice trailed off as she made another choking sound and dashed toward a distant section of the gardens with unladylike haste.

Bruce heard the lie in her stammer, saw it in the way she refused to look at him or the earl. She had neither a headache nor the desire to go to her room. He'd stake the abbey on it—

"I suppose you have an equally unconscionable excuse for causing Lady Melissa distress," the earl said. "The girl can barely function in company, and you delight in tormenting her."

There were many things about Melissa Bruce delighted in, but her distress wasn't one of them. He fully intended to make amends as soon as he could escape the earl without causing suspicion. He gave the earl a hard stare. "How heartwarming that you have repented your sins to become the champion of the weak and helpless. I know Kathy will be glad to hear of it."

The earl's face turned scarlet as his gaze shifted from one group of guests to another. "I welcomed you in good faith with the hope that you would behave yourself. I see that I was wrong."

"For fear you will burst a blood vessel, I will assure you that your ugly secrets are safe with me as long as *you* behave *yourself*," Bruce said while examining his fingernails. "Otherwise . . ." Allowing his voice to trail off, Bruce shrugged and strolled away as if he'd just enjoyed a pleasant chat with his host. From the rise of chatter about him, he thought it likely that members of the ton would be occupied for at least a week with the rumor that the Earl of Blackwood had reconciled with his "son." A lie the earl would be hard-pressed to deny, given his obsession with appearances.

No doubt he would swallow bile every time he was forced to bear the consequences of his unprecedented hospitality to his estranged heir unless Bruce ended the contrived truce by his own actions. The earl was not likely to proclaim the rumors false when so many had witnessed what appeared to be a welcome earlier in the day. Add to that his "selfless heroism" in saving Kathy and Damien from certain death at the hands of a madman not so long ago, and the earl would indeed be in a quandary. Who would believe that Blackwood—fine upstanding fellow that he was—could possibly despise those known as his offspring, much less wish them harm?

How ironic that the earl would be trapped by his own deceptions.

Perhaps Smithy would rest easier once Bruce related the incident.

Bruce pursed his lips in a soundless whistle as he deliberately took a path opposite the one Melissa had taken. Another deceit—one he hated. More and more, he found it difficult not to bring his odd relationship with Melissa out into the open. He didn't give a damn about gossip, but then gossip usually worked in his favor. Melissa would not fare so well.

It never failed to amaze Bruce how Melissa's fate

had become of paramount importance to him.

Judging himself far enough from prying eyes, he skirted the gardens and doubled back, alert for sight of golden hair and embroidered lavender silk. Instead, he crossed paths with Smithy.

"She's by the rose arbor," Smithy said sourly. "What now?"

Bruce smiled as he calculated the distance between arbor and maze. Not too far. "Now I spirit her away and lavish her with attention," he replied as he veered away toward the arbor, alert for anyone who might be admiring the blossoms.

"You had to go and fall in love with a woman who doesn't want you," Smithy complained as he came abreast of Bruce.

Love. There it was again—a reminder of his own quandary. Did he love Melissa or didn't he? Shouldn't he know? He might if he'd given it more thought than the more pressing question in his mind: Did she love him or merely lust after him? Weary of pondering a subject he'd worried to death, he glanced at Smithy. "I was bound to fall in love sooner or later. It has been my observation that nearly everyone does at least once. In any case, I'm much too fond of women to escape the affliction."

"And too fond by half of your prowess in making them fond of you," Smithy retorted.

"Are you accusing me of conceit?" Bruce asked with mock affront.

"If the codpiece fits . . ."

Amused at his friend's choice of words, Bruce shrugged. "Of course, I am conceited in regard to my ability to influence and to succeed. If I were not, I would have neither the initiative nor the gall to pursue my objectives."

"Always got an answer," Smithy grumbled. "Always twisting sense around till no one knows what it is except you."

"Exactly my point," Bruce said, and strode ahead, suddenly intolerant of the conversation. He'd been quite content with both himself and his conceits until recently. Until Melissa, who seemed to see through his flummery with ease. If he was in love with Melissa, he didn't mind in the least. As he'd said—it was inevitable that he should fall in love at least once in his life, and he refused to be a fool like his half brother, Max, and fight it to the point of absurdity. It was far easier to accept such things and make the most of them. It was also more convenient to marry for love. And marry Melissa he would.

The truth be told, he was ready to engage in domestic bliss. Since Max had married and reproduced, Bruce had been envious of the happiness he witnessed between Max and Jillian. After his sister, Kathy, had married and found a contentment he'd never expected to see in her, he'd been impatient to make his own place in the world, and in the future, with a family of his own.

Since the day the earl had beaten him senseless while revealing the truth about his and Kathy's parentage he'd understood that he really had no one, for inevitably his headstrong sister would pursue her own life in one way or another, and he would have to allow it. Since his mother's death, he'd had a hollowness inside him, as if he weren't connected to anyone or anything. And since Kathy had blurted out the truth to Max of their blood ties, he'd felt even more disconnected, as if he himself was a lie. For regardless of filial bonds, he and Max could only be friends in the eyes of the world—never brothers.

A lonely business, keeping secrets.

Shaking off such maudlin thoughts, he inhaled deeply the scent of roses that reached him as he arrived at the end of what was known as the morning garden, a soothing patch of flowers in hues of blue, violet, and periwinkle laid out in the pattern of a sky with yellow blooms arranged to represent the sun. He'd studied the layout carefully from his room on the third floor, amazed by man's refusal to allow nature to maintain her own designs.

The long-deserted abbey he had purchased and was renovating had wild, overgrown gardens that appealed to him far more. He'd instructed the army of gardeners he'd employed to weed and prune and little else.

He pictured Melissa there, her hair unbound and mussed by the breeze, her cheeks rosy from the sea air . . .

First, he needed to picture her in a chapel, repeating wedding vows.

"She's got you so addled you don't even know where you're going," Smithy said.

Bruce paused and glanced around. One more step and he would have been sprawled over a low stone wall, most likely breaking a leg in the process.

An odd muffled sound came from the other side of the wall. Stifled sobs? He cocked his head, listening intently. Not quite. Curious, he swung one leg over the wall, straddling it as he peered down at the source.

All he saw was golden hair and an embroidered lilac gown, both shaking in a scattered rhythm. Melissa's back was to the wall, her knees drawn up, her face buried in her folded arms.

She quieted abruptly and stilled for a moment,

then cautiously turned her head and peeked up at him.

The half of her face that he could see was flushed. Tears ran down her cheek.

He frowned, at a loss as to what to do. He hadn't thought his prank on Arabella would so overset Melissa.

Obviously he hadn't thought at all. He knew how sensitive and compassionate she was. He'd learned in their last two meetings how protective she was of her mother. *Mother is very fragile*, she'd said. He'd mused then that Melissa seemed more like the mother and Arabella the child—

Melissa covered her mouth with her hands and lifted her head to fully meet his gaze. Apparently the sight of him inspired another paroxysm of shaking shoulders, streaming tears and choked sounds punctuated by an unladylike snort.

Dumbstruck, he stared at the fine crinkles at the corner of her eyes and the indentations in her cheeks. Dimples. She had dimples.

She was laughing. Not giggling, but laughing, and trying very hard to hide it.

His heart lurched. Something thick and heavy climbed into his throat. His mouth trembled. He felt shattered.

"Don't," he said thickly as he leaned down and grasped her hands, drawing them away from her mouth. He swallowed hard at the burst of merriment that escaped into the air, and stared, fascinated by her wide smile that framed small white teeth— one of which slightly overlapped its neighbor. "Don't hide your laughter . . . *ever*." He blinked and averted his gaze.

Discovery was a hard, swift kick in his midsection.

He loved her. With fluttering stomach and sudden impulse to spout bad melodramatic prose, he loved her.

Her laughter eased into chuckles, then into nothing. Her smile softened into one of bemusement as she stared at him.

He stared back at her as he tightened his grasp on her hand and pulled her to her feet, then skimmed the tears of mirth from her cheeks with the backs of his fingers. Her eyelashes were dark and spiked with moisture.

She hiccuped.

Bruce bent his head, touched his mouth to hers, lightly, again and again, each time for a little longer until he could no longer draw away.

She shuddered and whimpered as she parted her lips and stood on tiptoes to deepen the kiss, her hands still held firmly in one of his between them.

Releasing his hold, he wrapped his arms around her waist, pulled her close, lifted her, swung her over the wall as their tongues met and mingled over and over. He swelled and hardened against his trousers and the stone he still straddled. By degrees he drew away from her and slowly raised his leg over the low wall to stand chest to chest and hip to hip against Melissa. He couldn't stop staring at her, studying her, thinking that she should look different to him now.

But she was the same—almost ethereal in her beauty, and frightening in her vulnerability.

Reluctantly, he stepped back. "Come with me," he said softly, hoarsely, somehow knowing she would not protest.

Again, she laughed, a single and brief gust of sound in the midsummer air.

*    *    *

Smithy stood where Bruce had left him a few feet away, watching with an unfathomable expression, then silently pivoted and led the way, turning his head this way and that, alert for unwanted witnesses to Melissa's laughter and what he recognized as Bruce's heart dangling conspicuously on his sleeve.

He'd seen it before, on rare occasions, when Bruce had been six and infatuated with a kitchen maid; when he'd been twelve, feeling betrayed and lying on the ground beaten to a pulp and listening to a truth no child should hear; when he'd last visited his sister and her husband and Kathy had placed his hand on her distended belly so he could feel the kick of his unborn niece or nephew. All of them chased by a yearning Smithy thought was too powerful for Bruce to bear. And so Bruce always tucked his heart back where no one could see or mock his vulnerability.

They'd been moments all too fleeting when Bruce had faced himself and recognized his true nature. As this one would be.

But one day Bruce would no longer hide behind the lies he'd been forced to live. He would finally know who he was and where he belonged. And it was about time, Smithy mused as he approached the mammoth maze, his gaze searching the surrounding area for intruders. It was getting harder all the time for Bruce to find challenges and projects to keep from dwelling on his dreams.

It had become obvious today that Lady Melissa Seymour *was* Bruce's dream. If Bruce wanted her, then Smithy wanted him to have her. And after that scene back at the wall, and the way she'd followed him with the light of happiness in her eyes, he had a feeling that the lady wanted more from Bruce than a tumble on the mattress from time to time. That she'd follow him anywhere, any time. Except to the altar.

That was a puzzle, to be sure, but Smithy had every confidence Bruce would solve it even if he had to cheat in the process.

He glanced back at the silent couple behind him, saw Lady Melissa's grave concentration on the maze ahead, deceptively straightforward from a distance, yet so intricate inside it was a tangle of winding paths, blind corridors, and dead ends.

He judged the setting symbolic. Nothing concerning Bruce was simple and straight, and appearances aside, nothing came easily to Bruce except his charm. Since the day the old Duke of Bassett had plucked Smithy off the streets as a boy of twelve and charged him to be a companion to Bruce, Smithy had pledged his devotion to the boy who had equal parts mischief, fear and defiance in his eyes. Over the years, Bruce had shared his privileges and education with him, and in turn Smithy had taught him the arts of dodging and dealing, as well as how to fight and when. He'd left Bruce to decide for himself what was worth fighting for.

Reaching the entrance to the maze, Smithy stood aside and watched Bruce and Melissa walk inside, still silent, still holding hands.

He shook his head and settled down to watch and to wait until they found their way out again. He hoped they would, for as sure as he knew that Bruce would fight hard for Lady Melissa for as long as it took, he also knew there would be more than one obstacle blocking his friend's way to peace.

And he knew that, no matter what happened, for good or ill, he'd not complain about Lady Melissa again.

# Chapter 14

**E**cstasy, Melissa thought as she studied her surroundings. Next to having Bruce inside her, nothing compared to privacy, space, and the freedom it afforded to be as one wished to be, unconfined by rules and prying eyes.

The maze was at least eight feet high at its lowest point and riddled with false exits and small nooks in which to rest. Bruce had led her straight to a small arbor carpeted with tall grass and canopied by unpruned leafy branches that arched overhead.

Like clasped hands.

She glanced down at her fingers entwined with his, then up at Bruce, and caught her breath. She'd never seen him like this, his gaze so intent it seemed to burn through her, searching for answers ... for secrets.

She realized she was in danger. It didn't seem to matter, yet she knew it must. A clandestine encounter in her bed was one thing, but it was broad daylight and her mother as well as two dozen members of the ton were on the other side of the manor. Hadn't she escaped their sharp gazes just so she could release her laughter? Laughter at her mother's predicament—an unkind amusement that would horrify the earl and his guests, and hurt her mother if she heard of it.

She should have been equally astute as to the hazards of giving Bruce the time of day, never mind a kiss and blind obedience to his command to follow him.

Yet it had sounded more like a plea than an order. And it had echoed her own need. To be with him. To be in his arms. To learn whether he feared her understanding or welcomed it.

"I must go," she said in sudden panic. "Mother will look for me."

Bruce became familiar again as he arched his brow and slanted her a wicked smile. "By now Arabella has been informed that you have retired with a headache."

"You didn't," she said, envisioning her mother fretting all afternoon over her health while coping with being alone. Her mother did not fare well without a familiar companion nearby. Melissa had often wondered if her mother wasn't as uncomfortable in public as she was.

"I didn't have to," he replied. "You provided the excuse yourself. As for any other excuses you might think of: No one will venture in here, and Smithy is standing guard—or I should say, sitting beneath a tree outside the maze—to further protect our privacy." He left her then, separating his hand from hers to bend down and reach for something beneath the foliage. "And since the earl appears quite taken with Arabella, he will seize the opportunity to have her to himself without her daughter to stand as chaperone." He straightened and shook the folds from a large woolen blanket, then spread it on the ground. "I imagine he will convince her to let you sleep off your *headache*."

She saw his smile mock her lie, but it barely registered as she realized that perhaps her mother was equally anxious to be alone with the earl. That perhaps the constant presence of her daughter might dampen the earl's evident interest in her. That given time and some of the privacy Melissa so coveted, some feeling might flourish between them, giving her mother the opportunity to develop what could become a lifelong attachment to someone other than herself. Melissa had often hoped for a man who would spark her mother's interest and devotion. It would be a good thing for her as well, for Melissa had known for some time that she could not forever live under her mother's thumb. She could accept being a spinster if she must, but she could not continue to be a shadow against the wall for the rest of her life.

"Stay, Melissa," Bruce said softly, and held out his hand to her.

She blinked and focused on the ground, at the blanket he'd laid out with bread and cheese and wine and a small vase of pansies in the center. She didn't question how it all came to be there. Bruce had resources that seemed as infinite as his smile.

"Please."

*Please* . . . as if the decision was truly hers and he would honor it. The truth of it was in his eyes, his expression.

Wicked and unpredictable he might be, but he was definitely a man of honor.

*Please* . . . a word that gave her the power to do as she wished.

She took his hand and stepped to the edge of the

blanket, held on to him as she sat down, her legs to the side, missed his touch until he sat beside her and lifted her hem to remove her shoes, one by one, and set them aside, then smoothed her skirts over her feet.

"You do not do things like this," she blurted, unbalanced by his gestures as well as his plea.

He reclined on his side, supported by his bent elbow. "Do I not? And how would you know?"

"I cannot imagine it."

"I assure you I am a most chivalrous and considerate man."

"Only when it amuses you."

He gave an aggrieved sigh. "On the contrary. I have never courted a woman before, and I find it nerve-racking rather than amusing."

"You can't be courting me."

"Can't I? Why not?"

"Why would you do such a thing?"

"Because I told you I would at our last meeting. Because I want to." He slanted her a wry smile as he turned her own words back on her.

Yet she'd known why she'd wanted Bruce to make love to her. She had no clue as to his motives in pursuing her other than to satisfy his sense of honor. "I have absolved you of responsibility and given you leave to walk away from me. Most men would have tangled in their own feet in their haste to do so," she said, voicing her thoughts without realizing it. "Why don't you?"

"I don't want to." With a knife from the basket, he cut a piece of cheese off the wedge and offered it to her. "I would rather see your tears and your smiles and hear your laughter."

She shook her head, declining the cheese. "I weep and smile and laugh like anyone else."

"No. Others contrive their emotional outbursts in order to fit in or to gain attention or to manipulate. Yours are honest." He popped the morsel into his mouth.

"How do you know?" she asked, thinking of how her mother would laugh when she wasn't in the least amused or show outrage when she really didn't give a fig if another had been insulted or slighted.

He swallowed before answering. "You keep them to yourself, or attempt to. Why?" Reaching for the bottle of wine, he popped the cork with smooth expertise.

She shrugged as she accepted the full glass he held out to her. "Because laughter can often be cruel." She couldn't help but give him a small smile then. "And I suppose because tears *are* so frequently contrived to manipulate. Emotions are private things . . . int—" She lowered her gaze, unwilling to complete her thought.

"Intimate?"

She nodded.

"And what of your smiles? Why do you not share them?"

"I do," she said softly as her shyness regained the upper hand, "when I feel like smiling . . . when it means something."

"Then I infer you are not often happy or pleased or even amused."

"I hadn't thought about it." But she had missed it. Over the years since her come out, she'd heard enough and seen enough to conclude that while others dwelled upon the worst aspects of their existence, Bruce wrested the absurd or the practical or

the favorable from life and wrung every last bit of
pleasure from it. The lack of such a quality in herself
seemed especially acute then. And now, talking
about it, she felt an odd sense of shame that she
followed neither course, but simply kept life at arm's
length. By her own choice, she existed rather than
lived.

Except when she was with Bruce.

She dipped her head lower, still not meeting his
gaze, afraid she would see pity or disgust for her
cowardice in his eyes.

His hand came into view and framed her chin,
forcing her to look at him. "Melissa, you have
brought me to my knees." The words were said gently with an edge of confusion. But in his eyes was
the same determination, the same promise, she'd
seen every time he'd spoken of marriage.

"Don't," she said hoarsely. "Please don't say it."

"That I love you?" he asked. "It's what must be
said, isn't it, if we are to resolve the matter between
us?" He winced and sighed heavily. "I don't believe
that came out quite right."

"It came out exactly as it is: gratuitous and cold
and contrived." Setting her jaw against the quiver
building in her chin, she widened her eyes and affected the blank stare she'd perfected to hold others
at bay, to keep the space around her to herself.
"Don't bother saying it again. I won't believe you."

He stared up at the sky, unblinking, sober, silent.

She'd seen that expression before, when he was
observing and listening and sorting it all out before
letting fly with an outrageous comment or bold
opinion. She'd even imagined in those moments that
he hatched his intrigues and plots as he absorbed
every nuance of what took place around him.

It occurred to her that she had spent a great deal more time studying Bruce, learning about him, than she'd dared admit to herself.

He shifted again to lie on his back and lowered his head to her lap.

Startled, she raised her hands, then didn't know what to do with them.

Bruce resolved the problem by arranging one on his chest and the other on top of his head. "May I tell you that I like you immensely?" he asked wryly. "That I think you are the most exquisite of women? That your depth of character and intellect fascinate me beyond anything I've ever experienced? That I desire you now and am quite certain I will desire you always?"

He rolled his eyes and gave her a sheepish grin. "And that never have I felt inclined to fawn upon a woman with such declarations before?" He felt along the blanket, picked up his glass of wine from the plate they were using as a tray, and raised his head to take a large swallow. "And never have I felt so bloody awkward."

She felt flustered and weepy with pleasure. She might have taken it all as so much flattering nonsense if not for his admission, accompanied by the flush creeping up his neck. But he had meant every word, she was sure. Words she could accept—perhaps because he had meant them or perhaps because she wanted to believe them. Perhaps both. It didn't matter. They were words that she knew were true. She could not escape the reality of her beauty. She did not think herself a shallow person, and though no one else had ever bothered to see it, she knew she had a good mind. As for his desire—it was all too apparent in the way he sought her out and touched her and swelled hard against her at the first onslaught of a kiss.

She grabbed her glass and gulped the entire glassful as heat radiated from her belly and her breasts began to throb, her nipples swelling against her bodice.

Bruce noticed and brushed his hand across her breasts.

She caught her breath and had to concentrate to exhale as the empty glass slipped from her fingers onto the blanket.

Idly, he reached up and toyed with the topmost button of her high-necked bodice, slipping it free from the loop fashioned of narrow silk ribbon and then circling the hollow at the base of her throat with his forefinger.

She barely moved, afraid to disturb his concentration as he freed another button and another, his fingers playing ever so gently over each bit of flesh he exposed. Fascinated, she stared at the glass, half full of wine, he held on his midsection, the way the liquid began to slosh with his breathing. And then she became aware that her hand was sifting through his hair, stroking his head, wrapping a tendril about her finger.

Abruptly he downed the rest of his wine and flung the glass away, then turned to her, wrapped his arms around her and bore her down on her back. His body angled across hers, his hands roamed down her spine as he covered her mouth with his, his tongue thrusting inside, taking her response and demanding more.

He tasted of wine and urgency, and she drank deeply of both until she was breathless and light-headed and drunk on Bruce.

He raised his head suddenly and tugged on her chemise beneath the opened bodice, freeing one breast, then the other.

Dimly she wondered how he had managed not to tear the fabric in his urgency, and then she didn't care if he ripped every shred of her clothing away as he opened his mouth over her nipple, drawing on her and tasting her until she cried out from the sensation shooting from breast to belly and back again.

He lifted his head and framed her face with hard, tense hands, staring at her. "You can be happy, Melissa. With me. I vow it. I will not leave you to waste away. You will never be bored, nor lonely. I will toss out your shoes and fit every room with thick carpet—"

Not wanting to hear more, afraid to be tempted, she arched her back and grasped the sides of his head, guiding him back to her breasts, holding him there, urging him to taste more fully.

The breeze rustling in the hedges and trees, the chirp of birds, the dull clink of a glass rolling into the basket—all were gentle sounds around them, like the calm before the storm, countering the driving rhythm of Bruce's hand sweeping up her skirts, finding her between the separate parts of her pantalettes, stroking and stroking until she flowed around him, liquid and hot and whimpering with sudden, shattering release.

He took her lips again, hard and deep as his hand left her to jerk the buttons of his trousers free. She bent her knees on either side of him, silently pleading, for him to enter her, to become hers in a way she could believe.

He took both her hands in one of his and slid down her body, leaned away from her to lift her skirts to her waist, descended to taste another part of her.

She neither fought nor protested. She couldn't. He was consuming her. She wanted to be consumed. She wanted him to do as he would, to wring every bit of pleasure from her as she wrested every sensation, every drop of ecstasy she could, from his mouth, his hands, his body.

Ecstasy. It was close . . . so close, growing like a midsummer tempest inside her.

With a groan, Bruce left her, rose above her, plunged inside her, hard and deep and fast, over and over again.

Ecstasy. It came like thunder in her chest and lightning in her blood. She sobbed with it as it went on and on, as Bruce poured into her, as she closed around him and wrapped her legs around his waist to hold him as long as she could.

He took her mouth and thrust again, burying himself so deeply inside her she thought nothing could ever separate them.

Ecstasy surrounding her like driving rain, then slowly drifting away like clouds on a breeze as Bruce lay over her, his body spent, his arms tight around her, his cheek pressed against hers.

"Melissa," he whispered. "I do not think I can live without this . . . without you."

She turned her head and caught her lower lip between her teeth. He offered her excitement, amusement, a place to walk barefoot and unconfined. He said he could not live without her body, her passion.

And she could not live with him. Not without his love.

\*     \*     \*

He loved her. Bruce knew it with a surety he'd never had before as he stared down at her dozing beside him on her back, her breasts and thighs and belly still bared. It amazed him how shy she was, yet seemed so at ease exposed to his gaze.

His and no one else's.

It amazed him no less that he so often behaved the dolt with her, yet felt no embarrassment for his clumsy words and reckless actions.

He did, however, feel frustration and impatience with himself for his inability to convince her of his feelings, to make her believe without doubt that his heart was hers. He couldn't blame her for her skepticism. Not when he'd dispensed the words so freely to so many over the years. He'd always believed that he did the right thing, giving his lovers the words and the tenderness they lacked in their everyday lives. None of them had misunderstood him or taken his declarations as being more than they were. But then they did not understand love to be a rare and lasting thing. Neither had he until now.

He hadn't understood that love arbitrarily offered became as cheap and common as the paste beads hawked at country fairs. And now he was trapped by his own misconceptions.

What words could he speak to make Melissa trust in what he offered her? He didn't know. A sad pass for the man reputed to be awake on every suit with a glib reply for every occasion and a solution for every problem.

A man helpless to communicate his own emotions.

It might help if he understood them.

He plucked a pansy from the small crockery jar and twirled it between his fingers, then feathered the varicolored petals over Melissa's flesh. Her eyes flew open and she yawned, widely and inelegantly. She'd never seemed more beautiful to him than as she was now, disarrayed and uninhibited and giving him a sleepy smile. "Pansies suit you," he said for want of inspiration to persuade her of his love. "More than one color, all bright and vivid and appearing different depending upon how one views you."

She blushed and fluttered her hands toward her lowered bodice and raised hem.

He skimmed the flower over the inside of her thighs, pleased to see her hands still and fall limply to her sides. "I cannot seem to resist you," she said.

"Only because you don't wish to resist"—he brushed the petals higher on her thigh and over the soft flesh between—"this."

He smiled without amusement as she gasped and shifted her legs. "You have no difficulty in resisting either my heartfelt declarations or my honorable intentions." He tossed the flower away, disgusted that he had fallen to using her passion as a weapon against her rejection of him.

"I will not marry you," she said firmly.

"And I will not settle for being your lover, Melissa," he said flatly. "I have never used a woman, and I will not be used."

She sat up abruptly and pushed her skirt down, then pulled the edges of her bodice over her breasts. "I'm not—"

"Aren't you?" Rising to his knees in front of her, he pushed her hands away and delved his hands into her gown to pull up her chemise, anxious to cover her before he gave in to lust yet again. "You spread your legs and bid me enter, then state your preference for an illicit affair rather than marriage."

Scooting around, she turned her back to him and proceeded to straighten her clothing. "I see no other way." She stilled and lowered her head. "And I'm not really certain I can do even that," she admitted, her voice so low he barely heard her. "I . . . I . . . like being with you and I want you, but—"

"You're afraid," he supplied.

She nodded.

"You should be," he bit out. "Need I remind you that neither of us has any control. If you're not breeding, you soon will be at this rate. Have you no regard for the child you might have? Are you so willing to bring a bastard into the world?" The very word *bastard* tasted sour in his mouth. He inhaled sharply and glared at the entwined branches of the overgrown hedges above them in an attempt to control the sudden urge to shake her.

"I think you want me to conceive. It would trap me, wouldn't it?"

Everything seemed to stop—birdsong and breeze and his own thoughts as he struggled to find an answer. An honest answer. It was there, in his mind, and had been since the night he'd climbed the trellis and hid under her bed. Pregnancy would force her to marry him.

Wouldn't it? With any other woman it was a certainty. But the more he learned of Melissa, the less certain he was of anything but his own feelings. She was unique in a world of conformity. And though she might be shocked to hear it, she was unpredictable.

"It's true, isn't it?" she said as she turned back to him, her gown fastened and smoothed and unbearably proper once more. "You had no intention of being careful."

"And you had no thought of it." Blindly, he rose to his feet and began a slow pace around the bower to calm his mood. "No, I wasn't careful. No, I didn't want to be." He swiped his hand over the back of his neck. "I won't again tell you I love you, Melissa, but I will, once more, tell you that I want you in my life, in my home, and in my bed. I want your trust and your devotion, and your children."

He halted and placed his hands on his hips to keep from placing them on her as he spoke without thinking, surrendering to impulse rather than calculation. Heaven knew, nothing else had worked. "I want you to consider carefully the consequences of our actions and come to a decision that will leave no casualties. Particularly when the most likely candidate for injury will be an innocent child."

She stood and faced him across the width of the bower, her hands twisted in the sides of her skirts. "I will consider it," she said softly, gravely, "*if* I find that I am increasing. Until then, I ask that you leave me alone . . . for both our sakes."

His stomach knotted and a chill washed over him. Pressure built in his chest and threatened to explode. It was all he could do to keep his voice low and steady. "As you wish, Lady Melissa . . . for both our sakes."

With calm, deliberate motions that seemed performed by someone outside his body, he picked up the blanket, folded it and stuffed it inside the basket along with the wine bottle. Something began to give way inside him. Something that felt too ugly and too strong for him to manage. He couldn't allow it to have power over him. He'd never allowed it.

He stared at her, focusing on her delicate frame and fragile expression, focusing, too, on his tender feelings for her. His composure returned, holding him steady and clearing his mind. He offered his arm. "I will see you safely to the side entrance of the house. From there you can take the servants' stairs, which are one door down from your chamber."

"I can manage," she choked out. "The earl gave me leave to explore the maze. Nothing will be thought of my presence here." She laid her hand on his arm. "It is you who must take care. I would not want to be the cause of more trouble between you and your father."

His chest heaved as he stifled a raw, bitter laugh. Instead, he seized her arms and hauled Melissa against him. "Save your concern for *us*, Melissa. And think hard. Think very hard about what has been said and what has happened here today. I cannot wait forever." Releasing her, he turned on his heel and strode blindly through the maze.

# Chapter 15

~~~◯◯~~~

**M**elissa knew she ought to feel quite lost and at odds with herself after Bruce left her standing alone in the maze, but she'd had the odd impulse to smile for no reason she could think of. Her mind refused to function properly as she lingered until daylight ebbed and twilight washed the bower in luminous silver. Wandering one way and then another, she finally found her way out and dashed to her room, unseen by the guests gathered in the grand salon before dinner.

She'd performed a little dance of triumph inside her chamber and giggled aloud. It was exciting to sneak about—though, she told herself sternly, she shouldn't like to do it again.

She remained in her room, soaking in a tub of hot water laced with soothing salts, then curled up in her bed, her eyes squeezed shut, numb to everything but a breathless sense of discovery.

She fell asleep and dreamed of Bruce. Odd dreams where she searched for him, seeing his back yet never reaching him. And then he would disappear and she came to a fork in the road and had to decide which to take before her mother found her.

She awakened once in the deep hours of night, alarmed and then filled with anticipation. She listened for the swishing sound she was certain had disturbed her sleep and watched for a tall shadow striding toward her.

Nothing happened. Concluding that her mother or Nicole had cracked open her door to look in on her and then retreated, she snuggled deeper under the covers, closed her eyes and again followed Bruce to the fork in the road.

The next morning broke with all the bright colors and fertile scents of late spring. She left her bed and stood at the window, drawing back the hangings to stare at the sun-gilded maze in the near distance. From there, she could see at least a dozen places where the hedges had grown to meet in the middle, and she wondered in which nook lay a basket holding bread and cheese, a half-empty bottle of wine, and a crumpled blanket. She'd left them there with the naughty thought that if anyone at the house party found them, speculation would run rampant through the somber assemblage as to who had engaged in such a clandestine tête-à-tête. Ashamed of herself for providing grist for the gossip mill she so despised, she'd run into a corridor of the maze before she could change her mind.

Her dream had been like the maze, turning this way and that and leading her around in circles and into dead ends. But in the light of day it didn't seem odd at all. In fact, it had been a rather obvious dream full of portent.

Last night she hadn't been inclined to heavy ponderings, and had allowed her mind to wander where it would while absorbing the discoveries of the afternoon with Bruce. But, now, her thoughts offered her no quarter as they stubbornly insisted on following their own path and taking her where she had sworn not to go.

*For both our sakes . . .* Bruce's voice had almost cracked as he'd repeated her words.

Somehow she'd hurt Bruce. She'd seen it in his eyes—a quick flicker of pain and helplessness. And then his voice had filled the small sanctuary, calm as always. But it had also been stiff and cold, as if he controlled something strong and undesirable, like anger.

Bruce's voice was never cold, never stiff, and never, ever, angry. His lack of bad temper was his greatest weapon and his most useful tool. He wielded wit and nonsense rather than fury, throwing his opponents off guard, forcing them to acknowledge his charm and try to best it.

Her weapon against him had been her ability to see through that charm. She could fight it because, in some way, she understood that he used it as she used her shyness to keep others from getting too close, to keep them from smothering her.

But every reason and every argument she had against marrying him had toppled with that brief flicker of vulnerability in his eyes.

She'd seen it and stood firm against it, telling herself that it was another ploy, reminding herself that Bruce would stop at nothing to have his way, that he was not hurt, and in the end he would not care that she continued to refuse him. She'd tried to remember all that while banishing memories of the words he'd spoken and how he'd spoken them. Sincerely. Emotionally. Bleakly.

She had tried and failed.

For every wicked grin and blithe retort he gave

her, Bruce had delivered several other messages to contradict them. It was those that she heard and saw and recalled with vivid clarity. It was those that compelled her to acknowledge the reversal of her resolve.

*I will not settle for being your lover,* he'd said, and it had cut her to the quick to comprehend that she'd unwittingly taken her selfishness too far, using him, even going so far as to suggest an affair so that she would not have to give him up. She should have comprehended that men and women had as many similarities as they did differences. That men could be hurt and feel shame and have the need to be taken seriously the same as women. Perhaps more so, for in her observations of men and women, she'd noted that the pride of a woman very often bent under strain, while the pride of a man most often broke with less provocation.

The stronger the man and his pride, the more painful the break . . . if the source of the injury mattered to him.

Spots blurred her vision as she dropped the edge of the curtains over the sunlight pouring in the window. In some way and for some reason, she mattered to Bruce. Of that she was convinced. Over the past three years, she'd seen him form several liaisons, and then walk away when it was over—all with the casual equanimity that was his claim to the affection of society. Never had she known him to actively pursue a woman once her attentions turned elsewhere.

Yet he pursued her relentlessly and then confessed to her that it was a nerve-racking experience.

She couldn't imagine him going to so much trouble just to satisfy his lust. Not when virtually every

woman he met flirted outrageously with him in the
hope that she would have the opportunity to share
a bed with him. Even dowagers long in the tooth
fluttered their fans and beamed with schoolgirl
blushes when he was near.

He'd removed her shoes. A silly thing really, yet
one that suggested an intimacy growing between
them that had little to do with lust. Rather it suggested that Bruce had been interested in more than
naked flesh all along. He'd not only meant to
achieve the intimacy of understanding, but he'd put
it into practice.

He'd noticed and remembered silly, little things
about her.

Absently, she opened the armoire and rifled
through the gowns she'd brought to the house party,
bemused by her reactions to what had passed between them yesterday.

She really ought to feel distressed or weepy or resigned to a future without Bruce. She ought to at
least feel the inclination to throw something in a fit
of pique. After all, he'd admitted that he'd wanted
her to conceive a child, thinking she would most certainly agree to marriage then. In itself, it was a
thoughtless, selfish, destructive act, disregarding her
feelings and her wishes. Yet, in Bruce's admission,
she'd heard something else. Something like desperation.

No man could place so much loyalty and devotion
to his family and close friends and be without conscience in his dealings with others. Even with herself, the daughter of a woman who hated him and
made no pretense otherwise. Though he taunted and
baited her mother, he had never stooped to malice,
unless one counted the pantalette incident, and Mel-

issa thought he'd done it more to remove her mother from the scene rather than to be vicious. Even with the earl, with whom he shared no love, he had employed sarcasm and irony rather than viciousness.

Bruce was not a spoiled boy who would tear down a life in order to satisfy a whim. She could only surmise that it was far more than a whim. That on some level she had yet to understand, he cared about her.

And if that caring did not extend to love, it didn't seem so important to her now. Instead, other considerations took precedence. She was not shy with him. She had blurted the most ridiculous things to him and he had taken her seriously, never once implying that she was foolish or ignorant. He craved her body and took what she so brazenly offered, yet cared enough to touch more than her flesh. With Bruce, she felt more herself than at any other time and with any other person, including her mother. He didn't care if she hated to wear shoes. And he appeared to be fascinated by her smiles and laughter and even her tears, rather than critical of her unprecedented displays of emotion.

He wanted her trust, her devotion, and her children. He did not love her but he liked her "immensely." He was "quite certain" he would always desire her. She fascinated him. And never had he felt inclined to fawn upon a woman with such declarations before. Never had he felt so awkward.

*Never....*

She believed him because she'd seen flickers of raw emotion in his expression. Because his actions with her suggested impulse rather than calculation. Sometime during the night, she had begun to wonder if he had not described love with both his declarations and his actions.

She would never know if she turned away from him.

And God help her, she wanted very badly to know. Badly enough to pledge to him her trust, her devotion, and her children. In return, she would have the same from him.

And perhaps his love as well.

Blinking, she focused on the sun-yellow muslin frock she had unconsciously pulled from its hook. Apparently, along with all her other conclusions, she'd also decided that she would not wait for her mother to "suggest" an appropriate gown, usually one that was a pale complement to her own attire.

Nicole arrived just in time to fasten the back of her gown.

"Mademoiselle, your *maman* wishes you to wear the blue percale today."

"How could I possibly know that?" Melissa said brightly. "I awakened with the birds and was dressed and gone before you arrived." Startled by her unfamiliar attitude, she stared anxiously at Nicole.

Nicole regarded her quizzically, then gave her a sober nod. "*Oui,* mademoiselle. I am quite distressed that you did not summon me," she replied as she quickly secured the buttons and tied the sash. She turned Melissa about and studied her critically. "And since you are gone from your room, I must search for you." Her mouth twitched and her eyes sparkled as she opened the window hangings.

Melissa's anxiety was replaced by a soft, warm sensation in her stomach. A sensation she'd never felt before, more than gratitude, and more profound.

It felt like fondness. Like the assurance of not being alone. Of being accepted and perhaps cared about in return.

It felt like what she'd perceived friendship to be.

She smiled and squeezed her maid's hand, trembling at the strangeness of reaching out to another person. "Thank you, Nicole," she said, and heard the thickness in her voice.

Nicole squeezed her hand in return, leaned forward to touch her cheek to Melissa's, then stood back, the proper servant once more. "For what, mademoiselle? It is my duty to see to your—how you say it—*your good*, is it not?"

With Nicole's words, Melissa realized that reaching out was good for her.

Bruce was good for her.

Feeling suddenly light and happier than she could recall being for a very long time, she caught her hair up on the crown of her head and secured it with combs and a yellow ribbon that matched the sash beneath her breasts. "I think you will find me taking breakfast with the earl's guests," Melissa said. *With Bruce*, she amended silently. Somehow she would manage a few moments alone with him. It would take only a few moments to say yes.

"Of course, mademoiselle, you could not wait for your *maman* since you sleep through dinner last night." Nicole picked up the clothes Melissa had shed the night before and frowned at the grass stains on the back of her gown and the small spot of wine on the hem. "The earl tells your *maman* that you have retired and wish not to be disturbed," she said carefully as she met Melissa's gaze. "She worries, but he tells her he sent you tea with a powder in it and to leave you to rest." Again she studied the stains, then looked up at Melissa.

Confusion over the earl's behavior came and went quickly as panic churned in her stomach and her hands suddenly felt cold. "Please don't ask, Nicole," she said with a quiver in her voice.

"It is not my place to ask, mademoiselle," Nicole said gently. "Even so, there was a *pique-nique* in the gardens, was there not? I believe there was wine at the meal and grass in the garden." She shrugged. "There is nothing to ask." Bundling up the clothing to hide the soiled areas, she walked to the door.

Melissa's panic died as Nicole opened the door. She frowned at the sound of wood swishing over thick carpet. "Nicole," she called. "Did you look in on me late last night?"

Nicole turned. "No, mademoiselle. I was instructed to let you rest undisturbed. Someone came to your room?"

"I thought I heard something like the door brushing over the carpet just now." She shook her head. "It was probably my imagination, being in a strange bed and all."

"*Oui.* One hears many unfamiliar sounds in a house as big as this one. They bounce off walls and drift through the air."

"Echo," Melissa said.

"*Oui,* they echo. Could that be what you hear?"

Willing to be convinced an echo was exactly what she had heard, Melissa nodded and dismissed the memory.

As Nicole left the room without another word, Melissa turned to the looking glass and discovered that she was smiling. She really should be ashamed of herself for enlisting Nicole in her deceit. The whole incident smacked of Bruce's influence on her.

Pleased with her appearance in the sunshine-yellow muslin gown that grazed her shoulders and frothed with short puffy sleeves and a deep ruffle at the hem, she patted the curls that tumbled from the top of her head and almost skipped to the door.

Surreptitiously peering out into the hall and finding it empty, she slipped down the servants' stairs Bruce had told her about and arrived at the dining room without incident. If only she had known which room Bruce occupied, she thought she might have had the courage to beard him in his den.

It didn't matter. Bruce would find a way to speak to her. He always did.

She gave her cheeks a quick pinch and smoothed her skirts, then entered the dining room with all the grace and dignity her mother would expect of her, all the while searching for a man with thick auburn hair towering above the others.

"Again, I have the feeling you search for someone," the earl said as he approached her.

Curbing her impatience to find Bruce, she smiled at her host. "My mother. Have you seen her?"

"I expect her any moment," he said. "How is your headache this morning?"

"I'm quite well, thank you." Again her confusion over his unsolicited aid surfaced. He'd lied for her about the headache powder and kept her mother from checking on her. Why? But then she remembered how he had compared her to his daughter. Could it be that he regretted losing so many years with his children while he'd been in America?

"No doubt your walk helped," the earl said, cutting into her thoughts. "I'm told fresh air is therapeutic."

"Yes, I find it so." She darted a glance toward the door as someone entered, and had to concentrate to keep from sagging in disappointment. It was the studious widow.

"I do hope you didn't take up my invitation to attempt the maze."

Her mouth dried to parchment. "The maze?" she said dumbly.

"Yes, a restless gardener found evidence of intrusion there last evening."

Her heart climbed into her throat. "I . . . I strolled to the stone wall by the rose gardens."

"I'm relieved to hear it. No matter how carefully one chooses one's guests, it would appear that mischief will occur." He offered his arm, giving Melissa no choice but to place her hand there. "At least you will not be plagued by his pranks for the balance of your stay," he said with a pat to her hand.

"Why is that?" she asked as a lump of dread settled in her chest. She held her breath, afraid of what she might hear. Her gaze shot to a scattering group of men by the sideboard.

Bruce wasn't there. The dread grew heavier, threatening to smother her.

"He left sometime in the night without a word to anyone," the earl said absently as her mother entered the dining hall. "Arabella is here. Shall we allay her concerns as to your health?"

Numb, Melissa allowed him to lead her to her mother, her mind preoccupied with the only thought she could grasp.

*Bruce had left in the night. Without a word.* Her stomach twisted and seemed to turn inside out. Her hands were suddenly clammy and cold. So very cold. The room began to spin as her chest constricted and a lump grew in her throat. She whirled and ran from the room. Her hand over her mouth, she stumbled up the stairs and down the hall. Sobbing, she fumbled with the door latch of her bedchamber and lurched inside, slamming the door shut and turning the key. She fell to her knees beside the bed and groped for the chamber pot, then bent over it and heaved for what seemed to be an eternity.

Tears ran down her face as she sat back on her heels, gasping and staring blindly at the wall, her arms wrapped tightly about her middle, barely aware that someone was pounding on the door and shouting for her to let them in. Her mother. And the earl.

She didn't care. All she could think of was that Bruce was gone.

He'd told her he could not wait forever.

He hadn't even waited until morning.

# Chapter 16

～○○～

**D**awn gave way to noon as Bruce pushed his mount beyond good sense in an effort to outrun the feeling pressing him from the inside out. The same feeling that had begun to build yesterday in the maze. Frustration. Impatience.

Anger.

If he had to ride hard and fast across the length of England, he wouldn't allow it to win.

He heard Smithy shout at him, but paid no heed. He had to outrun the emotion he shunned. He couldn't let it take hold of him. Not when he knew how it could terrify and harm. How it could destroy. Since Melissa had sent him away from her in the maze, he'd struggled against it, but still it crouched inside him, howling to get out.

Over and over again, he pictured Kathy as a child, turning ghostly white whenever a voice was raised, running when the earl went into one of his fits, hiding for hours at a time—she never said where for fear the earl would find out—until he and their mother were frantic. And when that didn't work, he relived the day the earl had become so enraged he'd pummeled Bruce to the ground and sat atop him,

233

beating him and shouting until Bruce wondered which would kill him first—the earl's blows or the truth.

*You are not my son. A bastard. The Duke of Bassett's bastard. He forced me to sell my name and my life to him, then gave them to his whore—your mother. Everything about you and your sister is a lie.*

He'd even reminded himself of how Damien's temper had not only battered Bruce but almost destroyed Max's marriage, and as a result, how Max's anger had damn near finished the job.

His stomach twisted into knots at the thought of losing control, of sending children cowering into dark places, of hurting those he loved, of becoming so blind to reason that hearts were shattered and lives were destroyed.

*Never.*

He spurred Solomon to greater speed as Smithy came abreast of him, still shouting. But his chestnut was tired, and his friend easily persuaded his own mount to pull ahead, then leaned dangerously far to the side to grasp Solomon's bridle and urge him to stop.

Bruce's hands relaxed on the reins as Smithy guided Solomon to the side of the road.

"Only reason to abuse a good horse is if you're running for your life."

He was. Life as he knew it. Life as he wanted it to be. . . .

Unchanged.

But it had changed. And so had he. Melissa had seen beyond the man he'd fashioned for society and forced him to do the same. A man who felt too much and too deeply for his own good. A man he had successfully outpaced for so long, he'd begun to believe the role he played was real. A man who craved to love and be loved and had begun to believe it would never happen.

It had happened, and he was at a complete loss as to how to go on with it.

"You going to woolgather all day or you going to take care of your horse?" Smithy asked mildly.

For the first time, Bruce became aware of Solomon's heavy breathing and sweat-slicked body. "I'm going to take care of my bloody horse," he muttered, and led Solomon off the road to a stream running lazily through the trees.

Smithy followed silently and chose a place a few yards away to feed and water his own mount.

Bruce didn't blame Smithy for avoiding him. As he removed the saddle and tack and wiped Solomon down with a damp cloth, he chafed with the knowledge that he had done the unforgivable. He had lost his reason and his control and taken it out on a helpless beast. It couldn't happen again. He had to organize his thoughts and contain his frustration before he reached Westbrook Castle.

Damn providence for decreeing that Kathy would suffer difficulties in the last month of her confinement. And damn himself for hesitating to set out immediately to be with the family at such a time. He'd wanted to remain at the house party, near Melissa, rather than answer his brother-in-law's urgent summons. He'd tried to convince himself that a few days wouldn't matter. After all, Jillian and Max were at Westbrook Castle, and Kathy had Damien.

He'd been so frantic to have Melissa, to wear her down as she'd worn him down, until she consented to be his wife, that, for the first time in his life, he'd been tempted to choose another over his family.

He winced at the callousness of it. Kathy was in dire need, and in spite of the family she'd acquired in Max and Jillian, he was the brother with whom she'd spent most of her life. He was the one to whom she'd clung in her fear and on whom she depended for comfort and understanding. He was the one who knew as no one else could how much they'd endured together.

She must be mindless with fear now with the baby she carried in danger. He should be mindless with fear for her, yet instead, his fear centered on Melissa.

For every mile he'd put between himself and Melissa, a sense of foreboding had grown inside him, as if his last opportunity to persuade her to marry him was being left behind.

"It's only natural, you know," Smithy said, still standing a small distance away, scooping grain from a cloth bag and feeding his horse from his hand.

Bruce glanced up and arched his brow. "If the wisdom you are about to share is so questionable that you feel you must remain out of reach, I'm certain I don't wish to hear it."

Smithy shrugged and spoke to his horse just loud enough for Bruce to hear. "He thinks he's the only one who ever had to choose between his family and the woman he loves. And he's beating himself 'cause he made the only choice he could. Lady Melissa will still be in London after Kathy has her babe. He'd be beating himself if he stayed and something happened to Kathy. You can't win in love. Come to think of it, guess you can't lose, either."

Silently, Bruce finished cooling Solomon down and reached for his own sack of grain, pulling out a handful and holding it to the horse's muzzle.

"Unless you botch it up," Smithy continued.

"Can't figure he did, though. Watched Lady Melissa until she was safe in her room like he said to. She got out of that maze by herself and got to her room as if she was born to sneak. Suppose with a mother like hers, it's only natural." He paused to lead his horse to the stream.

Bruce watched from the corner of his eye and spilled the grain. Solomon snorted and nudged his arm.

"You'd-a thought the lady would be in a fit, being left alone like she was. But no, she had a queer little smile on her face, and her eyes were all shiny bright, like she was happy. Can't figure what would do that to her."

Spilling more grain, Bruce muttered under his breath and attached the bag to Solomon's bridle. He glanced up at the sky, then down at the ground, and finally slid a sidelong gaze to Smithy. "Please define 'queer little smile,' " he said, and cleared his throat.

"How should I know what it means? Ain't seen it since your sister decided it wouldn't hurt none to be in love with her husband." Turning, he made a show of checking his horse's shoes.

"Maybe it didn't take Lady Melissa as long as it took your sister," Smithy commented. "Maybe not. Seems to take the gentry longer than most to figure out anything that's right in front of their noses."

Bruce raked his hand through his hair. *In love?* Not likely. Not yet. At the rate he was going, it would be never. Scowling, he strode to the stream, scooped up a handful of water and splashed it over his face.

"Take him." Smithy jerked his thumb toward Bruce as he returned to conversing with his horse. "Appears he's testy because his lady ain't eating out of his hand. He ain't figured out yet that if she did, he'd be bored in an hour. He's gotten too cocky, expecting everyone to fall in with his thinking . . . forgets some folks are smart enough to cut through his bull. Ain't figured out yet that's why he wants her. Ain't figured out that if she really didn't want him to convince her to marry him, she wouldn't give him the time of day. But then I don't suppose she's figured out that she's playing a game and having fun doing it. Imagine she'd be pretty shocked if she knew. Maybe not. Closed up as she's always been, she might be feeling proud of herself and a bit cocky in her own right."

Bruce's mouth twitched at Smithy's "figuring." He'd wondered the same thing about Melissa and had discarded it as wishful thinking. Still, he might give it further thought, since he'd have precious little else to do while waiting for Kathy to give birth.

Smithy spat on the ground. "He don't realize that a lady wants to be convinced she fell in love with the right man. And Lord knows, he'd have to do more convincing than most what with all his dallying over the years."

"Enough, Smithy. I surrender." Bruce rifled through the bag tied on his saddle and found the cheesecloth-wrapped packets of ham, bread and cheese he'd "charmed" out of the earl's cook before he and Smithy had left. Tossing one to Smithy, he chuckled as his friend missed and the packet rolled to the edge of the stream.

"Seems you found your good humor again," Smithy commented as he picked up the packet and strolled over to sit on the ground beside Bruce.

"It was never lost," Bruce replied, and knew it to be a lie. He had lost it and come dangerously close to breaking a vow he'd made while still in short pants.

Smithy grunted around a bite of cheese. "Best you leave the brooding to the Graces. It don't bother them to be out of sorts. You might say it almost suits them."

Bruce smiled faintly at the term coined by Jillian for Max and Damien, both dukes, both wealthy, and both given to brooding from time to time. Bruce preferred to jest, manipulate, connive and grin his way through a dilemma.

Except it didn't appear to be working. Not on Melissa, at any rate.

"She had a queer smile, you say?" he asked idly as he shredded a crust of bread.

"Mmmph," Smithy said around a mouthful of bread and ham.

Bruce cleared his throat and visited undue attention on folding a slice of meat into a piece of bread. "You saw a similar look on Kathy's face when she'd—how did you put it?"

"When she'd decided it wouldn't hurt none to be in love with her husband. You'd-a thought she'd just discovered the moon and wasn't sure what to make of it."

"It has been my observation that some things are common to all women. Like certain reactions to certain discoveries. . . ." Losing himself to his own musings, Bruce bit into his sandwich and stared at the stream bubbling over rocks.

"Men, too," Smithy said. "Remember how His Grace looked when Lady Kathy told him she was breeding?"

"Hmm. He had a"—Bruce's mouth stretched in a sudden grin—"a queer little smile."

Lighter in heart than he'd been since Damien's messenger had tracked him down with the news that Kathy had grown alarmingly large and had to take to her bed, Bruce finished his meal and saddled Solomon, even going so far as to whisper an apology in the beast's ear. "Take heed, Solomon, for I make it a point to never have cause to apologize."

"Aye," Smithy said as he climbed into his saddle. "If he had to say he was sorry too often the words would choke him to death."

Bruce mounted and turned Solomon toward the road, determined to think of how to entertain his sister. By the time he and Smithy arrived, she would likely be kicking in her traces to be up and about, and Damien, besotted as he was with her, would likely be turning upside down to entertain her. Max, on the other hand, had become so enamored of children since his own child had arrived that he was no doubt fretting like an old woman. Jillian would be the only calm one in the bunch, and ordering them all about like the tyrant she was when given the opportunity.

It would be up to him to neutralize them all. He strongly suspected that was the primary reason Kathy had insisted Damien send for him. He didn't believe for a moment that she was languishing in her sickbed. Rather she would be there kicking and screaming at regular intervals and tempting everyone in sight to tie her down.

And once her child was safely delivered and he had performed his avuncular duties of oohing, aahing and goo-gooing, and allowed the infant to do his business on his sleeve, he would make all haste back to London. To Melissa.

He glanced at Smithy, riding beside him at a sedate trot. "You're certain you delivered the note to Melissa?"

Smithy gave a long-suffering sigh. "Like I told you before: I slipped the note under her door rather than trust it to one of the earl's servants. Then I knocked on the door so she would find it right away."

Bruce wasn't entirely happy with that, but options had been scarce given the hour and location. As soon as he arrived at Westbrook Castle, he would devise a way to get another message to Melissa if he had to enlist His Royal Highness himself to deliver it.

Then all he could do was have patience while fervently hoping that she would greet him with a queer little smile on her face. And whether he found her with a gently rounded belly or not, he had better hear her say yes within moments of his arrival on her terrace.

For both their sakes.

# Chapter 17

❝❞**F**or Melissa's sake I think it best for you to remain here until she is recovered,'' the earl said as Arabella paced Melissa's bedchamber at the earl's estate.

"Really, Robert, you know it isn't seemly for us to remain after your guests leave. Speculation will run rampant." Arabella's brow furrowed as she stared at Melissa, lying silent in the bed.

"I've already taken care of it. Baroness Shipley has agreed to remain as well to act as chaperone." His mouth twitched. "She has been at loose ends since her husband expired, and appears to be enamored of my library. I daresay she will be quite invisible while protecting yours and Melissa's good names."

"Well, I do hate to move Melissa while she is so pale and obviously ill."

Melissa listened listlessly, not caring that her mother and the earl spoke around her as if she weren't present. She was trying very hard not to be present, at least mentally. For two days she had heaved incessantly until she barely had the strength to lean over the edge of the bed to cast her accounts into the chamber pot. Now a large porcelain basin lay beside her on the bed.

Unfortunately, some degree of alertness seemed to be returning to her. She had welcomed the sluggish drift between vague awareness and complete unconsciousness that had overtaken her yesterday morning and continued to linger throughout the day and night. With every moment that passed, the conversation taking place became clearer despite her efforts to block it out. Other things surfaced in her mind as well, persisting to be heard.

As to why she had taken so ill, the earl had deduced that it had been tainted fish served at his outdoor luncheon. The physician he'd brought in from London hesitantly concurred. The truth was that no one had any idea what had stricken Melissa, when the other guests were perfectly healthy.

If she'd had the strength, Melissa might have found it ironically amusing that no one even considered she might be increasing. Not shy, dull Melissa, who, as the joke went, was never away from her mother long enough to visit the privy.

Melissa had no choice but to consider the possibility. Her monthly course had not come when it should have after Bruce's visit to her room in London four weeks before. There were other signs as well since the night she'd found him sprawled beneath her bed with a bunch of pansies in his hand.

Of course, she had been so occupied with thoughts of Bruce that she hadn't noticed the absence of the curse until Nicole had given her an odd look last night as she'd helped her change into clean night wear. The maid had chattered away, which was even more odd.

"You will rest, mademoiselle, and this will soon

pass. It is a puzzle how you get sick, no? I tell the countess you have been well and all has taken place as it should." She plumped the pillows behind Melissa, leaning close to whisper in her ear. "She did not ask about the bleeding, so I did not lie. But the lie is ready if it is needed."

Melissa hadn't grasped Nicole's meaning immediately, but as she'd lain alone in her darkened room, comprehension had taken hold of her, shaken her, and prompted another bout with her head in the basin followed by her mother's insistence that she sip a cup of tea. Mercifully, she'd drifted off again, and was spared the anguish of facing the truth.

How obtuse of her not to have known sooner that something was amiss. What with Bruce's talk of children and his admission that he'd deliberately wanted to impregnate her, the subject should have been foremost in her mind. Any woman with a hairsbreadth of sense would have been beside herself with worry from the moment the possibility had been planted.

As recent events had proven, she had no sense at all where Bruce was concerned.

Her first mistake had been in indulging herself with him. Adding insult to injury, she had become quite full of herself with every subsequent incident. Despite her knowledge of making love, she had blithely ignored the reality in favor of the fantasy. If she were half as sophisticated as her knowledge on the subject, she would have taken her own precautions, as she was certain Bruce's other paramours had.

Her second mistake had been in taking Bruce seriously. Two days ago, she had decided to officially set her cap for him, disregarding how poorly it fit.

Apparently Bruce had taken note of it. In the face of her repeated refusals to marry him, she couldn't blame him, really. Any other man would have slunk away after the first rejection, as every one of her aspiring suitors had done.

As she would slink away as soon as she could stand without reeling.

For the moment, though, she was happy to be in the earl's home rather than her own. The earl had been more than kind and sympathetic where most men would have done their best to ignore her "indisposition." He seemed to care a great deal for her mother and had done a brilliant job of keeping her mother calm with his smooth handling of every detail.

The door opened to admit Dr. Mason and her mother. Anxiety instantly grew to such proportions, Melissa feared she would faint with it. She wasn't ready to have her suspicions confirmed. Not until she had time to adjust to her predicament. And she certainly didn't want her mother to learn of her condition from a stranger.

"Well, I see that the earl's potion has helped you some," Dr. Mason said as he peered down his pretentious nose at her through his pretentious quizzing glass. "Your color has improved and your abigail tells me you managed to keep down toast and tea this morning."

"I feel much better," she replied as firmly as she could manage.

"I wouldn't go that far, young lady." Dr. Mason checked her pulse and felt her forehead. "Not until we see you eating full meals without distress." He turned to her mother. "Since the earl's treatment seems to be helping her, I suggest you proceed with it. I must, however, return to London to attend my other patients." He snapped his bag shut. "Do feel free to call upon me if your daughter should go into a decline. Otherwise, time and rest will see her right again."

Melissa closed her eyes against tears of relief as the doctor left the room followed by her mother. Like everyone else, he barely noticed her existence, and since she was breathing regularly, he doubtless considered her less important than his other aristocratic patients.

Blessing Dr. Mason for his indifference, she managed a smile for her mother as she once again entered the room, this time carrying a tray with teapot and cup.

*The earl's potion.* Vaguely she recalled the earl suggesting they try a remedy he'd found efficacious in the treatment of mal de mer; perhaps it would benefit Melissa as well. Feeling completely overset by her predicament, Melissa hoped the medicine was responsible for her lapses into unconsciousness. At some point she would have to be strong and brave. But not yet.

She'd freely and foolishly gratified her whims thus far. What was one more indulgence?

"Here, darling, drink your tea," her mother said as she perched on the edge of the mattress and held the cup to Melissa's lips. "Your skin had become dry as parchment, and your eyes are still quite dull. You must have liquid."

Obediently, Melissa sipped as her mother chatted on in a strained voice. Remorse for the concern she had caused her mother, and for the greater concerns she would cause in the future, prompted more tears.

Unable to contain them, she leaned over and buried her face in her mother's lap and wept with all the misery and heartbreak and guilt that had been collecting since she'd learned that Bruce had gone.

"There now, darling," Arabella soothed as she set the cup down on the table beside the bed and gathered Melissa in her arms. "It will be all right. I promise. You'll be as pretty as ever in no time."

The tears came faster, and the sobs grew louder at her mother's assumption that Melissa was concerned for her beauty. "H-h-hang my eyes and my comp . . . complexion," she sobbed hysterically. "Is there n-nothing else about me important enough to c-cause concern b-b-but my appearance? D-do you not see b-beyond th-that to *me*?"

"Whatever do you mean?' Arabella asked thickly as she gazed down at Melissa and smoothed her hair away from her face. "How can you think I care nothing—" She gulped and pressed Melissa's face into her shoulder as she broke into sobs of her own.

Melissa clung to her and cried harder still at the hurt she'd caused her mother with thoughtless words. "I love you, M-mother," she said, raising her head and shifting positions to hold her mother in her arms. "I'm s-sorry."

"I love you." Arabella wailed. "How could you doubt it?"

Melissa couldn't. Calm descended on her as she stroked her mother's back and murmured soft "shushes" over and over again. Her eyes grew heavy and darkness crept into her vision. Her head felt light as air. Sighing, she allowed her eyes to drift shut, knowing she would drift in nothingness for the next several hours.

For just a little while longer, she was more than willing to take the coward's way out.

The chit was living up to expectations very nicely indeed. Not only was she playing right into his hands with her secret defiances, but she had taken to his potion with all the enthusiasm of a true coward. But the drug was dangerous, and he'd only given it to her because he'd feared she would expel her child during her incessant retching. That wouldn't do at all. Melissa's brat was the tool he'd been seeking to bring about Bruce's downfall.

Robert Palmerston, Earl of Blackwood, sat at his desk staring over his steepled fingers as he contemplated his next move. It would be interesting to see how Melissa handled the problem only he seemed to know about.

Countess Seymour and her daughter were certainly stupid not to have realized what was causing Melissa's "illness." But they would know soon enough, if he had to draw pictures for them. And then he'd set the rest of his plan into motion.

As if he'd have to exert himself, he thought smugly. Between Arabella's pathetic gullibility and her daughter's fainthearted escape into the opium he measured into her tea, events were unfolding with barely a twitch on his part. The opium, though he would have to watch carefully and give her the smallest amounts possible, had been true inspiration, settling the girl's stomach but also keeping her malleable and too quiet to do anything stupid.

It really was too easy.

As easy as it had been to worm his way into Arabella's heart. The stupid woman was already half in love with him. If he wasn't careful with how much solicitude, flattery and passionate kisses he doled out to her, she would end up clinging to him as tenaciously as she clung to her beauty.

There was that. Perhaps he would take advantage of her affections before it was over. The woman was surprisingly passionate, given her vanity and shallow nature. Taking her to bed might be an appropriate way to celebrate his ultimate victory over Bruce.

He smiled as he lowered his hands to flip open the missive on his desk.

*Melissa—*

*I am called away to my sister's sickbed. Her confinement draws near and she is not well. If you knew her you would also know that it will take the combined forces of the entire family to convince her that she is not well. In any event I am forced to leave immediately before I have succeeded in securing your promise to marry me. You have told me that I should not speak to you of love. Very well. Upon my return to you, I will instead be armed with a special license and the determination to honor and cherish you so long as we both shall live. I can only hope it will not take quite that long to convince you of my feelings for you.*

*Now that I have again stated my intentions and continue to feel bloody awkward doing so, I will bid you farewell for now and caution you to consider carefully what further embarrassments I will be required to visit upon myself to obtain a simple yes from you.*

*Say the word, Melissa. It is only three letters and rolls quite nicely off the tongue.*

B

The earl chuckled and leaned back in his chair. Bruce and his trained fool, Smithy, were slipping. It had been absurdly easy to retrieve the note Smithy had slid under Melissa's door. He'd had a man watching both Melissa's and Bruce's movements all afternoon and evening. The moment he'd received the report that a messenger in Westbrook livery had arrived with an urgent message for Bruce, he'd known that Kathy's time was likely near.

He had expected Bruce would steal into Melissa's room himself for a last tumble, and had stationed two footmen nearby to prevent it, but the note under the door had been far more convenient. It had been a simple matter to use his key, crack open the door, and retrieve the note, all without disturbing Melissa. That he'd been able to thwart Bruce without a confrontation had made it all the sweeter, and again, no one could accuse him of plotting against Bruce until it was too late, and then they'd fight the devil to prove it.

The earl poured himself a second glass of port, then lit a cigar in celebration of the unexpected *pièce de résistance* of his plan, namely that Bruce was actually in love with Melissa Seymour. Better yet, the chit hadn't the sense to see the obvious. Bruce climbing trellises and cornering her in the park and even going so far as to intrude uninvited upon a party hosted by the man he ordinarily took pains to avoid had gone completely over her head.

He supposed he shouldn't be too hard on her over the last. He and Bruce had made a superb show of being estranged father and son without giving away their mutual desire to escort the other into hell. It seemed an unspoken agreement between them that the past was done and could not be changed. There was no purpose in dredging it up for the sake of revenge.

Far better and far more entertaining was implementing a plan to set the course of the future. A plan Bruce had conveniently inspired by slipping into Melissa's bedchamber at the Longfords' house party. Their shared past would merely provide the soil in which Bruce would plant his own destruction.

The earl reached for his glass of port and mockingly toasted Bruce's brother-in-law, the Duke of Westbrook. *His Grace* would be hard-pressed to blame him for Bruce's downfall when all that transpired would be a result of decisions made by Bruce and Melissa themselves.

All he had to do was provide support to two ladies in distress—as any gentleman would—and display the proper amount of dismay over his "son's" latest peccadillo. He might even extend himself to hanging about for a while in an honorable effort to make amends to the Ladies Seymour . . . just for appearances, of course.

If Arabella proved acquiescent and submissive to his demands.

If not, he would turn his attentions to the rather homely widow Shipley, who spent an inordinate amount of time studying his private collection of erotic literature and art. He might even marry her and sire a son. Once he was finished with Bruce, no decent woman in England would consent to marry the man who had taken cruel advantage of poor Melissa Seymour. Bruce would certainly inherit the Blackwood title and entailed estates, but the earl fully intended to have an heir from his own seed waiting his turn. In time, he was certain a legitimate

Palmerston would once again hold title to Black-wood.

If all went well.

The earl raised his glass again, this time in toast to himself.

All *would* go well. Every sign thus far was in his favor.

# Chapter 18

The signs were all there.

For four weeks, Melissa had not been able to stray from the porcelain basin that seemed like a new appendage to her. She would awaken only to heave, try to eat only to heave again, then Nicole would bring her a cup of tea with the earl's remedy. She would begin to drift off again, only dimly aware that Nicole or her mother was spooning porridge or broth into her mouth and urging her to swallow.

And each day, morning and evening before she had the tea, the earl would come to visit, his countenance full of sympathy. "How are you today?" he would ask, and she usually replied by bending over the basin.

"I pray this ends soon," he'd say then. "Your health will suffer irreparably if it does not, and I will not have that."

She'd try very hard to stop heaving the remains of whatever bland food she'd been brought for breakfast. For him. For the man who leaned over her in fatherly concern and reminded her of her own father, whom she missed as sorely now as she had after he'd died, leaving her to console her mother and fill the void. She'd felt helpless then, as she did now. Helpless, and so very, very frightened of the world Papa had always kept away from his shy daughter.

The earl would remain for a while, settling into a chair by the window while Nicole straightened the room, watching as Nicole added medicine to a cup of tea, conversing about everyday things as Melissa drank it and began to drift away.

She'd measured the passing of days only by the sunrises she witnessed every morning before anyone else stirred. In those moments, she was lucid after a long night's sleep. Lucid enough to feel her belly beneath the covers and to calculate the passage of time.

She had missed her monthly course for the second time.

She was certain she carried Bruce's child. The thought had drifted on the edge of her consciousness, flitting like an elusive butterfly, barely touching her in her stupor, yet always there.

Far more persistent and tormenting was the knowledge that Bruce was gone and had not returned. If he had, he would have found a way to see her. There were no trees outside her window, nor a balcony, but that would not stop Bruce. Not if he truly wanted to see her. Obviously, he didn't.

Plagued by that thought, she welcomed the tea more enthusiastically.

But a week ago she had awakened more alert than usual, the headache that had been her constant companion thudding less than usual. Each day since, she had watched the sunrise with clearer vision and more focused thoughts. The first few days had been hellish as her stomach had cramped and she'd felt as if she were jumping out of her skin. Her body had prickled and stung everywhere until she'd wanted to scream with it. Perhaps she had.

And then Nicole would prepare the tea and she would slip into a fitful sleep.

Today, she felt almost herself except for the weakness in her limbs and a hunger that seemed to gnaw through her.

Nicole entered carrying a tray. "You are awake. I bring you toast and warm milk, mademoiselle." She set the tray down on the bedside table and helped Melissa sit up against the pillows. "You feel good, no?" she asked as she examined Melissa's eyes and felt her cheek. "You are not so—how you say?—feel like the clam."

"Clammy," Melissa replied with a weak smile. "And I feel *almost* well."

"*Oui*, and in good time, I think," Nicole said as she set the footed tray over Melissa's lap. "Your *maman* begins to talk of taking you to more doctors. She is very worried." She handed Melissa a finger of toast. "Eat slowly, mademoiselle. You do not want to make your *enfant* angry again."

Melissa dropped her toast and her heart began to thud. "My what?" she said carefully.

Nicole perched on the very edge of the mattress and took Melissa's hand in both of hers. "I know and you know," she said gently. "I take care of you. Now we must know what to do." She picked up the toast and held it to Melissa's mouth. "But first you must eat or there will be more tea and I think you should not want more."

Melissa didn't know what to say first as her mind raced, circling each subject Nicole had brought up, shying away from the one that brought fresh waves of anxiety with every thought. "Why shouldn't I want more tea?" she finally asked as she dimly recalled that Nicole had mentioned the absence of Melissa's course before.

"It is not good, too much of that tea. It helps the stomach and makes you sleep without rest, and then gives you the ache in the head, no?" She handed Melissa another finger of toast. "The earl gives it to you because you are so sick but he worries when you do not get better. He tell me to give you less each time until you get no more, n'est-ce pas? But still you suffer the needles of pain and the crying for help. The earl watched you every moment for many days until you sleep quietly again." Holding the glass of warm milk to Melissa's lips, she shook her head. "He curse himself for giving you the tea. He say too much 'would make problems later.' "

Frowning, Melissa tried to work through the information, but her thoughts continued to snap back to what else Nicole had said.

Her *enfant*. Her child.

Of course, Nicole knew.

As if she had read Melissa's thoughts in her expression, Nicole nodded and squeezed her hand. "*Oui*, mademoiselle, it is so. I think you must know this."

Melissa waited for cowardice to urge a change of subject, for fear to keep her silent, for mistrust to prompt a lie. Nothing came to her but the startling realization that she wanted to confide in her maid, that she needed to talk to Nicole, that she *could* without wariness to guard her tongue. She knew she could, yet did not know why.

She didn't care why. She only knew that she didn't want to be alone anymore.

She swallowed the last bite of toast and set the tray aside on the mattress. "I've known since I first became ill." The words came easily, followed by more. "And I've already decided what I must do. It only needs courage, and I am so very afraid."

With a matter-of-fact nod, Nicole met her gaze squarely. "You will tell the papa."

Tears rose and threatened to spill. She blinked them back, refusing to shed more than she already had every dawn for the past month. "I would have if he hadn't left me," she said thickly. "He knew the possibility existed and even mentioned it several times."

Nicole's eyes sparked. "I do not like men like that."

"It was my fault, Nicole. He wanted to marry me." Melissa turned her head toward the window, unable to say more. She'd berated herself and Bruce too many times since the morning he'd left without a word. And then she'd escaped into a stupor, which left her feeling worse than before. Now all she could do was lie in the bed she'd made for herself.

Tilting her head, Nicole studied Melissa's expression, then shrugged. "We will have much time to talk of him, mademoiselle. Now we must talk of you. Do you wish to run away? I have no one in France to help you, but my Ben will know of a place."

Overwhelmed by Nicole's show of unconditional support, Melissa blinked harder. "Why?"

Again Nicole shrugged. "I think we make good friends even if you are not a servant like me. I have no one and it makes a hole"—she flattened her hand over her chest—"here. You also have a hole, no?"

"I haven't any friends," Melissa whispered as she

lowered her head, ashamed to admit she'd never tried. Once, she'd wanted to try, when she'd met Jillian Forbes, sister to the Duke of Westbrook and wife of his and Bruce's friend, the Duke of Bassett. Sensing Jillian's innate kindness, Melissa had liked her immediately. She hadn't ventured beyond the wishing stage, using her mother's dislike and disapproval of Jillian as an excuse. More than once Jillian had gotten the best of Countess Seymour, and Melissa had both admired her and been intimidated by Jillian's quick wit and outgoing manner. She'd shied away from seeking friendship, certain she would not be equal to one as bright and lively as Jillian.

"We are both in need," Nicole said softly, tentatively. "I wish to help you, mademoiselle."

Just as tentatively, Melissa reached out and placed her hands over those of her maid. "You already have."

Nodding briskly, Nicole inhaled deeply and swallowed. "Tell me what you wish to do."

Melissa wished to run and hide, but she'd done that by drinking the earl's tea, by waiting for it and craving the escape it brought. Yet, even in that darkness she'd discovered that she could not escape herself. She raised her head and set her chin, determined that her cowardice would not be openly displayed in her actions. "I've thought of many things I could do and I've tried to avoid thinking at all," she said, her decision forming with every word. "I've made enough mistakes already, Nicole. Now I can only do what is right. First, I must speak with my mother. Secondly, I must find a place to go . . . where I can . . ." She clenched her hands together at the sudden realization that for once in her life, she was like others in the ton, scheming to deceive. Every year, at least one young lady would go to the Continent or far into the country and then reappear a year or so later with a child and either an indifferent husband or a sad story of how she'd been widowed. Some returned without a child, and Melissa had tried not to wonder about where or *if* a child existed. How ironic that she had at last truly "come out" of her shell in such a scandalous way.

She sighed and forced her hands to open and lie limply in her lap. "Thirdly, I will contact B—the father, to notify him of my circumstance. It is his right to know." She choked out the last as she remembered how definite Bruce had been about being a husband and a father, of living with his wife and child. How intensely he'd expressed those convictions.

Nicole snorted and sprang to her feet. "You English. So proud. So . . ." She muttered under her breath in French as if groping for a word. "So noble. So foolish."

How could she have ever thought Nicole timid? Melissa wondered as she watched the maid pace about the room, the movement of her hands punctuating every word.

"And for why are you so noble? You think your *maman* will thank you? *Non*, she will not. And you think the father will be happy to be found by the woman he left? *Non*. He is a coward to go when he knew this could happen." Her voice lowered and softened as she gave Melissa an apologetic look. "Please forgive. You love your *maman*, and you love this man, I think." Her arms waved again. "But you must think of yourself now, not others. You must be practical."

"I am being practical, Nicole. I must go somewhere and Mother will help."

"Only to save her own face," Nicole muttered.

"Does it matter why?" Melissa asked, knowing it did matter. Knowing that it would hurt her badly to learn that Nicole was right. It already hurt to suspect it.

"She will be very angry with you."

"Yes, she will be angry. And for the first time many years, I can do nothing to prevent it." That, too, hurt. Yet Melissa felt a certain sense of freedom in the realization. She was helpless to make the situation easier for her mother. For the first time in her life she had to be responsible only for herself and *her* child. For the first time in memory, Melissa felt almost normal.

Nicole smiled sadly. "Then I must help you prepare for your *maman,* and then after we have gone to the dirt—" She broke off her sentence and frowned.

"You mean 'gone to ground'?"

"*Oui*, I mean that. After that you will tell me where to look for this man you love."

Nicole made it sound so simple and straightforward that Melissa felt no need to deny the maid's assumption. Instead, she wanted to wrap her arms around her and hug her and cling to her strength and practicality.

But she'd made her own decisions today, without retreat into medicinal tea, without dependence upon someone else to tell her what to do and how. Oddly, it felt very good, cleansing almost. She would not have chosen to break away from her mother in such a way, nor would she have chosen to hurt her mother at all. Yet, hadn't she already made the de-

cision to break away by agreeing to marry Bruce?
She'd known then it would hurt her mother, and
had even accepted that she would very likely have
to elope to accomplish it.

But then, she would have had Bruce to help her.
He would have had a plan. With Bruce, she felt
brave.

Yet even alone and faced with the inevitability of
doing what she must, Melissa was anxious to see it
over and done. To get on with a life that suddenly
had become her own.

She eased her legs over the side of the bed and
took a deep breath, determined that the only
strength she would use today was her own.

Silence, deep and foreboding.

Melissa would not allow herself to back down, but
remained standing, facing her mother, sitting on the
settee beside the earl, staring at her in the wake of
her bald statement that she was pregnant. She had
asked the earl to be present, warning him that he
might not choose to remain, yet feeling he had a
right to know in view of his care of her.

Her mother had grasped the earl's arm so tightly
that the fabric of his sleeve bunched beneath her fingers. He had blinked, then studied Melissa thoughtfully, as if caught off guard by her boldness. In truth,
he did not appear in the least surprised by her confession.

The silence stretched tight like a chain about to
snap.

"How?" Arabella said in a strangled voice.

"In the usual way, Mother," Melissa said, surprised by her glib reply. But she'd been prepared to

answer "Who" rather than "How," and the words had just popped out.

The earl's mouth twitched.

Arabella's eyes narrowed as she took a deep breath. "This is not amusing, Melissa."

"No, it isn't, Mother. I'm quite terrified by the prospect."

Color bled from Arabella's face. "It's true then. Who raped you? When?"

"I wasn't raped . . . and I'm two months gone or close enough."

Her fingers tightening on the earl's sleeve, Arabella glanced away from Melissa as her features became hard and vicious as if she were facing an enemy. "I see. Then you played the slut. Did you spread your legs in the hay for a stable boy? Or did you raise your skirts and allow a footman to take you against a wall in the pantry?" she asked, taking the offensive as she always did when she felt threatened.

The insult chilled Melissa to her core, a relentless cold that stiffened her backbone and steadied her legs and gave her an odd sense of strength and calm detachment that seemed to remove her from the scene. Her mother was speaking of someone else, of something that was ugly and base. The moments Melissa had with Bruce had been rich and fulfilling and in no way sordid. She knew she should apologize to her mother for her actions, yet she could not demean the happiest moments of her life with any expressions of contrition. "No one in your employ, Mother. And it doesn't matter for whom I played the slut. Do not ask me to reveal his name."

The earl's brows arched.

"Melissa! How dare you speak to me so?"

"I've already dared a great deal more than that," Melissa said, feeling a stranger to herself. A stranger who was calm and certain and not in the least anxious. "I've dared to fall in love and to be happy about it. I never thought it to happen, you see. How could it?"

"Apparently you found a way," Arabella said, her color changing from pale shock to crimson outrage.

"Yes, I did."

"How? How did you manage it?"

That simple question answered many others for Melissa, confirming what she'd suspected and feared since the day they'd sealed her father in his crypt. Her mother would never have let her go. She would quite literally have to tear her life from her mother's grasp. "Quite easily," she said softly, firmly. "I chose to express my feelings when the opportunity presented itself."

"Feelings," Arabella spat out.

"Yes, feelings. The same feelings you had for Father. I wanted what you had, though I realize you did not want that for me. You didn't, did you?"

"Of course I didn't," Arabella said harshly. "You need protection from your own stupidity. Look at what your *feelings* have got you—a child by a man who I must assume has deserted you. Look what it got me—" She broke off on a choked sound.

Melissa almost faltered at that sound, recognizing it as pain and a grief that had not faded with the passage of time. But the earl shifted slightly, settling back as if he were quite content to listen without comment, and he removed Arabella's hand from his sleeve to hold it between his. He gave Melissa a discreet smile of encouragement.

Her father had done that—saying nothing and allowing her to work through her own thoughts and reach her own conclusions. And though she had rarely voiced her thoughts, it had been enough that she'd been encouraged to have any at all.

"It got you ten years of love and happiness, Mother. You have good memories that most women are denied by their adherence to traditions based upon greed and convenience. I think it is very sad that you dwell only on your loss and that you need a stupid girl such as myself to stand between you and loneliness."

The earl's brow arched again.

"As you will do now with your child," Arabella retorted on a shaky breath.

"No, I will not. I am neither stupid nor weak, as you wanted me and the rest of the world to believe. I am quite capable of making a decision and living with the consequences. In other words, Mother, I am no longer a child." Melissa paused, stunned by her declarations, and stunned, too, by her lack of anxiety and remorse. It occurred to her then that it was inevitable that she say what she had always feared to say—or even to think. She could not hang on to her mother's skirts forever. No matter how shy she was in public, no matter how hard she tried to hide from the world in her well-furnished chamber, the world had been bound to intrude sooner or later. That it had done so in the person of the man she loved had been a fortunate turn of events.

Perhaps it had been fate.

"Have you any notion of what you wish to do now?" the earl asked, speaking for the first time since he had escorted her mother into the salon.

"I think it best that I retire to the country."

"And return with a brat," Arabella said flatly.

"What will you tell our friends? That you were married and widowed? How many do you think will believe that old story?"

"I have little interest in what anyone believes or disbelieves, Mother. You know I dislike the crowds and frenzy of the ton." Having said that much, Melissa allowed the words to topple out. Words that had been gathering inside her for too many years until she could no longer contain them. "I have always wanted a quieter life, like the one we had when Father was alive. And I want my own life. I have just begun to discover that a person exists beneath all this froth." She brushed the skirt of her pink gown—a gown she'd deliberately chosen for the fripperies her mother dressed her in. "I would very much like to learn more about being a person rather than your doll. And," she added softly, sadly, "I would very much like for you to live for yourself rather than through me. As for my child, I will not adopt him to a prosperous farmer or hire someone to keep him out of the way."

"It might be best," the earl said thoughtfully, "since he won't have a father and he will be treated as an outcast by society."

The earl's comments increased the chill Melissa felt. Resignation added to her strength. She felt it like a cold empty place inside herself. A place she had to cross alone. She had no hope that her mother would understand or forgive her. She had no hope that in the earl she might have an ally.

Fear began to crowd out false courage. Meekness, she knew, might encourage her mother to take her in hand, to make arrangements and tell her what to do and how. But that was the old way. The wrong way. The safe way.

She'd turned her back on those ways the night she'd listened to her own wants and needs rather than the rules her mother imposed upon her, and she had found satisfaction even in her mistakes.

She pressed her hands to her waist, as if that might hold back the urge to plead and cower. "No," she said both to herself and to the earl and her mother. "The father of my child has asked me to marry him more than once. I plan to contact him and agree if he has not changed his mind."

"A marriage of greed and convenience," Arabella said, throwing her own words back at her.

"No, Mother. I will not tell him of the child until I know if he has changed his mind. If he has, I will not tell him at all. If he has not, I will tell him about the child and gladly marry him . . . for love and no other reason."

"I suppose you think that if he wants to marry you without knowing of the child then he must be doing so out of love." Arabella sneered, her features as cold as Melissa felt. "How childishly melodramatic you are, Melissa. It is far more likely he wants you for a showpiece and an heir. Every unmarried man in the ton has approached me for your hand. They wanted your beauty and your dowry and found your biddable nature an added advantage. No doubt this man is the same."

"The same beauty and biddable nature that you have found so appealing, Mother." Unable to control her flinch at the cruelty of the truth, Melissa lowered her arms to her sides, not caring that her mother instinctively scowled in disapproval of her posture. "But my lot will be improved just the same. I will be the one setting the rules in my household. I will decide where to go and how to dress and even how to stand properly—"

"I've heard quite enough. You will do me the courtesy of listening to me without comment." Arabella rose stiffly and regarded Melissa with all the hauteur and silent criticism she bestowed on others who did not meet with her approval. "Though at this moment, I am tempted to wash my hands of you, I will not be accused of abandoning my daughter. I insist that you reveal the name of this man."

"No." The cold became worse, hurting Melissa, turning her brittle and fragile, threatening to crack and shatter her if she didn't soon escape.

"At least tell me if he is of good family. Is he titled? Does he have money of his own?"

"His lineage is impeccable, Mother, and his wealth impressive," Melissa said. "Though you may not like him, he will not disgrace you."

"Very well," Arabella said. "I will do as your father would have wished and give you your dowry to do with as you please. If you marry this man, I will expect the courtesy of an invitation to the wedding. Beyond that I will leave you to dress yourself and stand as you please." She turned and walked toward the door.

Melissa's heart sank as she realized, too late, that her defiance had trapped her. If she ran after her mother now, she would surely fall apart and plead for understanding and forgiveness. If she did that, she would be placing herself back in her mother's hands, a coward once more, too defeated to do anything but what she was told.

Too late, she realized that courage was like an unbroken horse that must be trained not to run away with its master. She had gone too far, speaking her mind without care for the heart of her mother. She had struck out blindly, not considering the damage that might result. She had found courage in herself and wielded it without mercy. She had wanted independence and had taken it without a care as to what it might cost others.

She wanted to make it right, yet didn't know how.

She opened her mouth but no sound escaped. She inhaled and tried again. "Mother . . ." No words came. What could she say in the wake of all that she had already said?

Arabella stilled and turned enough to glance at her.

Melissa licked her lips but they remained dry. Her tongue felt thick and her eyes burned. She swallowed. "Mother . . . I love you."

Arabella turned away, her back straight, her head high.

The earl slipped out of the room with an encouraging nod.

Sighing, Arabella remained where she stood. "I have always loved you, Melissa. If I had known you thought me a monster, I might have found a way to change your opinion."

Melissa shook her head and ran to her mother, stopping just behind her. "You're not a monster. We . . . we just don't care about the same things. I do need you. I need you to advise me rather than tell me what to do. I need you to understand rather than condemn when I am wrong." Helplessly, she reached out and touched her mother's shoulder. "I need you to allow me to be an adult rather than keep me a child. I need you to share my life rather than overwhelm it with yours."

Arabella's shoulders heaved and she seemed to

sag. "I was so afraid of losing you that I drove you to this, didn't I?"

Melissa grasped her arms and urged her mother to turn and face her, feeling once again as if she were the adult and her mother the child. "I fell in love, Mother. I made love. I knew I could become pregnant. I didn't care. You had nothing to do with it."

Arabella swiped at her eyes with the back of her hand and sniffed. "We've made a mess of it, Melissa. I'm quite lost as to what to do to clean it up."

Something warm grew inside Melissa at her mother's words. She framed Arabella's face with her hands. "I want to clean it up myself, Mother. I would, however, like your company along the way. We know we love one another. Perhaps it is time to learn to like one another."

Arabella rested her forehead against Melissa's. "Perhaps it is." She gave an awkward little laugh that mingled with a sob. "It would appear you know a great deal more about me than I know about you."

The door opened and the earl stepped in, followed by a footman carrying a tray. "If we may interrupt for a moment, ladies, I thought we could use some tea and cakes." He directed the footman to set the tray on the table in front of the settee, then waved him out.

"Now, Arabella, Melissa, I see that you have reached some accord. Shall we all sit down while Arabella serves?" The earl led Arabella back to the settee, then nodded at Melissa. "Please do sit down, my dear."

Melissa stood rooted by the smile he gave her, so gentle and full of concern. She met his gaze and saw nothing of disapproval or condemnation. She sat on the edge of the nearest chair.

The earl strolled to a point between Arabella and Melissa, his gaze sliding from one to the other. "Though this matter really shouldn't concern me, your request that I remain during your conversation implies a certain need for my counsel." Without waiting for confirmation, he continued. "I am not unfamiliar with family spats and how easily they are forgotten and forgiven, so do not misapprehend that I am shocked by what has taken place here. I am instead deeply concerned by the situation."

Arabella visibly relaxed as she poured tea, apparently comforted by the civilized ritual.

The earl accepted a cup of tea and handed it over to Melissa, then took another from Arabella's hand for himself. As if he were about to discuss the repairs on a roof or tenant's cottage, he sipped leisurely until Arabella finished preparing her own cup.

"Cake, Melissa?" he asked. As she shook her head, he rocked back on his heels. "Now, if you ladies will indulge me, I will offer a solution that I strongly suggest you both accept."

# Chapter 19

```
       ∽◝◟◜◞◝◟∽
```

**B**ruce sprawled in a chair in the sitting room
that was part of Kathy's and Damien's apart-
ments at Westbrook Castle, and stared out at the
gardens below the window. Naturally, the garden
had to sport a bed of pansies. Why he'd turned his
chair to face the windows he didn't know. But then
the alternatives were either to swelter in front of the
fireplace stoked up to keep heated water at hand or
to stare at the door behind which his sister was la-
boring to deliver her first child.

It was about bloody time.

He'd been playing the charming and droll elder
brother for his sister's entertainment for six bloody
weeks now. Six bloody weeks away from Melissa,
wondering what she was doing, and how she fared,
and what thoughts were going through her beautiful
head at his silence. He'd tried to think of a way to
get a message to her and failed. Smithy had even
consented to ride hell-bent for London to try to deliver a message himself.

Smithy had grumbled and groused about having
to leave Kathy, saying he didn't know who looked
the most pathetic—Kathy, sinking to the depths over

271

her enforced confinement to bed, or Bruce, languishing—languishing of all things—over a woman.

Bruce had taken great exception to that. Frail females given to swooning languished. Missish fops given to poetic fawning languished. Belonging to neither species, *he* did not languish. He merely turned his intellect and creativity to scheming and plotting, a dignified enough occupation for a man worthy of the name.

Smithy had snorted at that and packed a few bits of clothing for his journey and cautioned that if Lady Kathy's bun popped from the oven while he was gone, he would take appropriate revenge.

Bruce had known how badly Smithy wanted to be present. He'd attended every important day in Bruce's and Kathy's lives since the old Duke of Bassett had fetched him to Blackwood Manor as a boy, and he wasn't about to break tradition. Besides, it tickled his fancy that Kathy and Damien both insisted he would be an honorary uncle to their child. Imagine that—Smithy being called "Uncle" by a future duke.

But Kathy's condition had alarmed Bruce enough that he knew he had to remain and do his part to keep his stubborn sister in bed. He'd never seen a pregnant belly as large as Kathy's. And not only her belly but her ankles and feet and hands were swollen to the point of bursting. Every time she'd tried to stand, her face contorted with pain in her back, her belly and her legs. Though Bruce would swear she carried a child large enough to heft a tankard of ale moments after being born, the midwife insisted that Kathy remain in bed and delay the birth as long as possible.

Smithy had actually paled at first sight of her, and

spent a great deal of time investigating the midwife and calculating distance to the nearest physician. He'd even thought that Kathy's outrage that the physician had wanted to use leeches to take down the swelling had been unreasonable. Smithy, who despised physicians.

Yet, knowing how much Smithy wanted to remain near Kathy—behaving as if he could hold disaster at bay with his large cudgel—Bruce had bedeviled him into going anyway. He could admit to himself that if he didn't have word of Melissa soon, he would likely fall headlong into a decline.

Love, he'd discovered in the past month, was not only a bloody bother but it robbed a man of his dignity as well.

But that would end as soon as Kathy gave birth and they could be on their way back to London. Back to Melissa.

"I've never seen you brood before," a feminine voice said from behind him.

He rolled his eyes. It would be Jillian, come to torment him. Jillian, with whom he'd shared an affinity since their first meeting.

"I never brood," he said without turning around. "How is Kathy?"

"Kathy is holding up very well. She sent me to look after you."

Hearing the swish of skirts, he raised his cup of coffee and took a bracing sip. "I am merely restless, Jillian. Nothing more."

"Restless?" Max's voice boomed from the door. "The man who would wait a year or more to wear someone down to your way of thinking? I'd say it was damned remarkable and even more unlikely."

"Business," Jillian scoffed. "It's a game to Bruce

which has no value to him beyond momentary amusement. I'd say that he is stomping in his traces to return to whatever we tore him away from. Who is she, Bruce?"

Resigned to Jillian's acuity in sensing his thoughts, Bruce set his cup down and leaned his head against the back of the chair. "Be a good girl and go help my sister."

"Your sister has insisted that her husband help her. He put the babe in her belly and she feels it's only fair that he help get it out. I have been banished in his place."

Bruce's mouth slanted in a wry smile at his sister's defiance of convention. "Then pace or drink yourself senseless in Damien's place."

Max chuckled and dragged one chair, then another, into a semicircle near Bruce.

"I wish I could, but he will no doubt swoon within minutes and I must be prepared to drag him out of the way." Her skirts swished again, then appeared as she stood in front of the chair next to his. She widened her stance and backed down into the seat, then shifted several times until she found a comfortable position and placed her hands on her growing belly.

Fortunately, Jillian's belly seemed of normal size for a woman six months gone.

"I'll wager Damien prefers being with Kathy to wearing a path in the carpet," Max said, and took his own seat facing Bruce. "What do you think, Bruce?"

Bruce immediately thought of Melissa and how beautiful she would be carrying his child, how beautiful she might already be carrying his child, and how intriguing an experience it would be to aid in the birth of that child. "I think it's bloody demeaning and frustrating to be treated like studs who have done our jobs and are sent out to pasture while the females congregate to deride us for our indifference and lack of understanding." Bruce winced at his outburst and sank deeper into his sprawl, refusing to confirm his suspicion that his half brother and sister-in-law were exchanging meaningful glances in the heavy silence.

If he didn't get away from here soon, he would surely go stark, staring mad. Everywhere he looked a woman heavy with child fixed him with a puzzled or inquiring stare. And all he had done every time his gaze fell upon said women was slip into one fantasy or another of Melissa growing round with his child, of a minute hand or foot pressing upward until it could be felt through her flesh, of Melissa smiling up at him as he caressed that tiny hand or foot. . . .

"I think I will drink myself senseless, then," he said, and cursed as he remembered that the liquor in the room had been depleted the night before as they had all congregated there to entertain Kathy.

"He is definitely brooding," Jillian stated.

"Hm," Max murmured. "And I am less interested in the lady's identity than in what she has done to him."

"I do hope she has made him fall in love," Jillian said around a sigh.

Bruce closed his eyes, choosing to ignore their speculations rather than confirm them. If he were so foolish, Jillian and Kathy would be hatching plots as well as babies. And the last time Jillian had hatched a plot, she'd dragged him into it by appealing to his sense of loyalty to the half brother who was also his friend. At the time it had seemed quite sane to help her trap Max into marriage. Bruce had already realized that Max was head over heels for Jillian, and Max certainly hadn't known what was good for him. What could possibly be wrong with helping Jillian make Max see the light?

He hadn't counted on Damien's working it out, nor Jillian's admitting to it. He hadn't counted on Damien trying to take it out of his hide nor Max wanting to finish the job.

Still, Jillian's plan had worked in the end, and *he* hadn't come up with a bloody idea in weeks.

He opened his eyes to slits as the thought expanded. He'd been putting off a request to Max that he exert his influence to secure a special license from the Archbishop of Canterbury. He might have to marry Melissa in secret, but he was determined it would be in a proper chapel, preferably at Westbrook Castle or Bassett House, since the abbey he'd purchased was still in havoc. What God joined together, let no man—or outraged mama—put asunder and all that. He'd discovered in himself a wide streak of propriety when it came to such things.

In any case, the silence in the room spoke of looks and signals being exchanged between Max and Jillian, a circumstance that promised he would be under siege until he explained his queer behavior over the past six weeks.

Sighing in resignation, he surrendered to the inevitable. "She has," he said blandly.

"She has what?" Max asked.

"Oh!" Jillian gasped. "Max, it *is* a woman and she *has* made Bruce fall in love with her."

"She's done nothing of the sort," Bruce said. "I

fell in love with her quite on my own."

A wail of pain came from the next room, followed by a most unladylike grunt.

"Push, damnit!" Damien shouted, his voice not the least muffled by the closed door.

"Blast it, Damien, it's your child, too. *You* push." Kathy's retort ended in another wail.

Bruce winced and then grinned. "And this is what I have to look forward to."

He opened his eyes in time to see expressions of shock on Max's and Jillian's faces.

"Don't tell me she's increasing," Max said in disbelief.

"Of course not," Jillian said. "Bruce would never do such a thing. He's speaking of marriage."

They turned questioning stares on him.

"Well?" Max said with cocked brow. "Is she?"

"Aren't you?" Jillian asked at the same time.

Bruce had a sudden urge to squirm in his seat. Was Melissa pregnant? He hoped she was. He feared she was.

God, he was becoming cork-brained.

He flinched as another, more prolonged grunt issued from the next room.

"Oh, Bruce," Jillian said. "You didn't."

Heat climbed up the back of his neck as he avoided Jillian's gaze. How could he admit that he had broken his cardinal rule to never sire a child out of wedlock? He fixed his gaze on the door, behind which Damien was cursing and his aunt, Lady Louise Forbes, was giving orders and the midwife was shouting for quiet.

"I need you to get me a special license, Max," he said tersely as images of Melissa bearing his child haunted his thoughts. She was so delicate. Would she scream? Or would she stoically try not to bother anyone with her pain? "The sooner, the better," he added as he lunged from his chair and began to pace.

Jillian and Max rose in unison to approach him. Jillian took his hand and kissed it. "You do love her, don't you, Bruce?"

"I take it you're in a rush." Max clapped a hand on his shoulder.

"Yes," Bruce said simply in answer to both their questions.

"Damien, when I told you to push I did not mean for you to actually knead it from my . . . oh . . . oh . . ." Kathy's voice rose to a shriek.

The wail of an infant followed. Then sobs and another shriek.

"Damnit! What in bloody hell?" Damien shouted. "Kathy, you can't—"

Bruce headed for the door. Max pulled him back. Jillian stilled, her eyes wide and afraid.

"Watch me," Kathy gritted, then grunted loudly.

A second wail joined the first.

"Are there any bloody more?" Damien asked.

"I've had quite enough, thank you," Kathy snapped, then broke into sobs.

Bruce stood with Max's hand gripping his shoulder and Jillian holding on to his hand for dear life while tears spilled from her eyes onto her distended belly.

"Oh my," she whispered. "Oh my."

"Kathy, I'll buy you a dozen houses for this day's work," Damien shouted happily.

The door burst open and Damien crossed the threshold, an infant in each arm. "Twins! One of each!" He grinned foolishly and tried to wipe his eyes with his shoulder.

Bruce broke free in time to steady Damien's hold on a wrinkled mite with hair as black as his sire's. He took the baby from Damien and glanced at the other as Damien passed it to Jillian—an equally wrinkled mite with flaming red hair.

Forgetting everything else, Bruce carried his charge to the window, turning his back on the room and its gibberish-spouting occupants. A tiny hand latched onto his finger and tried in vain to shove it into its mouth.

For the life of him, he couldn't see a dratted thing through his own tears. As he cradled his nephew to his chest, he imagined a child with golden curls and innocent blue eyes.

A sense of urgency jumped in his chest as thoughts he'd tried to suppress came to life. He'd been gone too long. Smithy might be unable to get another message to Melissa. He had to get to her himself. Quickly.

"Kathy?" he asked.

"She's weary but fine," Damien replied.

"She would also like to hold her children," Kathy called from her bed.

Bruce plopped a kiss on the baby's head and turned to hand him over to Max. "I hate to put a damper on the festivities but I must go."

"You can't," Kathy shouted. "Go where?"

Striding into the bedchamber, Bruce smoothed hair from his sister's brow and kissed her on the nose. "To marry Melissa Seymour," he said as he straightened and crossed the room.

Kathy's mouth fell open.

"What about Melissa Seymour?" Damien asked.

"I'll have the license delivered to your house in London," Max called.

"Melissa Seymour? Oh my," Jillian whispered as Bruce passed her and left the sitting room.

In the hall, Smithy pushed away from the wall and fell in step beside Bruce.

"Twins," Bruce said. "Were you successful?"

"I heard. The whole countryside heard." Smithy reached the door to Bruce's rooms and pushed it open. "And no, I wasn't successful."

Bruce had been afraid of that. It wasn't as if Smithy could climb the trellis into Melissa's room. If caught, he'd be locked in the deepest pit of Old Bailey and forgotten, or worse. "Did you try wrapping the message around a rock?" he asked, thinking that an equally absurd way to deliver a note, yet the only thing he'd been able to come up with.

"Tried and missed," Smithy muttered, avoiding his gaze. "Then the constable walked by within spittin' distance—" He broke off and shoved his hands deep into his pockets as they entered Bruce's room. "We need another plan—"

Bruce strode into the dressing room to collect his riding clothes, tossing off his coat and waistcoat and flipping open the fastenings on his trousers as he went. "We're off to London. Have Cook pack enough food for the journey. We ride straight through. Max is getting the license from the archbishop."

"She ain't said yes yet," Smithy said. "You might have to carry her off like His Grace did with your sister." He mumbled something under his breath that Bruce couldn't hear.

Grinning, Bruce shrugged out of his coat and

reached for his riding clothes. "Whatever is required, Smithy. Whatever is required."

Smithy lowered his head and muttered again.

Though he still couldn't distinguish the words, Bruce caught the tone and finally registered Smithy's discomfort.

Something was wrong.

Feeling as if doom had just perched on his shoulder, Bruce stilled with his doeskins partially unfastened and his shirt tucked in on one side and hanging loose on the other. "You did at least catch sight of Melissa," he said, not daring to voice it as a question.

"No." Smithy dipped his head lower.

Doom began to feed off Bruce's control and claw him with panic. "What is it?" He inhaled sharply, calming himself. "Just . . . tell . . . me . . . what . . . happened," he said slowly, holding his voice to barely above a whisper.

Smithy raised his head, bleakly met his gaze. "The house is closed up—no servants around and dust covers on the furniture. They went back to London, packed up and went on a 'jaunt,' or so Constable Gordon said. Didn't know where. Looks like the earl and Countess Seymour had a tiff and parted ways. Gordon said she seemed 'quite undone.' " He sighed and jerked his hand from his pocket to run it over his face. "There's more. Gordon said that Lady Melissa took sick at the earl's party. She was looking real peaked and frail-like when he saw her. Said it might've been tainted food but no one else suffered."

"How long?" Bruce asked, still barely above a whisper, still holding on to his control.

"She was abed at the earl's for a month, then the

countess and her went back to London, packed, and lighted out a fortnight ago,'' Smithy mumbled, and lowered his gaze again.

A fortnight. Forever. And Melissa had taken ill while still at the earl's. Ill enough to have to remain there for a month. And, now, she was gone. He'd missed her by two weeks. Bruce's mind reeled as he thought of all the places Melissa could be by now, of how large the world was and how long it might take to find her.

Forever.

She was ill . . . perhaps carrying a child.

His sense of doom picked him clean, leaving him nothing but barely restrained panic as he tried to think, to plan around the knell that echoed in his head and the anger that pounded inside him for release.

Melissa was gone, spirited away by her bitch of a mother.

"What now?" Smithy asked.

Methodically, Bruce tucked in his shirt and finished fastening his pants, then pulled on his boots one by one as he forced his mind to rationality and calm. The world was large but not infinite.

"I am going to speak with Max and Damien." He shrugged into his riding coat, looked up at Smithy and continued with a deadly calm. "And then I am going to find Melissa before it is too late."

As he strode back toward the sitting room adjoining Kathy's bedchamber, he thought of all the times he had tried to pry more than one or two words from Melissa. It was an odd thought to have, yet Melissa's silences had drawn him to her, both fascinating and exasperating him. Later, he'd discovered how eloquent she was in those silences, and how profoundly her ventures into conversation had affected him. He'd had to listen closely, and he'd had to study her expressions carefully to understand the layers of herself she revealed in those moments. In the past weeks he had recalled every one of them and loved her more in the memory. Just her presence had given him a sense of peace he'd never known. With Melissa, he felt no need to keep several steps ahead of himself to prevent his mind from slipping into a past best forgotten, or at least avoided. With Melissa, neither the violence nor the loneliness of the past mattered. With Melissa, he'd viewed the future as a promise rather than another challenge to be met to keep him from seeing the emptiness of his days. He'd accepted that he loved her, and now he admitted that he needed her. Desperately.

But she was gone. Vanished.

He would give his entire fortune to again experience the peace she gave him even in her silence.

# Chapter 20

*Late January 1822*

The months passed in ennui and silence. Over six months since Melissa and her mother had left the earl's, and then London a few days later. Six months of listening to her own thoughts. Her worries. Her fears.

In a daze after revealing her circumstances to her mother and the earl, Melissa had agreed to the earl's plan without weighing the consequences. It hadn't registered that the hunting lodge he offered them for the duration of her pregnancy would be so isolated, nor that the village five miles away would be so small, though the earl assured her it would be best, as the villagers were dependent upon him and would keep silent about her presence in the lodge. It hadn't occurred to her that she would be surrounded by craggy hills and bleak moors. And, relieved that her mother had not washed her hands of her, Melissa hadn't thought of what it would be like to be cooped up with her for so long without society to divert them.

To her mother's credit, she had taken Melissa se-

riously that day in the earl's salon. And for the last
six months she had cut off more than one sentence
upon realizing that she was about to criticize or demand. Instead, she made subtle comments which
weren't subtle at all about what she would do—or
had done—in Melissa's place.

One day, Melissa would have to tell her that she
had no talent for subtlety.

Melissa never dreamed that she would actually
wish to be in London during the Season. It gave her
an entire new appreciation for the advantages of life
in the city, such as friends that made her mother feel
secure, social occasions that diverted her mother's
attention, and crowds that occupied her mother's
critical eye, which skittered away guiltily whenever
Melissa glanced her way.

It was altogether unsettling to see the formidable
Countess Seymour guilty and trying so hard to
please someone other than herself. It was heart-
breaking to see her reach out, then hesitate and pull
away as if she were afraid to touch Melissa, especially in a display of affection.

Neither the reaching out nor the hesitation was
natural to her mother, who hadn't overtly exhibited
affection since the day they'd laid Melissa's father to
rest. Nor was her mother's lack of complaint at being
separated from the earl until Melissa's time became
imminent.

Nor was their isolation and enforced exile natural.

As much as Melissa had always craved privacy
and peaceful moments, she now wished for conversation and company—specifically, Bruce's conversation, both nonsensical and serious. Bruce's
company, both in passion and in quiet moments.
She'd lived in constant hope and expectation that

she would soon have what she wanted.

She'd kept that hope alive by going into the village every other day with Nicole in a pony cart the earl provided to shop for food and necessities and post a letter to Bruce. And then she'd return to the lodge, devastated and aching with emptiness.

No newcomers had come to the village inquiring about her. No answering letter awaited her.

She'd said no to Bruce once too often, telling herself that she had to be certain, that she couldn't marry for any reason other than love. In truth, she'd enjoyed Bruce's pursuit of her. His attentions and efforts resembled a courtship of sorts, and she'd wanted to make the most of it. She suspected that somewhere in a corner of her mind, she'd known she would relent. Her convictions, it appeared, lacked the same courage that she did. Ideals, she'd realized, were fine and high-minded until put into practice. Then they became unreasonable and stubborn and wanted compromise.

She'd realized, too, that a compromise resulting in a life shared with Bruce was far preferable to a life shared only with memories. She'd had the romantic and rather girlish notion that the memories might be enough, that to have even that much was better than nothing. But she couldn't hold her memories, couldn't feel their warmth and passion, couldn't laugh or banter with them, couldn't build on them. Memories couldn't surprise her or amuse her or challenge her.

She'd discovered she was indeed selfish. She didn't want to settle for anything less than loving Bruce in person every day for the rest of her life.

She rested her hands on her belly in silent apology to the child she carried. Soon, she would have a son or daughter with whom to share her life, but that, too, brought fear and anticipated loss. Fear that she would cling to her child out of loneliness as her mother had done with her. Loss because she would not shackle another life in such a way. When the time came, she was determined to nudge her offspring out of the nest and encourage him to fly—

"Mademoiselle, it is time, I think, that you stay home while I shop," Nicole said beside her.

Panic struck swiftly and completely. "No!" she said shrilly, then struggled to catch her breath. "I-I look forward to these jaunts. I'm certain they are quite good for me." She couldn't remain at the lodge, couldn't stop trying to reach Bruce, if for no other reason than she needed to know that just once she had not given up, accepting her lot in life rather than face resistance.

"The air is damp and cold and yet you are making the—" The maid frowned as if concentrating on locating the proper word. "You are making wet on your skin."

"Perspire?" Melissa said absently, then lifted her hand to her face. She *was* perspiring even though Nicole drove the cart.

Nicole nodded and pulled the horse to a halt. "It is time," she said firmly. "At first I think you should go no matter what your *muman* say. Peasant women breathe the fresh air and do the walking and they do not have so much trouble with their bellies as the ladies do, but your belly has dropped lower and I think your *enfant* is wanting to come out sooner than he should."

Melissa had suspected as much lately as her lower back ached constantly and the pressure of the child did seem very low. She would have considered miscalculation, except that there was only one time with Bruce that could have borne fruit before the earl's house party—the night Bruce had waited for her beneath her bed. "I'll be fine," she said as firmly to Nicole as she did to herself at least a dozen times a day. "I am quite fit."

"*Oui*, you are as healthy as the horse," Nicole agreed as she set the reins down. "But that does not mean you cannot have the baby too soon." She turned to take Melissa's hands in one of hers. "I will send your letters, mademoiselle."

Melissa shook her head. "Nicole, you know I won't let you do that. I don't want you to know the identity of the baby's father. The less you know, the better for you. If Mother found out—"

"His name is Bruce Palmerston, Viscount Channing. The earl, your friend, is his papa though *they* are not friends. No?"

Melissa felt the blood drain from her face. Had she made a mistake? Had she inadvertently said or done something to give her secret away?

Nicole grinned brightly. "I know this, you see? But I do not tell your *maman* or anyone else—not even my Ben when he comes to visit next week, if you say no." She sat back.

"Ben is coming? Here? Next week?"

Nicole's head bobbed and her eyes sparkled and a flush rouged her cheeks. "He comes, but you must not tell your *maman*."

"No, I must not," Melissa said as she battled a sharp stab of envy. "But how will you keep it from her?"

"I have cleaned the woodcutter's cottage, and Ben will stay there. He will not even go into the village."

"Will you . . . I mean . . ."

"No, I will stay in the house and only meet Ben for the talk and the kisses."

"But—"

"Mademoiselle," Nicole said gently, "Ben wants marriage, you see. I have said yes to that, and so we can wait."

*We can wait. . . .* Melissa averted her gaze and for the first time felt shame for what she had done—not for making love with Bruce, but for the reasons behind it. The wrong reasons. She'd done it because she hadn't expected more, because she was snatching moments rather than fighting for years. . . .

*A lifetime.*

She'd expected too little out of fear that she could not handle more. Yet Nicole's Ben was traveling to the farthest reach of England, an extraordinary measure just to talk with and kiss Nicole, to see her.

Bruce had climbed walls and trees and risked humiliation to see her, extraordinary measures for a man who had only to smile to have what he wanted from a woman.

"Please, mademoiselle, we must go, but first you listen." Nicole snapped her fingers in front of Melissa's eyes.

Melissa turned her head and focused on her maid. "What did you say?"

"I say there is no reason for you to go into the village. You must stay home and rest now. You have the threads and cloth and yarns to make pretty things for your little one, and time grows short." She patted Melissa's belly. "And you grow very, very big. I do not want to help you push out the *enfant* here in the pony cart."

Something swelled inside Melissa as she glanced down at her stomach. It burst as the bulk suddenly shifted from the center to one side and her skirt rippled with the forceful kick of a tiny foot. Nicole was right. Her baby would soon be born. A beautiful baby with Bruce's dimples and engaging smile. A boy as big and fine as his father and just as restless to get on with the next stage of his life. A baby to hold and love and care for.

She battled down the anxiety that came every time she thought about it. Anxiety because she didn't know how to care for a child. She didn't even know what she was going to do after they left the lodge.

She'd been so certain she'd hear from Bruce. It was really her fault that she hadn't.

Tears began to flow, spilling down her cheeks faster than she could swipe them away. She gulped and sobbed and babbled every curse she could think of. "Oh, blast and damn and drat. I am so bloody, blasted weary of weeping at the drop of a-a hat."

Nicole gathered her in her arms and patted her back. "You make the rhyme. Did you hear it?"

Raising her head, Melissa hiccuped and blinked and began to laugh while tears continued to pour down her face. "How did you know about Bruce?" she asked, afraid to hear the answer.

"I peek at one of your letters. You will need help, I think, and I cannot help if I do not know."

She hadn't given herself—or Bruce—away. Her secret was safe. Melissa's sobs doubled and increased in volume. "B-blast it, Nicole, you can't help me. No one can."

"If you are going to use the cursing, I must teach you more words," Nicole said lightly. "And I will find a way to help. But I must know more." She fished a handkerchief—which she had taken to carrying for Melissa's fits of weeping—out of the pocket of her voluminous white apron and began to mop Melissa's face. "Now, tell me if your Bruce is the one who came to the earl's party and everyone welcomed except his papa."

Melissa nodded miserably as she thought of Bruce being rejected and scorned and vilified by his own father. By the same token, it hurt her to see the earl's pained expressions when Bruce had spoken to him with such indifference and a barely veiled lack of respect. "I d-don't know why the earl doesn't like him or why he doesn't like the earl. They are both such fine men."

"Hmph," Nicole snorted. "We will see who is fine and who is not. This I do not decide yet. Your Bruce, he is the one you were in the maze with?"

"How did you know?"

"It is my place to look after you, no? So I look when you do not go to your room with the headache. I see this big man with hair like dark red wine and holes in his face"—she pushed her index fingers into her face on either side of her mouth—"here."

"Dimples," Melissa said.

"Yes, dimples. And he had clouds in his eyes. I look more for you and then go back to the maze. You come out with your gown all covered with wrinkles. I think what is happening but I do not say."

"He had clouds in his eyes?"

Nicole nodded gravely. "Clouds with no wind to push them but with not enough water to rain. It is fear I see, and worry. Such clouds do not know where to go or what to do. They are lost, I think."

Lost. *Bruce?* Melissa couldn't fathom it, yet she had come to trust Nicole's instincts over the months. The small Frenchwoman possessed a practical wisdom Melissa envied. If she'd had such wisdom to apply to her actions, her defiances might have been less unruly and more effective. As it was, she had gotten exactly nowhere—if one didn't count a hunting lodge on the edge of the world and a mother who had forsaken her overbearing ways in favor of covert manipulations.

But even Nicole had to be wrong at some point, and Melissa was certain this was the time. Bruce Palmerston had never been lost in his life. And if he had been, he would make it a point to convince the rest of the world that he was exactly where he should be and everyone else was misdirected.

"He looked worried and afraid?" she asked, having almost as much difficulty grasping that concept as the other.

"It look so to me," Nicole said with a shrug.

Melissa had seen Bruce bluff his way through confrontations, smile his way through troublesome moments, and turn a calamitous situation back on itself, scheming as he went along. To be worried, one had to face the possibility of defeat, and Bruce did not know the meaning of defeat, much less fear it. . . .

Unless she had been the one to introduce him to the concept—a heady and improbable notion that was only possible if his heart had been in the battle. If he wanted her so badly that he could not imagine life without her. That, like her, he was willing to do anything, go to any lengths, to ensure that didn't happen.

Obviously, that was not the case, or he would have replied to her missives either in writing or in person. A nasty canker of disillusionment had been growing in her mind as a result of his silence. She'd had faith that he would reply, even if only to reject her. She'd believed him possessed of too much honor to do otherwise.

She'd assumed he would continue to pursue her.

"You were mistaken, Nicole," she said as she fought back a fresh supply of tears.

"We do not think of this now, mademoiselle. Now we must care for you and the little one and then we find this man and see if he thinks with his brains or the pouches in his pants."

Melissa frowned and then giggled as she comprehended Nicole's meaning.

"There," Nicole said as she patted Melissa's knee. "Now you will say you stay home while I send the letters for you."

"Thank you, Nicole," Melissa said thickly as she conceded to her maid's good sense. It was becoming difficult to endure the jostling of the pony cart. Even more difficult was returning home from the village each time with one more disappointment adding to her despair.

As Nicole set the horse into motion once more, Melissa glanced around at the landscape, seeing it— really seeing it—for the first time.

The dark hills seemed like tortured souls, jagged and hunched with the wind tearing through them with an agonized wail. The trees were gnarled and twisted and bare, the moors bleak, and beyond, the sea crashed against rocks in impatience and defiance, all of it forsaken, as she'd been forsaken. Yet it had all endured—the hills and trees shifting and bending and growing in spite of the wind and gloomy sky, the rocks standing defiant in spite of the sea.

Suddenly, she felt it inside herself, a strength she'd only begun to realize before Bruce had left her. She felt the defiance and impatience, and she felt anger. Anger at herself.

She'd been floundering in her own misery, defeating herself with her own despair. How easily she'd become what she had been before Bruce had sauntered into her life. How quickly she'd surrendered to her own weakness because Bruce had not appeared to prop her up.

*We find this man . . .* Nicole had said. She made it sound so simple, as if it was a natural assumption.

It should be.

Melissa sat back and ran her hands over her belly. If she was so willing to go to any lengths to be with Bruce, then she would have to do more than write pathetic little letters and wait for him to find her.

She would have to give birth to his child first, but then she had to find him, face him, fight for him. If she did not try, then she deserved to live with her mother and be dominated by her. She'd deserve to be alone with her memories.

She couldn't have been wrong about Bruce. There had to be a reason why he'd left so precipitously. A reason why he had not responded to her missives.

One way or another, she had to know.

The more time passed, the more convinced Bruce became that Melissa was carrying a child.

Yet not knowing for certain was driving him mad. Again and again he calculated the time—over six months since she and Arabella had closed the London house and vanished, and two months before that since he'd climbed into Melissa's bedroom and made love to her on cushions on the floor. More than eight months total since he'd first lost control and spilled his seed into her.

It made sense. Melissa had become ill at the earl's house party, an illness that had lasted a month.

Eight months.

He had to know.

It would be simple enough to wait and see if she and Arabella returned in a few months with the tale of a runaway marriage and sudden widowhood to explain the presence of an infant.

If they returned with an infant. If they did not, it would either mean that there had been no child or that Melissa had left it tucked away somewhere or given it to some prosperous merchant's or farmer's wife to raise. It happened all the time. With Arabella in the equation, God knew what Melissa might be driven to do. It was one thing to secretly defy her mother by kicking off her shoes or even by having an affair with him, but quite another to single-handedly take on the world with a child in her belly.

His blood ran cold at the prospect. His fists clenched in denial. He had to find her before it was too late. He had to help her and take care of her, and never let her out of his sight again.

He'd run out of ideas as to how to go about it.

For over six months, he'd tried everything he knew to locate her.

Melissa, it seemed, had dropped off the face of the earth.

And Bruce had reports from all corners of the known world as a result of his search for her. His family had helped, of course. In the tradition of the Dukes of Bassett and Westbrook, Max and Damien had closed ranks behind him, providing aid before he'd had the chance to ask for it. Damien sent men to search the south of England and the Continent. Max posted men to the north and into Scotland and

Ireland. Bruce hired agents to search America and the islands of the Atlantic.

But first, he had dispatched Bow Street Runners to each of the earl's properties with instructions to use whatever means—fair or foul—to go through every room at every house, cottage and hovel in the earl's holdings. Smithy had taken on the job of personally directing the search, and even now, two Runners resided in Blackwood Village taking note of every coming and going as well as the gossip of servants at the manor.

If Smithy's suspicions hadn't already been alive and nagging in his own mind, they would have taken root with Melissa's disappearance. As Smithy had said: It was too easy. Too easy for the earl to become involved with Melissa's dilemma and offer aid for purposes that were all too obvious. Purposes that resurrected every torment, every fear, and every demon from Bruce's past.

His mind had been in a frenzy ever since, conjuring thoughts of an elaborate plot hatched by the earl to obtain long-awaited revenge. Rationality suggested that it was unlikely the earl would have gone to such lengths. That Bruce's relationship with Melissa had sprung from a bizarre and spontaneous collection of events that could not have been orchestrated by even the most devious mind.

Coincidence was another matter entirely. The earl *had* been in the hallway as Bruce had crept from Melissa's bedchamber at the Longfords' house party. Had that been enough to spawn a scheme to destroy Bruce?

Bruce knew all too well how a random occurrence could be shaped into a plot. He'd done it enough times himself. And though it galled him to draw any comparisons, he had to admit that he had learned some of his methods from the man he abhorred for his cruelty and lack of conscience. He'd had to learn at an early age in order to survive, warned by instinct rather than articulate knowledge that one must fight fire with fire. But there the comparison ended. He'd refined the method as he grew older, learning to use it in business as well as for entertainment, always careful to keep cruelty and destruction out of it. The closest he had come was in threatening to ruin Melissa three years ago, and that had been to protect Max and Jillian. It had also been pure bluff, as had his threat to Melissa that he would not wait forever.

A thoroughly stupid bluff.

Obviously, she had taken him seriously.

*Eight months. Forever.* It seemed so since he'd held her and talked to her, discovering yet another layer of her with each moment they were together. It seemed longer than forever since he had mounted a search of cosmic proportions for Melissa.

He was beginning to understand why wars were fought and civilizations crumbled for love of a woman. He'd bloody well torn a good portion of the world apart to find Melissa, employing what amounted to an army of footmen and solicitors and bankers and agents to accomplish it.

Each man involved in the search had submitted reports on where he'd been and what he'd learned.

Which was exactly nothing.

It would have helped if Melissa had been dark-haired or bucktoothed. Eyebrows inevitably lifted when one of his or Damien's or Max's men inquired after a blond, blue-eyed Englishwoman. There were any number of refined young ladies fitting that description in the country as well as traveling abroad with their parents. He'd received detailed information on them all.

Smithy had remarked that finding a woman who fit a glass slipper would be easier.

How could she have so completely vanished? he wondered as he scanned the betting book at White's, searching for clues. A desperate measure, not to mention a lost cause, but he had run out of ideas, and the book had often provided him with valuable tidbits of information.

Not this time, though he had found wagers posted concerning the state of his mind, his wealth and his manhood. The ton had apparently taken note of his grim preoccupation with gossip from which he'd hoped to pick up a thread of information about the Ladies Seymour. But, again, he'd heard nothing but what Smithy had initially gleaned from Constable Gordon coupled with expressions of relief that Arabella was absent and clucks of sympathy for "poor Melissa," who had to cope with her mother's broken heart over losing the affections of Robert Palmerston, Earl of Blackwood.

The Earl of Blackwood had been in London the entire time, his manner no different than it had been. And with his usual calculated charm, he turned aside tactless questions concerning his brief romance with Arabella. The ton not only deemed him a hero for saving Kathy's and Damien's life, but a true gentleman as well.

It was unreal.

Everything seemed unreal to Bruce. The longer he searched, the stronger the sense that his time with Melissa had merely been the fantasy he'd played out the first night he'd made love to her, a shadow in the darkness holding him in thrall. Melissa as a passionate, complex woman had never existed. His moments with her had never happened, and there was no child, couldn't be a child.

Yet if that were so, why did he feel as if a part of him had been brutally ripped out? Why did he feel as if he were alone on a vast and dead ocean, becalmed and hopelessly, helplessly, lost?

He'd never felt helpless before. Hope had always been the strength that got him through his childhood at the hands of the earl.

"Looking for someone to fleece?"

Bruce glanced up to find the earl standing a few feet away. He contemplated leaving, but his nagging suspicion of the earl urged him to remain. "Idle curiosity," he said as he motioned to a steward to bring him a brandy. Inspiration struck out of nowhere, prompting him to slant his mouth in a mocking smile. "I see an old wager in here concerning you and Arabella. Longford risked twenty pounds on his conviction that Arabella would browbeat you into marriage. Lindsey believed you would simply use her and discard her." He paused as the steward served his brandy. Cupping the bowl with his hand, he swirled the liquid, seemingly intent on the aroma of fine spirits. "I was considering adding to it. The timing offers intriguing possibilities."

"Really?" the earl said. "I wasn't aware of any timing, nor of any possibilities."

Bruce hid a triumphant grin. The earl had taken the bait. "Then you disappoint me in your lack of acuity. I was certain you could at least count to nine."

The earl stiffened and seemed to pale, but it was so fleeting Bruce couldn't be sure.

"Pray continue," the earl said blandly. "I might enter the wager myself. The idea of fleecing *you* holds a certain appeal."

Bruce took his time in sipping his brandy. "It is not like Arabella to miss the Little Season, yet she was notably absent. Nor did she have her usual gathering for the holidays. It has been—what?—six months or so since her rather abrupt departure," he mused idly, then took another sip from the snifter. "She is still young enough to bear children, and you are the only man in whom she has shown interest. . . ." He allowed his voice to trail off suggestively.

The earl snorted in disgust. "I have had quite enough *bastards* in my life to sire one on a cow such as Countess Seymour." His expression quickly altered to one of boredom. "But by all means place your wager. I would enjoy countering it and relieving you of some of your money . . . say, ten thousand pounds?"

Bruce stared at the ceiling a moment, giving the appearance of being deep in thought. "Do you protest too much, I wonder? After all, Arabella is not one to flee unless she has been forced into an uncompromising position. In any event, she has a way of making her presence known regardless of where she is or why."

"Perhaps it is not Arabella who needed to flee," the earl said. "She would do anything, even live in obscurity, to protect Melissa. That chit is so brainless, any man with half a mind could convince her to spread her legs for him."

Crimson flooded Bruce's vision at the insult to Melissa, hot with rage and dark with the desire to spill blood. The earl's blood. He tightened his grasp on the snifter and forced himself to drink, to hold on to his control. "Yes, well, I daresay if that were true someone would have accomplished it before now . . . if he could get past Arabella, that is. I'm certain you were right to shake off such a dragon. No doubt she would have eaten you alive." Unable to continue, he drained his glass and handed it to the earl. "Take care of that for me, will you?"

Bruce turned and walked away, his stomach tied in knots, the haze of fury still roiling in his mind, and a sense of hopelessness growing in his heart.

# Chapter 21

**B**ruce was past praying for . . . almost.

If he were in the privacy of his home, the earl thought he might have given in to the urge to dance a triumphant jig at the bleakness he'd seen in Bruce's expression as he turned away.

It wasn't every day one's nemesis gave one the perfect opportunity to heap insult upon innuendo. Bruce must indeed be desperate to approach him in a bid for information after his spies had come up short in searching Blackwood holdings.

The earl had known almost the minute the Runners had arrived at each of his properties, and had found it immensely entertaining to allow them to carry on, knowing they would neither find nor hear a thing to implicate him in Melissa's disappearance.

He'd counted on it.

It paid to be feared, he thought in satisfaction as he strolled to a chair in the club and settled in. So feared for his cruelty that not one of his servants dared to breathe a word about their master. Not that they knew anything to tell.

Still, he had to admit that he'd suffered a bad moment when Bruce had alluded to pregnancy. But then Bruce had botched it, being too obvious in his baiting. It did the earl's spirits good to see Bruce losing his touch, and if he didn't miss his guess, his control as well. For a split second, the earl could have sworn Bruce was about to throttle him.

Yet, as everything else in his plan, all was going as it should.

The hunting lodge had been another sign that he would succeed in getting revenge at last. He'd heard of the place from his tailor, whose cousin had inherited it and wished to sell. No one wanted a lodge in a godforsaken backwater known for its remote location and dismal landscape. It had taken very little effort on his part to lease the place for a year— anonymously, of course.

No one could trace it back to him.

If his plan were any easier to execute, he'd be bored stiff before Melissa dropped her brat.

*Her bastard.*

What a pathetic little mouse she was, constantly sending letters to Bruce and languishing in misery when he didn't reply. How amusing it was to spend his evenings reading each one of them and then locking them away in his desk. It was worth the exorbitant sum he paid the villagers to keep silent about the Ladies Seymour and deliver all of Melissa's letters to him rather than sending them to Bruce.

And then there were the letters Arabella wrote to him—fawning, romantic affairs that turned his stomach. She even doused them with perfume. Never again would he be able to abide the scent of roses. Roses! The woman had no imagination.

That particular conclusion had discouraged him from taking advantage of her. A woman who lacked imagination would never respond properly in bed. A woman as desperate for love as Arabella would likely lie there like a stone, as meek as her daughter, accepting whatever pain he inflicted without a whimper.

He preferred screams alternating with retaliation.

Soon. If the midwife in the village near the lodge was correct, Melissa would deliver within weeks, perhaps days. In fact, the earl planned to leave for the lodge tomorrow so that he would not miss such an auspicious occasion. He supposed he would have to allow Arabella and Melissa to remain while Melissa recovered from the birthing. No doubt, they would hate every moment of their enforced confinement. It pleased him to think so.

Soon, he would take great pleasure in serving his revenge on Bruce very cold indeed. And then he would hear Bruce roar in pain.

The earl smiled and rose, suddenly anxious to return to his manor and await news of a blessed event that would be a curse on Bruce for the rest of his life.

Soon Bruce would know what true hopelessness was like.

"Nothing?" Smithy asked as Bruce climbed into his coach and took the seat across from him.

"Nothing," Bruce replied, and wearily rubbed his hand over his face. "I even cornered the earl and danced around a bush or two. I'm beginning to believe he has nothing to do with this . . . what the devil?"

The door opened and a young man climbed inside.

Smithy lunged for the intruder, grasped him by the collar and drew back his fist.

"Please, Lord Channing," the young man whispered frantically. "I mean you no harm, and we are being watched. Tell your coachman to drive so we will not be overheard."

Bruce squinted in the pale light from the lanterns hung outside the coach. "I know you . . . Ben, isn't it? The baker's son?"

"Yes, my Lord." Ben tugged his forelock. "Please, sir, tell your coachman to—"

Bruce interrupted him by giving the roof a thump. The coach lurched forward and then swayed into a steady pace through the London streets.

"You in trouble, boy?" Smithy asked as he settled back into his seat and gestured for Ben to sit beside him.

Bruce frowned at Ben's filthy clothes and week's growth of beard.

"No, sir. I've just come from visiting my fiancée in Northumberland."

"If you arrived there looking like that," Bruce said, "she no doubt sent you packing."

Ben shook his head and gulped in air. "I have ridden straight through with stops only for fresh horses. My Lord, her name is Nicole. She is maid to—"

"If you have a point, make it," Smithy said impatiently.

Bruce couldn't blame him. Ben emanated at least five days' worth of unwashed body odor.

"I'm trying, sir. Nicole is Lady Melissa's maid," he blurted.

Bruce stilled even as his heart thundered and his blood raced as swiftly as his mind. Northumberland.

He had reports from all over the area, but the natives there were a closemouthed and suspicious lot. No doubt they felt that anyone who traveled there in the dead of winter ought to be suspected of something.

A trick. It had to be. But whose?

"Lady Melissa Seymour?" he asked casually.

"Yes, my Lord. Nicole . . . she told me you . . . that is, I know." He shook his head, seeming at a loss for words. "Nicole sent me to fetch you back before it's too late. She says that if you truly do care for Lady Melissa and want to marry her, you must hurry."

Every bone in Bruce's body chilled. He felt brittle, about to snap if he exerted even the smallest bit of hope. "All right, Ben, who is twitting me?" he asked flatly, though he knew it wasn't a joke. It couldn't be. No one knew of him and Melissa. Not a word had drifted through the ton about his search for her.

"Damnit, my Lord, sir, Lady Melissa is increasing, and you're the father," Ben shouted, then lowered his voice. "Nicole says the baby is restless and wants to come out early. She says I should bring you back any way I can whether you like it or not."

"And you do everything Nicole tells you to do?" Bruce asked carefully. The young man's urgency was getting to him, convincing him of what he feared to believe. If he went to Northumberland and it was a trick, he might be gone when reliable news came in of Melissa's whereabouts. And time was growing dangerously short.

"No, my Lord. I do what is right." He pulled a pistol from inside his coat and leveled it with a wavering hand, first on Bruce, then on Smithy, and then on Bruce again. "Any man who hasn't the decency to answer a single one of the letters sent to him by a lady in distress doesn't deserve—"

Bruce leaned forward and sank back again as the muzzle of the pistol threatened to jam up his nose. "What letters? I've received no letters."

"The lady sent them. Nicole was with her every time, and Nicole doesn't lie."

Smithy spat loudly out the window. The coach lurched as Smithy turned his head and wrapped his arm around Ben's neck. "Drop the pistol, boy, before I snap your head off your shoulders."

"No, sir," Ben gasped as he held fast to the gun. "I've sworn to Nicole to help Lady Melissa or die trying. If you don't come, Nicole threatens to shoot off your balls, and I can't have that."

Bruce felt his bones thawing. His heart steadied to a beat of anticipation. "That won't be necessary, Ben. We'll pack provisions, get fresh horses, and be on our way to the north ... as soon as you've had a bath."

Ben's hand fell, his fingers limp. The pistol dropped to the floor. "Thank God."

Bruce leaned his head back and closed his eyes. "Yes," he murmured in a thick voice, "thank God."


It could not be. God would not be so cruel as to foil him now.

But then the earl admitted that God had forsaken him long ago.

"Who in the devil is this Ben?" he asked his man, Tommy, a Neanderthal he'd brought with him from America, a man he'd plucked from a life of wrestling for money. Tommy's brutish appearance fooled others into thinking him a slow-wit when in truth he had remarkable powers of observation and logic. It would have been a tragedy if that talent had been beaten out of him.

"A baker's son," Tommy replied in characteristic brevity. "Keeping company with Lady Melissa's maid."

"Ah, so he visited his love." The earl sneered as he paced the floor in his study. "And the men I hired to watch the lodge did nothing to chase him off."

"Thought he was just riding through. Didn't know he was at the lodge till they saw him with the maid just before he left. He'd been staying in the wood-cutter's cottage back in the woods."

"Well, at least they had the sense to send word to me right away." He glanced up at Tommy and tossed back his third glass of port since Tommy had begun his report. He cursed under his breath as he thought of the time wasted while he'd been at White's and Tommy had been going from one establishment to another looking for him. "Have horses saddled and waiting. We leave for Northumberland at once and will stop only for fresh mounts."

"Now?" Tommy glanced out at the gray fog that shrouded the night.

"Immediately," the earl gritted. "If the baker's son rode straight through, it was for a purpose. His invasion of Bruce's coach confirms it. We must reach the lodge before Bruce."

Without a word, Tommy left the room and issued terse orders to the house steward to alert the stables and awaken the cook to prepare food.

The earl poured another glass of port and then threw the whole at the hearth. His entire plan might be foiled by a damned, besotted baker's son.

But the game wasn't over yet, he thought as he

strode from the study and up to his bedchamber to instruct his valet to pack a small bundle of clothing for him. If Melissa hadn't given birth by the time he arrived, he'd charge his men to lock Bruce in a box until she did. If she had, the pieces would fall into place as anticipated.

Perhaps it was another sign that justice would be done on the soul of the old Duke of Bassett and blight the life of Bassett's bastard son. A bastard who not only dared to claim the Palmerston name and titles but flaunted them like a gauntlet dropped between them.

The earl smiled at the sound of activity in the stables below.

Finally, he'd found a way to pick up that gauntlet. Finally, the battle was joined.

Perhaps the baker's son had done him a favor.

And Bruce would compound it by being in place and saving him the bother of sending for him and having to endure Arabella's affections while waiting for Bruce to arrive.

He'd made a mistake in selling his name to Bassett's trollop. He'd endured years of playing the husband to a woman who looked through him, years of pretending paternity to Bassett's by-blows, and then ten years exiled in America, forbidden to set foot on English soil by both Bassett and Westbrook on pain of death.

Well, the old dukes were dead, drowned during a yacht race. The earl chuckled at the thought of small fish feeding off their carcasses. He could imagine it in vivid detail, their arrogance reduced to bones scattered over the bottom of the sea, their salted flesh being torn away from them a piece at a time. It had kept him going when he'd had to cool his heels longer still after returning to England and being promised ruin by Westbrook's heir. Bassetts and Westbrooks—always guarding one another's backs, always vanquishing those who sought retribution from them.

But not this time. The sons might have inherited the titles and power of their fathers, but they had also inherited the sins. They might have accepted Bruce and Kathy into their family circle and extended their high-minded traditions to them, saving Kathy from his wrath, but there was nothing they could do to save Bruce.

Not now. Events had gone too far. The sins of the father would indeed be visited upon the son. He would have the pleasure of watching Bruce pay every day for the rest of his life.

He'd waited a long time. He'd been prepared to wait longer. Who'd have thought that a baker's son would unwittingly become the wheel that would speed the process, saving him both aggravation and time?

The earl's chuckle expanded until it filled the room, the entire second floor and then drifted down to the public rooms and kitchen.

Little would Bruce know, as he sped across the country, that his time had run out.

Impatience gnawed on Bruce like a child cutting his first tooth. The farther north they went, the more appalling the roads and the weather. He'd alternately spent the first fourth of the journey chafing in the coach he'd insisted on taking for Melissa's journey back, ordering Ben to relate every detail he knew of the last six months and reviewing the mea-

sures he'd taken to be certain he hadn't missed
something.

He'd silenced Smithy's complaints about taking
the coach with a snarl.

He'd dispatched a trusted footman to Westbrook
Castle to inform Damien and Max of current devel-
opments and advise them of the earl's complicity—
at the very least in arranging for Melissa's and Arabella's location, and at the most in manipulating
events for a purpose Bruce didn't dare entertain at
the moment. If he did, he would end up delivering
two blows to the earl for every one inflicted on him
as a boy, and then he might bother to confirm his
suspicions.

He'd collected the special license Max had ob-
tained for him within a fortnight of his request and
contemplated—then discarded—an idea to abduct a
vicar somewhere along the way to conduct the marriage before Melissa could say no, which, in any
case, was no longer a choice for her to make.

He'd sent his stableman ahead to choose the best
cattle he could find and have it waiting when they
pulled into previously determined inn yards.

By the time they reached the halfway point, he
had advised Ben that holding a barker on a viscount
was a poor way to play knight to his lady fair, and
counseled the young man in the futility of trying to
save a woman from herself. If Nicole had been determined to shoot Bruce's balls off, she would
bloody well do it regardless of her fiancé's efforts to
prevent it.

Ben had asked if Bruce was worried about that.

Smithy had snorted and made a remark to the effect that Bruce's balls were made of Toledo steel and

the best anyone could do was take a nick out of them.

Bruce hadn't answered, loathe to make a cake of himself to a young man who had elevated him to the status of hero. Aside from that, Bruce wasn't nearly as concerned for his balls as he was his heart, which was hopelessly mired in emotions he had no idea how to handle.

But, he assured himself, he didn't need to handle them; he merely needed to act upon them and let the rest take care of itself, or so Max and Damien had instructed.

That memory had pushed him over the edge of restraint. At the next town, he bought two horses and the accompanying tack for an exorbitant amount, ordered Ben to mount, directed Smithy to bring the coach and find his own bloody way to the hunting lodge, and then rode ahead with a reluctant baker's son at his side.

# Chapter 22

❦❦❦

**"M**y Lord," Ben called two days later as they reached the turnoff leading to the lodge, several hundred yards ahead. "Men ahead." He pointed to four men acting as a fence across the short road, one brandishing a pitchfork, another a cudgel only slightly smaller than Smithy's large one, the third a stout walking stick, and the last balled fists that looked like hams.

Having anticipated such an eventuality, Bruce reached into the leather bag tied to his saddle and retrieved a brace of pistols he'd loaded some five miles back. "Do you have your pistol, Ben?"

Ben gulped and nodded. "Please recall, my Lord, that I spend my days preparing and delivering confections."

"They are hired bullies, Ben. You're a strapping lad. Did you never dispatch a bully in your youth?"

"Yes, my Lord. I fought dirty." He shuddered as if the memory was not a prideful one.

"If there is such a thing as a clean fight I have yet to hear of it outside of highly romanticized epic poems," Bruce said as he tucked the pistols into the waist of his pants. "Follow me and shout for Nicole.

No doubt she will emasculate at least two of them. And if you don't fight dirty, I'll throttle you myself." He spurred his horse into a gallop.

One man ran to meet him, his cudgel upraised. Bruce mowed him down, hearing bone crunch and a shout of pain as a hoof connected with the man's shoulder.

The remaining three advanced. Bruce pulled a pistol, aimed and fired. The man jerked, then swung at him, catching him on the elbow with his cudgel. Agony shot through his arm. His fingers numbed. The pistol fell to the ground.

The man's cudgel followed as he fell, clutching his thigh.

Ben fired at another man and missed.

Bruce kicked out at another, catching him under the chin before he could drive his pitchfork home.

The door to the lodge opened and the earl appeared, standing in the threshold like a king surveying his realm.

A woman knocked him down and waddled out into the yard.

Melissa.

A second woman followed, her white apron billowing. A third ran out, her arms outstretched toward Melissa.

Distracted by the sight of Melissa leading with her belly, Bruce failed to see the man he'd kicked recover from the blow and lunge toward him. Hands twisted in the front of his coat and dragged him from the saddle. Ben leaped from his horse and clubbed him with the butt of his pistol. The man stumbled backward, nearly colliding with Melissa.

The first man staggered to his feet, his arm dangling uselessly, and lurched toward Bruce. Nicole leaped on his back, yanked on a handful of his hair and sank her teeth into the lobe of his ear.

The attacker with the walking stick swung at Ben. Ben ducked and butted his head into his groin, then charged the man trying to dislodge Nicole from his back.

From the corner of his eye, Bruce saw Melissa drawing close to the two men still standing. Behind her, the earl rose to his feet and ran after her.

"Get out of the way, damnit!" Bruce shouted to Melissa.

She halted and looked as if she would topple forward from momentum and front-heavy weight.

"You stupid bitch," the earl snarled as he reached her and took her arm. "You'll ruin everything."

Arabella ran into the yard and grasped the earl's shoulder, whirling him around. "Don't touch her."

The earl backhanded Arabella across the face. She fell to the ground, her eyes glazed.

Nicole tumbled from the back of her victim. Ben pummeled him with both fists.

Backing up, Bruce urged the bullies toward him, drawing them away from Melissa and her maid.

As they passed her, Melissa stuck out her foot. The ham-fisted man fell facefirst onto the frozen ground. Melissa picked up a rock and crashed it on his head. He fell limp and silent, his hands open.

She staggered backward with a gasp. "Not now!" she screamed.

*Not now.* It echoed in Bruce's head. The time for brawling was past. He had to end this now. A sudden, deadly calm descended on him. He drew the second pistol from his waistband, pointed it at the last man standing and pulled the trigger.

The man howled and clutched his knee, then

howled again as the knee struck hard, frigid ground.

Ben stood beside Bruce, his chest heaving and great gusts of air billowing from his mouth as he exhaled.

Bruce envied him the ability to breathe as he stood frozen, staring at Melissa, drinking her in, absorbing her altered appearance, unaware of how cold it was and barely remembering the struggle and the four men littered about the yard.

He'd known she was increasing, and had thought of it constantly, yet the sight of it shocked him. She was the same, yet different as she straightened, staring back at him, her arms lowered and cradling her belly.

Her belly. His child.

She paled and shook her head as fluid suddenly gushed into a puddle at her feet. Her belly seemed to gather into a hard tight ball as she swayed, then stiffened, her face pinched with pain.

The earl reached for her. "We must get her inside," he said, then sneered at Bruce. "Or do you prefer she drop your bastard in the dirt?"

Bruce stepped forward. "Touch her again and I'll kill you," he said, his voice low and feral.

Arabella struggled to stand, a bruise spreading over half her face and blackening her eye.

Melissa doubled over as Bruce reached her and began to lift her in his arms.

"No," she gasped, "don't move me yet." Her gaze raced around the yard. "Nicole," she pushed the words through gritted teeth, "the pains . . . they're coming . . . on top of each other." Her belly tightened even more, then began to relax into a more natural shape.

Bruce picked her up, cradled her in his arms and

strode toward the lodge. "Ben, truss these animals up to a tree, then take a horse and go to the main road to watch for Smithy. Nicole, is there a midwife? Arabella, boil water, get blankets." He pinned the earl with a hard stare. "You, get inside."

"With great pleasure." The earl bowed and smiled. "I wouldn't miss this for the world."

Ignoring him, Bruce carried Melissa inside as another pain gripped her. "Where is your room?"

Arabella raced past him.

"No time," Melissa panted. "Please . . . any-where . . ."

Nicole rushed in behind him. "The midwife is in the village. The earl was about to send for her to stay until—"

Melissa cried out.

Bruce lowered her to the floor in front of the staircase and sat down, spread his knees, then pulled her back against his chest. "Help her," he ordered, still in a low, calm voice.

Nicole dropped to her knees, pushed Melissa's skirts above her belly and arranged her legs. "*Merde*, I see the head."

The earl strolled in and sat on the third stair to Bruce's side.

Arabella ran in with blankets and linens piled in her arms. "Help me get this under her," she said briskly.

Bruce leaned over as far as he could and slipped his hands beneath Melissa's hips, lifting them as Arabella slid a thick quilt and then a sheet under her. She spread another sheet over Melissa's belly and legs, making a tent.

Melissa gripped Bruce's hands and held tight as another pain seized her.

"Push, mademoiselle," Nicole ordered. "He has the large head and will not come without your help."

"Amazing how everything has fallen into place," the earl commented idly. "I couldn't have planned it better myself."

Melissa leaned forward and pushed hard.

Bruce winced at the sound of her effort and pain. His skin broke out in a cold sweat as Melissa's fingers clenched harder around his hands. She felt so fragile in his arms, he thought she might snap with the next pain.

Before she recovered from one pain, another began. He tore his hands from her grip and wrapped his arms around her chest, hoping to still her trembling. Impressions sped through his mind as he gathered his strength and mentally pushed with her. Her skin felt like ice. She'd been outside in only her gown. She drew up her legs and grunted with a deep sound in her chest. She didn't even have pantalettes on to warm her legs. She was barefoot, and a hideous bruise was swelling on her foot from tripping one of the earl's men. Her lips were blue.

Arabella ran out and returned with a red-hot knife and a hank of embroidery silk.

"Watch it, Bruce," the earl taunted. "Watch your bastard being born. Think of it—a bastard. He won't inherit the title. Society will tolerate him but not accept him. He will belong nowhere. He will, in fact, suffer what you should have suffered."

Bruce's heart pounded and felt as if it were shattering in his chest.

"Shut up," Melissa screamed. And then she screamed again as her belly domed, and Nicole ordered her to push even harder.

"You'll always remember that the woman you love did this to you," the earl continued. "She ran from you. She didn't love you enough to trust you. She trusted me instead. And she knew she was breeding even when she dallied with you in the maze. She deceived you by her very silence."

Bruce felt colder still, as if his soul had died and lay buried deep inside himself.

"The head is out; we must hurry," Nicole said.

Arabella poured hot water into a basin of cold, then knelt beside the maid, her eyes filling with tears as she held a blanket ready to wrap around the baby.

Melissa gulped and strained and whimpered between compressed lips as she doubled up and pushed.

"Madame," Nicole said to Arabella, "thread the needle. She is tearing very much . . . the shoulders are coming . . . yes . . . push now."

Melissa opened her mouth and screamed, a blood-curdling sound that reverberated in Bruce's ears, in the empty shell he had become. He held Melissa, supported her, pushed her forward again, and whispered encouragement to her as she sobbed and labored. He wiped her forehead with his hand and shushed her, and prayed she would not split apart.

A wail mingled with her next scream.

"A big, beautiful boy," Nicole exclaimed, and passed a wriggling pink body to Arabella to clean.

"A boy," the earl gloated. "Perfect! A bastard son for the bastard." He angled forward to look at Melissa. "Thank you, Lady Melissa, for falling in so nicely with my plans."

Melissa sagged back in Bruce's arms, turned her head and spat in the earl's face.

Bruce barely noticed as he stared at the baby, at

his covering of blood. His gaze shot to Nicole as she wiped her hands and arms with a length of linen, staining it with blood. So much blood.

Melissa's blood.

He registered her weight cradled by his body. Dead weight, limp and cold. Her chest moved. He held his finger over her mouth, then her nose. She still breathed, yet she felt lifeless in his arms.

She sobbed. "I'm sorry . . . so sorry . . . so weak . . . tired." Her voice was a thin sound like frayed thread about to break. It sounded like defeat, like good-bye.

"Don't," Bruce growled in her ear. "Do you hear me? Don't . . . even consider running from me again. Fight for once in your life. Have the courage to face me and settle this between us."

"That's enough," Arabella said tightly. "Melissa, your son is making enough noise without this. He needs you. Take him, please. I have things to do." She thrust the bundle into Melissa's arms, then edged closer to Nicole. "What must be done?"

"I need light, madame, to do the stitching."

"Are you certain you should?" Arabella said. "I was not stitched when Melissa was born."

"I think it will help, like stitching a cut on the head. We must do something or she will not heal."

The door crashed open and Smithy barreled inside, then abruptly halted. He stared at Melissa and the needle in Nicole's hand and fainted.

Ben dragged him aside and walked in.

"Get light," Arabella ordered, and threaded another needle.

Running outside, Ben returned with the coach lantern in his hand and held it close to Nicole.

It all skated over Bruce's head as he watched Melissa hug the baby close and kiss the red pelt of hair covering his head, his dimpled cheeks as she exposed one tiny foot, then the other, covering each body part back up after examining it. "He's perfect." She sighed, then tilted her head to meet Bruce's gaze. "I won't run away. I promise." Her eyes closed, her breathing even and deep.

"There, we are finished. The bleeding is slow now. Most come from the tearing, I think." Nicole rose to her feet with Ben's help.

Water splashed as Arabella tossed the needles and thread and knife into the basin, then rose beside Nicole. She stared down at Bruce, then at the baby, then at the earl. "I do believe I have a clear picture of what has been going on," she said flatly. Very slowly she approached the earl. "Robert, will you please stand in the presence of a lady?"

With a puzzled expression, the earl obliged.

Of a height with the earl, Arabella met his gaze eye to eye, drew her arm back and down, then arced it upward, her fist catching him beneath the chin.

His teeth snapped together; his eyes showed startlement a split second before they rolled back in his head. He fell backward on the stairs, his arms and legs spread.

"I will prepare Melissa's bed. Please recover yourself, Channing, and carry her up to her room." Arabella stepped over the earl and climbed the stairs.

In a daze, Bruce ordered Ben to revive Smithy and lock the earl in the cellar, knowing only that he could not allow the earl to return to London, where he would spread the tale of Melissa's ruin. Then he did as he was told, carrying Melissa upstairs to her bedchamber, standing helplessly in the doorway as Arabella and Nicole bathed her and helped her into a nightgown, making certain she was all right, then staring at the cradle beside her bed.

He knew Melissa watched him the entire time, knew she wanted him to meet her gaze, to say something. But he couldn't. Not now. His mind felt battered, his senses numb. Yet something ugly lay waiting inside him, waiting for him to release it. If he looked at her, it might swell and explode and leave nothing of the man he was.

Arabella turned and discovered him. "She needs her rest, if you please, Lord Channing," she said, her expression indecipherable, her voice devoid of inflection.

He left and found his way downstairs to a small room intended as a study and shut and locked the door, locking himself in where the hideous thing he'd thought long dead could overwhelm no one but himself.

*Bassett's bastards.* The words returned to assault him like the fists that had beaten him over and over again as he'd lain on the ground, refusing to flinch, willing himself not to strike back as the earl hammered the truth into him with his words and his fists. At sixteen, he'd already been taller and broader than the man he'd thought was his father. He could have killed him if he'd wanted. But he'd suffered a lifetime of blows from the earl. A lifetime of being struck for no reason other than he existed, struck, too, with the cruelty of disapproval and hatred without knowing why. He'd wanted to strike back, to pound and pummel and kill.

But the part of him that knew the gentle love of his mother, the adoration of his sister, the part of him that loved them back, that needed to be there to protect them from harm and heartbreak, had lis-

tened to his mother's cries and his sister's screams
and vowed to lie still, to deny his fury, to refuse to
hate anything but the anger wanting power over
him.

That part of him had somehow known that therein
lay the victory. He'd understood that the choice was
his. He'd made his choice and abided by it, fighting
when he had to without rancor, protecting because
he loved rather than hated.

He felt nothing but defeat now, and the anger he'd
always fought with calm and reason and humor as
if it were a primitive child to be tamed.

A child. His child. A bastard son for the bastard.

*Think of it—a bastard. He won't inherit the title. So-
ciety will tolerate him but not accept him. He will belong
nowhere. He will, in fact, suffer what you should have
suffered.*

He'd watched his son being born and it had
moved him. He'd held Melissa as she labored and
he had loved her all the more. He'd listened to the
earl's taunts and hated him as he'd vowed never to
hate anyone.

*You'll always remember that the woman you love did
this to you . . . ran from you . . . didn't love you enough
to trust you. She trusted me instead . . . deceived you by
her very silence.*

Bruce understood that Melissa had been used and
manipulated. He understood that she'd been ill and
afraid and he'd been gone. He even realized that she
might not have received his note, that the letters Ben
said she had written to him had been diverted. But
she'd made the choice not to wait, not to give him
a chance. She'd chosen to believe he didn't—
couldn't—love her. She hadn't trusted him with
anything but her body. She'd believed the worst

about him, used him and then run away.

And as his son had emerged into the world, breathing, crying, flailing his arms and legs at the indignity of it, hatred awakened and seized power.

He hated the earl because he had spoken the truth.

And he hated Melissa even as he loved her, passionately, mindlessly, helplessly.

He knew it wasn't rational, that he had to make a choice between the two.

He clenched his hands and fought the ugliness inside himself as he had never fought anything in his life.

But, God help him, he didn't know how to fight his own weakness.

# Chapter 23

**S**ilence. Ominous and smothering.

It surrounded Melissa as she lay in her bed, listening for Bruce, waiting for him to come and afraid that he would. It had been four days and she knew nothing of what went on in the world around her—whether the earl was still there, whether his men were still trussed to a tree outside.

Whether Bruce had left the study directly below her room.

She'd heard him there the first two days, small sounds of moving about, occasional knocks on the door and low voices muffled by the floor between them, and then silence again.

At first, she hadn't had the energy to do more than wonder as she'd floated in the weary euphoria of admiring her son, of holding him and feeding him and watching him sleep.

Little had been said by either her mother or Nicole as they'd tiptoed in to see to her needs and to stare down at the baby if he slept and make comical sounds and touch him if he did not. Both women all but pounced the moment he made a sound remotely resembling a cry. Melissa rather enjoyed watching her mother behave in such a ridiculous manner.

She gazed down at her son, nursing at her breast, his small hand kneading her flesh like an affectionate kitten. Such a beautiful child with hair that caught fire in the sunlight and eyes that were dark blue, like midnight. "Has your papa held you yet?" she whispered. "Do you know if he is about?"

"He is," Arabella said as she swept into the room, the bruise the earl had given her on the side of her face faded to a sickly yellow, the rest of her immaculate as always. She carried a robe of cherry-red velvet over her arm. "The last thing I wanted after you were born was to wear let-out clothes. Your father gave this to me the day you were born. He said nothing was more striking than a fair woman wearing red." She laid the robe on the bed beside Melissa.

Melissa stared at the rich velvet, at the vibrant color unsuitable for a young maiden. Her mouth tipped in a small smile as she skimmed her hand over the thick nap of the lustrous fabric. The robe, she realized, was her mother's unspoken acknowledgment that she was no longer innocent, no longer a child. In a way, she supposed it was also a statement of acceptance.

The baby sighed with a sound like the "baa" of a lamb, then latched back onto her breast to suckle with loud gulps.

"That child's appetite is just short of gluttony," Arabella commented as she stroked the baby's head. "I am going into the village today to fetch a wet nurse."

"I don't want a wet nurse."

Arabella swept the robe aside and sat down on the edge of the bed. "I know you don't, Melissa. I refused one and fed you myself until you were old enough to wean."

"You did?" Melissa marveled at the information. She'd always assumed that her mother would not have wanted to risk her figure in such a way.

"I treasured those moments with you. I would chase everyone but your father away and we would talk and sing silly songs to you as you fed, and then Edward would put you in your cradle and take his time in helping me fasten the front of my gown . . . and then we would—" Arabella shook her head as a pretty blush stained her cheeks. "I've been remembering so many things these past few days. Lovely things that you should experience." She arched a brow. "Obviously you have experienced some of them."

Melissa tilted her head, saying nothing. It was the closest her mother had come to admitting that perhaps she'd been right to assert her independence, that her mother understood what she'd tried to tell her that day at the earl's.

"He has stopped gulping, Melissa, yet he is still hungry," Arabella said gently. "You bled a great deal and I suspect you haven't enough milk to sustain him. He is wanting to feed every hour. You are healing nicely but that will not continue if you insist on nursing him this way."

Melissa laid her son on the mattress beside her and buttoned up her gown. "I *am* healing nicely," she argued. "I feel quite well, actually. Surely, I will produce more milk—"

"Melissa, Nicole and I have been feeding him goat's milk while you sleep." Lifting her hand, Arabella smoothed Melissa's hair away from her face. "He must have a wet nurse, darling. It is best for both of you. You'll not do him any good if you waste away, you know."

Melissa stared at her son as he struggled to get his fist into his mouth. He was fretful after she fed him, yet quieted later. Now she knew why. She also knew her mother was right. Unable to speak for the thickness in her throat, she nodded.

Arabella leaned over to stroke the baby's cheek. "I will send the wet nurse back with Ben, as I plan to remain in the village for the day."

Melissa frowned. "What could you possibly do there all day?"

"I shall find something to occupy the time." Arabella rose and strolled to the window. "I've been quite good in dealing with Channing thus far, but if I remain while you speak to him, I will likely want to hit both of you and then tell you what to do. I am in no mood to sacrifice more of my dignity than I already have."

Melissa's mind reeled as she absorbed her mother's revelation. "You've dealt with Bruce?"

"Actually, very little. I've sent him food and drink through Smithy, and refrained from barging into the study or catching him on his way back from the privy to give him a piece of my mind. And that is all the dealing I wish to do with him. That particular chore, I'm afraid, belongs to you."

"And you're telling me I must speak with him today?" Panic fluttered in her chest at the thought.

"I would not presume to tell you any such thing," Arabella said flatly as she turned from the window. "I merely assumed you would wish to since you are feeling so much better. And I brought you the robe because I thought you might like to look pretty, as well as stay warm, while you did it." She shrugged.

"It is, of course, entirely up to you how and when you come to terms with the father of your child."

Melissa didn't know whether to laugh at her mother's version of subtlety or hide under the bed at the idea of confronting Bruce.

"I will, however, risk your displeasure by telling you that the longer you wait, the worse it will be. Channing has locked himself in the study like a wounded animal. Wounded animals are dangerous in their anger."

"Bruce is never angry," Melissa said as the flutter of panic increased to a wild beating.

"After what was said and done, he would be quite inhuman if he were not angry," Arabella stated, then sighed. "I wish I could find fault with it, but I cannot. Neither can you, or you would not have been hiding from him these past four days." Arabella stepped around the bed, pried loose the baby's grip on Melissa's finger and lifted him in her arms. "If it were me, I would make myself as attractive as possible—perhaps wear that pale pink silk nightgown to soften the strength of the red velvet—and beard him in his den. I don't think he expects you to go to him. Men do not cope well with surprise."

"I would have thought you'd want me to get away from him; you dislike him so."

"It's a bit late for that, Melissa," Arabella snapped. "And much as I hate to admit it, Channing has been hurt in a most hideous way. I'd say he deserved it, but no one deserves what has been handed him. If you had given what took place after he arrived any thought, you would agree with me."

All Melissa had done was think about it. But the whole day had an unreal quality, as if it hadn't really happened or she had merely viewed it with exaggerated emotions. The brawl in the yard had been nothing more than a misunderstanding; the earl's words had not been nearly as vile as she remembered. Bruce's silence and odd behavior were nothing more than immersion in thought, or perhaps the same overwhelming awe she'd felt upon first sight of her son.

Little of what had happened made sense other than the earl had somehow used her to hurt Bruce. She shuddered at the hatred she'd heard in the earl's voice. Hatred for Bruce, and for her. Instead, she'd come to trust the earl in his understanding, pity him for what she'd perceived to be his loneliness, even grown fond of him and compared him to her father. How could she have been so wrong? Why had she not recalled the cruelty in his eyes and the scorn in his voice as he'd spoken of his son the first night she and her mother had met him? Why had she not given more credit to Bruce's manner toward him?

"Do you understand what happened, Mother?" she asked.

"You and I were duped. I was lonely and fell in love with the wrong man. You were confused and frightened and trusted the wrong man. Beyond that, I am not going to enlighten you. That is for Channing to do."

"He will do nothing but become a piece of furniture in that room if he does not come out soon," Nicole commented as she bustled through the door.

"Nicole, you are impertinent," Arabella scolded as she nuzzled the infant in her arms and allowed him to suck on her finger.

"*Oui, madame*," Nicole agreed without a trace of repentance. "Ben has asked when you are ready to leave. He has the pony cart ready."

"I will see to satisfying this child's appetite first, and then we will go. Cook will watch the baby until Ben returns with the wet nurse," Arabella said as she walked toward the door, then paused and turned. "Melissa, you have no doubt romanticized Channing. You certainly are not alone in that. The whole of society admires in him what they would condemn in any other man. Even the wisest of dowagers find him exciting and, I daresay, near to perfect." She reached for the latch. "I will caution you to remember that no one is perfect, least of all a man who has refined control of both himself and the world about him to an art." With that, Arabella swept from the room.

Melissa sank back on the pillows and knew she was cowering in the face of her mother's warning. Bruce was angry and wounded, her mother had said. Bruce, who never displayed temper, who disarmed his opponents with smiles and quips, and met adversity with calm logic and more smiles and quips.

*Control. He'd refined it to an art.* She'd failed to see that he would not have done so if the need did not exist. If a wounded animal did not lurk inside him, howling to escape. She'd heard it in his voice when he'd warned her not to run from him again, and in his silence afterward. She'd seen it in his blank expression as he'd stood in the doorway and stared at the cradle, stared anywhere but at her—not in awe or some overpowering feeling of love, but in anger held in check.

Anger at the earl. At her.

She'd known it and denied it, telling herself that she delayed speaking with Bruce because she wanted to sort everything out, to know why such horrible things had happened, why Bruce had not once ventured into her room since he'd carried her upstairs.

He'd been in the study for four days. . . .

Alone. . . .

Silent.

Reminding herself that he had come for her, fought to see her, held her while she'd given birth on the entryway floor, she managed to ease out of bed and gain her feet. She allowed herself to hope that it was a good sign, clinging to that hope until she could talk with him. She would go to him, she reasoned, and they would sort everything out together.

Her heart jumped into her throat and beat a frightened tattoo as other memories rose to bait her.

*Are you so willing to bring a bastard into the world?* he'd asked in the maze, and she'd had no answer for him.

*I won't again tell you I love you, Melissa. . . . I want you in my life, in my home, and in my bed. I want your trust and your devotion, and your children . . . consider carefully the consequences of our actions and come to a decision that will leave no casualties . . . the most likely candidate for injury will be an innocent child.*

He'd said it with emotion in his eyes but she'd been too full of her own fears to heed him. He'd said it gravely with not a sign of mockery, yet she had not taken him seriously. Instead she had accused him of tricking her.

*You cheated first.*

Nothing was as she'd perceived it to be.

In her usual cowardly fashion, she'd convinced herself that she should wait to speak to him until she could think clearly and remain awake for longer than it took to nurse her son. Yet, if she had not been thinking so much, she would have acted on instinct and run to him the moment she could stand without the room spinning beneath her feet.

She'd been quite successful in hiding from herself and Bruce, from the lurking fear that all had happened as she remembered.

But there was no place to run, no place to hide, no more excuses to do either one. No longer could she shove troubling thoughts aside, refusing to dwell upon what she did not yet comprehend. Bruce was downstairs, waiting, she knew, for her to come to him.

She took one step and then another, confirming that she did feel quite well if she did not count the pull of the stitches or the cramps that came and went in her abdomen, reminders that she had a child depending on her to make his world safe and happy. She had a life to live.

And suddenly, she had the urgent sense that she had only one opportunity to live it as she wished and with whom she wished. Bruce was a reasonable and good natured man. Everything would be all right.

It had to be.

Nicole gave her a sideways glance. "I have the confession, mademoiselle."

"Mother told me about the goat's milk, Nicole. It's all right." Melissa wobbled to the stand holding a porcelain basin and pitcher full of warm water.

"I ask Ben to bring your Bruce here," Nicole stated baldly. "I give him my papa's old pistol to make sure."

Melissa's heart dropped to her feet as the bar of soap she'd picked up plopped into the basin. "You sent Ben? With a gun? Bruce didn't come here on his own?"

"He come. The moment Ben tell him where you are and that you send him so many letters, he bring the coach for you to ride in and then he is not so patient inside and buy horses for him and Ben to ride. Ben say your Bruce pay too much and ride too fast." She slipped the pink nightgown—a Grecian style caught at the shoulders with wide, flat bows and tied beneath her breasts with a thin braided cord—over Melissa's head. "He did not receive the letters, mademoiselle. Ben believes him when he says this."

Melissa stared at the floor as if she could see Bruce through the boards. "None of them?" she whispered. "He knew nothing of what happened, why I came here?"

"None. Ben say he has been searching for you across the country and across the ocean." Holding the robe, she helped Melissa shrug into it. "He search first at the earl's places, but this one was not known to him. Ben say even dukes help to search."

Melissa's hands trembled as Nicole urged her into a chair at the makeshift dressing table and began to brush her hair. She clamped her teeth together to keep them from chattering with sudden cold. Bruce hadn't known anything until Ben went to him with a gun. All this time he'd searched for her and dukes had helped him. The Dukes of Westbrook and Bassett, of course. It had to be.

"He want very much to find you, mademoiselle. This Ben says."

Bruce had known before he arrived that the earl had helped her, that she had accepted his help. He'd been "not so patient inside." Inside, where no one could see.

*She ran from you . . . trusted me instead.*

Of course, Bruce was angry. Perhaps more than angry.

And though she'd always quailed at any display of temper, she thought she might welcome it from Bruce, for she'd discovered that nonsense was not so easily uttered and truths not so easily masked in the presence of anger.

She rose abruptly from the chair and walked to the door, opened it and made her way down the stairs, ignoring Nicole, ignoring everything but the need to see Bruce. She'd known that something was wrong, something she didn't understand. It was time she understood just how wrong.

# Chapter 24

**S**omething was very, very wrong.

Melissa knew it the moment she entered the study without knocking and quickly shut the door behind her before she could turn away and take refuge in her room. Her mouth was dry and her knees felt like pudding. She shivered at the utter silence and stillness of the man standing at the mantel with his back to her, his chin propped by his clenched fist, so isolated in the dark, as if he wanted nothing to touch his senses.

She stepped into the center of the room and bumped against a table. The drapes were drawn. Not a light burned. The grate in the fireplace was bare and cold.

Bruce stiffened, his back and shoulders rigid like armor against her.

"Bruce," she said softly.

He lit a candle and held it high as he turned, his gaze sweeping quickly over her, then fixing on a point over her shoulder. "You're feeling well?"

"Yes, thank you."

"Sit down."

She shook her head. "No . . . I would rather stand."

"As you wish," he said with a trace of sarcasm.

She stared at him, at a loss as to what to do, what to say.

He took a step toward her, keeping parallel to the mantel, an expression in his eyes she did not recognize. "Thinking of running?"

"I told you I would not."

Another step. "So you did."

She realized then that she didn't recognize his expression because he had none. His face was smooth, his eyes dark and flat with only the barest flicker of light reflecting from the candle, as if every emotion was banked. His knuckles were white as he lowered the candle holder onto the mantel and straightened again.

She moistened her lips with her tongue. "You said we had things to settle."

He smiled, a predator stalking her with politeness and a soft voice, waiting to spring the moment he came within reach of his prey. "I have already settled them. You have but to comply."

She knew then that she had again waited too long in her fear. That she'd had good reason to hide, that all the while her instincts had been warning her, aware of what she was not.

Her fear was justified. It stood before her now, tall and tense and cold with banked emotions. An angry man who had no practice in dealing with his own fury.

Bruce watched her from the corner of his eye, watched her lace her hands at her waist, watched her gaze dart around quickly in alarm.

He didn't care. Every part of him felt like brittle ice. His heart was a frozen lump in his chest. He only cared about surviving this meeting without cracking. Surviving Melissa without shattering.

"You didn't receive my letters," she said.

"No," he replied, and pointed to the desk, to a sheet of parchment lying there. "I found that in the earl's pocket. Read it."

He counted her footsteps as she walked to the desk, skirting him with room to spare. He counted each crackle of paper as she unfolded the note Smithy had slipped under her door in what seemed another lifetime. A fantasy. And then he counted the seconds while she read. Anything to keep his mind orderly, controlled.

Tamed.

"Yes," she said, her voice both firm and quavering at the same time.

He turned toward her, faced her fully for the first time since he'd met her gaze in the yard. He saw the pain in her face and knew it was too late to stem the thaw of emotion inside him, too late to detach himself from it, from her. "Yes?" He advanced on her, driven by a force he could not resist.

Not any longer. Not with her standing before him wearing both power and innocence. Not with such fear in her eyes. He could not stand the fear. Not when it wore his name.

She stared directly at him, unflinching, though her eyes were too wide and her hands trembled as she held up the letter he had written with hopes so high he'd been giddy with them. "As you said in the letter, yes rolls quite easily off the tongue."

"Just like that," he said as he approached her step

by slow, measured step. "After your refusals, after running away without trying to find out what had happened, after—" He paused just out of reach of her. "After what, Melissa? Did you think I abandoned you? That I'd had my fun and chose to move on to someone else? That I lied to you in the maze for my own amusement? Were all those sins added to the one to which I admitted?" He took another step. "A nasty sin, that. I cared for you and wanted to spend my life with you and acted out of desperation. For that I am the worst kind of wretch. A liar. Heartless and without conscience. A user of innocents."

She ran her tongue over her lips as she shook her head and backed away. "I never thought that."

"No?" He advanced on her again, backing her against the wall. "Liar. The only thing about me that you did trust was what fit so nicely into your body and gave you such pleasure. It's all you wanted of me."

She flinched and averted her gaze.

He grasped her chin and forced her to look at him. "Unfortunately, you got more than you bargained for. You got my bastard son."

She wrenched her chin from his grasp. "Don't . . . call him that."

"Why not? He is"—the words caught in his throat but he wrenched them free, tasting their bitterness—"a bastard. What did you plan to do with him, Melissa? Did the earl promise to provide for him as he provided everything else? Or were you going to leave him somewhere? An orphanage? A hired family in the country?"

"No! He is mine." She squeezed her eyes shut. "He is *ours*. I could never—"

"The choice is no longer yours to make. Bastard or not, he is *mine. I* will provide for him. *I* will raise him. *You* are free to do as you wish."

"I won't leave him. You can't take him from me."

"But I can. Or did you think I would turn my back on him? Is that on your list of my sins?"

"Bruce—"

"Be quiet." His control splintered, thawed into rage, flooding through him, threatening to drown him. He allowed it to spill out, releasing the pressure that had been building in him until he thought he would go mad with it. "I did not say I love you because you decreed it. I did not shout my feelings to the world because you feared your mother. I did not carry you off as I was tempted to do because you wanted to marry for love and I thought—*I thought*—you would believe me in time. *If* I displayed it rather than spoke of it." He slanted his mouth in a sneer. "Besotted fool that I was, I wanted to give you the trappings—a wedding in the finest church overflowing with guests. I trusted you to realize what I could not prove except through my actions. I waited for you to choose between my love and your fear."

"I did," she said so quietly he could barely hear her. "I went downstairs the next morning to tell you and you were gone."

He flattened his palm against the wall by her head. "And yet again, you believed the worst."

"I believed nothing. I was too ill then. Later, I believed that you had reason to leave. That I had been the fool, enjoying the game too much to end it, enjoying your pursuit of me and . . . and how special you made me feel. I had behaved like a silly schoolgirl and I believed that you wanted a woman."

"At last, you speak the truth," he snarled.

"Did you not enjoy the game also?" she asked, startling him with the attack, with the sudden uptilt of her chin and the steadiness of her voice. "Did you not speak of courting me? Was I so wrong to want to be courted?"

"Touché," he said, and pushed away from the wall, away from her, his fury increasing at her logic. He'd had enough of logic the past four days. It had betrayed him, failing to stand firm against his anger and then deserting him altogether, leaving him with nothing but blind emotion.

"Renovations at the abbey are almost finished," he said harshly. "I am taking my son there."

"When do we leave?"

"We?" It came out on a breath he hadn't known he held, shuddering with a relief he didn't want to feel.

"You said I am free to do as I wish. I wish to remain with *our* son."

"Very well. I still have the special license. We will be married en route." He glanced at her over his shoulder. "You understand that a public ceremony is out of the question."

She stepped away from the wall and approached him. "Bruce, I wanted to marry only for love. I wanted to marry you. For love. I could have done it with the knowledge that all you felt for me was lust and perhaps fondness." She swallowed and held her arms rigid at her sides as if she steeled herself against a blow. "But I cannot marry you, knowing you hate me." She turned her back to him, facing the door.

He grasped her arm, whirled her around and jerked her against his chest. "Hate?" He framed her face with his hands. "I wish I hated you." Lowering his head, he covered her mouth with his, plundering her, claiming her. "I want to hate you," he said, his lips a whisper away from hers. "But I can only hate what you did."

He tore away from her and returned to the mantel, his back to her, not wanting to see her as the words spilled out as rapidly as his anger. "It isn't logical when I know I am as much to blame as you are—perhaps more so. I knew the consequences. I risked it out of conceit. I risked it because I convinced myself that history would not repeat itself." He balled his fist and struck the mantel. "I was too complacent. It was one thing for me to be a by-blow with a legal name and title, and quite another to father a bastard who has neither." He struck the mantel again as his voice broke. "That is what I hate, Melissa."

"A bastard son for the bastard," she quoted. "I didn't understand it." She drew near to him, laid her hand on his arm. "I still don't understand."

"Then allow me to enlighten you." He shook her off and strode to the far end of the study, staring at windows that were covered, keeping the world out. "In short, Kathy and I are the by-blows of the late Duke of Bassett. In the eyes of the law, we are legitimate only because our sire had the wealth and power to ruin the earl and then blackmail him into marrying his mistress, our mother. We were conceived out of lust, born with the wrong name, and raised with hate." He heard Melissa gasp and ignored it. She would be shocked. And then, when she'd heard it all, she would turn away. Yet, still he continued, needing her to know. Needing the finality of it. "That is the reason for the earl's cruelties and his senseless quest for vengeance. Still, Kathy

and I have a legal name and a place in the world."
Dimly, he was aware that his shoulders heaved, that
his eyes burned. He blinked rapidly and forced himself to go on, to finish it. "A privilege I have ex-
ploited to make my own fortune so that while I
might keep the name I was born with, I would never
depend upon it. So that I could bloody well purchase
my own place in the world whether the world liked
it or not."

"You hate that, too," she said.

"I hate it," he admitted as the burning increased
behind his eyes. His head felt as if it would burst.
"I hate having to call Max friend rather than brother.
I hate that I play a role, deceiving everyone—deceiving you—because society values a man's name
rather than the man himself." He glanced at her over
his shoulder and smiled thinly at the tears streaming
down her face as she stood in the middle of the
room, her hands over her mouth, her face pale.
"Most of all, I hate knowing that my love and wealth
combined with all the power of Bassett and Westbrook will not protect him or give him a name. That
he will be held accountable for the sins of the two
generations that preceded him. I cannot protect him.
No one can." He didn't move as he waited for her
to walk away from him, hoping she would so that
he might hate her, too. "Ironically, our son is possessed of some of the bluest blood in all of England.
A pity it will not serve him as it has me."

"I'm sorry. So sorry," she said. "I didn't think—"

"No, well, neither of us thought, did we? And
now our son will pay."

"He will survive, as many such children have survived. As you and your sister have survived. He will

be loved by both of his parents, and he will have a home." She reached out, then lowered her arms. "But I can see that it won't be enough for you. That perhaps he is less a victim than you are."

He spun around, feeling as if he'd been struck. "I have made it a point not to be a victim."

"But you are, and our son will see it one day, and he will believe he is the cause." She swiped at her eyes and fixed him with a determined glare. "I will not have it, Bruce. I cannot change what you have been through, but I can see to it that our son does not suffer for it."

"I wait with bated breath to hear how you will accomplish such a feat," he said bitterly, resenting the innocence and idealism that allowed her to hope.

Uncertainty crossed her features. Her glare faltered, yet she stood firm. "I . . . I don't know how. But there must be a way. . . ." Her voice trailed off as she lowered her head to stare at the floor. "I'll find a way."

He laughed then, a hollow sound that reverberated in his head. "There's a way," he said viciously. "Undo it, Melissa. Make my son not a bastard."

She paled and backed away. "How?"

"I don't know bloody how!" he shouted as his head throbbed and his chest tightened. "Now get out." He struggled to soften his tone, to hold on to some shred of composure. "For God's sake, Melissa, leave me with some pride."

Her mouth worked as she continued to stare at him, shaking her head.

He stared back, willing himself to freeze again, to feel nothing, to acknowledge nothing. "I'll give you a choice. Take your son and leave now. Or remain and give power over him and yourself to me. You have until the count of five."

She whirled and ran, colliding with the door, struggling with the latch, then jerking it open and disappearing into the entry.

As the door slammed behind her, Bruce picked up a small table and crashed it against the wall. She had made her choice. It was over.

He sank into a chair, his hands dangling between his knees, his head bent. His shoulders heaved and heaved again.

The wail of a helpless infant filled the air and mingled with the strangled sobs of his father.

# Chapter 25

⟨∼⟩◡◡⟨∼⟩

**S**omeone stood in the threshold of the sitting room, yet Melissa paid no attention as she halted just outside the door, paralyzed by the crash of porcelain and wood. She turned and gripped the latch handle, but it wouldn't turn. "Bruce!" she cried and pounded on the door, then stilled as she heard it. A deep, wrenching sound so tortured, it seemed almost inhuman. "Let me in," she whispered, knowing he wouldn't even if she had shouted. Knowing that the sound she heard was because he had already opened himself to her more than to anyone else.

A small hand grasped her wrist and eased her fingers from the door handle. "Let him be, Melissa. It is time Bruce stopped fooling himself along with the rest of the world."

Melissa swept the hair from her face and held it as she looked up and focused on a woman she had never seen before. A woman with rich auburn hair and sapphire eyes.

Kathy, Duchess of Westbrook, and Bruce's sister.

"He'll be fine, Melissa, truly," Kathy said as she led Melissa into the sitting room and urged her into a chair. "I've waited a long time for my brother to face the truth rather than treat it as some cosmic joke. I am Kathy, by the way. I believe you know Jillian and Max and Damien."

"I believe she knows a great deal more," Max, Duke of Bassett, said dryly. "Hello, Lady Melissa."

"Lady Melissa." Damien, Duke of Westbrook, bowed over her hand. "You've given us all a nasty scare."

"We came as soon as we received Bruce's message that he had discovered your whereabouts," Jillian added.

"Your Grace . . . s," Melissa said, dazed by the ease and familiarity with which they treated her, and a bit hysterical at the awkwardness of trying to address two dukes and their duchesses at the same time. "I didn't hear you arrive."

"You hear that?" Kathy said. "Already she is part of the family. She called us 'Your Graces,' which of course is far easier than repeating 'Your Grace' four times."

"What?" Melissa said, confused.

"Never mind, Melissa. We are all a bit addled from too little sleep and too much traveling," Jillian said. "And you didn't hear us because Smithy met us in the yard and let us in. As to the rest, we *are* family, or about to be, so to you we are simply Jillian, Kathy, Max, and Damien . . ." She leaned over to study Melissa's face. "You are quite done in."

"Of course she's done in. She has just recently given birth, and after what Smithy told us about it, I am amazed you are on your feet at all," Kathy said. "I hope you don't mind, but I found Cook and ordered tea to be served early. We are all famished."

"Of course." Melissa lurched out of the chair, feeling dizzy from the onslaught, and desperate to find some silence. "I really must go."

"Go?" Kathy stepped in front of the doorway. "Surely you didn't take those ridiculous choices Bruce gave you seriously?"

"You heard?"

"We couldn't help but hear," Max said as he gently pushed her back into the chair and took a place standing beside her. "The inside walls of this place are thin as paper, and Bruce, being Bruce, would make a good show of losing his temper even if he hadn't intended it. It's ingrained, you see."

Damien's jaw clenched and his eyes hardened as he flanked her other side. "Speaking of temper, I understand the earl is locked in the cellar."

"Ease off, Damien," Max said. "Blackwood will keep until we get around to him."

"I think we should forget about him entirely and leave him to rot," Jillian stated from the settee directly across from Melissa.

Suddenly exhausted by the banter that Bruce's relatives exchanged so easily, Melissa leaned back in the chair. She stared at each in turn, feeling hemmed in by them, nonplussed by the way they had moved as if orchestrated to keep her from escaping them.

Bruce's relatives. A family so close they were attuned to one another, overlapping their sentences and adding a bit more to the conversation on each go around. A family that en masse, dropped whatever they were doing to rush to the aid of one of their own. She'd always wondered what it would be like to be part of a large family, but then she'd decide that the frenzy would drive her mad. She'd been wrong. She felt comforted, protected. Not lonely.

She focused on Max and wondered why she hadn't noted the resemblance between him and Bruce before. She'd certainly seen him with Bruce enough times during her three Seasons. But, then apparently, no one else in the ton had seen it either. It might be Max's tawny mane compared to Bruce's chestnut hair that threw everyone off. Or perhaps Max's more serious mien in contrast to Bruce's mischievous one.

"Are you planning to leave, Melissa?" Jillian asked softly.

Melissa frowned as she realized she'd been inching forward in her chair, preparing to escape. "I ... no. I was just going to my room. I need to think," she blurted. "I have to find a way to help Bruce."

"And yourself," Kathy added.

"It's one and the same," Max observed. "We all know how much Bruce loves you."

Jillian leaned forward. "Do you know, Melissa?"

"I—" Did she know? Melissa wondered.

"Of course she must," Kathy replied, saving Melissa from answering. "The evidence is wallowing in his own guilt as we speak." She nodded toward the study.

"Why must she know?" Damien asked.

*Because he had risked everything to persuade her to marry him,* Melissa said in the privacy of her own mind. Because he searched the world for her and then held her against him on the floor, sharing in the birth of their son. Because he had shared his dark secret with her, then thrown furniture against the wall and wept after she'd run from him ... again. Because he'd wanted to marry her even though it could not help their son, and then he'd given her a choice, regardless of what he wanted. She knew he loved her, believed it, and the realization was as simple and inexplicable as a single word.

*Because . . .*

"She didn't believe him," Max cut in. "A result of her hearing him say it to other women."

Allowing the conversation to wash over her, Melissa lowered her gaze and willed herself to concentrate on doing something—anything—to make things right. She wanted Bruce to be as he was—a man who enjoyed life and had no place in his world for bitterness and anger. A man who smiled readily and saw the absurd side of every situation.

". . . should have carried her off and married her before she had a chance to say no."

"Damien!" Kathy scolded. "Just because it worked for us—"

Melissa blinked. "Hush," she blurted as she scooted to the edge of her seat, barely aware of the sudden silence. "Please forgive me, but I must think." She lowered her head and closed her eyes as an idea took root and flowered. An insane idea she had no hope of carrying out. A wonderful idea that she had to carry out. She pushed her hair away from her face and lifted her gaze. "Your Grace—Damien—how far is Gretna Green?"

"A day's journey if you keep at it. Why?"

She met each bemused gaze in turn. "Can you keep Bruce here for two days? I don't care how. Lock him in with the earl and let them thrash it out if you must. Just keep him here." She rose from the chair and paced the short distance between the hearth and the window opposite, knowing four pairs of eyes followed her progress.

"You can't mean what I think you mean," Kathy said. "Melissa, you are barely out of confinement."

"What is it Melissa can't do?" Arabella asked as

she strode into the room, one glove off and one on, her cloak still about her shoulders.

"I'll require funds," Melissa said, ignoring them all. "Quite a lot of funds, I should imagine." She reached for her mother's reticule and peered inside. "Not nearly enough. I understand that bribes are costly." She glanced around at the gazes seeming to watch her in awe. "They are, aren't they?"

"Good God, she's serious," Max said and rubbed his hand down his face.

"You've made up your mind then," Arabella stated flatly. "You're quite set on having Channing, wretch that he is."

"I love him, Mother, just as you loved Father."

Arabella nodded. "I'll find something for you to wear." She passed a critical eye over Melissa. "Something loose but flattering. Your figure is still rather like a pillow with half its stuffing gone. You'll need to look your best if you are going to indulge in bribery." She halted in the entry hall. "Where are you going, by the way?"

"Gretna Green," Damien said. "And Max and I are going with her."

"No," Melissa cried. "No," she repeated more quietly. "I must do this myself, and if you go you will take over and do it for me."

"She has you there," Kathy murmured.

Arabella shook her head. "I had hoped you would take after me, but obviously you have inherited your father's whimsical and impulsive nature. He didn't often indulge himself but when he did, all I could do was help or be left behind." With that, she climbed the stairs, discarding her cloak and bonnet and laying them over the banister.

"You can't go alone," Jillian protested.

"This from a woman who tricked me into marriage, using both fair means and foul," Max commented idly.

"I'll go with her," Kathy said. "Someone must and I want this whole business settled so I can return to my babies."

"I'll go, too," Jillian said.

"No one is going with me," Melissa shouted, startling herself. "Except Nicole and Ben. They can marry while we're at it." She paused on her way to the door. "Oh! My baby."

"He'll be fine and utterly spoiled by the time you return," Jillian said with an edge of resignation. "Kathy and I have both left infants behind, so we will be quite happy to cuddle yours, not to mention the wet nurse who arrived just behind us."

Melissa smiled at the four people who did indeed seem like family, though she barely knew them. "What did you have?"

"Twins—a boy and a girl," Kathy said.

"Another boy," Jillian said at the same time.

"I'm very happy for you," Melissa said.

Max pressed a leather pouch in her hand. "Funds—quite a lot of them. Just do the thing right and tight so we can be happy for you."

Melissa rushed through getting into a gown, afraid that once reaction set in, she would turn coward and lock herself in her room. She took more time with her son, begging his forgiveness for leaving him and promising to give him a proper name as soon as she returned. Assured that the wet nurse was competent and could satisfy the infant's appetite, she looked in on her mother, who was lying down with a cold cloth over her eyes, and asked her not to worry.

"Would it do me any good?" Arabella asked with an aggrieved sigh. "Just get this done so I can return to civilization."

It occurred to Melissa that her mother might actually be enjoying the whole thing. It was, after all, reminiscent of her father's rare but flamboyant attacks of whimsy, and it took responsibility out of her mother's hands. Melissa thought it must be a terrible strain for her mother to keep up appearances. Perhaps she needed an occasional excuse to relinquish control and simply drift with an erratic tide.

Winter chill slapped her in the face as she left the lodge. The sight before her stunned her into abruptly halting. Not one but two grand coaches stood side by side, each bearing ducal crests. The one bearing the Bassett lion had an equally grand and freshly groomed sextet of horses hitched to the traces. Ben sat atop the driver's box.

To the side, Bruce's coach stood with a wheel half on, half off, evidence of his race to reach her once he'd learned of her location.

Smithy stepped in front of her, a pistol in his belt and a small cudgel in his hand. He cleared his throat. "I'll be going with you. Ben is a mite young and has more experience making cakes than protecting ladies."

"Are you familiar with Gretna Green, Mr. Smithy?"

"I was with His Grace and Lady Kathy when they eloped. If you're about doing what I think, I know just the place." He belatedly doffed his worn cap, and again cleared his throat. "I care about him, too, and don't want to see him hurt any more than he already has been. I'll be getting you back safe and sound for him."

"Is that a warning, Mr. Smithy?" she asked, touched by the concept.

"I'll let you know," he said gruffly as he handed her into the coach.

She sat down and waited until he'd helped Nicole inside as well. "Your company will be most welcome," she said softly. "Thank you."

The coach jerked as he climbed into the box beside Ben, then lurched forward.

Melissa arranged her skirts and the bulk of her heavy woolen cloak and sat back, her heart thumping in tune with the pace of the horses. She breathed deeply, waiting for doubts and trepidation to take hold. But, rather than her usual cowardice and anxiety creeping in and dragging her down, excitement and anticipation gave her a sense of floating just above her seat, bouncing with the ruts in the road. She had come up with an idea. Her mother had not tried to browbeat her into being sensible and proper. She was actually doing something to influence the course of her life.

Right or wrong it was a good feeling.

# Chapter 26

**B**ruce parted the drapes just as Melissa entered the coach, watching as it lumbered away, out of sight. Max, damn him, had provided the means for her flight. Smithy, damn him, had gone with her, doubtless thinking she required an able escort.

Smithy was right. She would be safe with him. Ben was a good lad but more inclined to wrestling with pastry dough than opponents.

Bruce hadn't thought she would go. Not so soon. He'd thought he'd have another chance, after he gained control of himself, after he worked out what to say to her to convince her he loved her. But nothing had come to him, neither witty nor profound.

And now she had left.

In spite of the choices he'd given Melissa, and vowed to honor, his first instinct was to snare the nearest horse and ride after her. His second was to, for once, do the honorable thing where she was concerned and let her go.

He didn't know how he would live without her, let alone ignore the existence of his son.

He swiped his hand across the back of his neck. It seemed he didn't know much of anything. For months, he'd tried to make sense of it all. For months, he'd failed. He was still failing.

"Kathy is right. He is wallowing in his own misery." Max strolled in carrying a bottle of brandy.

"Languishing to his eyeballs in muck," Damien said as he followed Max inside with three snifters in his hand. "A pity how a woman influences the location of a man's brain."

"Bassett blood always did have more nobility than sense," Max said.

"How did you get in here?" Bruce asked wearily.

"I should think that was obvious," Damien replied.

"We found the master set of keys," Max said. "It's dashed insulting to be locked out of the only room fit for a man in the place. Hunting lodge." He snorted. "Not with lace curtains in the bedchambers and flowered coverings on the walls. Give me bare stone and hunting scenes any day."

"Before you gentlemen set your back teeth awash," Arabella said as she brushed past Damien and Max, "I have collected something for Channing in the village." She shoved a thick packet of letters at Bruce. "It appears that the entire population of that miserable place was in Robert's employ. These were confiscated the moment Melissa or Nicole dropped them off for the mail coach. I find it quite disgusting that the citizens have no compunction when it comes to withholding letters from the mail coach, yet keep those same letters unopened out of respect for a body's privacy."

Bruce stared down at the packet of single sheet letters, neatly folded and sealed with wafers. "Why?"

"Why am I giving these to you?" Arabella raised

her chin and took a deep breath as if girding herself for something unpleasant. "I love my daughter and she would want you to have them, though only God and Melissa know why at this point. Also, that child upstairs needs a father. I am resigned to tolerating you for his sake—"

Bruce lifted his gaze to Arabella. "My son is upstairs?" he said hoarsely. "Melissa left without him?"

"No, Lord Channing, she did not leave without him. She left him in our care until he is old enough to travel."

Max loudly cleared his throat.

Arabella sighed. "It isn't as if he won't know an infant is under this roof. Like his father, the child is adept at making his presence known. And if you had any sense, Channing, you'd know that Melissa had to go away." She patted her hair. "I suggest you read those and consider your behavior of this afternoon." She cast a disdainful glance at the rubble of porcelain and wood littering a corner. "It is not good for a child to be exposed to violence. You startled him so he screamed in fright for a full ten minutes." Her nose high enough to scrape the ceiling, she executed an exit every bit as grand as her entrances.

"Who would have credited it?" Damien mused.

"The ice-breathing dragon has a soft underbelly," Max said.

"It comes from having an infant around," Damien said as if his recent fatherhood had added sage to his wisdom.

"No doubt," Max said with his usual dryness. "Though I suspect Melissa is not the mouse she is thought to be and had a hand in it."

Damien groaned. "I just had a ghastly thought. Do

you realize that Arabella is now bound to our family by blood?"

"Melissa is returning for the child?" Bruce said.

"Well, it's hard to say. She might come herself, or she might not. Depends on what she comes up with while she's away."

"I came in here to drink and relive my days of youth and freedom," Damien grumbled.

"Shall we make a toast to that effect?" Max poured brandy into each glass as Damien set them down on the desk.

Absently, Bruce took his glass as he scowled at the packet of letters.

"Aren't you going to read those?" Damien asked.

"No." Bruce pushed them aside. He didn't need to read them. Everything had been said. She had tried to reach him. He needed no tangible proof that she had not deceived him. In any case, it mattered little.

"You might like to know that Blackwood has been dispatched," Max commented idly. "The only way he'll return to England is in a pine box."

"Where?" Bruce asked, though he didn't really give a bloody damn. The earl had his revenge.

"New South Wales and beyond," Max said. "Some sort of titular governorship, I believe."

"An offer he could not refuse, coming from the palace as it did," Damien said. "Seems someone in a high place won some very valuable pots and elected to make a trade—an exchange of favors, so to speak."

"What did you win and throw away, Max?" Bruce asked, knowing that his half brother's delay in getting to Northumberland involved a deliberate wager with said "valuable pots."

Max shrugged. "A few properties, a shipping venture, some railroad stock. Nothing I didn't already have in abundance."

"Well, it appears you have taken care of everything."

"Not quite everything," Max said pointedly. "We've left some of it for you."

Bruce tossed back his brandy in one gulp, feeling the fire in his gut and the jolt in his brain. "I'll draw up papers giving Melissa property and lifetime allowance and the same for my . . . son."

"Max wasn't speaking about Melissa and the boy," Damien said, and poured another measure in his glass. "What are *you* going to do?"

What indeed? Bruce wondered as he fitted his mask into place and gave Damien and Max a mocking smile. "Finish the abbey, then watch it rot again."

Damien shook his head. "Jillie was right. He's gone soft on us."

"Lost his taste for adventure," Max said.

"And challenges. Without him, they'll all pile up in various corners with no one to meet them."

"A lost cause," Max murmured. "Let the biggest challenge of all get away."

"Well," Damien said as he rose from his chair. "Nothing to do here but watch him *rot*. I'll find warmer company with the ladies."

Bruce let them go as the anger he'd thought expended began to heat again.

It continued to scorch him as one day gave way to another. And yet another. He rode with Max and Damien, discussed the merits—or lack thereof—of having a hunting lodge in the middle of nowhere and speculated that it had been built as a love nest by some henpecked sod who wanted to conduct his affair as far as possible from his wife. He shared meals with his family, bantered and exchanged gossip with them, and realized he was trying too hard to be himself.

Nothing was said about Melissa, even when his son was brought to him and sucked on his finger while he tried even harder not to feel like the odd man out.

And when he became too maudlin, he retired alone to the study and stared out the window . . . at the stable . . . the road, his son still in his arms.

Anything to hold himself in check, to keep the anger that so persistently simmered under a tight lid of control. Anger at Melissa. At himself. Anger that had no excuse for itself, a parasite that sapped men of decency and humanity. They were sentiments others sneered at, but Bruce had lived by them, and as a result, was able to live with himself.

Heaven help him, but he was turning into a pompous ass, he thought as he stood by the window, watching the moon arc in a winter gray sky. "Snow is coming," he murmured to his son. "Surely she has the sense to find a suitable shelter." He reminded himself that Smithy had gone with Melissa.

The infant began to fret. Bruce pulled a fresh napkin from his pocket and laid his son on the desk to change him. "Your mother has a great deal more courage than I to brave such appalling roads and hideous weather," he said in the steady cadence that never failed to soothe the babe. "I shouldn't have let her go, you know." He folded the napkin and slipped it beneath a tiny bottom before removing the damp one. "To tell the truth, I didn't think she would. I prayed she wouldn't." He sucked in a breath and held it as he opened the napkin just in case it held more than liquid. It didn't. "That's the trouble with honor. It's a trap, and once you fall in you're done for. I always avoided women like Melissa for that reason. They're too fond of concepts such as chivalry and romance and 'Death before dishonor.' "

And fools such as he were all too eager to please. It was why he'd made it a point to speak words of love to his paramours. To give them—for a few moments, at least—what they did not have from their husbands. And look where it had gotten him. The one time he'd delivered them from his heart, he'd been accused of lying. He, of all people, should have remembered the power wielded by words.

Still, Melissa could have given him the benefit of the doubt.

That, too, added heat to his anger.

He'd been damned if he did and damned if he didn't.

"Bruce, I've had quite enough of this," Kathy said with her usual tact as she stormed into the room. "You cannot live without Melissa."

"Of course I can," he replied as he secured the napkin and pulled the baby's gown over bowed legs that were filling out nicely.

"All right. You don't want to live without her. Try to argue with that."

"I wouldn't dream of it."

"You've given up, Bruce."

"I never continue a lost battle. What is the point?"

"Battles such as this are never lost until one surrenders."

"Who said that?"

"You did." She scooped up her nephew and cradled him close. "Blast it, Bruce, I miss my children. I want to go home."

"Then do so."

"You know I can't." She met his gaze with tears shimmering in her eyes. "It's too much like Mama, Bruce. She gave up after the duke died. She wasted away because she was afraid to be alone. I see that fear in you when we're all together and you sit apart and hold your son close. You may think you can live without Melissa, but I know how hard it is to face life without the one you love. Mama *couldn't* face it, and you don't even try." She leaned her head to the side and raised her shoulder to catch her tears. "I wish . . . I wish Mama had felt anger rather than resignation, Bruce. With all the children—Jillie and Max's and mine and Damien's and now yours—she missed so much joy by giving up. So much *life*."

Every word she uttered was tinder tossed on the fire, burning him. He wrapped her in his arms, his sister and his son, holding them, sharing the grief he had never shared with anyone. Grief for his mother. For himself.

"I've been waiting for your anger to come back," Kathy whispered. "I see you fighting it as if it were a demon, and it's not. Sometimes we lack the courage to do what must be done, to say what must be said. Anger can hurt, but it can also make us honest when we would deceive ourselves. It doesn't have to destroy."

The baby began to fuss in earnest. "You see, he is angry. It's how we know he is hungry or in need." Kathy held him closer still, soothing him with incoherent sentences, then looked up at Bruce. "He hasn't a name yet."

The simmer bubbled higher and hotter, scorching him. "I know," he said baldly.

"I mean a Christian name. When is someone going to give him something to take pride in? Are you so busy trampling your own pride that you care nothing for his?"

It was the final stick on the flame. "Take him to his nurse, Kathy. And have one of Max's or Damien's footmen saddle a horse."

Seemingly intent on leafing through a book, Jillian strolled in, halted and grinned. "Oh, good. He's vexed again. I was beginning to think he'd given up."

"I . . . have . . . not . . . given . . . up," he said, enunciating each word, goading himself into believing it and acting upon it.

He didn't bother to change or to collect provisions. He just strode out to the stables and mounted the horse waiting for him. Odd that, when there hadn't been time to issue orders.

"It's about time," Max said as he appeared in the stable door.

"Shut up, Max."

"Where are you going?"

Bruce frowned and cursed. "I don't bloody know, but I'm going just the same."

"She went west and up into Scotland. I doubt she'd make good time in that behemoth I use for transport. Add the weather and her . . . rather tender condition, and you should find her easily enough."

Max was still rambling as Bruce spurred his mount and cantered down the road, maintaining a steady stream of thoughts to fuel his anger. He'd played the coward long enough.

Languishing in muck. Rotting. Given up. Trampling his own pride.

Melissa was heading for Scotland, of all places. To find a place to live in relative obscurity? Alone with his son?

Over his dead body.

# Chapter 27

**B**ruce's life flashed before his eyes as a coach lumbered toward him from a turn in the road only minutes after he left the lodge. His horse reared and squealed and sidestepped, nearly unseating him in the path of the wheels.

Smithy and Ben put their combined weight into reining in the team.

Bruce leaned over and caught the harness of the lead horse. The coach groaned to a halt.

*"Mon Dieu,* Ben!" Nicole exclaimed as she threw open the door. "I would like the honeymoon before I die." She looked up. "Oh, my Lord. You have scared my wits. Do you not look where you are going?"

*Honeymoon?* Melissa had gone on a jaunt to Scotland so her maid could get married? He blinked and frowned trying to make sense of it. He was off to track Melissa down and the coach was returning. If Melissa knew what was good for her, she would be inside said coach.

"Nicole," Ben said with a skittish glance at Bruce, "you can't talk to him like that."

Nicole shrugged. "I think it is too late. I have said it and he has heard."

"Where is she?" Bruce said in a grating voice.

"I'm here, Bruce," Melissa called from inside the coach.

He directed his horse toward the open door and peered inside. Relief swept all else aside. He studied her color and found it the usual roses and cream and velvet textures. Her eyes were clear, though seductively drowsy as she tilted her head and gave him a little smile.

He wanted to kiss that smile. Thoroughly.

Melissa lay on the seat, swaddled in cushions and blankets, her hair in disarray, her skirt hitched up to reveal a pretty leg.

His body stirred and awakened and began to rise against his trousers. He wanted to crawl inside with her, press her into the cushions with his weight—

But she had given birth a bare week ago and he was supposed to be furious with her. A fury that felt good rather than troubling. A fury that would not destroy.

"What have you been doing?" he demanded.

"Sleeping, for the most part."

"Sleeping," he said flatly. "Are you ill?"

"No. I was just so weary after we left." She propped herself up on her elbows and struggled to break free of the padding surrounding her. "I feel quite well, except for these dratted stitches."

*Chitchat*, he thought in disgust. They were making idle chitchat in the middle of the road, where they had almost ended up a tangled mass of cattle and bodies. Leaning over, he scooped Melissa up, scowled, and lowered her to the ground. It wasn't likely she could ride with him even the few hundred yards to the lodge. Stitches—*there*, of all places.

He dismounted and slapped the horse's rump to send him back to the stables, then grabbed Melissa and crushed her to his chest, the front of his great-coat wrapped around her, enclosing them in a co-coon of warmth. "Don't you *ever* do that to me again." He cupped the back of her head and covered her mouth with his in a hard, fast kiss. "Do you hear me?" he said against her cheek. "Never again." He plunged his tongue into her mouth, ravishing it, claiming Melissa once and for all. "Please," he choked out, "don't leave me again."

The door opened, spilling light into the yard. One by one, the entire family trooped outside in various states of dress. Arabella brought up the rear with her hair curled around strips of rags.

Bruce tore away from Melissa and grimaced as frigid air froze the twin spots of moisture on the front of his shirt. He glanced at the front of her gown and saw larger spots on her bodice. *Mother's milk,* he realized. She was leaking. Closing the edges of her cloak, he grasped her hand to tug her toward the house.

"What are you doing?" Melissa asked, looking flushed and dazed and completely mussed from head to foot. She was breathtaking with her gold hair wild around her face and her gown wrinkled beneath her cloak and her bare toes peeking out from her hem.

She was barefoot—such a natural state for her he hadn't noticed.

"I am taking you into the house where you will bloody well remain until we get married," he barked, remembering that he was annoyed with her for a multitude of reasons that made no sense, excepting his persistent erection, which made perfect sense.

She stopped dead, bringing him up short a step ahead of her.

"What now?" he asked impatiently as he turned around.

"Nicole, my reticule," she called, halfway between him and the coach.

Nicole popped her head into the coach, then back out again and ran to Melissa with the small bag and a pair of shoes.

Bruce grabbed the shoes and bent down to slip them on Melissa's feet. Melissa tore open the bag and rummaged for a packet of papers that couldn't have been difficult to find in such a small space. Dropping the bag, she pressed the packet to her waist and smoothed it out with her hands.

"Melissa," he warned. "In the house. Now."

She marched up to him and winced as she stumbled over a pebble.

"You did say 'until we can be married,' didn't you?" she asked evenly.

"I did," he replied tersely. "No choices, Melissa. Not anymore."

"Well, it's too late," she snapped as she thrust the papers at his chest and marched on with a hobbling gait.

He caught the papers and then caught her in one long stride. "You have no reason to refuse me, damnit! None! You—"

"I've already married you," she shouted back, and poked him in the chest, where he still held the packet. "You're the one with no choice in the matter. It's done and I'll have no arguments about it. And if you would stop bellowing for a moment and read those papers, you might realize that I did not leave you." She paused for breath. "It seems," she said in a heartbreakingly soft voice, "that no matter how hard I try to do otherwise, the only place I can run is toward you, Bruce."

He swallowed and blinked and quickly bent his head to blindly stare at the packet. His hands shook as he opened the oilskin and unfolded a sheet of paper and read.

It was a certificate of marriage. . . .

His hands shook harder and air was difficult to come by.

It was dated five months before, and signed by a Mr. Isdale in Gretna Green.

"I undid it as you requested," Melissa said smartly. "Your son is *not* a bastard. His name is Edward Maxwell Smith Palmerston. *My* name is Lady Melissa Belle Lucinda Palmerston, Viscountess Channing, whether you like it or not. I spent an inordinate amount of energy, time and money to make it so. And if you hadn't been so busy . . . *anguishing*, you would have no doubt thought of this yourself." Her mouth seemed suspended in the open position, as if she wanted to say more yet didn't know what, then snapped shut.

"Anguishing?" he said for lack of anything coherent.

"You know what I meant," she said with chattering teeth, and propped one foot on top of the other.

He stuffed the paper inside his coat and swept her up into his arms, his gaze never leaving her face, fascinated by the sparks of defiance in her eyes. "You attended our wedding without me," he accused.

"It was a neat trick," she replied, "and of course

it lacked something. . . ." Her voice trailed off as defiance turned to concern. "It is all perfectly legal, Bruce, if you don't count the three hundred pounds I paid to bribe Mr. Isdale."

"Three hundred pounds! It only cost Damien and Kathy ninety." He sighed and smiled down at her. "Am I worth so much to you?"

She caressed his cheek with the backs of her fingers. "More," she whispered for only him to hear. "You are worth so very much more."

He paused to kiss her with gentle strokes of his mouth over and over again. "I love you, Melissa."

She swallowed the words with her mouth, then pressed her fingers to his lips. "You needn't say it, Bruce. They are only words. Your actions are far more eloquent."

"For heaven's sake, Bruce," Kathy called. "It's freezing out here. Can't you do that inside?"

With a mocking smile, he rolled his eyes. "You married them, too, you know."

"I know," she said as she laid her head on his shoulder. "Brothers and sisters and an assortment of nieces and nephews. A large family."

"You don't like crowds," he reminded her. "And we're a thoroughly unconventional and unruly lot. Can you bear it?"

"For a lifetime," she said.

The spectators gathered in front of the door parted as Bruce carried her inside, looking at Melissa, only Melissa.

For a lifetime.

# Epilogue

**P**eace.

It was the early mornings Melissa and Bruce shared in one another's arms as dawn peeked over the horizon beyond the abbey, silent, yet shaded with color and life. It was the distant roar of the sea and the rolling meadows dotted with Bruce's sheep and cattle and horses. And it was knowledge that being alone was now a choice rather than an irrefutable fact.

And perhaps it was a bit too complete at the moment.

Alarmed, Melissa waddled down the long roofed terrace opening into the gardens with a series of stone archways, seeking the activity that should be reaching its zenith this time of the afternoon. Impatient with her increasing girth, she leaned against an arch and pressed her hand to the stitch in her side. "Bruce," she called. "Where are you?"

"Hush." His voice drifted to her from a miniature castle set among hedges and beds of pansies.

She approached the whimsy—though some called it a folly—that Bruce had built for their children to play in. Long legs stretched out from the drawbridge. A giggle followed by another came from the courtyard inside the walls. She leaned over the stone and peered inside.

Bruce lay on his back in his shirtsleeves and doeskins, a two-year-old boy sleeping soundly on his chest and a paper crown tilted over his eyes.

Two pair of eyes—belonging to Kathy's twins—stared out at her from the tower. Another two pair—unmistakably Jillian's boys—waved from around the corner. "Hello, Auntie 'Lissa," they piped in loud whispers. "We are Uncle Bruce's prisoners and we must be quiet to get out."

"It's time to wash for tea," Jillian called as she strolled in from the rose garden, followed by Max carrying their third child—a daughter this time—on his shoulders.

"Where is everyone?" Damien asked as he and Kathy returned from the meadow, matching daisy rings on their heads. Damien carried a willow basket where an infant slept with his thumb in his mouth. "Oh, there you are."

The boy on Bruce's chest stirred and rubbed his eyes, so much like his father's.

"Melissa, darling. Tea will be in half an hour," Arabella said as she and LadyLou, Jillian's and Damien's aunt, arrived from the direction of the kitchens. No doubt, Melissa's mother had been trying to supervise Ben's preparation of the twins' birthday cake while LadyLou had been trying to pry her away. "And where is Nicole?" Arabella fretted. "That girl has gone empty in the attic since her fourth month. You'd think she was the only woman on earth to carry a child."

"I sent her for a nap, Mother."

"Well, I trust she is sufficiently rested by now."

Arabella glanced around, counting heads under her breath. "At least the children are all in one place. For once we won't have to comb the grounds searching for them all."

"I told Ben we would have the p-a-r-t-y out here," Bruce said as he set his son aside and sat up, his legs still extending across the drawbridge, the paper crown toppling from his head as it jutted above the castle walls, built low enough for children to climb over.

"Out here?" Arabella sputtered. "But no one is washed and you, sir, are in your shirtsleeves."

LadyLou sucked in her cheeks.

Damien stared at the sky.

Max and Jillian suddenly appeared fascinated by a particular pansy.

Kathy glared at Arabella and opened her mouth, obviously intent on burning the countess's delicate ears.

"Arabella," Bruce said mildly, cutting his sister off and placing the crown back atop his head. "In case you hadn't noticed, I am a king and this is my castle. If I decree that we will have the twins' party out here, then we shall do so."

"My party, Papa," Edward squealed in glee as he clapped his hands.

"Now see what you've done," Bruce said without heat. "No, Edward, a birthday party for your cousins." He glanced up at Melissa. "Where is Smithy?"

"Collecting the p-o-n-y he purchased for our offspring."

"A what?" several voices said in unison.

"You heard me," Melissa said with a grin. "Smithy insists that you had one at that age and *he* will be the one to provide his namesake with his first mount. It was Max's fault, since he had presented the twins with theirs this morning."

A procession of footmen, led by Ben bearing a large cake and Nicole bearing a large belly, arrived carrying tables, chairs, trays of all manner of food and pastry and pitchers of water and milk for the children and wine for the adults.

Damien immediately began to organize the children and oversee the footmen. Max fixed his eldest son with a stony glare as Alexander argued with his uncle.

Bruce disengaged himself from the castle with a series of contortions and arched his back.

Melissa stood out of the way, observing the three men who were so close they often thought alike, yet behaved so very differently. Damien erupted and ran over a problem with impatience. Max glowered a problem into submission. Bruce convinced the problem that it was not a problem at all.

She studied Kathy and Jillian and drew similar comparisons. Like Bruce, Jillian was driven by her instincts, always following them with good reason and better intentions. Kathy was like Max, circling her instincts with wariness as if they might jump out and attack her. Melissa tried to sum up herself and decided that she was like none of them in her habit of patiently hoarding her instincts, taking them apart for examination before choosing the proper time to follow them. Yet, as different as she was from the other members of the family, she knew she fit in quite nicely. Someone in the raucous group of relatives had to be silent and observing from time to time.

Bruce stretched his arms above his head as he caught her eye and gave her a thoroughly naughty wink. "The prisoners are released," he proclaimed, then grasped Melissa's hand and drew her off into the bushes.

"Really," Arabella gasped. "He is too primitive."

"I certainly am," he agreed as he pulled Melissa into a maze of tall hedges some distance away. "We'll be back by the time everything is ready."

"Bruce, you are every bit as much a child as your son," Melissa said breathlessly.

"You won't think so in a moment," he murmured as he took her mouth in a hungry kiss and unfastened her bodice at the same time. His hand parted the edges and dipped into the neckline of her chemise, freeing her breasts for his gaze and then his mouth.

Melissa fumbled with his trousers and encouraged his erection to spring free, stroking him, over and over again, faster and faster as he lowered them both to the ground and lay flat, accepting her ministrations while exploring her through the opening in her pantalettes.

"I can't wait," he growled, "until this child is born and we can—oh, God, Melissa . . ."

She replaced her hand with her mouth, inciting his response, enjoying his helplessness beneath her.

He stiffened and gripped her arms, sliding her up his body to delve into her mouth and tease her nipples with his fingers. And then he tore away from her and rolled to his stomach, his breath coming in short pants and then nothing at all for a few short moments of release.

Childish squeals and adult shouts drifted on the air.

"Whose idea was it to have the lot of them here?" he groaned.

"Yours. You wanted to show off the abbey before my confinement began."

"Your confinement." His expression was suddenly uncertain as he tucked her breasts back into her clothes and fastened her bodice. "I'm sorry it happened so soon, Melissa."

She smiled at him as she tucked him back into his trousers with a last caress. "I'm not. I'm quite determined to have a very large family and celebrate every birthday in chaos."

He swallowed, then kissed her forehead. "Melissa, I—"

She pressed her fingers to his lips. "I know, Bruce. I know every moment of every day."

She sat back and listened to the squeals increase as an argument commenced between the birthday twins. Max's laugh rumbled over the grounds. Kathy shouted in exasperation. She heard all the other voices as well, joined by Smithy.

Melissa rose with Bruce's help, anxious to join the fray.

Where there was family and love, there was often chaos . . .

And peace.